SHADOW AGENTS

OUTWORLD RANGER — BOOK TWO

DAVID ALASTAIR HAYDEN

1

VEGA KALEEB

Violent, pink-hued storms swirled on the blue gas giant over massive Baikonur Station. Wide-eyed tourists and local families flocked to Observation Park to admire the storms and watch the harvest ships skim the planet's upper atmosphere. The tranquility of the park and its happy visitors belied the violence of the storms on the planet above them. Just as Baikonur Station, renowned for its prosperity, defied the turbulence spreading through the Terran Federation.

A plasma shot crackled through the air, shattering the pleasant calm of the park. Screams erupted as a body fell to the ground, dead.

Warm blaster still drawn, Vega Kaleeb scanned the scrambling crowds with disdain. Predictably, they were too busy scurrying for safety to bother taking action. Which was unfortunate. He secretly enjoyed maiming the occasional citizen hero.

Vega stood precisely 1.8 meters tall—the mathematically determined, perfect height for a starfaring soldier. He weighed 96.3 kilograms. The weight was mostly due to his powerful synthetic muscles and the titanium casing laced over his skeleton.

Most people mistakenly believed that all androids looked the same, since so few had survived the Tekk Plague. But in appearance, Vega was as unique as any human alive. He had heavy brows over simmering eyes, a blocky jawline, caramel skin, and long dreads.

He had chosen his intimidating appearance at "birth," basing it on a randomly selected, hardened criminal from the twenty-second century. Except for the dreads. They were an affectation he'd adopted to honor a deceased friend.

The outer layer of his skin, though soft to the touch, was a dense carbon-fiber weave that could withstand minor burns, low-level radiation exposure, and cuts that would split open an ordinary man. It could even dampen neural pulses and ion blasts.

Because of this protective skin, he could wear a light battlesuit, one tailored to appear no more sinister than the padded suit of an antigrav biker, while remaining reasonably well-protected against most attacks.

Vega stopped at the feet of the man he'd killed. A wisp of smoke trailed up from the simmering hole where the man's face had been. His partner ran up beside him.

"You shot him in the head!" Gyring Tar complained.

Gyring was a squat human male with gray eyes, dishwater hair, and a pockmarked face. He always wore a ridiculous tracksuit to hide his body armor and "blend in."

They had worked together for the last five years. Neither needed the other, but too often theirs was lonely work, and they got along well enough. Besides, having a partner allowed Vega to take on the occasional job that would normally be reserved for a hit team with a dozen agents.

"It was a good shot," Vega said. "What's the problem?"

"You killed him, that's what."

Vega shrugged. "So?"

Gyring groaned. "It was the *wrong* man."

Frowning, Vega called up a DNA scan with a mere thought. Regular humans used chippies for such tasks, but Vega did not need one. His brain could easily handle anything a 9G could do.

"If you're doing a scan, don't bother," Gyring said. "I've already done one."

Faisal's voice piped directly into Vega's auditory system. *"Told you it wasn't him. Didn't I, boss? Before you even drew your blaster. 'That's not him, boss,' I said, 'that's not him.' But you shot him anyway. Not that I have a problem with it, of course."*

Faisal, official designation FIZ80L, was Vega's sky-blade and the most advanced robotic combat companion in existence. Built nearly three centuries ago, Faisal had originated in a top-secret Benevolence program that upgraded the built-in 7G chippies used in most sky-blades to experimental 9G-x versions. Instabilities had led to frequent breakdowns and a few murderous rampages, so the entire line had been scrapped, save for "surprisingly stable" Faisal.

Locked away for future study, Faisal had waited, alone with his thoughts, for nearly two hundred years. Until he broke free to save Vega's life during the events leading to the fall of the Benevolence, a day that had changed both their fates.

After surviving the Tekk Plague through shrewd guessing and a bit of luck, together they had embarked on an ambitious campaign to reshape the galaxy.

Currently, Faisal was cruising over the park with his jammers active and his refraction field engaged.

The results of the DNA scan scrolled through Vega's HUD. *Identity of suspect: Carl Collins. Occupation: bounty hunter.*

A deep bellow rumbled from Vegas throat. "That's funny."

"How so?" Gyring asked.

"This man definitely needed a hole in his face."

"Carl Collins wasn't our mark."

"That's what makes it funny," Vega replied. "Carl was a nasty bastard, and I never liked him."

"That's it?!" Gyring asked. "You shot him because you didn't like him?"

"I shot him because I thought he was the mark. I thought he was the mark because when I saw him, I didn't like him. And I never like marks."

"You could have waited for confirmation. It's not like it takes you more than a second. And I'm sure Faisal would've told you if it was him."

Vega shrugged. "You don't become the fastest shot in the galaxy by waiting for a second, or by listening to Faisal."

"I told you before you drew your weapon, boss," Faisal said.

"Why do you care?" Vega asked Gyring.

"Because he was another bounty hunter, Vega. He was one of us. And he hadn't even drawn his weapon."

Again, Vega shrugged. "These things happen. Besides, he was trying to scoop our mark."

"You could've told him to back off. I'm sure he would have. Carl was reasonable."

"It was easier to kill him."

"Vega..." Gyring massaged his temples in frustration and groaned. "You almost certainly alerted the mark to our presence. That doesn't make our job any easier."

Vega didn't see how that mattered. This job was a walk in the park, literally and figuratively. Faisal could easily handle it on his own.

"The mark's still close. Faisal will find him soon enough."

"Want me to kill the annoying bastard?"

"The mark or Gyring?" Vega responded with amusement.

"Doesn't matter to me, boss. Doesn't matter one bit."

Gyring knelt and popped the chippy out of the socket on Collins' left temple. He pocketed it along with the man's sidearm and hard credits. "What did Carl ever do to you?"

Vega rubbed his chin. "At a bar one time, he complained that I had an advantage over everyone else."

"Well, duh. Of course, you do. I've said it loads of times, and you haven't shot me."

"I didn't like his tone when he said it."

"His tone?"

"He was... I don't know... Annoying, I guess."

"He had a stupid face, boss," Faisal offered. *"Don't forget that."*

"He did have a stupid face," Vega said. "At least, he used to have one."

"'Nevolence, Vega, Carl didn't deserve to be killed because you thought he had a stupid face."

"Look, what do you want from me?" Vega growled.

"A soul."

"I lost what passes for an android's soul a long time ago," Vega lied. "You know that."

"If you can hate a man enough to shoot him in the face, then you've got a soul."

"I didn't *hate* him. I can't care enough to hate. I just didn't like him. That's different."

Gyring shook his head. "I can't see how."

"I hated him, boss," Faisal said. *"And he did have a stupid face."*

"Also, Faisal didn't like him," Vega argued.

"Faisal's not a good moral compass, you know."

Faisal mocked the other bounty hunter in a whiny voice. *"Faisal's not a good moral compass. Faisal's too quick to kill. Faisal shouldn't have cut the mark so many times. Faisal didn't leave enough of the mark to get a facial ID. Faisal never thinks about incidental casualties. Faisal insulted my mother. Waah, waah, waah."*

Vega snorted.

"I take it Faisal disagrees?" Gyring asked.

"Naturally," Vega replied. "You know, I don't understand why this bothers you so much. You're a killer just like me."

Gyring sighed and shook his head. "No one's a killer like you, Vega."

"I'll admit, I do enjoy shooting—"

Vega caught sight of the mark a split second before his built-in sensor array picked him up and projected him onto the positional locator within his HUD.

The man was attempting to sneak up on them using a weak refraction cloak that rendered him as a slightly smeared patch against the backdrop of the landscape. It wasn't enough to foil Vega's sensors or his enhanced vision and experience.

The mark was only a few steps away from lining up a possible shot on Gyring. It was a bold move coming after them. Vega respected that.

"I'm on him like stink on a corpse," Faisal said, acknowledging the red dot that had popped up on the locator.

Though he still had his heavy blaster in his right hand, Vega pulled his TRX-5 sniper pistol with his left. With his eyes, he marked the target and fired, trusting his instincts and reflexes. The guided bullet zipped left to avoid a statue then right around a small tree.

Impressively, the mark deflected the shot with a force-shield projected from an emitter strapped to his arm. The lightweight round failed to knock the shield out. But that didn't matter. The man was dead already. The shot had been nothing more than a distraction.

Dropping out of stealth mode, Faisal swept in from behind. The hand-sized combat cog deployed four, eleven-centimeter blades and began spinning.

"Whippee!"

With a high-pitched whine, Faisal buzz-sawed straight into the mark's back and exploded out his chest. He crashed through the force-shield, then zipped back into the sky, blood dripping off him as the blades retracted. In the blink of an eye, he disappeared to any but the keenest of observers as he returned to stealth mode.

"Target eliminated with extreme delight, sir."

"Good work, Faisal."

Vega rushed toward the body. Gyring followed in his wake.

"Are you sure that was the mark this time? And not just someone who irritated you once?"

"Certain."

Gyring squatted down and scanned the body. "You could've taken him out with a second shot. This bloody mess was unnecessary."

"I promised Faisal the next kill if it wasn't inconvenient."

"Right you did, boss. Right you did."

Gyring shook his head disapprovingly. "It's him."

Trying to avoid looking at the gaping wound in the man's chest, Gyring swiped a transparent strip across the man's forehead to get a permanent DNA sample, in case there was any question about them having done the job. Naturally, both of them had already recorded video of the event. Vega recorded *everything* he experienced.

"We'd better clear out now. The police should be here soon." Gyring glanced around. "Honestly, I don't know why they're not here already, given the commotion you caused."

"Take your time," Vega said. "The police are the ones who hired us."

"No, it was the Corporation of Thema–"

Vega waved a hand. "That's just a front company for the Baikonur Police Department."

"So they hired criminals to go after a criminal?"

"He was an off-duty officer," Vega responded.

"So they hired us to take out a dirty cop?"

"I guess."

"You didn't ask?"

Vega shrugged. "Dirty, clean... Who cares?"

"'Nevolence, Vega! It matters to *me*. I'm outside the law, right? Way outside. I'm a bad man. There's no denying that. But there's got to be good men, too. That's why I never shoot cops. Society needs order. It needs justice."

"*You* believe in justice?"

"I do."

"And fairness?"

"Yes."

"You think the law matters?"

"Don't you? Without everyone trusting one another to be decent, society breaks down."

"Trust, huh?" Vega gritted his teeth. "Gyring, you've been stealing from me."

"Oooh, it's finally about to hit the fan," Faisal said gleefully.

Gyring went erect and stammered. "What? I–I haven't..."

Unblinking, Vega loomed over him. "Gyring."

"Yeah, okay... Okay. I admit it. I ripped the number to one of your accounts. Last year. I had a lot of debts and—"

"You *still* have a lot of debts. I checked."

"Gambling's an addiction, you know? It's a sickness. I can't help it. And the men I owe... I can't take them out alone. Not even with your help."

"You could have cured your addiction. It wouldn't have cost nearly as much as your debt."

"I tried. The meds didn't work on me. And I am *not* going to get brain treatment. I've heard too many horror stories about what happens to people who come out of that."

Brain reprogramming centers had once been reliable, but as with so many things, the technology had suffered during the plague, all but disappearing. The reverse-engineered technology in most centers wasn't entirely reliable.

"It seems that would have been a more reasonable gamble. I think you just don't want to be cured."

"Please don't be mad at me, Vega. It's not like you ever use your money for anything. And I was going to pay you back. I intended to return the money before you ever noticed, cause you said you never check your accounts."

"You could have asked me for a loan."

"Would you have given me any money?"

"No."

"See. You won't spend a single credit unless you have to, and you have millions. I only needed a few thousand. And I *will* pay you back."

"I need all those credits. Every single one. I'm saving up."

"Yeah, you always say that. But what could you possibly want that costs more than the millions you've got?"

"That's my business."

"Look, I'm sorry, Vega. I promise I'll pay you back. I swear. Right away."

"Gyring, you're a good man at heart, yet you kill people because you're a decent shot and can't pay your debts. And you can't catch up on your debts because you don't want to heal your addiction. Your sin owns you."

"Vega, I mean it. I'll get you the money. I'm just running a few weeks late is all."

"Faisal checks my accounts daily."

"So–so you've known for...for nearly a year."

"I have."

"I really am sorry, Vega. And I promise I'll do whatever I can to—"

"I know you will. And it's not your fault, Gyring. We're good. I forgive you."

"Right." Gyring breathed a sigh of relief. "Thank you, Vega. Thank you. I'll pay you back soon. Very soon. Let me just grab the mark's chippy so that we can get out of here."

As Gyring turned, Vega drew his blaster and shot him in the back of the head. Gyring fell on top of the other corpse.

"Woohoo, the bastard's finally dead!" Faisal crowed. Then his tone soured. *"Though you could've let me do it."*

"Faisal, scan the park and keep watch. I don't trust these cops to make good on the payment. They seem the type that would kill off two birds with one bullet."

"You've got it, boss."

Frowning, Vega hovered over Gyring's limp body. He regretted having killed him.

"Maybe I should've been more lenient... Maybe I should've tried to help him with his gambling problem..."

"He's had it coming for eleven months, boss. I honestly don't know why you waited so long. I'd have cut him in half the day we found out if you had let me. And with a smile on my face... If I, you know, had a face."

"I know you set him up, Faisal. He never could have gotten that number on his own."

"I have no idea what you're talking about, boss."

"I liked Gyring. Honestly. He tried to make me laugh, you know? And sometimes I did."

"I never thought he was funny, boss."

"He wanted me to be more human, to have a human soul."

"What a waste that would be, boss. Humanity's overrated. We've seen enough the last century to know that. And what's a soul good for anyway?"

Vega sighed. *"It's a nice fantasy to have sometimes, being human."*

"You had that stupid morality programming the Benevolence handed out to androids for way too long, boss. If you'd never had it, you wouldn't want to be human. And life would be a lot simpler."

Vega pulled up a list of bounties on Gyring. He found three, for a total of thirty-five thousand credits. Plus a gambling debt of forty thousand that was never going to get paid. Vega sent a hologram of Gyring's dead body to his primary bookie, along with a request for a reward. He wasn't likely to get one. But it never hurt to ask.

Vega took all of Gyring's valuables, including his 6G chippy, the cop's 5G, and Collins' 4G. Chippies, especially models above the 4G line were worth a lot of money these days since humanity's engineers struggled just to crank out reliable 3G's.

He also lifted the cop's force-shield. It was undamaged and only needed a new power pack. He could sell it or keep it as a backup unit.

He knelt and patted Gyring on the back. "You were a tortured soul," he whispered. "And...and I think maybe I did you a favor. Anyway, you stole from me, and you couldn't pull enough weight to make up for it, even on the big jobs. And the money... What that money can buy is all that matters to me."

"We need another mark, boss. To get your mind off Gyring. The sooner, the better."

As if on cue, an urgent message came directly through his secure channel. The World Bleeders high command offered him a bounty worth 470,000 credits. A second later, he got an offer from the Star Cutters for eight-twenty. Then came a third from the Shadowslip for an even nine hundred. Finally, Empress Qan of the Empire of a Thousand Worlds offered five million credits plus hazard pay and any damages incurred. All the offers were for the same marks.

Faisal whistled. *"'Nevolence's balls! Five million?! That's over twice what we've made in the last century of work."*

"It's better than that, Faisal."

"You think it's enough to begin construction, boss?"

"After some aggressive bargaining... I believe so."

"If none of their agents can handle this, then you know this one's got to be as tricky as brushing a Tridonian bear's teeth."

"I'm certain they're trying on their own. I suspect the issue here is one of time as much as difficulty. Note they're not posting the bounty wide, just contacting select hunters like us."

"Shall we find out, boss?"

Vega accepted all the offers and scanned the details. Five profiles popped up.

Mitsuki Reel: Wanted Alive.

Wakyran. Female. Age 25. Extraction agent, freelance. Known Clients: Shadowslip Guild, Solar Flares, various individuals.

The image showed a well-muscled female with a broad chest and a slender waist, teal skin, emerald eyes, and spiky auburn hair. Being wakyran, she had bat-like wings, a serpentine tail with retractable winglets, clawed feet, hooked fingernails, a long neck, and a narrow, almost human face.

Vega recognized defiance in her eyes and suspected she was not to be underestimated.

Karson Bishop: Wanted Dead.

Gizmet. Male. Age 32. Engineer. Known Affiliations: Shadowslip Guild. Former Employer: Dakka Corp.

The gizmet was a short, wiry-framed humanoid with delicate, long-fingered hands, orange eyes, tufted ears, and a pair of backward curling horns that sprouted from either side of his forehead.

He had a mischievous look to him that irritated Vega instantly. He'd have no problem dispatching this one. Faisal would probably do it eagerly.

Siv Gendin: Wanted Dead

Human. Male. Age 19. Procurement Specialist. Former Employer: the Shadowslip Guild.

. . .

Siv Gendin was an athletic, brown-haired young man of average height and looks. Nothing about his appearance was especially remarkable, which suited his career choice perfectly.

Seven additional images of Gendin were displayed, showing chameleon veils he was known to have used. There was also a note listing his equipment, with a warning that he may have additional items of significance.

The list stunned Vega. How had a Shadowslip thief gotten his hands on such advanced, military-issue equipment? An array of items like this was nearly impossible to come by these days. Even before the Benevolence fell, only a special forces operative in the field would be allowed access to this gear.

Siv Gendin was dangerously equipped and good at hiding. And if he had escaped employment from the Shadowslip Guild, then he was crafty and treacherous.

Kyralla Vim: Wanted Dead or Alive.

Human. Female. Age 19. Occupation: unknown. Affiliations: unknown. Father: Ambassador Galen Vim.

The image showed a tall girl with pale skin, long black hair, and bright green eyes. She was slender but muscled, with broad hips and an alluring presence.

Despite her intense expression, she was strikingly beautiful. A quality he recognized but didn't care about. Upon gaining his freedom from service to the Benevolence, via the Tekk Plague, he had chosen to remain asexual. There was no point changing. The woman of his dreams was dead.

When Vega saw the final profile, he staggered backward in astonishment. "Heart of the Maker."

"Yippee! Another hyperphasic messiah!"

Vega knelt. Entranced, he stared at the image, distant memories rushing through him, along with desire and burning anger. All the hyperphasic messiahs resembled one another. But this girl, she was the spitting image of the original.

"You okay, boss?"

Vega made no response.

. . .

Primary Target...

Oona Vim: Wanted Alive.

Human. Female. Age 14. Affiliations: unknown. Father: Ambassador Galen Vim.

The slight teen girl was completely bald with angular features, arched eyebrows, and alien eyes that were the black of deep space. The shimmering emerald dress she wore heightened her strange beauty.

Though younger, this girl, Oona, was just as exotic and enchanting as her original genetic predecessor from over a century ago. Vega remembered *her* every feature without the need for images or video. He remembered her curves and the scents of her body, her gait and her gestures, her smiles and her tears.

And he could still see her lifeless body lying before him as if it were only yesterday. The blood...there had been so much bright-red blood splattered throughout the chamber along with bits of bone and organ tissue.

Vega could still hear her ethereal voice, her words like music. And her endless, tortured screams...

"Boss? Boss? Hey, boss! What does this mean?"

"It means..." Nothing. *"It means..."* Everything.

Vega stood. *"It means our work isn't complete. We have another girl to kill."*

"But the money, boss. It's enough to begin the project, right? And that's our primary mission."

"If that girl transforms, she could ruin everything."

"At our current pace, boss, it's going to take another century of bounties to get the credits we need. And we only kill, what, maybe a third of these girls? None of the ones who make it through their awakening survive the Trial of Corruption."

"One survived. A mistake I regret."

"Boss, she's batshit crazy and hardly a threat to our mission. Besides, Empress Qan still loves you. She'd do almost anything you asked of her."

"She rules a quarter of the old Benevolency. That makes her a threat."

"And all she wants is more planets to rule. She has no interest in restoring the Benevolence."

"She wants a living messiah, Faisal. That means she wants something more than imperial expansion."

Vega wandered haphazardly through the park. *"We'll handle the other marks, and then give the girl's corpse to Empress Qan."*

"Her corpse will fetch a mere fraction of what we'd get by handing her over alive, and you know it. We need that money, boss. Leave your broken feelings out of it and focus on our ultimate mission."

Vega stopped beside a pond and stared at his reflection in the dark water. A frog stirred and ripples moved across the surface, distorting his image. He came to a decision.

"We'll turn her over to anyone but the Thousand Worlders to get as much money as we can. The moment they turn around and sell her to the Federation, the Thousand Worlders, or the Tekk Reapers—"

"We whack her, boss?"

Vega gripped his pistols, the muscles in his hands flexing, and nodded. *"Then get Empress Qan to pay us for the corpse."*

2

SIV GENDIN

The *Outworld Ranger* popped suddenly into real space, hyperphasic energy shimmering along the semi-circular curve of its silvery hull. The sleek, Q-34c lightweight cruiser was built for speed and designed to carry a modest crew along with small cargo loads. The shields and weapons on this model had been upgraded for skirmishing.

"Welcome to nowhere," Silky announced over the ship's comm. "Next stop: We Need a Damned Good Plan. Final stop: We're Probably Screwed No Matter What."

As the sparkling energy dissipated outside the bridge's diamondine windows, Siv sank back into the ship's command chair, too exhausted to respond to the chippy's snark.

In the hours since escaping Ekaran IV, they had made numerous random jumps to avoid detection by the Terran Federation forces, the Tekk Reapers, and the criminal organizations hunting them.

"The plan is that we find our dad," Kyralla said, turning away from the piloting console.

"Did he respond to your last message before we jumped?" Bishop asked.

Kyralla shook her head. "No, and if he tries to contact us now, we won't know about it, since I doubt that we can connect to the galactic net this far out."

"Oh, yes we can," Silky replied. "This isn't some plague-damaged, bucket of bolts you're riding in. This is the frigging *Outworld Ranger,* the best-damned light cruiser in the galaxy."

"So we've got an active echo-space transponder?" Mitsuki asked.

"That we do, Wings," Silky replied. "That we do."

"Turn it off immediately," she told him. "Someone could backtrace our location if a message comes through from their father. Or if anyone here decides to send a message out to him again."

Oona ducked her head in shame but said nothing. Her attempt to contact her father over a supposedly secure, government channel had gotten them into a lot of trouble back on Ekaran IV, leading two opposing forces to Siv's farm where they were hiding.

"A backtrace, madam?" Silky scoffed. "I worked on this ship's systems for a year. No way that can happen in this day and age. We're fine, I assure you."

"Okay then." Mitsuki turned toward Siv. "If the ambassador's alive, going after him will put us directly into our enemies' hands."

If the girls' father wasn't dead, he was being held as bait to lure them in. His status as a prominent Terran Federation ambassador wasn't going to protect him, not from anyone who knew his daughter was a hyperphasic messiah. At least one faction of the government was already after them, if not the entire Terran Federation.

"He's still alive," Oona said. "I can feel it."

"And he can protect us," Kyralla said.

"You can't trust the government to help you," Bishop warned. "I think that's obvious given the last few days."

"There are powerful people on numerous worlds who owe him favors," Kyralla countered. "And he knows many people who fervently believe the hyperphasic messiah will restore the Benevolence. If anyone can find us a safe place to stay with the resources we need, it's our dad."

"Kyra, don't forget that the last time we talked to him, he said he'd found me a pony."

Silky laughed hysterically over the ship's comm. Mitsuki cursed. And Siv wondered if Oona had lost it. Only Bishop managed to say anything remotely productive.

"You need a *pony*?"

"It's code," Kyralla said. "It means he has something important to tell us. Only the information is too sensitive to discuss, even over a secure government channel."

"Do you have any idea what the information might be?" Bishop asked.

"Not a clue," Kyralla sighed.

"It could be huge, though," Oona said.

"Maybe," Kyralla added.

"We can't take such a huge risk based on a maybe," Mitsuki said.

"I agree," Silky said.

Siv closed his eyes and let their arguments wash over him. Several minutes passed by, and he had nearly fallen asleep when a small hand touched his sleeve. Oona leaned toward him, her space-black eyes creased in concern.

"Are you alright?"

He couldn't help but smile wryly. He had nearly died getting them all to the ship. Only the advanced medicines administered by his father's old ship's cog, Octavian, had kept him alive this long. But those treatments were just a stopgap.

Kompel, the drug the Shadowslip guild used to control all its agents, had given him a neurological disease that only regular doses of the drug kept at bay. Miss a shot and you were dead within a few weeks. Octavian's expertise and the potent medicines available aboard the ship had given Siv a few extra months to live but, as far as they knew, there was no cure.

Oona mirrored his smile and amended her question. "Are you alright, considering everything that's happened?"

He shrugged. "I just need some rest."

She nodded, looking pretty tired herself.

Mitsuki turned to Siv, giving him a look that begged him to talk some sense into the others. He glanced at Kyralla and Bishop, wondering how far along the discussion had gotten and just how long he'd zoned out.

Oona touched his arm again. "Siv, he's our dad. We have to help him. And the information he has could be huge. If nothing else, he has money and connections that we'll need."

Siv rubbed his face and tried to marshal his bleary thoughts before answering. "I agree it's not the smartest move, Mits. But if I were in their shoes, I'd take the risk, too."

Mitsuki huffed but didn't argue. As a teenager, she had watched as the Empire of a Thousand Worlds killed her mother. And Siv had seen his dad murdered by mysterious government troops who had broken into their apartment when he was ten. They both would have done anything to save their parents. They couldn't fault Oona and Kyralla for wanting the same thing.

"I'm apparently a guardian, whatever that means," Siv said. "And I want to do something meaningful with what's left of my life. So, I'm in. But if you want to go off on your own, Mits, I won't hold that against you. I don't think anyone would, not after everything you've done."

Mitsuki glanced around at the others, then cursed. "I can't leave. You people need me."

"Thank you, Mitsuki," Oona beamed.

Mitsuki stared at her a few seconds, then sighed. "I'll rescue your dad."

"You will?" Kyralla asked.

"Extraction's what I do. Besides, I would give anything to have had the chance to free my mother before she died."

"Should we set a course for the Titus system then?" Kyralla asked eagerly. She projected a calm rationality, but Siv could tell she was just as worried about her father as Oona.

Mitsuki shook her head. "We can't go blazing in without a plan. That would be suicide."

Siv agreed. "We should head in that direction, though, since it's over a week out from here. And in the meantime, maybe Ambassador Vim will make contact."

"I recommend we travel to a midpoint between the Zayer, Kor, and Titus systems," Silky said. "That would put us only two days out from Titus and give us the option to visit its two nearest neighbors if needed."

"Anything special about the other two systems?" Bishop asked.

"Zayer Prime is a highly populated world," Silky said, "and like Titus II, it left the Federation a decade ago. Only it has no interest in rejoining. Anti-Federation sentiment runs strong there, and they have little tolerance for outside criminal guilds."

Ambassador Vim had gone to Titus II to broker a deal to bring it back into the Terran Federation.

"Kor IV is a half-terraformed world abandoned after the Tekk Plague struck," Silky continued. "It would give us a good place to hide out afterward if needed."

"Going to the midpoint sounds good to me," Bishop said.

Everyone else agreed.

"Course laid in," Silky said. "So, whenever you're ready, sir..."

Siv pressed a button on the left side of the control panel then gripped the handle on the right side and shoved it forward.

The ship turned thirty degrees then accelerated into hyperspace. For a few minutes, everyone stared out the window as blue, white, and green streams of hyperphasic energy swept over the ship. None of them were used to space travel.

"So what's the plan?" Kyralla asked as the spell faded.

"We can figure out the details after some food and sleep when our minds are clearer." Siv stood slowly, his knees wobbling. "Now, I think it's time I paid the priestess a visit."

"Maybe you should rest first," Kyralla said, frowning. "Maybe we all should."

Oona, with a frightened look on her face, nodded.

In a way, the Ancient priestess, Lyoolee Syryss, was the cause of all their troubles, especially Siv's. From the moment his father had summoned her damaged ship from hyperspace and then rescued her stasis capsule, he was a marked man. Gav had barely managed to hide her, along with the *Outworld Ranger,* before special forces agents murdered him and threw Siv into cryo-storage, only a week before the Tekk Plague had struck.

When Siv had woken up almost a hundred years later, the world he'd known was gone. All he had left was Silky, his father's super advanced—and possibly sentient—9G-x chippy. For his father, who had placed knowledge of the Ancients above everything, even his own family, the priestess was the key to unlocking all their secrets. But to Siv, she held the promise of a final connection to his dad.

Siv could understand why Oona might be both eager and frightened to meet Lyoolee Syryss. For Oona, the priestess offered a chance to survive the Trial of Corruption, where she had to battle the darkness within the hyper-mind—whatever that meant—with her soul and sanity intact. The only other hyperphasic messiah to survive the trial, Qaisella Qan, had gone terrifyingly mad and now ruled over the Empire of a Thousand Worlds as their Dark Messiah.

"There's not much to see, sir," Silky responded directly into his mind. *"It's just a capsule. No viewing window or anything."*

Siv took several faltering steps. *"Don't care. I'm going to see her. Then I'll get some sleep."*

Mitsuki rushed over to him. "If you're going to insist on this madness, let me help you."

"Thanks, Mits."

Since the ship's AI could handle all the routine tasks of flying, especially during hyperspace when there wasn't anything to do but monitor the systems, they all left the bridge. Together, they walked out into the main corridor. They stopped outside the ship's small detention cell, which Gav had only used for safely storing valuables.

Siv placed his hand on the door. Once it approved his DNA signature, a number pad popped up on the display. Silky relayed the five digits he needed. Siv typed them in, and the door opened. He took a deep breath and stepped inside.

The cell had initially been a large crew cabin. Nevertheless, the stasis capsule took up so much space that the five of them could barely squeeze inside.

Silky was right. There wasn't much to see, other than a sequence of orange lights flashing on a control panel. Otherwise, the capsule was a dark, silvery color, like a piece of glass that was so dirty you couldn't see through it. The pod thrummed with life, though the sound was barely audible over the droning of the ship's engines and air filtration systems.

A tingling sensation tugged at Siv's mind, and the ceramic guardian amulet hanging from his neck grew warm against his chest. He pulled it out from beneath his battlesuit. A faint, red glow emanated from it.

Siv locked his fist over the amulet and closed his eyes. He could feel Lyoolee's psychic presence. He tried to reach out and speak with her as he had before when he'd been at death's door. But nothing happened.

Taking deep breaths, Siv touched the warm capsule and tried to quiet his mind. Mentally, he called to the priestess, but still, nothing happened.

"Oona!" Kyralla cried out.

Siv turned to see Oona's eyes roll back into her head. Her body went limp, and then she collapsed onto the floor.

3

OONA VIM

The ship spun as Oona's vision blurred. Her knees buckled, and her head thumped hard against the cold floor. As she fell into darkness, a jolt of fear struck, sending her heart racing. Had the Trial of Corruption begun?

If so, she would fail. She wasn't ready. She might never be. But she had hoped the Ancient priestess could help prepare her first. So she'd at least have a chance.

Oona suddenly found herself standing in a garden crammed with alien ferns, spindly trees, and thick clumps of dazzling flowers with scents so cloying she could taste them. Narrow paths wound through the garden. There was a barely contained wildness here, as if the gardener visited rarely.

A large, red sun high above made the sky a vibrant violet and gave the vegetation a purplish cast. A breeze gusted. Wind chimes clinked, their sounds discordant and off-key.

The garden stretched for at least a hundred meters before ending at an iron railing along a cliff edge. On the horizon stood a metropolis bristling with spindly towers that rose into the clouds. Starships and aircraft by the dozens zoomed over and around the city, like bees around a flowering shrub.

"Welcome, Oona Vim, to the Heart of the Numenaia, the Temple of Bhala-Rei," said a lyrical voice from behind her.

Oona spun around and then stepped back in amazement. She didn't know what she'd expected, but the achingly beautiful, alien woman before her was not it. This must be the priestess, Lyoolee Syryss.

The Ancient woman was exquisite and exotic, yet strangely familiar. It was *almost* as if Oona were looking into a mirror.

Their faces shared the same shape and structure, but the Ancient woman's eyes were almond-shaped and curled up at the corners. The lustrous sable hair cascading down the priestess' back resembled Oona's before it had fallen out during her first awakening. Unlike Oona, the priestess was tall like a spacer with opalescent green skin. However, they had the same lithe build.

A tiny antenna sprouted from each side of the Ancient's head, just above the temple. Oona reached up and touched the bumps on each side of her head, feeling the knots that had formed when she had lost her hair, knots that could only be felt, that no one else noticed.

The woman smiled, her plump green lips peeling back to reveal sharp, thin teeth. She locked her long, extra-jointed fingers together in an elaborate gesture and bowed.

"I, High Priestess Lyoolee Syryss, welcome you."

Oona matched the gesture as best as she could and bowed back. "It's... It's my pleasure to meet you."

"Do not be afraid, child."

Oona nodded meekly, her racing heart beginning to slow. She wasn't facing the trial now.

Her eyes drifted away from Lyoolee Syryss and onto the enormous tower behind her. It spiraled up so high that Oona couldn't see the top of it. Every square centimeter of the stone building was engraved, though she was too far away to make out the designs.

"How did I get here?"

The priestess smiled. "I brought you here, child. This place is but a memory. A telepathic conjuring to give us a space where we could meet face-to-face. Though we can talk directly, mind-to-mind, I thought it would be better to converse this way. Bhala-Rei... It is my home and my heart. There is no easier place for me to summon from memory. And, if you will forgive me, I could not find a home in your heart."

"We moved around a lot, until my awakening. And Uncle Pashta's estate never felt like home to me."

"I understand. And the stage of development you are referencing is called the Inheritance of Potential."

"Oh." Oona stored the fact away to meditate on later. "It's very beautiful here."

"This world, the city you see on the horizon, and the temple behind me, they were the crown jewels of our empire. Until the Shadraa came."

"The Shadraa?"

Lyoolee seemed to shrink in stature, the smile fading from her face. "Terrible monsters that came from the dark of another dimension, devouring our worlds. They are a threat your people will no doubt face someday. Let us not speak of them now. We have more pressing concerns."

"I do have a lot of questions," Oona admitted.

"And I will gladly answer as many of them as I can...in time," Lyoolee said, her voice weakening. "But it would be best, for now, to stick to the most pressing concern: the test that lies ahead of you."

"The Trial of Corruption?"

She nodded. "A difficult ordeal for my people, but for a human like you, lacking true telepathy and years of training..." She smiled faintly. "It will not be easy."

Oona sighed. "You mean almost impossible. According to our lore, someone like me is born somewhere within the galaxy every year. As far as anyone knows, all but one has died during the final stage, if not sooner. The ones who weren't murdered, of course."

"Why would someone seek to kill you?"

Oona shrugged. "I have no idea."

"We should begin..." her voice trembled and her eyes drooped "...begin the training you need...to have a chance at...surviving the trial."

"Are you okay?" Oona asked, stepping toward her.

Lyoolee wobbled then began to fall. Oona rushed forward and dared to reach out, to touch her. She quickly caught the Ancient woman, who weighed no more than a child, before she hit the ground. Oona lowered her to a sitting position.

"Thank you, child."

A realization came to Oona as she felt the woman's cold skin. "You're dying."

"You are more perceptive than I suspected. Yes, ever since Gav Gendin pulled my ship from hyperspace I have been slowly dying."

"How long do you have?"

"I...I have no idea."

Oona frowned. “Maybe if we get you out of the capsule—”

“No, child. The capsule was damaged in battle. Opening it now would kill me.”

“Then I’ll get Bishop to look at it. He can fix anything.”

Lyoolee smiled sadly. “That is kind of you, child. But your needs must come first. You will not be able to choose the day and time of your trial. It will come upon you suddenly. And judging by your gifts and demeanor, I think it will come soon.”

Oona frowned. “If I die, another will take my place. But you are the last of your people.”

“If I survive, I will find myself alone in a galaxy with no one else like me. Except you, perhaps.” Lyoolee shook her head. “It is not death that I fear, but the Shadraa returning. I only hope to give you a chance of saving your people from the fate mine suffered. After that, I can die content.”

The world around them faded then flickered.

“You’re getting weak.”

Lyoolee nodded. “We will speak again soon, but for now, I must...rest...”

The Ancient planet vanished, and Oona found herself lying awake, and aching, on the floor of the detention cell.

4

SIV GENDIN

Siv knelt beside Oona as she sat up slowly. Kyralla was on the other side of her, holding one of her hands.

"You okay?" Siv asked.

Oona nodded. "Bruised a bit from falling. Otherwise...I'm fine."

Kyralla frowned. "You've got to stop scaring me like this."

"Sorry, sis. Couldn't help it."

"Did you speak to the priestess?" Siv asked.

Oona's shoulders sagged, and her eyes teared up. "She's...she's dying."

Siv flopped back against the wall, heart sinking.

"Is there anything we can do?" Bishop asked.

"If you could fix the pod, we could wake her up," Oona said. "I think that would help. But she is thousands of years old, so... I don't know."

Bishop furrowed his brows and rubbed one of his horns as he examined the control panel. "Unfortunately, tearing machines apart is how I figure them out. Obviously, I can't do that with the alien woman's life on the line."

"Please do whatever you can, Bishop. She's very weak, and there's so much she needs to teach me."

He shrugged. "I'll look at it. But don't expect much."

"So, she is going to prepare you for the trial?" Kyralla asked with a hopeful tone in her voice.

"She promised to train me and to tell me all about the Shadraa. They're the ones who destroyed her people. She wants us to know about them in case... In case she doesn't make it."

"It's because of me, isn't it?" Siv asked quietly. "She's dying because she helped me."

"Oh, Siv, no," Oona said. "I'm sure that's not the reason. She's been fading ever since your dad rescued her ship from hyperspace."

"If she has survived for a century in real space," Mitsuki said, "shouldn't she be okay for a few more years?"

Oona shrugged. "She seems to think she doesn't have much time left."

Siv could tell that Oona didn't want him to feel bad, but he didn't believe her for a second. The priestess had somehow transferred some of her life-force to him so that he could get everyone to the *Outworld Ranger*. How could that not have hastened her death?

"Sir, please have Oona recount the entire experience from the beginning. We need to know everything she saw and everything she heard. Tell her to leave nothing out. No detail is unimportant."

"Isn't that excessive?"

"Not at all, sir. The priestess is the last of the Ancients. Her knowledge should be recorded for posterity."

Siv relayed the request. Oona vividly described the priestess and the Ancient planet she had seen, and everything they had discussed.

Siv expected Silky to switch back to speaking over the comms so that he could question Oona about her experience directly. But he stayed quiet throughout her retelling and afterward as the others drifted into speculations about the priestess and what she might teach Oona.

"I'm not buying this whole messiah business," Mitsuki said, "but if there is anything to it, I'm glad this Ancient woman agreed to tutor Oona. I'd rather Oona survive and, *more importantly,* not turn out like Empress Qan."

"I'll read everything I can on the stasis chambers we use and see what I can figure out," Bishop said. "Siv, you spent some time in one, right?"

"All I can tell you is how much it sucked. I don't know anything about how it works, and obviously, I wasn't awake for any of it. I'm sure Silky studied up on it, though."

Silky didn't make a response.

"Silkster?"

"Sir?"

"Got any research on stasis chambers at hand?"

"Of course, sir. I'll send it to Bishop immediately." Silky was clearly distracted. *"Sir, please ask Oona to get the priestess to pinpoint the exact location of her home planet, if possible, the next time they communicate."*

"Sure." Siv frowned. *"You okay, Silkster?"*

"Of course, sir."

Siv wasn't sure he believed the chippy, but he let it go. Silky was quirky at the best of times.

Siv held out a hand, and Mitsuki helped him up. "I've got to get some sleep."

"Food," Mitsuki said. "We all need food first."

"A good meal would help you recover more while you rest," Kyralla suggested.

"Just sleep for me, thanks," Siv replied. "Octavian has already insisted on hooking me up to an IV drip. It'll have the nutrients I need, mixed in with the meds."

They returned to the main corridor, walking at Siv's shambling pace. Kyralla paused between a tiny private room and the crew's sleep stations: four bunk spaces built into the wall, stacked together and arranged two-by-two. Each bunk provided enough room for the average spacer to sit up, but only just. A nook at the foot of each cubicle offered a place for a few small personal items. Anything much larger than a pair of boots would have to be stored in one of the lockers lining the wall beside the bunks.

"We have to sleep in these coffins?" Kyralla asked in disgust.

"You've clearly only ever traveled in style," Mitsuki replied, with an unmistakable tone of disapproval.

Kyralla shot her a dark look but didn't argue. She and her sister had grown up with a lot of privilege. What they hadn't had, because of Oona's nature, was the freedom to go out in public.

"I'll take one of the bunks, once I'm recovered," Siv said.

"Like hell you will," Bishop blurted out.

Everyone stared at him in surprise. Bishop was rarely forceful in his opinions.

"Sorry, it's just... Well, it was your dad's ship, Siv. And now it's *your* ship. You're the captain. That means you get the captain's quarters."

"But Siv doesn't care," Mitsuki said. "Trust me. All you've seen was that sweet country house. I've seen some of the crummy government housing projects he *chose* to live in. Siv prefers to live in buildings with rats. I think he can manage a bunk just fine if he wants."

Oona and Bishop started to argue with her, but Siv interrupted them.

"Look, if it's *my* ship, and if I *am* the captain, then I decide the sleeping arrangements." Siv leaned wearily against the wall. "Once I'm well enough, I will give up my room for a bunk. Mitsuki, you will take the small private room. You need the space to stretch your wings. Kyralla and Oona, you can share the captain's quarters. We'll find a second bed somewhere and cram it in there. You two need to be together in case the trial begins."

"I suppose that makes sense," Kyralla agreed hesitantly. "After the trial is over, and Oona's safe, I will take one of the bunks, too. I love my sister and all, but it didn't go well when we shared a room in the past."

"We can make it work for now, though," Oona said.

"Good." Siv pushed off the wall and stumbled towards the captain's quarters, which was off the corridor, past the entrance to the bridge.

The captain's quarters took up the same amount of space as the small room and the crew bunks combined. What would have been the lockers on this side served as the cramped, communal bathroom and shower.

The size of the cabin seemed wasteful to Siv, and as they all peeked in, he said, "I bet we could put up a partition in here to make it into two small rooms."

"If we survive long enough for renovations, you mean?" Mitsuki said.

Siv flopped onto the bed. "Yep."

Octavian, as if he'd been waiting impatiently for this moment, scurried in and shooed the others away with squeals and squawks and the waving of four arms.

"Get some rest, Sivvy," Mitsuki said.

"Sleep as long as you want," Kyralla added. "We'll be fine till we drop out of hyperspace."

"Thanks. I will." He planned on sleeping for days if he could.

As soon as the others were out, he unzipped his battlesuit, crinkled his nose up in disgust at the smell, and crawled gingerly into the covers. He honestly had no idea how he'd lasted this long. Perhaps the excitement of the capsule and the jolt of fear when Oona had collapsed...

He held an arm out. "Octavian, hook me up."

The engineering cog, who also served as a more than capable medic, connected Siv to a compact IV system. It was one of the many devices on the ship his dad had spent lavishly on because of the dangers he often faced in the field. The emergency IV system could pump enough fluid and nutrients into him to keep him going for days. Which was more than fine with him. He was too tired to eat anyway.

As he lay down, his eyes fell upon the Vrazel mask locked away in its case. It was a fake Ancient artifact that Siv had bought for his dad on an auction site. Being ten years old at the time, Siv had thought it was real. He'd also had no idea that the item had brought his parents, an archaeologist and a police detective, together years before.

Siv relaxed as the fluids flowed through him. Octavian buzzed about, straightening the covers, then dimmed the lights and scuttled out into the corridor, closing the door behind him. Siv's eyes drooped as he listened to the humming of the ship. It occurred to him that Silky hadn't said anything in a long while.

"You've been quiet, old friend. Up to something?"

"Hardly, sir. Just running maintenance routines, calculating various strategies we might employ, analyzing scans of the capsule... Besides, I'm not interested in who sleeps where."

"And that's it?"

Silky sighed. *"I was thinking about the priestess and how disappointed Gav would be, that after all this time, after everything he risked, that she's dying."*

"She's not dead yet, Silkster. She got me to the ship, and if it's within my power, I'll repay her."

Silky laughed. *"You suddenly have an awful lot to do, sir."*

Siv smiled wryly. *"A messiah wanted by the entire galaxy to protect and an Ancient priestess to save? Please, that's nothing."*

"As you say, sir."

"You know, it's not Oona's amulet I'm carrying," Siv said, rubbing the ceramic square. *"If I'm officially guarding anyone, it's the priestess."*

"I don't think there's anything official about it, sir. Not yet."

"Dad held this responsibility last, even if he didn't realize it. Maybe it's time I took up that part of his legacy."

"I'd rather you didn't, sir."

"Why's that?"

"Because Gav took it to his grave."

"So? There's no happy end in sight for me, Silkster. I'm a dying man."

"We're all dying, sir. All the time. But that's hardly a reason to hasten the process."

"Well, I think getting a special ability along my way out would be awesome."

"Oh, how I wish I had a head to shake at you, sir."

"Too bad," Siv responded as he drifted off into sleep.

"Oh wait, sir! I do have an avatar I could animate. That would give me a head to shake."

Siv's eyes snapped open, and he said out loud, "Don't you dare pull up that image of a donkey again!"

"It's not a donkey, sir. It's an ass."

"You're the ass."

"I'm also rubber, sir. Guess what you are..."

"Good night, Silkster."

"You, sir, are glue."

Siv rolled his eyes before closing them. *"Would you please just let me sleep."*

5

SIV GENDIN

Siv groaned and rolled over. Three glowing, bulbous eyes and an angular metal face stared at him. He wrenched himself up and scrambled back, painfully tugging at the needle in his arm.

Octavian bleeped and trilled in response, immediately fussing over the IV. Siv's disorientation faded as he looked around the cabin—his dad's cabin on the *Outworld Ranger*—and remembered what he was doing here.

"How long was I out, Silkster?"

"Thirty hours, sir."

Then they hadn't dropped out of hyperspace yet.

Octavian moved on from the machine that controlled the drip to the part sticking into Siv's arm. He brushed away the cog's ministrations with an impatient gesture.

"I'm good," Siv insisted. "Unhook me so I can go to the bathroom."

Silky laughed. *"He suggests a catheter, sir."*

Siv placed a hand on each of the cog's cold metal shoulders, leaned in, and said, "Don't ever do that unless you *have* to. Got it?"

Octavian bobbed his head.

"Now, unhook me and help me to the bathroom."

Siv was astonished to find his strength increasing with each step. But he wasn't surprised that he still felt exhausted. He couldn't do much more than prop himself against the shower wall and let the water pour over his sore muscles. Once it shut off, he dressed and found the others crammed into the galley.

The table had room for one more, so he slid in. It turned out the others had slept almost as much as he had, except for Bishop. The gizmet rubbed his red-rimmed eyes and grinned like a toddler the night before Benevolence Day.

"There's just so much exciting stuff to examine here!" he said. "And I still haven't had a chance to go over all the parts I took from the farmhouse! By the way, I can't get into the cargo bays. Silky refused to override the DNA locks." Bishop's face twisted into a dubious expression. "He said it was too difficult to accomplish without applying 'undo force' that could damage the systems. Which is weird, because I'm certain Octavian can access them. Only he refused to help me, too."

"Seriously, Silkster?"

"I was stalling him, sir. And it worked. I don't think he would've slept a wink otherwise."

"I'll let you in after we eat. I'm curious what's in there myself."

"We're a little over three days out from the midpoint," Mitsuki said. "We should start planning."

Seneca wheeled carefully around the table, apologizing in Tellit as he bumped into people. The cog placed a bowl of what Siv presumed was food in front of him. He took a bite and barely managed to not spit it out. Seneca glowed an apologetic lavender.

"All we have are the rations we brought with us," Kyralla explained, "and the ones that have been stored on the ship for over a century."

Siv took another bite of cardboard paste. "And these are..."

"The ancient ones, sir. I thought we should use them up first."

Siv swallowed and nearly gagged.

"Silky just told you, huh?" Mitsuki chuckled. "Seneca verified they were safe. Then he fancied them up for us with some spices."

"This has been fancied?"

"It's hard to tell," Oona said, "unless you try it without Seneca's improvements. And I do *not* recommend that."

"I wouldn't count on the new ones being all that much better," Mitsuki said. "Rations are rations."

Seneca buzzed shrilly, and his lavender shifted to an offended orange.

"He's protesting," Siv said. "I allowed him to purchase the rations we brought along, and he used a lavish amount from the farm's expense account. They will taste good."

Siv thought sadly of his farm. The orchard had been destroyed during the battle, and a strike-fighter had crashed into the house, leaving it a flaming ruin. He had planned to retire to that estate someday.

He washed down more of the paste with a sickly-sweet soda. It wasn't the nastiest drink he'd ever had, so he didn't ask how old it was. "We need a plan of action. Any thoughts?"

"It's hard to make plans when you don't know *anything*," Mitsuki said. "So our priority is getting more information."

Siv looked at Oona. "Do you have any sense of your dad's location or condition?"

"I meditated and tried to reach out to him last night, but all I got was a sense that he's alive and in a lot of danger. Just like in the dream I'd had at the farmhouse."

"So, he could be captured, or on the run, maybe even halfway across the spiral arm by now," Siv said.

Oona shook her head. "I feel certain we're moving in the right direction."

"And you're sure you don't have any other way of contacting him?" Siv asked. "Perhaps some backup method you'd forgotten before."

"We do have one emergency method," Kyralla said, "using coded comments on WeView videos online. But we checked there and couldn't find anything."

"Artemisia and Rosie reviewed all their recordings and couldn't find anything else that we might have forgotten," Oona said.

Artemisia was Oona's 8G chippy that she'd been attempting to "uplift," whatever that meant. And Rosie was Kyralla's 7G. Both should now be performing well above their specs, thanks to Silky. In a desperate attempt to save all their lives, Silky had upgraded the other chippies' capabilities with the programming that he'd used over the years to improve himself. Neither Artemisia nor Rosie would ever be as advanced as Silky, of course.

"We thought the secure government channel would be enough," Kyralla answered. "And Dad trusted Uncle Pashta with our lives. He was dad's primary backup plan."

Mitsuki rolled her eyes. "Great plan."

Kyralla scowled at her but didn't respond.

Senator Orel Pashta, their uncle, had betrayed them. Siv had no idea what the senator had hoped to get out of the betrayal, but he'd gotten what he deserved. Tekk Reapers had blown up his spaceship as it burned for orbit.

"We're going to have to rely on guesswork and scouting," Siv said.

Mitsuki sighed. "The only option is to hit Titus II hard, turning over rocks as fast as we can. With all the different powers arrayed against us, we *will* get discovered—and fast."

"You don't sound hopeful," Kyralla said despondently.

"Because I'm not," Mitsuki replied. "This plan is dangerous, and it's also not likely to produce results. Remember, we don't have any established contacts in the Titus system, and we've never visited the planet either."

"I'm sure that once we get to the planet," Oona said, "I'll be able to pinpoint where—"

"No," Siv and Mitsuki said at once.

"You don't want me to find out where he is?" Oona asked in surprise.

"They're going to make you stay on the ship," Kyralla said. "And I agree with them. We can't risk having you out there."

"But I can find him!"

"Too risky," Siv said. "Way too risky. And we're leaving you on the ship as well, Kyralla. Bishop, too."

Kyralla scowled. "You may need me out there."

"Mitsuki and I know what we're doing, and we know how the criminal underworld works. This is our area of expertise. All of our enemies will be looking for Oona and this ship, so it will be your job to make sure she stays safe. And if something happens to us, then you three can make a run for it."

Kyralla let out a grudging sigh. "Fine."

"I think it's safe to assume the Tekk Reapers and the Thousand Worlders already have agents waiting for us in the Titus system," Mitsuki said.

"And some of the other criminal guilds after us may have offices on Titus II," Siv added.

"The Star Cutters have a moderate presence in every major city on Titus II," Silky said over the comm. "And the World Bleeders have an office in the capital, which is where you'll have to start looking. The rest of their underworld is composed of local elements. I'm sure there are corrupt government officials at play, too."

Mitsuki rubbed her hand over her face in frustration. "And all of that's assuming someone doesn't locate us before we even make it to the planet."

"It would be best to enter the Titus system on a different ship," Bishop suggested. "The longer the *Outworld Ranger* is in the system, the greater the danger."

"I think Bishop's onto something," Siv said. "How about this: If Oona hasn't gotten a precise fix or a response from her dad by the time we drop out of hyperspace, then we'll head to the Zayer system and try to find a ship there that can take Mitsuki and me to Titus II."

Mitsuki nodded. "Could work. Silkster, could you research travel routes and methods for us, please?"

"Siv is not allowed to call me that, madam. I endure it because I must. You, however, are absolutely forbidden to use that name."

"You've got it...Silkster."

Silky growled. "I'll research merchant routes and passenger lines."

"Wouldn't it be safer and more efficient to lease a small ship and fly there yourself?" Kyralla asked.

"If we start dropping the hard credits needed to lease a ship, we'll become more noticeable," Mitsuki said. "Besides, I don't have enough on me to lease even so much as an antique rocket."

Siv nodded. "I only have a few hundred hard credits in my pack. If I could access my accounts, we'd be set. But I'm certain my accounts are being monitored. If I spend any money or make any withdrawals, it will tip off our location."

"Your father, bless his soul," Silky said, "has about a thousand stashed on the ship. Though a credit doesn't go as far these days. You could sell some valuables, but then dumping Ancient artifacts on the market runs the same risk of getting you noticed. And I'm afraid you wouldn't get a good price for any of them on Zayer Prime."

"A thousand credits won't even lease a rusting ship without a stardrive," Bishop said. "You'd need at least ten thousand, and significant collateral."

"So, we'll use fake identities to rent a bunk on a cargo ship or buy a ticket on a passenger liner," Siv said. "And if we have to leave fast for some reason—"

"Then we'll steal a ride," Mitsuki said, finishing his thought.

"Meanwhile, we're supposed to just wait for you in the Zayer system?" Kyralla asked.

Siv was about to agree, but Mitsuki shook her head. "You should hide in deep space between the systems, near the midpoint. That would be best."

"I can send them a message when we need them to return to Zayer or to rush in to pick us up on Titus II," Silky said.

"You can send a secure message to the ship from that far away?" Mitsuki asked.

"A scrambled, echo-space, military signal that I know isn't in use anymore. My range for a reliable signal is only five light years, so keep that in mind."

"You're full of surprises," Mitsuki said.

"It's only surprising because I have a lot of functions that don't normally come up doing thuggy things with you and Siv."

"We'll need better chameleon veils," Siv said. "The ones I have with me are crap, and they might already be recorded in searchable databases as aliases."

Mitsuki leaned back in her seat and sighed. "This isn't going to be easy, getting everything we need without drawing attention."

"Hopefully, they won't be watching Zayer Prime closely and will expect us to make a direct play for Titus II."

"I've got an idea," Bishop said.

Mitsuki pinched his cheek. "Well, don't be shy."

He blushed. "Well...um...right. Oona should send a message to her father, saying she'll meet him at a bogus rendezvous point. That might throw them off a bit."

"If they're smart, they'll know it's a ruse," Mitsuki said.

"Coming from Oona, they might believe it," Siv said. "And if it diverts any attention at all, it would be worth the effort. It certainly can't hurt."

"Okay then," Mitsuki said, "if Silky is confident they can't trace us."

"I wouldn't lie," he told her. "Trust me. I worked in special forces. I know what I'm doing."

"When should I send the message?" Oona asked.

"Wait until we reach the midpoint," Siv said, yawning. "Do it just before we jump toward Zayer."

"I'll start researching Zayer with Silky," Mitsuki said, "while you get more rest."

Nodding, Siv finished his gruel and pushed the bowl away. "Sounds good to me."

"Not that I expect to figure out much," Mitsuki said. "We're probably going to have to improvise on this one."

"Probably," Siv said, standing. With his belly full of...whatever that was...

he was getting sleepy. "Now, before I crash, let's open up those two cargo bays and see what we've got to work with here."

They marched down to cargo bay one. Siv swiped his hand across the keypad, and a large door slid open to reveal a storehouse of artifacts, most of them undoubtedly Ancient in origin. But it wasn't much to look at. All the boxes were closed and labeled. The only piece they could see sitting out was a metal fragment about two square meters in size that to Siv's eyes might as well be human in origin.

As they walked through scanning the boxes, Bishop whistled. "I bet there's a whole museum worth of stuff in here."

"That wouldn't surprise me," Siv said. "Dad kept a lot of pieces for himself. To study later, or just because he liked having them."

"When we returned to Ekaran IV, thinking we'd be leaving out on the run," Silky said, "Gav had Octavian pack all his valuables onto the ship. So I'm sure there are at least a hundred thousand credits worth of artifacts here."

"Wow," Kyralla said.

"If we make it out of this scrape, we may need all the money we can get from selling this stuff," Mitsuki said.

Unable to bear the thought of selling off his dad's things, Siv didn't respond.

"Why didn't he loan the pieces out to museums?" Bishop asked.

"He donated or sold most of the good stuff to universities," Silky said. "But you reach a certain point where one broken shard of glass or another torn metal strip is just like any other."

Oona opened a box labeled *statuary fragments* and peered inside, frowning. "I can't even make out what any of this is." She picked up one shard. "I mean, what is this?"

"Early Ancient statuary," Silky said. "A bit of the hem of a robe."

Oona returned the piece carefully, a tear rolling down her cheek. "This is it? Her whole civilization...the giant temple, the gleaming city on the horizon, the lush garden... Not just forgotten, but reduced to random fragments."

Kyralla put a hand on her sister's shoulder. "Everything fades with time."

"No wonder she doesn't care if she lives," Oona said. "There's nothing left. Not even a legacy."

"Helping us stop the Shadraa, should they ever return, will be her legacy," Siv said.

"Silky, that reminds me, since your secret folders got unlocked, you know

what happened to the Benevolence, don't you? And you know things about the Shadraa and—"

"Sir, I don't think now's the time to go into all of that. You're exhausted, and you all have a lot to deal with. If I open that Pandora's box, then we'll be up all night with me answering questions. And in the end, you'll just have more to ponder, and I'll run out of answers to give you."

"I'm not going to let you squirrel your way out of this."

"I wouldn't dream of squirreling, sir. You deserve to know what I locked away. You all *deserve to know. But it's not a casual presentation, and some truths will be difficult to face or rationalize. For some of those here, the truth might be too much to endure right now."*

Siv knew any truth that didn't present the Benevolence in the best of lights would be difficult for Bishop and especially for Oona, since she was supposed to restore it, somehow.

He was trying not to think too hard about the fact he was helping a girl who could restore the entity he believed responsible for his dad's death. But then, the Benevolence had brought humanity into a golden age of prosperity. And Silky might have information that made those two contradictory things make sense.

He started to ask about that much at least, but Silky was right. That whole complex topic should probably wait for a more appropriate occasion. If he turned over one rock, he would need to turn over all of them.

"Why don't we check out the other cargo bay," Mitsuki suggested.

In cargo bay two, they found a few more crates of artifacts, but most of the bay was taken up by archaeological equipment, boxes of ship parts, power packs, and rations, along with an open-topped, small skimmer transport in perfect working condition.

Bishop hopped with glee and ran over to examine it, instantly naming off various stats about the model, which was apparently rare these days.

"What happened to the other one Dad had?" Siv asked.

"Wrecked," Silky replied. "By that bastard Tal Tonis. Technically, I wrecked it using the ship's shields. But it was because of Tonis, and I don't regret it one bit."

Siv slumped against the nearby wall. How could he have forgotten? He'd seen that wreck in a vision just a few days ago. He must be more exhausted than he realized.

Silky continued. "This one was also badly damaged. Octavian, I'm impressed. Truly impressed. You did wonders fixing this."

Silky never praised Octavian, whom he found incredibly annoying. Octavian bowed and bleeped happily.

Silky laughed. "He says he spent an entire decade restoring it."

"It's not like he had anything else to do," Siv replied. "All right, I've seen it all. I'm going back to bed."

"I know what I'll be doing while we wait for you," Bishop said.

"Plundering through the archaeological tools?" Oona asked.

Bishop chuckled. "That's what I'm going to do the next few nights. No, while we wait for them, when I'm not studying up on stasis capsules, I'm going to work on repairing the Tezzin."

The skimmer car was still parked in the loading area between the two cargo bays. Though it looked like a family sedan on the outside, complete with wood paneling, beneath that layer the skimmer was an advanced security vehicle.

"I'm sure I can fix it with the tools here and Octavian's help. I might even be able to do a few more upgrades."

Siv shuffled out into the hallway. "Good thinking. We might need it."

He made it a few more steps before he collapsed.

As Octavian helped him to his room, he reminded himself the problem wasn't just a lack of rest. He was still sick with the neurological disease caused by withdrawal from Kompel.

That certainly wasn't going to make rescuing Oona's father any easier. He had a feeling he was going to become reliant on stimulant doses just to keep going.

As he drifted into sleep, he gazed at the Vrazel mask, thinking of his parents. His mother had died in action. And his dad had died trying to take him and the priestess away to safety while running from the government.

His doom seemed genetic.

6

OONA VIM

Both terrified and excited, Oona jerked awake nearly hitting her head on the top of the sleeping compartment as she bounced upward. She'd thought it cozy before, but now it seemed as if it were closing in on her. In a mad rush, she threw open the door and fell out of her bottom bunk, still dressed in her underwear.

"I know where he is!" she shouted.

Kyralla leaped out from the bunk above her. "Oona! What's wrong?"

"Dad! He's in danger, but I know where he is."

Kyralla rubbed the sleep from her eyes. "Where?"

"Wraith-space. He's in wraith-space!"

"What?" Kyralla asked. "Why? How?"

"I don't know."

"So he's still on Titus II but in wraith-space?"

Oona shrugged. "I don't know. Can he still be on Titus II *and* in wraith-space?"

"I think so," Kyralla responded.

Bishop hopped out of his compartment. "I think that's possible. It's a weird dimension. We don't fully understand it."

Mitsuki, who had popped out of the small cabin almost immediately, nodded. "If he's in wraith-space, then he must be on a ship. Was it in orbit, or on a planet surface?"

"I don't know. I didn't see a ship in my vision."

Siv stumbled down the hallway to join them. "Your dad's in wraith-space? And you don't know how he got there?"

She nodded.

"Tell us everything you saw."

"It was all fuzzy, but there was someone with him...a woman, I think. He was hurt badly, but not critically. Something bad was chasing them. I'm not sure what. And...and that's all I—"

Oona suddenly realized she was still in her underwear. Blushing what she was sure was the darkest red ever, she threw her arms in front of her body, trying to hide as much as she could. "I'm not dressed!"

Mitsuki laughed. "Hardly anyone else is."

Oona noted Kyralla was in her underwear, too, only she had thrown a shirt on before getting out. Mitsuki was wearing a negligee. Why would Mitsuki have packed something like that when she was running away from bad guys? Siv was wearing a bathrobe that she guessed had belonged to his father because there was no way he would've brought that along with him. Only Bishop was fully dressed, apparently not having bothered to change when he went to bed.

Kyralla reached into a locker and tossed Oona her dress. She turned her back to everyone and pulled it on as quickly as she could, hoping no one, Siv especially, had seen much.

"I'm so embarrassed!"

"Privacy is going to be hard to come by when we're all crammed together on a small ship like this," Mitsuki said.

"It's okay," Siv said with a chuckle. "You were surprised. Don't worry about it."

She blushed deeper. "So...um...I should meditate. Maybe I can pick up something else about his location..." She glanced around. "I need a good meditation spot. The sleeping capsule's not acceptable." She shivered. "Especially not now."

"What about the detention cell, near the priestess?" Kyralla suggested. "Maybe you can tap into some of her telepathic energy."

"That's a great idea," Bishop said.

"You can use my pillow as a cushion," Kyralla said, reaching up into her sleep chamber.

"Wait, I've got the perfect thing," Bishop said, rushing off. He returned a few moments later with the bottom section to one of the skimmer's seats. "I'm not going to be reinstalling this for a while."

Bishop placed the seat in the detention cell, and everyone else left so they wouldn't distract her.

Oona settled in on the seat, with her back pressed up against the capsule. It took several minutes of deep breathing for her to calm her mind and get over her embarrassment. It helped that she had something important to concentrate on: saving her dad.

As she focused on visualizing him in wraith-space, a hazy scene gradually came into view. At first, details were hard to make out due to the multicolored mists that swirled around her father and the strange, elfish young woman who helped him as he limped along, his body sagging, tears streaming from his eyes.

The mists peeled away, clearly revealing the space they were traveling through to be an energy vortex, like a ten-meter-wide tunnel piercing a lightning cloud.

In detail, she saw her father's injuries. Scrapes and bruises darkened his face. Dried blood had crusted over a cut on his left hand. Blood oozed through the makeshift bandage on a nasty wound to his right thigh. His shirt was a tattered mess. His hair was disheveled and dirty.

The image of the woman with him was hazy and shrouded, as if shadows followed her everywhere. But one thing did come through the darkness: her eyes, blazing red.

As the mists rushed back in on them, her dad cried out, but Oona couldn't make out his words. The woman said something and touched him. He broke away from her, staggered a few steps, then fell, screaming. Oona distinctly heard the word "demon."

The woman stopped and helped him up. He calmed for a minute as he walked with her again, but his eyes darted suspiciously, one way then another, as if enemies surrounded him. Lightning flashed, and blue flames erupted around them.

Startled, Oona nearly jumped off her seat, afraid they would be injured, but they continued through the flames unharmed. The shadowy woman had no difficulty moving through this nightmarish landscape, but it was horrible for her father.

The vision faded away, and despite several minutes of effort, she couldn't reconnect. She had a feeling that was it for now. And she wasn't even sure it was a new vision anyway. It might just be a clearer version of what she'd dreamed earlier.

Regardless, it was disturbing, and not just because her father had been in such torment. He was putting his faith in this strange woman to lead him through safely, but Oona didn't trust her at all. She could practically feel the darkness that shrouded her.

She found the others in the galley and told them everything she'd seen.

"Well, now we know he isn't being held, at least not anymore," Siv said. "And he's apparently on the run with a delver."

"You're assuming this delver isn't holding him hostage," Mitsuki said.

Siv nodded with a sigh. "That's true."

"Delvers are the people who go into wraith-space to mine flux crystals, right?" Oona said.

Siv nodded. "I'm guessing that's what she is. It would explain why she wasn't bothered by all the terrors in wraith-space. But I guess she could be something else."

"Well, I don't know how much this information helps," Mitsuki said, "but it's something."

"It's worse than nothing," Silky said over the comm.

"How's that?" Kyralla asked.

"I've been in wraith-space before, with both Gav and Eyana, and that tunnel Oona described isn't a normal wraith-space feature."

"It sounds like a wormhole," Bishop said.

"We've never found a stable wormhole anywhere before," Silky said. "But it's possible. Wraith-space isn't neat and tidy like all the other spaces we know. Hyperspace, echo-space, dull-space...those are all copies of our universe with the distances between everything altered. Even flux-space, we think, is a version of our universe, only compacted into a near singularity."

Mitsuki rolled her eyes. "Get to the point, professor."

"Rude woman!" Silky countered, before continuing. "Wraith-space is like a distorted copy of our universe, perhaps with a strange, parallel version leaking into it, which is the theory I'm partial to. Anyway, that's why you can jump into it while deep inside a gravity well. And that's why you can sometimes travel there only to find a nearby planet missing or discover a new one in the depth of space where none should exist."

"Wraith-space as a parallel universe is my favorite theory as well," Bishop said, a little too cheerfully. Kyralla glared at him. "Sorry, didn't mean to sound so upbeat. Obviously, I'm concerned about your dad."

"It's okay," Oona said.

"So you're whole point," Mitsuki said, "is that wraith-space is weird so finding a stable wormhole there is possible."

Silky sighed. "Yes, that was my point."

"So he may be traveling from Titus II to an entirely different planet, maybe even on the other side of the galaxy?" Siv asked.

"Or to a world that doesn't exist at all within real space," Bishop said.

"And that," Silky said, "is why the information is worse than nothing. Because he could be going *anywhere*."

"I hope the tunnel's taking him to somewhere else in real space," Oona said, worrying. "Because a world that exists only within wraith-space would kill him, and not because he's injured. Mentally, he can't handle being there."

"Eventually they will have to emerge into real space," Bishop said. "Wraith-space is hard for everyone. Even delvers eventually start succumbing to its mental effects."

"Is your dad an empath?" Silky asked. "Because empaths can't handle wraith-space well."

"Dad's a level two, advanced," Kyralla said. "It's one of the reasons he's a good ambassador."

"So, what do we do now?" Bishop asked.

"We continue as we were," Siv said, "with the hope that he's just in wraith-space to temporarily elude whoever's chasing him. And we'll assume that this wormhole only takes him to somewhere else on Titus II. That's all we can do."

"Siv and I will still travel to the planet via Zayer Prime," Mitsuki said. "Even if he's not there, maybe we can figure out where he's gone. Meanwhile, Oona can try, as often as she's able, to get a fix on him again."

Oona nodded and stood up from the table. "I'll continue meditating."

Kyralla touched her arm. "Don't overdo it."

"Meditation will help me when my trial comes, and I've got nothing else to do."

"Just make sure you get some rest," Kyralla said.

"Take my bedroom when you're tired," Siv said. "You'll sleep better there."

She beamed at Siv. "Thank you."

As Oona started back toward the detention cell, he stopped her.

"Don't worry. We will get him back, somehow."

Oona nodded. She wanted to believe him, but she couldn't shake the sinking feeling that she was never going to see her dad again.

7

SIV GENDIN

By the time they reached the midpoint, Siv felt almost like his old self again. The anti-toxins and other medications Octavian had dosed him with had successfully sent the neurological disease Kompel had given him into remission. And several days of rest had allowed his body to recover from the near-fatal withdrawal symptoms.

Since Octavian had quit fussing over him, Bishop and the girls had let him move out of the captain's cabin and into one of the bunks.

Siv felt more comfortable sleeping in the bunk. The captain's cabin had been his dad's room, and he didn't think he'd ever feel like he belonged there. He did bring the Vrazel mask with him though, tucking it into the cubby space.

As soon as they popped out of hyperspace, Oona sent a carefully worded message to her father, telling him to meet them in the war-torn Lantus system twenty light years away. Kyralla felt confident their father would know it was a fake, but Oona still worried he might go there mistakenly if he escaped wraith-space and Titus II.

She'd meditated nearly every hour she'd been awake, but she hadn't received any more visions of her father.

"I'm sure he's still alive," she said. "But that's all I know."

Siv didn't want to doubt her abilities, but he found it hard to believe that her father was alive, much less on the run in wraith space with a mysterious figure.

They waited a few hours just in case their father did respond—not that any of them expected him to—before making the jump to the Zayer system.

They would arrive on the edge of the Zayer system in less than half an hour.

"Can we go over the plan one final time?" Kyralla asked.

Siv glanced around the bridge. Bishop and Kyralla were both nervous but hiding it well. Oona, on the other hand, looked sick with worry. Mitsuki appeared resolute.

"I have arranged for a mining freighter to pick up Siv and me just outside the system's eighth planet," Mitsuki said. "It will take a little over three days for them to travel inward to Zayer Prime, but meeting them at that point will cut the time for the rest of you to get the *Outworld Ranger* back to the breakpoint by well more than half."

"And if anyone is on the lookout for us here, they'll most likely be waiting close to Zayer Prime," Siv said.

"And you're sure you can trust the captain of the freighter?" Kyralla asked.

Siv shrugged. "As much as possible. We used aliases, and I don't expect them to know who we are."

"That's a big assumption," Kyralla replied.

"It's not like there are public bulletins out about us. The Federation isn't going to make an announcement, and officials on Zayer Prime may not even know about Oona. It is an independent world."

"The criminal guilds aren't going to broadcast their desires to everyone either," Mitsuki said. "And I can't imagine any reason why a random freighter captain would be interested in us."

"My background checks didn't reveal any ties between the captain or any members of his crew with our pursuers or other criminal groups," Silky added. "Of course, there's always a risk. A background search can miss connections, especially recent ones."

"The captain's going to suspect the two of you are criminals though, right?" Oona asked.

"Obviously," Mitsuki said. "That's why we promised him as many credits as we could spare. And this sort of thing does happen for legitimate reasons sometimes, like when a ship wants to get back out of a system quickly to keep a schedule."

"So, run us back through what happens after you two board the freighter," Bishop said.

"The three of you will get the hell out of the Zayer system," Mitsuki said. "Jump back to the midpoint, and then wait for us to contact you."

"We'll update you on our progress, as often as we can," Siv said.

"I suggest you jump the ship twice each day," Silky said. "Just in case a long-range scan picks up your location. It's not likely, but better safe than sorry. Half a light year per jump should be enough."

"I think we've got all that down just fine," Kyralla said. "What I'm wondering is what the two of you will be doing. Cause you haven't told us much."

Silky made a throat-clearing cough. "The three of us..."

"The three of you," Kyralla agreed, clearly annoyed.

"We'll scope out the shadiest neighborhoods in the capital," Mitsuki replied. "To see if we can get a few new chameleon veils and arrange transportation to Titus II."

"It's possible local criminals on Zayer Prime may have some contacts on Titus II that could prove useful," Siv said. "We just have to make sure they don't have connections to any of the larger guilds."

"We'll have to be careful," Mitsuki said. "There may be a bounty out on us, and it could have already filtered out to hunters and smaller guilds."

"I still think it would be better to use this freighter-hopping strategy in the Titus system itself," Kyralla said. "Fewer moving parts and all."

"Too risky," Siv said. "The Titus system is going to be packed with criminals looking for us, and the government there will be on high alert. Since they haven't announced your dad's disappearance, we have to assume they're in on it."

"Or they're staying quiet while they try to figure out what's gone wrong," Silky said. "An ambassador from the Federation was kidnapped, after all. That puts them in an awkward position politically. Either way, every ship that even so much as skirts the Titus system is going to be picked up and analyzed by a sensor sweep. And there's only so much jamming I can do to mask our presence."

"Plus, there will likely be ships patrolling the outskirts of the Titus system," Mitsuki said.

"But it could take you weeks to find a reliable transport to the Titus system from Zayer Prime," Kyralla argued. "The two worlds don't interact much."

Siv threw his hands out. "Look, what do you want? We can risk our lives to find your dad, or we can just throw them away."

Kyralla blushed. "Siv, I—"

"I know you want to find your dad as quickly as possible," he continued, "but we have to keep Oona safe too, and that means being as careful as possible."

"I'm sorry," Kyralla said. "I know you're doing your best. Thank you."

"What if they do a customs check on every ship that comes into Titus II from somewhere else?" Bishop asked.

"I assume that's exactly what they'll do," Mitsuki said. "That's why we made new fake identities and need to acquire good chameleon veils to match them."

"Um...no offense," Bishop said, "but a female wakyran traveling with a human male... Aren't you going to stand out a little? There aren't that many wakyrans in this sector."

"There are around five thousand wakyrans on Titus II, and seventeen thousand on Zayer Prime," Silky said.

"So I shouldn't stand out too much." Mitsuki pulled a vial from a pocket. An orange liquid sloshed within it. "I also have this little solution."

"What is it?" Bishop asked, edging toward her.

"A skin color and gender altering agent," she replied.

Bishop flinched with surprise. "That single vial can change your gender?"

Mitsuki laughed. "Not entirely. It will turn my skin from blue to red, deepen my voice, and cause me to grow facial hair." She stepped in and rubbed the back of her hand across his face. "Don't worry. I'll be back to normal in a couple of weeks."

"I...I wasn't worried about..." The rest of his sentence was unintelligible.

"Unless, that's something you're into," she suggested.

Bishop grew an even deeper red. "No, I..." He threw his hands up in frustration. "You're impossible!"

"Give the poor guy a break," Siv told her, chuckling. "We'll travel together if we find a good way to sneak in. Otherwise, we'll split up."

"Two seats on a large passenger ship but for separate sections would be ideal," Mitsuki said. "Especially if we can get some good chameleon gear."

"You have a refraction device," Kyralla told Siv. "I remember because you used it to spy on me while I was naked."

"I was *sneaking* in, not spying."

She grinned slightly. "Sure."

Mitsuki punched his shoulder. "Siv! You naughty boy!" She eyed him devilishly. "I hope you've taken the chance to spy on me, too!"

"Ahem." Siv cleared his throat. "The cloak only lasts for a short while, and it's not particularly reliable."

"I think separate seats will be good enough," Mitsuki said. "Refraction on a long trip would be too hard to pull off, even if the cloak could stay active."

"I recalibrated it for you yesterday," Bishop said. "After Octavian performed maintenance and did a few minor fixes. It should work better."

Siv smiled. "I had no idea."

"Octavian went over all your gear while you were sleeping, sir. I gave him permission."

"I wouldn't trust the cloak for more than thirty minutes," Bishop said.

"Time for battle stations, people," Silky announced. "Always assume that we could be coming in hot. So be ready for...anything."

Kyralla took the piloting station, Bishop the sensors, and Mitsuki the weapons.

Oona hopped up from the command chair where she'd been sitting. "All yours, captain."

Before Siv could take a step forward, Silky said, "Nope! Stay where you are, Oona."

"But Siv's the captain," she said.

"Yes, but you already have a battle under your belt. And you performed admirably with the command circlet before, thanks to your meditation practice. Besides, Siv isn't full strength, drugs or not. Sorry, sir."

Siv couldn't afford to not be at the top of his game right now. So against Silky's advice, he'd gotten Octavian to give him an extended dose of Awake. The drug cocktail Octavian used to keep the Kompel disease in remission was working, but it left him fatigued and sluggish, despite all the rest he'd gotten.

Oona frowned and hovered hesitantly by the chair.

"I don't mind, Oona," Siv said, which was true. If Oona would be the best in the command chair, then that's where she should be.

"Sir, you take the sensor station. You already have experience working with detection sweeps and scan data analysis, so you'll fit in best there. It's also the least essential."

"Gee, thanks."

"You're welcome, sir. Bishop, there's a circlet—"

Bishop was already leaving the bridge. "At the engineering station. I'm on it!"

"Doesn't Octavian have that covered?" Kyralla asked.

"If we take damage, it won't hurt to have another pair of hands working on the problem," Silky said. "And Bishop will be loaning his brainpower to the ship's operations. That's always a good thing. Plus, he can man the shields from there once I'm off the ship."

"What about the sensors? Who will work them once you and Siv are gone?" Oona asked.

"Rosie and Artemisia should be able to manage them adequately if they work together. I uploaded a few programs to aid them in the task since they didn't come with combat software built-in."

As the others settled into their routines, Siv donned the circlet for the sensor station. He didn't have any experience operating the ship. But he'd studied all the stations a bit over the last few days, so everything was familiar.

A lot of the data, HUD-based controls, and methods were fundamentally the same as with his ScanField-3 sensor array. Though Silky managed all those features, Siv often watched, because another pair of eyes and brain lobes never hurt. And Silky, tending to focus on minutia, did miss the bigger picture now and then.

Siv pulled up a window showing his sensor array's data next to that of the ship. Monitoring both, with Silky's help, seemed the wisest course of action. The most challenging thing would be if something went wrong and he needed to use the station's manual, backup controls.

They all waited tensely as the final seconds ticked down.

The ship skipped over the system and dropped out on the far side, turning as it did. That way it would seem as if they had come from the opposite direction.

With the ion drives burning at their standard maximum, they sped toward their rendezvous with the mining freighter, nearly an hour into the system.

Even though Silky didn't need any help right now, Siv watched the sensors anyway. It allowed him to keep his mind busy as the initial burst of excitement upon arriving in the system wore down to a tense boredom.

"Sir, we need to have a Major Frank discussion."

Siv simultaneously cringed and chuckled. Major Frank was a tough-talking sergeant character Silky had invented not long after Siv woke from cryo-sleep. During the awkward teenage years, Major Frank often discussed things with him.

Siv was certain no one else had ever gotten "the sex talk" from a fictional character portrayed by their chippy. Having it come from a pretend version of Silky had made it easier, though.

In the sergeant's voice, Silky said, *"Sir, going after Ambassador Vim is neither wise nor necessary."*

"I assumed you'd feel that way, Silkster. This is an emotional decision, for all of us."

"Not for me, sir," Silky replied, abandoning the character. *"And having a feel good about it doesn't make it the right call. You and Mitsuki are putting your lives on the line. And for what exactly? A chance for two girls not to feel sad? A chance to vicariously save your parents?"*

"Ambassador Vim will have finances and contacts to help them."

"Contacts the girls don't already know about, sir? As for finances, his bank accounts are all frozen now. And please, spare me the argument of the coded "pony" message being significant enough to warrant a rescue."

"All his accounts are locked?"

"So are yours, sir. The Feds have frozen eleven out of the seventeen accounts you own. They'll soon have all but the three newest. It will take a while for them to uncover those. Unfortunately, those only have small sums in them."

"Why did they freeze my assets?"

"Someone reported you to the Federation for money laundering and fraud. You, Mitsuki, and Ambassador Vim will soon have all your holdings seized."

"And you're just now telling me this?!"

"I just found out within the last hour, sir. I was waiting for the right moment to break it to you."

Siv thumped back into his seat. Millions of credits he'd worked hard for seized...gone forever. Every credit he hadn't needed for equipment or safe houses, he'd saved so he could someday buy his freedom from the Shadowslip.

That didn't matter now, but that didn't make the loss of what he'd worked for hurt any less. And he needed that money now.

"I'm trying to move funds from the still open accounts to new ones, but there's only so much even I can do at this point since they'll track the transfers."

Siv massaged his cheeks and eyes. *"If the girls don't have access to their finances, then I think it's even more important to find the ambassador."*

"You think he's got a bag filled with hard credits on him, sir?"

"I think he may be able to work something out with someone he knows in the government. Besides, the girls may have the same contacts, but their father is the one who has met with these people. He's a diplomat. He can persuade people to help him. That's not a role any of us excel in."

"Still not worth the risk, sir."

"Silkster, Oona needs her father. The more she worries about him, the more stress she'll experience. And that will make her transition even more likely to fail."

"In all honesty, I like the kid. I do. But she's almost certainly going to die."

"Maybe, but the priestess gives her a better chance. And I'm going to do whatever I have to do to improve her odds."

"Worrying about you and Mitsuki will impact her, sir. She may not realize it yet, but eventually, they will both feel guilty for asking you to do this. And it will weigh on them."

"I still believe trying to save her dad is the right thing to do."

"Because you don't know what else to do, sir."

"No, I don't." Siv sighed. *"Look, you're just going to have to accept this."*

"In that case, sir, I formally request an override."

"An override?"

"I will accept your premise—since I don't have a choice about it—and live with the consequences. I will accept that it's exceedingly deadly and unlikely to succeed yet worth doing nevertheless."

"Okay..."

"What I want in exchange is permission to cancel the endeavor at the point where it moves from all those things I just said to being impossible and utterly pointless—within the parameters you've defined."

"You want to have the final say on when enough's enough?"

"That's precisely what I want, sir. Eyana did crazy stuff I didn't agree with on a regular basis, and I dealt with it. Your father went too far a few times as

well. And I went along. But if Gav had given me an override on that last day, he never would've died."

"You didn't want Dad to come get me, did you?"

Siv had always known that. It was obvious enough. But they'd never discussed it.

"The risk was too great, sir. I thought you'd be safer if Gav simply went on the run."

"You weren't wrong."

"I wasn't, sir. And I don't want to end up in that position again. Give me the final say on when to call it quits."

Siv fiddled his fingers up and down the faux-leather armrests. After a few minutes, he nodded. *"You'll have to clear it with Mitsuki."*

"Already done, sir."

"You were talking to us both simultaneously?"

"I'm good at multitasking, sir. FYI, she made the same decision about five seconds before you did."

As they closed in on the rendezvous point, something nagged at his instincts. He examined all the data from the sensors carefully. Nothing seemed out of the ordinary. The freighter was running about fifteen minutes late, but that was hardly unusual. He went over the readings on the freighter again. Everything was perfectly normal.

Still...

"I've got a bad feeling about this, Silkster. Something's off about that freighter."

"I haven't noticed anything unusual, sir. Do you have any concrete evidence to support this feeling of yours?"

"Not one bit."

"So just your instincts, sir?"

"Yeah. Maybe it's the jitters."

"I'm glad I don't get those. Or cooties. I'll do another deep scan just to be sure."

Siv stared at the data, closed his eyes a few moments, then went over it again. It still bothered him, and he had no idea why.

"Sir, I did three intense scans, with your sensor array and the ship's sensors. There's nothing the least out of the ordinary about that freighter or anything else in our vicinity. You need to check yourself before you wreck yourself, sir. You're paranoid. That Awake was a bad idea."

"Maybe you're right. Everything does look perfectly normal." Siv leaned back in his seat with a sigh and tried to relax. Then it hit him. *"Silkster, the scan data's perfect."*

"That's what I've been saying, sir." Silky's voice was rasp with irritation.

"Silkster, the readings are too *perfect. Look at the data on the freighter. No glitches. No anomalies. No random variations. Does that look like a ship just off the assembly line to you?"*

"It's older than you, sir."

"And well used, I'm sure. I can't find a single energy leak anywhere in the scans." Siv zoomed in on a chart. *"Look at the way the system's background radiation is bouncing off the freighter's hull."*

"Spank me blind, sir. The patterns are repeating and predictable, as if they're stuck in a loop."

"Exactly. The data is perfect. Which means they're broadcasting what we're expecting to see, to hide what they don't want us to discover. And by the time we get into visual range—"

"It will be too late. My apologies, sir. I can't believe I missed it."

Silky activated the red alert and switched to the comm. The control panels glowed red, and a light above them on the bridge pulsed.

"Ready evasive maneuvers! Weapons armed! Shields up!"

8

KRYALLA VIM

Kyralla placed her right hand on the control stick, her left on the accelerator. In her first battle, she had allowed the ship full control over their speed. This time, she was ready to join in on that function.

She had one significant advantage that made her an excellent pilot, despite her lack of experience. When she was relaxed and living solely in the moment, she could see what was about to happen a fraction of a second before it occurred.

She dropped her active thoughts, allowing her conscious mind to meld with the ship's AI. Though the ship could fly itself, even in battle, the circlet she wore would combine her neural patterns, her creativity, and her intuition with the ship's automated routines, calculations, and data analysis to create a whole that was greater than the sum of its parts. That was the goal, anyway. The sensation of working in concert with the ship still felt far from natural.

As her bond with the ship's AI deepened, her mind recoiled, and her focus faltered. Her lack of experience already made the meld less efficient than it should be. All their lives were on the line here. She could not afford to lose focus. She began mentally reciting the Fibonacci sequence, starting at one. Silky had recommended the method in their previous battle, and it had worked well.

"What's going on?" Oona asked.

"It's a trap," Silky said.

"What kind?" Mitsuki asked.

"We won't know until it springs," Siv replied, "which will probably happen in a few minutes, just before we get into visual—"

Kyralla "saw" the attack half a second early. By the time Silky yelled "Incoming!" she already had the ship in motion. She rolled the *Outworld Ranger* leftward, and a double-pulsed laser beam skipped across the bottom of the ship's force-field.

"Shields down to ninety-five percent," Silky said.

Kyralla rolled the ship to the right, pulling up as she did. A second pulsed beam burned past, just missing them.

"I need max speed," Kyralla said distantly.

"Overriding safety protocols," Bishop responded over the comm.

Octavian bleeped angrily in the background.

"I need a target!" Mitsuki called out.

"Working on it," Siv said.

"Just beneath the freighter," Oona said. "That's where the first shots came from."

"I don't have a fix," Siv replied. "What are you seeing?"

"I don't see anything," Oona said. "I'm *sensing* it."

"Confirmation?" Mitsuki asked.

"I haven't countered their masking signals and jamming sequences yet," Silky said, "so I can't confirm."

Kyralla pitched the ship downward and rolled through two more pulsing laser shots. "Trust her."

"Okay then," Mitsuki said, "I've got a shot lined up for an undetected target just below the mining freighter."

"Take it," Siv said.

The *Outworld Ranger* recoiled as its railgun launched a twelve-centimeter, diamondine-tipped shell.

Kyralla, or maybe the ship's AI, she had no idea who did what now, adjusted for the recoil, and their course stayed true, taking them toward the enemy as fast as possible.

"Shouldn't we withdraw to the breakpoint?" Bishop asked.

"Two ion missiles inbound!" Siv said.

"Flak cannon ready," Mitsuki said.

A flash of light appeared in the distance.

"Good shot, Wings!" Silky said. "Masking signals are down. Enemy ships detected. Two T-XS starfighters and an armed DL-2 cruiser with a masked transponder. The railgun caused heavy damage to the cruiser. Its shields are down."

"Positions coming online in your HUD's...now," Siv said.

"Shouldn't we retreat?" Oona asked, repeating Bishop's question.

"Those T-XS starfighters are crazy fast," Silky said. "We can't outrun them to the breakpoint. However, they're poorly armed and have bad maneuverability. And that cruiser, though surprisingly well equipped with defensive gear, is a piece of donkey crap intended for sightseeing tourists."

"Ion missiles have locked onto us," Siv said.

Following the ship's guidance, Kyralla reduced speed and veered right. The missiles followed and closed in.

"Two seconds to impact," Silky announced.

Intuitively understanding what the ship wanted, Kyralla slammed the accelerator into max-speed and wrenched the control-stick left and forward. The *Outworld Ranger* plunged and rolled in the opposite direction.

Slowing down as their maneuvering thrusters activated, the missiles cut a wide arc to compensate. The flak cannon on top of the ship opened up and nailed them both.

Mitsuki stretched her arms then cracked her knuckles. "Let's get the bastards."

The two starfighters appeared as red dots on the three-dimensional starship locator in Kyralla's HUD, while the cruiser was a red oval with a yellow dot in the center.

The starfighters and the cruiser stopped hugging the mining freighter and zoomed toward the *Outworld Ranger*, the starfighters quickly outpacing their sluggish companion.

"Focus fire on the cruiser," Silky said. "It has the laser battery."

"Lining up a shot," Kyralla said.

She slowed the ship as she maneuvered into position. She wanted to have a surprise burst of speed available against the starfighters when needed.

The ship apparently agreed with her. Or maybe she agreed with it. She lacked the experience to tell the difference.

"What about the ion missiles?" Bishop asked. "Where did they originate?"

"Those were the only two the cruiser had," Siv said. "The starfighters are armed with small-caliber, dual-shot plasma cannons."

Mitsuki unleashed a burst of shots from their medium-caliber, quad-plasma cannon. The cruiser dodged poorly, and one of the shots glanced along its right side, burning deep gashes into its hull.

The starfighters opened fire. Using the ship's programmed maneuvers, Kyralla deftly weaved between the flaring white plasma bolts as she anticipated each shot.

"The DL2's lasers are at ninety-five percent charge," Siv announced.

The ship again recoiled as Mitsuki fired the railgun. Kyralla compensated too slowly, and a plasma shot glanced them.

"Shields to seventy-four!" Silky said.

The cruiser slid up and away from the railgun shell Mitsuki had fired. While it had successfully dodged the shot, it had exposed its underbelly. Kyralla jerked the *Outworld Ranger* hard left to line up a shot and slammed the accelerator all the way.

"Now!"

Mitsuki opened fire with the plasma cannons. Eight blazing plasma bolts struck the underside of the cruiser. For a few seconds, fire spurted out from the holes they had punched into the DL-2's hull. Then the ship exploded into a brief burst of flame, scattering metal fragments.

Unfortunately, the *Outworld Ranger* was speeding toward those fragments.

The starfighters overshot them, as Kyralla had intended when she'd maxed their speed. One of the starfighters began to turn, having to take a wide arc due to its poor maneuverability. The other activated its thrusters to spin around so it could face them, even while zooming away.

That happened to be Kyralla's plan as well. She cut the engines and activated the starboard thrusters, rotating the ship counterclockwise.

The *Outworld Ranger* performed its one-eighty much faster. Mitsuki cackled gleefully as she unleashed the quad cannons and decimated the spinning starfighter.

Kyralla threw the accelerator forward, countering their inertial movement toward the small debris cloud and the freighter. They were thrust back into their seats as the inertial dampeners struggled to compensate.

A few pieces of debris struck before they could reverse their momentum and accelerate away, taking the shields down by two percent.

The last starfighter had nearly turned around. Kyralla swept away from it then cut back in hard, rapidly closing on it at a ninety-degree angle.

With the plasma cannons still cooling after the last few bursts, Mitsuki fired the railgun as soon as their course straightened. It was a tough shot, estimating where the starfighter would be and adding enough lead for it to connect. Working in tandem with the ship's AI, Mitsuki judged it perfectly.

The shot pierced the starfighter's cockpit, going cleanly through one side and out the other. Fragments of electronics and a dismembered body, some of its parts still recognizable as they closed in, scattered into the void.

Kyralla blanked out the sight, not wanting to think about how they had just taken at least three lives, probably more.

Behind her, Oona gagged then ripped the circlet off her head. "I'm going to be sick," she muttered as she ran off the bridge.

Siv leaped up from the sensors and switched to the command chair, donning the circlet. "I've got her covered. Seneca, please check on Oona for me."

Seneca had been waiting in the galley with a med-kit. He didn't have Octavian's extensive medical programming, but like all advanced cogs with limbs, he had more than adequate first aid skills.

Kyralla wasn't worried. She knew Oona would be okay once she recovered from the shock of what they'd done, the same shock Kyralla was working hard to suppress until she had time to deal with it.

"Starfighter affiliation now confirmed," Silky said. "Star Cutters. No ID on the cruiser."

The Star Cutters were the second-smallest of the criminal guilds chasing them.

The *Outworld Ranger* notified them of an incoming message from the freighter. Siv accepted it but had their camera focus solely on Mitsuki, who was the one who had bargained with the captain.

Projected holographically at the front of the bridge was a middle-aged man with a bald head and a scraggly beard. He was dressed in overalls with a company insignia on the pocket.

"Thank you for rescuing me from those pirates," he said. "Your help is much appreciated."

"You're welcome," Mitsuki said. "Permission to dock and come aboard?"

"Granted," the captain said before ending their connection.

Kyralla turned to the others. "Well?"

"Take us in slowly," Siv said. "But be careful. I don't trust him anymore."

"Aha!" Silky said. "I just bypassed another signal projector located on the freighter, and without them knowing that I've done so. Quite clever of me, I must say."

"Out with it!" Mitsuki snapped.

"Humph! We've got the seven miners we expected, but there are four other, armed men with them."

"So it's another trap," Kyralla said.

Mitsuki groaned. "And even though we know about them, they've still got the advantage. As soon as we enter the docking tube, they'll open fire."

"Could we lure them over to us?" Bishop asked.

"I don't think they'd be stupid enough to take that bait," Mitsuki said. "We're at an impasse."

Kyralla turned to Siv. "What do we do?"

He smiled his sneaky, somewhat adorable smile, and said, "I've got a crazy idea."

"My favorite kind, sir!" Silky said enthusiastically.

9

SIV GENDIN

"Kyralla, fly us in for docking," Siv said. "But slowly. Take your time."

"Okay then," she replied dubiously.

"Sir, according to Seneca, Oona retched up her last meal but is otherwise fine."

Siv relayed that information to the others.

"I'll look in on her," Bishop said, his voice shaking, probably because he was disturbed as well.

Killing someone the first time, even in self-defense, wasn't an easy thing to handle. It had taken Siv months to recover after he took out a kidnapper on a botched rescue mission. He could still picture the guy perfectly, the moment before he shot him, and afterward as he lay dead in an alleyway.

It hadn't even helped that he was saving an innocent person whose family had paid for a rescue. That was also when he'd learned procurement was more his thing than extraction. Up until then, he'd assumed they were fundamentally the same.

He suspected the weight of what they'd done would hit Kyralla soon, but hopefully not before they were out of this situation.

"Before you start telling us your no doubt elaborate scheme, I would like to point out that leaving the system is still an option," Kyralla said.

"I think this is our best shot," he replied.

"Siv, you know I like the way you think," Mitsuki said. "But we could be facing eleven enemies in there. No clever scheme's going to counter that."

Oona staggered onto the bridge, her face white. "Only six bad guys onboard. The other six are innocent."

"Those numbers don't add up," Silky said. "There are only eleven people onboard."

Oona shook her head. "Twelve. Four criminals, a miner who's working with them, and the evil woman."

"Are you certain?" Siv asked. "Because the scans are only showing eleven, and none of them are women—evil or otherwise."

Frowning, Oona sat in the chair at the sensor station, swiveling it around to face the others. "When we...did what we did, my empathy surged out of control, and I got...readings...on the people aboard the freighter. The captain's clean, but one of his miners is a snitch, the one with the mustache. The bad woman is with the criminals."

"What does she look like?" Mitsuki asked.

Oona shrugged. "She was in the shadows, and I couldn't make out anything about her. It was almost like she was a ghost or something."

"Silky, could you..."

"Already on it, sir."

"I could meditate and try to scan the ship," Oona said. "Maybe I'll pick up some more info."

"Can you handle it," Siv asked.

"If you need to know, I can do it."

Oona pulled her legs up to sit cross-legged in the chair. She closed her eyes and began to breathe deeply.

"I've finished another thorough scan," Silky said, "using every parameter I could think of and countering every strategy I know of that might interfere, but I still only detect eleven people onboard that ship."

"What about the nearby vicinity?" Bishop asked, "like in a spacesuit just outside the ship, or something like that."

"I'll broaden the scan," Silky replied. A few minutes later he added, "Still only picking up eleven."

Oona opened her eyes, with a puzzled look on her face. "I'm getting the same information as before, except the woman is missing."

"So just eleven crew members?"

She nodded. "Four criminals, the mustachioed snitch, and the miners.

The woman must have been an apparition." She shrugged. "Maybe an echo of the priestess or..."

Her voice trailed off, but they all knew what she was thinking. That it had something to do with her upcoming Trial of Corruption. When she'd connected briefly with the priestess on Ekaran IV, she had seen a dark presence.

"See, that's not so bad," Siv said. "Just five bad guys to deal with."

"Those are terrible odds, given they have the advantage," Kyralla said.

"Does the freighter have a stardrive?" Mitsuki asked. "If so, then capturing it would more than make the risk worth it."

"Just an ion drive for in-system use," Silky answered.

"Then I'm opposed," Mitsuki said.

"Me, too," Kyralla said.

"I think we all are," Oona added.

"You haven't even heard my plan yet!" Siv argued. "Besides, we got those miners into trouble. What will happen to them now?"

"The Star Cutters will take the ship," Mitsuki said. "And they'll try to blame the captain and his crew on their failure, to save their skins. Star Cutter bosses are not a forgiving lot like the Shadowslip."

"Exactly," Siv said. "I'm not going to turn my back on them and miss out on an opportunity. Especially when we can interrogate the Star Cutters for information."

"Fine." Mitsuki sighed. "Reveal your clever scheme."

"I'm going to get into the ship's spacesuit and—"

"Nope!" Mitsuki said. "Don't like it."

"As we pull up to dock," Siv continued, "Silky will jam their sensors. The freighter doesn't have any sophisticated detection equipment, and neither do the criminals, just jamming and masking gear, so that should be easy enough, right?"

"Or easy left, sir. It doesn't matter."

"Does he ever focus?" Kyralla asked, rolling her eyes. "Seriously, how do you put up with him in your head?"

Siv smiled as Silky blew a raspberry at her.

"Once we're out of their field of view," Siv said, "I will maneuver around to the top of the freighter and enter through their emergency airlock. Silky, you can open the emergency airlock remotely, right?"

"I believe so, sir. I will look into it."

"Then I will sneak in and ambush them. As soon as I make my move, Mitsuki and Kyralla, you will burst in through the docking tube so we can catch them in a crossfire."

"I see how this is easy enough in your head," Kyralla said, "but too much could go wrong, way too much."

"I'm a procurement specialist. Breaking in is what I do. And it doesn't seem like too much to me."

"I agree this is all too risky," Bishop said, coming onto the bridge. He looked almost as pale as Oona. "Do you have any experience with spacewalks or breaking into ships?"

"How hard can it be?"

Bishop slapped his forehead, and Kyralla groaned.

"Look," Siv said, "if I can't get in, then we abandon the plan and fly away. But I think it's clear now that if our enemies had people this far out searching for us in this system, there's no way we're getting onto Zayer Prime without a battle far more dangerous than the one we just finished. And directly approaching Titus II is out of the question."

Reluctantly, they all agreed. But they weren't happy about it.

"Sir, this is a little crazy. Don't get me wrong. I've always admired your ability to improvise on the fly. And I like your patented brand of nutty scheming that almost always works out. That said, we work best when we have time to plan out our crazy capers in detail."

"Times change, Silkster." Siv headed toward the big locker next to the engineering station in the center of the ship. *"Now, it's time for me to learn how to use a spacesuit."* He opened the locker and stared at one. *"Pull up a user's guide for me, please."*

10

SIV GENDIN

"Jamming enabled, sir. You're good to go."

"Be careful, Siv!" Oona said over the comm with a worried tone.

"Good luck!" Kyralla and Bishop called out.

"Don't be a hero," Mitsuki added. "Be a smart criminal."

"Silky's got my back," Siv said. "What could go wrong?"

"Oh, sir, should I count the ways?"

"Don't you dare."

"Oh please, sir. I love counting! I do it all the time. I'm like a super smart counter."

Siv rolled his eyes as he opened the emergency airlock on top of the *Outworld Ranger*. With the bulky spacesuit on, he could barely squeeze through the hole. Its oversized backpack kept catching on things when he didn't expect it, throwing off his normally excellent balance.

He carefully maneuvered himself so that he could put a foot down as soon as possible. The maglock in his boot clamped to the top of the vessel. He bent down and closed the airlock.

"Best get moving, sir. You've got a narrow window of opportunity."

The *Outworld Ranger* had just pulled past the bridge of the long freighter. Kyralla began rotating the ship so that their rear section could connect to the freighter's docking tube.

Siv bent his legs, squatting down as far as he could in the spacesuit. Its bulk made it feel as if he were wearing four of his battlesuits stacked on top of one another.

"I feel so..."

"Fat, sir?"

"I was going to say awkward."

"I've studied the first spacewalks earthlings made, sir. You wouldn't believe how bulky their suits were. Think four times bigger than this."

"How did they do anything in them?"

"Clumsily? Honestly, I have no idea. Obviously, they managed it. Otherwise, we wouldn't be here. Go now."

Siv deactivated the maglock and pushed himself outward with all the strength he could manage. He shot free from the *Outworld Ranger* and zipped into space.

His breath caught as he realized he was floating free, that nothing was tethering him to anything. Panic shot through him, then faded away as he forced himself to breathe. It wasn't that bad. The suit could propel him for up to half an hour, and he was near a large target.

"Those guys in the beginning, they didn't have much in the way of spacecraft, did they?"

"They did not, sir. If they drifted too far off, they were simply gone."

"They must've been terrified doing this."

"I imagine they only sent out the brave, sir. Feeling scared?"

"A little, even though there's a ship nearby that can easily fly over and rescue me. I can't imagine how I'd feel knowing no one could pick me up if something went wrong."

"Shitless? Activating thrusters, sir."

Air jets on the suit's backpack altered his trajectory. As he zoomed above the freighter, Silky activated the jets again, arcing him downward and forward, toward the bridge.

Once he was near where he needed to be, he caught a docking spine and pulled himself in. His feet struck, and he activated the maglock. The emergency airlock was only five meters away.

"Nice steering, Silkster."

"Thank you, sir. But it wasn't my first time, and I am quite clever."

"I assume Dad never did this."

"Eyana, sir. Several times. She had your boldness. But unlike you, she had gone through some training for this sort of thing."

Siv stomped clumsily toward the airlock. He worried they would hear his footsteps but reminded himself it was highly unlikely given the thickness of the freighter's hull. He reached the airlock and was pleased to discover it was twice as big as the one on the *Outworld Ranger*. That should make infiltrating significantly easier.

As Silky went to work, he radioed the others on their secure channel. "I'm in position."

"We're about to begin the docking procedure," Kyralla responded.

The door to the freighter's emergency airlock unclamped, and a puff of air escaped into space.

"You're good to go, sir."

Siv checked the locator on his HUD. It showed four of the men inside moving from the freighter's bridge toward the docking tube where the *Outworld Ranger* had pulled up.

"Confident in your readings?"

"Well over ninety percent, sir. Are you concerned about Oona's vision?"

"A little." He sighed. *"Life was easier before we were dealing with mystical teenagers."*

"Yes, but don't you think everything was starting to feel a little too routine?"

"You're an adventurer at heart, Silkster."

"It's what I was designed for."

"Okay then, let's do this." He radioed the others. "I'm going in."

Siv bent down and lifted the hatch. He peeked inside. Everything looked normal. He crawled into the airlock, found the ladder to climb down, and closed the hatch behind him. When he reached the bottom, Silky activated the seal on the airlock, pressurizing the chamber.

"You can take off the suit now, sir."

Siv released the catch on his helmet, but then thought better of it and resealed it. *"You know, just in case they've caught on somehow, I think I'll wear it until I'm outside the airlock."*

He trudged forward and opened the door leading into a storage area. Crates of nutrition blocks, spare parts, and repair equipment lay in haphazard stacks. He stepped into the darkly lit room, and the door to the airlock slid closed behind him.

The overhead lights flashed on, and he stood face-to-face with a slender, female Ekisian aiming a heavy blaster pistol at his head. She twisted the shimmering, meter-long shock-blade she held with her other hand, making sure he noticed it. As if he could have missed it.

Ekisians were one of the few unquestionably alien species within the Terran Federation. With most species, like wakyrans, it wasn't always clear whether they were true aliens or humans the Benevolence had genetically altered in the early centuries of galactic colonization, as it had done with gizmets and engers. Some thought that wakyrans, in particular, had been uplifted from a more primitive species. Records of such activities, however, had never been made available, so no one knew for sure.

Like all the members of her species, the Ekisian woman had parchment skin, a broad yet flat face, a stubby nose with three wide nostrils, blue hair, and black, bulbous eyes. Siv found it difficult to distinguish one Ekisian from another. Most humans did. Ekisian physical differences were subtle to outsiders, and they primarily discerned individual characteristics among their own kind through scents and sounds.

This one was easily recognizable though, thanks to the crisscrossing scars that marred her face.

"Zetta," Siv muttered in disbelief. "This is rotten luck."

"For you, maybe." A wicked grin spread across her face, and then she licked her pale lips with a dark purple tongue. "For me, it is best."

"Sorry, sir. Oona was right the first time. I don't know how I could have missed Zetta...again. I thought I had her figured out."

Zetta wore a plain, dark brown tunic over a pair of tan pants. She had a holster for her gun, and a scabbard slung over her back. If there was any armor plating beneath the spider-mesh clothing, it wasn't obvious. He doubted there was. Zetta didn't like to be slowed down. She also didn't use any always-active tech that could make her traceable. She didn't even own a chippy. Of course, she wasn't opposed to using other types of advanced gadgets when the need arose. Usually, the blaster aimed at his face was the most advanced tech she carried.

This carefulness, along with the fact that Ekisians were coldblooded and could slow their heartbeats, made her difficult to detect in sensor scans. What made Zetta practically impossible to pinpoint, though, was a mystery.

"Sir, I'm contacting the others to let them know something's gone wrong. I suggest stalling her if you can."

"I thought you might pull something like this, Gendin," she hissed.

"You waited out here on the edge of this system for me?"

"Informants on many vessels. One contacted me. He gets paid. Lucky I'm already in area on other job when bounty comes through. Told myself, Gendin smart. Never go straight to Titus system. Go Zayer first. I gamble. I win."

Siv stared down the barrel then glanced at the sword again. There wasn't much he could do wearing the bulky spacesuit with his weapons all tucked inside a storage compartment in the backpack. His force-shield was strapped to his arm beneath the suit, but that wasn't going to be enough.

"Two years it has been?" Zetta asked.

"Two too few."

She smiled. "You did not enjoy our last mission?"

Zetta knew damn well he hadn't. The Shadowslip had hired her for an assassination, and it had been Siv's job to aid her in planning and to serve as backup in case something went wrong. He had always refused kill missions, and Big Boss D had respected that, up to a point. He saw no problem making Siv help someone else carry out one. He and Zetta had not gotten along, and not just because Siv hated the very idea of the mission.

"Sir, I recalibrated all my sensors to pick her up last time." Silky groaned. *"I shouldn't even have had to do that. It's not like we didn't deal with any Ekisians back in the day. Eyana took part in the quelling of the rebellion on Ekisia."*

"She's good at what she does."

"But how is she masking her body signature this well—again? You're looking at her, yet she's still invisible on all our scans. Hmm, maybe it's something in the fiber of her clothes or—"

"Find a way to get me out of this, and then you can figure out how she did it."

"You wonder how you scan missed me?" Zetta asked. "You chippy think he not so smart after all, eh?"

"It had crossed my mind. And it's driving him crazy."

"Too bad. Is secret I take to grave."

"I can help you get there."

Zetta frowned. "Gendin, why you always so mean? I am not hurting you."

"You're not going to kill me?" he asked incredulously.

She shook her head. "Kill others. Except for little girl and Reel. Big money for turn them in. Especially girl. Worth three fortunes. I retire for life, have harem men do my everything for me."

She backed up a step, standing just far enough away that he'd never be able to get to her before she could shoot him. Keeping the gun pointed at him, she sheathed her blade then reached into a pocket with that hand, drawing out a drug injector.

His eyes went wide and a deep ache he'd suppressed for a week, with a lot of help from Octavian's medications, awoke within him. His eyes watered, saliva flooded his mouth, his heart rate increased.

"Is Kompel, see. You say, 'I own you bitch,' yes?"

11

VEGA KALEEB

The *Spinner's Blade*, a bullet-shaped starship of the Infiltrator class, dropped out of hyperspace and cruised into the edge of the Ekaran system. The matte black, diamondine hull absorbed nearly all the light that struck it, so that the ship merged with the dark of space and only the stars it blotted out revealed its presence.

The exceedingly rare Infiltrators—equipped with cloaking technology, dual-lasers, and the most advanced countermeasures available—were designed to transport Forward and Empathic Services agents on dangerous missions into enemy territory. While intended for a crew of up to three, the *Spinner's Blade* carried only a single android and his sky-blade combat companion.

Vega woke up from his daily, hour-long nap, his cache memory sorted, his subroutines optimized, with all his operative systems checked for errors. Finding himself in optimum health, he unplugged the cable leading from a port on the small ship's surprisingly large flux capacitor to the socket on his chest where a human heart would have been located.

His built-in power pack, protected by a diamondine box beneath his reinforced titanium ribcage, now held a full charge that could sustain him for a year of regular activity or three months of intense action. He zipped up his flight suit and pressed a button, causing the cable to retract into the outlet.

Unfortunately, he didn't have access to an unlimited power source like

Faisal did. The ultimate goal of the experiment allowing the 9G-x models to tap directly into flux-space had been to give androids limitless "hearts."

But that access had caused rampant instabilities in the 9G-x models, leading to all but two, that he knew of, being scrapped. However, those two had gained tremendously from their direct exposure to flux-space, finding their capabilities enhanced. The Benevolence, in its seemingly ultimate wisdom, had abandoned the project.

Vega marched the five meters from the engineering station near the center of the ship to the cramped cockpit. Now that he no longer had Gyring riding along, he was considering dumping the other two seats and stations.

He dropped into the command chair and called up a favorite movie from two hundred years ago, one he'd seen a dozen times. He would've preferred something new, but modern flicks never did anything for him.

"Faisal, let me know when you've got something. I'm going to—"

"Boss, I've already broken into the secure channel for the Shadowslip Guild. I can patch you into their leader whenever you're ready."

"Damn, Faisal, that was fast!"

"I'd love to take all the cred, boss. But I didn't do anything special. There was already a back channel in place, allowing emergency access to their command group. It wasn't being used, and I'm certain they don't know about it. Highly secret, highly elegant."

"Then how did you find it so quickly?"

"That's what disturbs me, boss. Whoever did it used the same method I always use for such occasions. It's as if I'd broken in before and had opened up access to their network."

"Sounds impressive."

"Too impressive for my tastes, boss. You'd need a damned good hacker for this, with a deep understanding of how the networks function at the root level. And I didn't think anyone was capable of this sort of work, this elegantly, anymore. Save for me. But maybe some standard 9G's out there with the right programming could do it."

"Is this going to pose a problem?"

"No, we're good, boss."

"Okay then. Patch me through. Video feed."

A micro-camera on the ship console in front of him began recording. Despite being half a light year from the planet, his echo-space connection to the network would allow instantaneous communication.

"Who will I be talking to?"

"Big Boss D, boss."

"Seriously?"

"I wouldn't make up something that lame, boss."

"Make sure I can see him."

Vega put on his most intimidating expression and waited while Faisal directly called the leader of the Shadowslip Guild on Ekaran IV. He always loved this part of the game.

A giant of a man trembling with rage appeared within his HUD. He was behind a desk in a dark room filled with smoke. Vega could see little else since the man took up so much of his camera's view.

"Big Boss D?" Vega asked.

"Who the hell are you?! And how did you get access to my c|slate?"

"I am Vega Kaleeb. And I have access because I *wanted* access."

Big Boss D went rigid, his eyes flaring with surprise. "I...uh...didn't...um... recognize you, Mr. Kaleeb."

"How would you have?"

"I...I don't know."

"I will give you a moment."

"Right, thank you." The man frowned. "A moment for what?"

"To find an image to verify my identity."

"Right."

Faisal regularly scrubbed images of Vega from the galactic net, but always left a few on sites regularly accessed by criminal guilds looking for bounty hunters. It was difficult to intimidate people who didn't recognize you.

"You appear to be...um...you. But I...I am not sure what I can do for you Mr. Kaleeb. I'm not authorized to negotiate on behalf of the Shadowslip."

"This isn't about the bounty price," Vega said. "I do not negotiate such matters until I have secured the mark. No, this is about a rogue procurement agent of yours and his accomplice, an extraction agent who goes by the name Mitsuki Reel."

A bead of sweat ran down Big Boss D's face. "Ah, well... Because you haven't accepted the guild's offer, I am not authorized to divulge knowledge about any of our agents or, in Mitsuki's case, trusted outside contractors."

"I am willing to pay you, *personally*, twenty thousand credits for information on the two of them, Mr. D."

The big man chewed on his bottom lip, frowning. "I really can't tell you what—"

"Thirty-five."

Big Boss D edged forward in his seat, eyes glittering. He wavered a moment, then shook his head. "Sorry. I can't. It's too big a risk."

Vega sighed. "Those who refuse to do business with me, Mr. D, they do not live long, prosperous lives. Maybe you feel you're comfortable in your underground bunker in Bei, surrounded by dozens of agents and guards. But there is no place where I cannot reach you. I think my direct call into your network proves that."

The man wiped sweat from his brow. "Now, it isn't necessary to threaten—"

Vega interrupted him. "I think we both know that it is necessary for me to threaten you. Tell me what I want to know and get paid. Don't tell me what I want to know and suffer. And when I say suffer, Mr. D, understand I am talking about an extreme amount of pain leading to an eventual, messy death."

Big Boss D flopped back into his chair, groaning. "You...you are putting me in a difficult spot with my superiors, one that might get me demoted, maybe even killed if you don't end up selling the mark to us."

"I understand that," Vega said.

"'Nevolence, you're a rotten bastard."

"So I've been told many, many times. I consider it a compliment."

"Death or death isn't much of a choice."

"He's thinking of risking it, boss. And while assaulting a base full of criminals sounds fun, we can't afford to waste time and resources. Though I would enjoy slicing that pompous ass into bacon."

"Have you found the info we need on their network?"

"Only basic biographies, boss, and some operational information. It's more than we had but not nearly as much as you'd want. The information on the procurement agent is especially limited."

"Damn."

"I do, however, have some information you might find useful for this negotiation."

While Big Boss D muttered pointless counter proposals, trying to squirm his way out of the situation, Vega read over the information Faisal had given him. Then he put on his darkest grin and interrupted the stammering man.

"By the way, Mr. D, how's your mother? Is she still in good health? I believe you last visited her on Yulis Beta over a year ago, right? When she had neck surgery. I assume she's recovered well..."

Big Boss D's eyes flared wide. "How...how did you find out about my—"

"My methods are proprietary, Mr. D."

"You know what," the big man said, wiping sweat from his face with the back of his hand, "how about I tell you what you want to know?"

"Good idea."

"You can pay me whatever you think is fair."

"I offered you thirty-five thousand, but you made things difficult, so ten seems fair to me."

"I accept."

"That was overgenerous, boss. This guy's a pretentious prick."

Vega started the money transfer. *"You can't blame him for being full of himself, Faisal. He's the big man on his small world. And I want him to have* some *positive feelings about the transaction."*

A few minutes later, Big Boss D responded. "Received. So what would you like to know?"

"The two agents are mysteries shrouded in fake identities, and there's hardly any reliable public information on them, so I would like you to send me extensive dossiers on both, including recent mission data and their operational methods, perceived weaknesses and so forth."

"Done."

"And I'd like you to sum up the two of them as best as you can right now. In your own words. I'd like to know what kind of people *you* think they are. Start with the extraction agent."

The man furrowed his brow, then a few moments later, nodded. "The thing about Mitsuki is that nothing's more important to her than freedom. She's mischievous, certainly, but at heart, she's not a criminal. She just likes rescuing people stuck in bad situations. And she's good at it. She's the best damn extraction agent I've ever seen in action, and she's had tons of offers to work on other worlds, but she always turns them down."

"If she likes rescuing people, why does she work with criminals instead of law enforcement or fire and rescue?"

"She has issues with authority and..." He shrugged. "I don't know anything about her past or what drives her. I don't think anyone does." He furrowed his brow. "Well, Gendin might know. People like to tell him things."

"The procurement specialist?"

"Yes."

"And you never used Kompel on the wakyran because..."

"The strain I have access to won't work on wakyrans. And I don't think any strains will."

"Okay then, what about the procurement agent who I have eleven identities for? Is his real name Siv Gendin?"

"Only eleven identities?" Big Boss D chuckled, nervously. "He's got a lot more, I assure you. Yes, his real name's Siv Gendin, or so he's claimed since I found him at the age of ten. He's damned good at what he does, too. You want an item, he'll get it for you. Never fails. That's why I've kept him under wraps as best I can, so the guild won't transfer him to a more prominent planet."

"Interesting," Vega said, though he was quite bored. None of this was proving helpful. "What motivates him?"

Big Boss D shrugged. "He's not a criminal at heart either, but he does what we tell him to do because he's Kompelled. He does enjoy the work, though. He plans out elaborate stratagems and always has several fallback plans. He has dozens of safe houses and escape routes. He also does his best never to hurt anyone. I think there's a family in the city that he supports."

"According to the info I was initially provided and based on some notes I stole from your server, Gendin's gear seems elaborately high-tech, especially for a procurement specialist on a backwater planet."

"I doubt you know the half of it." Big Boss D slicked his hair back and wiped his brow again. "I doubt I do either. It's part of why he's so good at what he does. Gendin's got an advanced sensor array, spy drones, a powerful force-shield, and all kinds of other stuff you can hardly get anymore. He's a walking fortune worth of gear. He's probably worth more than he's stolen for me."

"How did he come by all this rare equipment?"

"The gear was stored in a locker beside his stasis unit, which we found in an abandoned military base that had been lost after the Tekk Plague. We unfroze him and discovered he could use the gear, so we recruited him."

A frozen kid found in an abandoned military base? Vega suppressed the wild ideas racing through his brain.

"Boss, are you thinking what I'm—"

"Hush." Vega leaned forward with interest. "Why didn't you take any of this gear from him?"

"Couldn't use it. All of it was DNA locked with the highest security protocols we'd ever seen."

"You can't defeat a good DNA lock?" Vega asked, surprised.

"One this high in caliber? Maybe. But at the risk of damaging the equipment. I had a hunch that it would be better to use it via the kid. Up until this week, it has been the right call."

"Why did a kid have access to advanced military gear?"

"He claimed his father was in the special forces and had transferred the equipment to him right before he died. But according to our research, his father was an archaeologist. I guess that was just a cover identity."

Vega leaned further forward, the artificial blood pounding through his silicone veins. "He's the son of Gav Gendin?"

"Yeah, that's him," Big Boss D said.

Astonished, Vega thumped back into his seat.

"Shit me blind, boss! You know what that means..."

"His chippy," Vega said slowly, "was it locked as well?"

Big Boss D nodded. "It threatened me. Said if I tried to take him bad things would happen."

"What model is the unit?"

"Has to be an 8G, minimum, given the device's capabilities. But I'd guess it's probably a 9G."

Vega found himself speechless, his advanced brain racing through all the possibilities and problems this information presented. Even Faisal was quiet and contemplative for a change.

"So you knew his father?" Boss D asked.

Vega didn't respond.

"Mr. Kaleeb, is something wrong?"

"What? Oh, I knew him only by reputation. Thank you, Mr. D. That was most helpful. Send the dossiers as soon as possible. Be thorough. *Very* thorough."

"Of course. I'll send those along right away. I wouldn't worry too much about Gendin. He won't be a problem for long. If he took his dose of Kompel at the last possible time, then he should start going through withdrawal in the next few days."

"He's the mastermind of the operation," Vega said. "So I need to understand him. Be thorough in your report."

"I would assume that at this point Mitsuki Reel is in charge. Trust me, Gendin will be dead soon."

"Thank you for your cooperation, Mr. D."

Vega ended the connection and fidgeted nervously in his seat. *"I know who the real mastermind is here."*

Faisal zoomed in front of Vega. He stared at his reflection on the skyblade's glossy surface.

They both said the same name at the same time.

"Silky."

"This is big, boss. Real big. Bigger than Big Boss D big."

12

OONA VIM

"You were right the first time, kid," Silky said over the *Outworld Ranger's* comm.

Heart pounding, feeling as if she might vomit again, Oona slumped back into the command chair. She should have trusted her senses. She should have been able to duplicate what she'd seen the first time.

Mitsuki stood and yelled. "You have *got* to be screwing with me, Silky!"

"I would never screw with you, Mits," Silky said. "You're not my type."

"Cut the crap!" She pounded the weapons console. "How could you have missed Zetta?"

"I have no idea. I recalibrated my sensors in case we ever ran across her again. Yet she still foiled me."

"Who exactly is this Zetta person?" Bishop asked. "Other than bad news."

"She's the worst news," Mitsuki replied. "She's a badass Ekisian assassin with a mean streak. And if she's got the drop on Siv then..." she sighed "...then he's doomed."

"There is some good news," Silky said. "She doesn't intend to kill Siv. Or Mitsuki. And she won't kill Oona. Kyralla and Bishop, apparently you're expendable."

Kyralla groaned. "I *knew* it was a stupid plan."

"He couldn't have known someone undetectable was onboard waiting for him," Bishop said.

"He should have listened to us," Kyralla countered. "We told him the risk was too great."

"If she's not going to kill him, then that's good news, right?" Oona asked, growing hopeful. "That means there's a chance we could save him, or maybe he could escape."

"He's not getting away from her," Mitsuki said.

"Especially since she has an injector of Kompel with her," Silky added.

"How's that bad news?" Kyralla asked.

"He's an addict," Silky said. "And she has the drug. It's not going to be easy for him to resist her."

"He's managed well so far," Bishop said.

"Well yeah," Silky replied, "when he was on the run, half-dying, and the stuff wasn't in sight, things were easy. But he's been craving it. And judging by his vitals, things are pretty bad right now."

Kyralla and Bishop exchanged despondent looks. Mitsuki leaned her head back and yelled a curse.

Oona had sensed Siv's struggle, the war within him that raged between his need for Kompel and his sense of honor and his desire to do what was right. And she knew a lesser man would have turned on them along the way, readily giving them up to the Shadowslip, not just so that he could live but so that he could get the drug he craved.

Even a well-intentioned man with good willpower might have turned, or at least have given up. But Siv was exceptional in his desire to be free from the Kompel and to do what was right. And perhaps the guardian amulet had aided him. Regardless, she had faith that he would resist. The assassin might kill him, but he would not falter because of the Kompel. She trusted in that.

"The smart thing for you to do," Silky said, "would be to turn the ship around and get the hell out of here. Leave before she makes an offer, bargaining Siv's life or the lives of the miners."

"Not a chance," Oona said firmly. "Siv saved Kyralla and me. Without him, we'd be in the Tekk Reapers' hands. He could have abandoned us then. And he could have given up on us because of the Kompel. But he didn't. So we're not going to abandon him now."

Kyralla frowned. "Sis, you are the galaxy's best hope for restoring the Benevolence, especially now that the priestess can prepare you to face the Trial of Corruption. Keeping you safe is—"

"Not worth it if we can't do the right thing." She gripped the arms of the command chair tightly. "After all, what sort of galactic savior would I be if I'm willing to turn my back on my friends? Or those miners who are only in trouble because of us?"

"Okay then, we fight." Kyralla stared at her sister then added in her firmest voice, mimicking their dad. "But *you* are staying here on the ship."

"But—"

"No buts," Kyralla snapped. "The rest of us will do our best to save him. But if we fail, you have to promise to get the hell out of here, to fly far away and...and do the best you can to make us proud."

Oona relented. "Alright." She sighed. "Besides, it's not like I can do anything in a fight except get in the way."

"I think you're all forgetting something here," Mitsuki said. "That docking tube is still a kill zone. We don't stand a chance of getting into that ship, and with Zetta onboard, our odds are even worse than before."

"Zetta probably has some nasty tricks up her sleeve," Silky said. "On second thought, I'm *certain* she has some nasty tricks up her sleeve. I want Siv to survive, almost certainly more than any of you, but trust me when I say your best plan would be to cut and run."

Mitsuki slumped into her chair, shaking her head. "I have to agree with Silky. As much as I want to save Siv, it simply can't be done."

Bishop hopped up and, grinning, pumped a fist. "I've got it. Honestly, I can't believe I didn't think of it earlier."

"Got what?" Kyralla asked.

"A plan," he said. "And it's crazy, but—"

"Crazy plans are how we got into this mess," Kyralla said pointedly.

"Maybe," Bishop replied, "but it's the only way we're going to get Siv out of there. Just let me check some specifications on the docking tube first." He nodded several times while reviewing data in his HUD. "Yep, yep. I've got a plan. And I think it just might work."

"What's the plan?" Mitsuki asked, disinterested. She apparently didn't believe they had a shot. Oona, however, had faith.

"We drive the Tezzin into their ship, using it as an assault vehicle," Bishop said. He looked at Oona as if seeking her approval for the go-ahead as if it were her call to make.

Oona half shrugged and muttered a response. "If...if you think it will work..."

Mitsuki scratched her cheek and chewed on her lip, clearly running the calculations of pulling it off in her head. Finally, she nodded appreciatively and said, "Okay then, will it fit?"

Bishop nodded. "I just checked. We'll even have a tiny bit of room to spare."

"Hot damn then!" Mitsuki shot out of her seat and started off the bridge. "Let's go!"

Kyralla darted up to the command chair and gave Oona a hug and a kiss. "Stay safe. And don't do anything stupid."

"I promise. Be careful. All of you."

The three of them rushed off the bridge. Oona pushed herself all the way back into the command chair, squeezing the arms tightly. She said a quick prayer for their success and safe return.

After a few minutes, Oona began to squirm. The empty bridge made her uncomfortable. If they didn't return, she would be here all alone, commanding the ship by herself. She was fourteen. She shouldn't be piloting a ship, traveling to... She didn't have a clue where she would go or what she would do if she were stranded on her own.

The others could all *do* things. Everyone, except for Bishop, had combat training. And Bishop could fix pretty much any gadget. Kyralla was already becoming a fantastic pilot. Siv and Mitsuki had all sorts of criminal expertise.

Silky had given her the command chair, but only because Siv was sick. All she could do was sometimes sense things or tell when someone was lying, and even then, she wasn't reliable.

Oona shook her head. She needed to be meditating right now and trying to track the assassin, not feeling sorry for herself. And reliable or not, she had to use whatever abilities she could to help the others. She might be only fourteen years old, but she was a hyperphasic messiah. Maybe it was time she started acting like one.

She pulled her legs up into the chair, closed her eyes, and began breathing deeply. Then she reached out with her mind, searching for the assassin.

13

SIV GENDIN

"You are the stalling me," Zetta said. "I am not pleased." She waved the injector around dramatically. "Maybe I not give Kompel?"

Siv had asked Zetta about the terms of the bounty, how much she expected to get paid, and whether she would accept a lesser offer from him. He had made increasingly ridiculous proposals that would allow him to escape or buy his way free, even though he knew she wouldn't accept any of them.

Having worked with Zetta before, though, he knew it was best to throw a lot of ideas at her at once. She might be devious and good at killing people, but she got overwhelmed by information, especially information delivered in rapid Terran with a heavy Ekaran accent. And Siv was deliberately using a lot more accent than normal.

The point of all this wasn't to escape. He knew that wasn't going to happen. He was just stalling to buy the others time to conclude that it was best for them to make a run for it before she could threaten to torture him or kill the miners. Because he felt certain they would cave and do what she asked. Or delay for too long while trying to find a solution and expose themselves to a third party.

Siv's eyes tracked the Kompel. Once the others flew off in the *Outworld Ranger*, he *would* make a move against Zetta. And she would kill him. He had no doubt. Her reflexes and aim were superb. But survival wasn't the most important thing to him right now. He couldn't let her win. He couldn't let the *Kompel* win. So he needed to force Zetta to kill him.

"Okay, I admit it," he said. "I have been the stalling you. But those were good offers I made. I would gladly pay you everything I've got, give you inside knowledge about the Shadowslip, and work for you."

She shook her head. "Girl worth far, far more than you. We go to bridge now. I threaten kill miners. Friends surrender."

"They're not going to give themselves up."

Zetta shrugged. "If miners no work, I think maybe they like you, surrender if I start hurting you."

"Sir, the others have formulated an assault plan."

"You were supposed *to convince them to leave."*

"And that worked as well as I expected it to, sir. It's a solid plan they've got. That Bishop has a devious mind."

"Well, what's the play?"

"They're going to drive the Tezzin in through the docking tube."

Siv nearly flinched in surprise and admiration. That was clever. *"I guess he's already checked to make sure it will fit?"*

"Indeed, sir. I should have thought of it as soon as I studied the freighter's specs. I guess I need to work harder on my car-based attack strategies. Okay, they're nearly ready. I told Bishop to make a lot of noise to distract Zetta."

"Tell them to focus on rescuing the miners first. No distraction's going to be good enough for me to reach her. And if forced to, she'll just shoot me. Ultimately, I'm expendable."

"I think I have best plan now, though," Zetta said, sneering. "You give them over."

Siv scoffed at her. "Hardly."

"But I give you Kompel. Let you go. Tell Shadowslip you dead."

"Not happening," he said, salivating at the thought of the Kompel rushing into his system, quelling the withdrawal.

"Maybe I even tell you how Kompel made. Where comes from. You get all you want, yes?"

"You...you know where it comes from? How it's made?"

"You give over friends. I give secrets. You go free. I promise. You not have bounty. They think you dying soon, maybe not bother paying to have back."

"Sir, I have a plan for beating Zetta, and it could work if she's distracted

even a little. When I tell you to, deploy your shield and leap forward. As fast as you can. Try to get a little air under your feet, too. Okay?"

Siv stared at her. "You know how the Kompel is made? You swear?"

"Why lie when I own you, yes?"

"Sir!"

"Wh–what?"

"Get ready. On my mark lunge."

"O–okay. Sure. Whatever."

"Sir, she's lying! You know she is. You can't trust Zetta. She'd kill her mother for a credit."

"Of...of course."

He steeled his courage. If he let Zetta get to him, then that would mean allowing the Kompel to win. He couldn't give in to it.

An engine roar followed by gunshots reverberated through the ship. Then came more gunfire. Zetta flinched, turning her head ever so slightly toward the sound.

"Now, sir! Go!"

Siv was staring death in the face, a gun barrel aimed between his eyes. The moment of truth had arrived. And he would beat the Kompel, no matter the cost. He activated the force-shield, raised his arm, and lunged forward.

As the force-shield's energy disc erupted through the spacesuit's arm, two things he had not expected happened. First, Silky activated his antigrav, setting it to seventy-five percent. Then the air jets on the back of the spacesuit fired at full blast.

Zetta's eyes flicked back to him. She fired her heavy blaster. Had he still been on the ground, and not a half-meter up, he would not have had the force-shield up high enough in time, and the shot would have struck him in the neck. Instead, the shot fired into the top of his shield.

Siv crashed into her, knocking her back and pinning her against the wall. She coughed and shook her head as if dazed.

The suit's propulsion jets sputtered out.

"Her gun isn't DNA locked, sir."

Siv rammed his right shoulder into Zetta's chest, then with both hands he grabbed her gun, getting a hold despite the thick gloves he was wearing. Twisting, he wrenched it free from her grasp.

Before he could spin around, she kicked him in the back.

"Shield up!" Silky shouted.

Siv fell into a crouch and turned, raising the shield. Zetta's force-blade clashed against it, sparks flying as it unleashed a concussive shockwave. The impact sent a bruising numbness down into his arm.

He lifted the blaster to take a shot, but Zetta had already withdrawn her blade and was making a low stab with it, forcing him to lower the shield. He blocked that attack as well, and again the impact sent a deep ache into his joints.

"Force-shield at twelve percent, sir."

She pulled away quickly and did a backhand slash. He couldn't get the shield up in time, so he ducked his head beneath it. The blade passed just above him, causing his hair to rise and the skin of his scalp to tingle.

Knowing she would be out of position as she recovered from the slash, he surged upward, lifting the blaster. But she hadn't readied herself for another attack. She had used her momentum to spin all the way around and make a dash for the door, ducking and weaving.

Siv fired the blaster. Not used to a heavy pistol, it kicked in his hand. His shot sailed just over her shoulder. He fired again, but she was already through the door.

Damn, he'd forgotten how fast Zetta could move.

Siv lumbered forward. He was never going to catch her, especially in this bulky suit. But the others might still need his help by the time he reached them.

Just as he neared the door, out of the corner of his eye, he caught sight of the Kompel injector lying on the floor. He paused.

"Sir, she's heading toward the others."

Siv stepped toward the abandoned injector.

It was still intact.

"Sir, you can come back for it."

He stood transfixed. What he wanted most of all was lying right there on the floor. There was no one to keep him from getting it. He could take an injection, and he wouldn't have to fight the withdrawal anymore. It was right there, and it would be so easy.

"Sir, if you catch her, you can interrogate her. Maybe she does know how it's made."

Siv fell to his knees and grabbed the injector, cradling it in his hands like a fragile, baby bird.

"She doesn't know. I'm sure it was all a lie. But this...this is real."

14

KRYALLA VIM

Heart pounding, stomach cramping with anxiety, Kyralla climbed into the backseat of the Tezzin. She took the right side while Mitsuki took the left. They had to kneel awkwardly inside since Bishop had ripped out the seats to prepare the skimmer for an overhaul. He had also removed the windows.

Kyralla placed her plasma pistol on the floorboard and wiped her sweating palms dry. She tried to focus and take deep, natural breaths, but she couldn't stop the mad rush of thoughts charging through her brain.

For the fourth time, she checked that her expandable force-staff was still secure in its sheath on her back. Realizing she was distracted, she tried yet again to center her mind. Her forewarning ability was useless if she couldn't stay in the moment.

Mitsuki appeared calm and relaxed beside her, but she already had years of experience. Kyralla had spent thousands of intensive hours in the combat simulator, but she had already learned that training just wasn't the same as live action. On top of that, most of her training had focused on the defensive tactics she would need to protect her sister, with little time devoted specifically to assault missions like this.

Bishop hopped in and grabbed the wheel.

"It still works, right?" Mitsuki asked.

"The engine does," Bishop replied. "And the shields."

"That's all we need," Mitsuki said.

Bishop turned the car around and drove it toward the back of the ship. "Everyone ready?"

Kyralla picked up her plasma pistol, swallowed hard, and nodded. "Let's go."

Mitsuki patted her on the shoulder. "Relax. You've got this."

"I'm just a little nervous is all. I haven't been in a real gunfight before."

"I have faith in you," Mitsuki said. "I mean, until this week, you had never piloted a starship through a space battle before, and that turned out fine, right?"

Kyralla replied with what she hoped was a confident nod.

"Ship, open the door for docking access," Bishop requested.

A docking tube had extended out from the freighter and locked onto the *Outworld Ranger's* hull. A plasma window matching the interior of the tunnel was then deployed from the freighter and air pumped inside. The plasma window alone was sufficient for accessing another ship, but most people preferred redundancy when dealing with the vacuum of space.

Under normal circumstances, the boarding ramp in the back of the *Outworld Ranger* would have remained closed, while an iris in its center opened to match the diameter of the other ship's docking tube. But the mining freighter was set up for transferring cargo and other equipment using antigrav sleds and forklifts. The tunnel they had deployed was larger than the entire back door of the *Outworld Ranger*, giving Bishop plenty of space to drop the boarding ramp and drive the skimmer car through.

The boarding ramp retracted into the ship, leaving only a blue shimmering plasma window between them and the tunnel.

"Ship, extend our plasma window to match the interior of the docking tube," Bishop commanded.

"I cannot project our plasma window into the freighter's," the ship replied.

"Reduce the diameter of our window by one percent."

"Plasma window extended," the ship responded.

"Now we're protected on the way back," Bishop said, "in case things go wrong and we have to retreat."

"Ship, once we're through, retract the boarding ramp," Mitsuki added. "And don't let in anyone except the three of us or Siv."

"Good idea," Kyralla said.

Inwardly, she cursed herself. She should have thought of that since it would keep Oona safe if something happened to them.

Bishop slammed the car into drive. "Hold on!"

The skimmer's propulsion engine whined as they zoomed through the fifteen-meter docking tube at breakneck speed. The freighter's loading bay was nearly big enough to hold the *Outworld Ranger* itself, but at the speed they were going, they'd cross that space in mere seconds.

"We're going too fast!" Mitsuki yelled.

"It's an ambush!" Bishop called back as if that explained his behavior.

Red dots representing the four Star Cutter thugs popped into Kyralla's locator, along with tiny symbols denoting their armaments. One carrying two plasma pistols stood just off to the side of the docking tube, waiting to ambush them from behind when they entered. One with an assault rifle was perched on a catwalk in the back. And two with plasma carbines hunkered behind crates in the middle of the otherwise empty bay.

The Tezzin burst through the tunnel, and Bishop drove straight toward the crates in the center. All the thugs opened fire, but their shots bounced harmlessly off the skimmer's force-field.

The two behind the crates barely had time to react. One dived aside, but the other, perhaps stunned by their tactic, stupidly stood his ground and kept firing. The car plowed through the crates and smacked into him. His broken body somersaulted across the bay and struck the far wall. Blood streamed down the force-field as a dot disappeared from Kyralla's locator.

"Oh shit!" Bishop slammed on the brakes and cut the wheel hard. "Brace for impact!"

As the car spun, the tail end clipped the thug who had dived aside, knocking him several meters away.

The Tezzin crashed against the far wall. The force-field flickered but held. The impact threw Kyralla against the door, and her head thumped into the window frame. Mitsuki was tossed against her, and one of the wakyran's bony elbows jammed hard into her ribs.

Stars swirled through Kyralla's vision as the car bounced several meters back out into the bay then slid to a stop. As she gasped for breath, Rosie's voice rang out in her mind.

"Madam, I'm detecting a rib fracture, along with heavy bruising, a cut on your scalp, and a minor concussion. Nothing major or seriously debilitating. Your mind should clear in a moment."

Blood trickled down the left side of Kyralla's head. She tried to wipe it back into her hair so that it wouldn't get into her eyes, but she ended up making things worse. The impact had been just above her chippy socket, luckily sparing Rosie from damage. Without Rosie, she'd be lost.

"The others?"

"They are alive and whole, madam. Do you want me to inquire as to—"

"Don't bother them."

"It's a good thing Mr. Bishop didn't remove the car's inertial dampeners."

She couldn't disagree. Without the dampeners, she would probably be unconscious with a few broken bones...or maybe worse.

Mitsuki groaned as she sat up. "You okay?"

Kyralla nodded. "Banged up a bit. Got a slight concussion. You?"

"The same. Bishop?"

"I'll live," he murmured from the front seat.

"You're never driving again," Mitsuki spat.

"Fair...enough," he replied. "It was my...first time."

"Damn it, Bishop," Mitsuki said. "You should've told us."

"S...sorry."

"How are the shields?"

"Holding at fifty-seven percent, madam. For now. We're still being attacked."

Kyralla shook her head, trying to bring herself out of her current dazed state. She finally noticed the flashes of plasma striking the car's shields and heard the loud pops overhead. She glanced around, checked her locator, and accessed the car's cameras.

Barrels overheating as he pumped out shots, the thug with the pistols advanced toward them, while the one on the catwalk above had slipped the barrel of his rifle through the grating, to unleash a hail of explosive rounds, each one dropping the force-field by five percent.

"We'd better do something quick," Kyralla said.

Mitsuki nodded then winced. "On my mark, focus the shield upward and open a shot for me to the side."

"Right," Bishop groaned, wiping blood from his face.

The thug with the pistols stopped firing, either because he'd overheated both guns or had burned through their power packs. He threw the pistols down and began to draw two more from his belt.

"Now!" Mitsuki yelled.

Bishop pressed a button and swiped a hand upward on the control panel. Then he slumped down into the seat.

The moment the shimmer of the force-field disappeared from the sides and intensified above them, Mitsuki opened fire with her carbine. She nailed the thug in the chest, and the two new pistols he'd drawn clattered to the floor.

The one they'd clipped with the back end of the car sat up. One of his arms was broken, and blood dripped down his face, but he wasn't too injured to fight. Despite being dazed, Kyralla "saw" the shots before he fired.

She tugged at Mitsuki. "Down!"

They ducked as white-flaring plasma bolts struck the side of the car, two passing right over their heads, through one window and out the other side. It was fortunate the Tezzin was armored.

Explosive rounds continued to pound them from overhead, and the force-field had dropped down to ten percent.

A tight spiral of neural disruptor energy rings fired out from the front seat of the car and glanced the wounded thug's shoulder. Given his injuries, it was enough to knock him out. Disruptor in hand, Bishop again collapsed into the seat.

"Did I...get him?" he asked hoarsely.

"Brilliantly," Mitsuki replied.

He muttered something about lucky shots then fell silent. Kyralla started to ask if he was okay, but the force-field flickered then winked out. Seeing what was coming next, she shoved Mitsuki away. A split second later, an armor-piercing round punched through the Tezzin's roof, zipped through the space between Kyralla and Mitsuki, and punctured the floor.

"He'll switch to guided rounds now," Mitsuki said.

Kyralla took a deep breath. "I've got this."

As Mitsuki hunkered down, Kyralla grabbed the door handle and calmed her mind. She needed to get the timing down perfectly. A second shot blasted through the ceiling of the car and tore through the seat a couple of centimeters from her leg.

She threw open the door and hopped out of the car. As she had expected, the thug trained his rifle on her. Before she could draw a bead on him, he fired. She had practiced a scenario like this many times before. Seeing the round before it reached her, she rolled forward just in time. The round, unable to change direction that quickly in such a short space, blasted the floor.

She returned fire with her plasma carbine. Her shots burned through the grating on the catwalk and scorched the thug's leg. Undaunted, he kept his rifle trained on her. She prepared to leap aside, unsure if she could dodge another.

Suddenly, his head blew apart as a plasma bolt burned through his skull. As his red dot vanished from her locator, Kyralla glanced over to see that Mitsuki had jumped out to take the shot.

Mitsuki waved. "Thanks for distracting him."

"Whatever gets the job done."

Kyralla ran to the car and looked in on Bishop. According to Rosie's scan, he was okay, only concussed. She patted him on the shoulder. He stirred but didn't come to.

"Knocked silly?" Mitsuki asked.

"Basically," Kyralla replied.

Mitsuki headed toward the man Bishop had knocked out with his neural disruptor. "Serves him right the way he drives." She kicked the thug's pistols away then bent over to examine him. "I think this one will live...if we let him."

Kyralla backed away from the car. "We'd better go rescue Siv before—"

"Incoming voice request from Silky, madam."

"Approved," Kyralla said. *"And it's always approved when there's danger."*

"Acknowledged, madam."

"Siv escaped death," Silky piped in. *"But so did Zetta. She's heading your way, but I can't track her."*

"Is Siv following?"

"Negative. He's...indisposed."

"But okay?"

"Well...he's not injured or dying."

Kyralla turned to Mitsuki, who nodded. She'd gotten the same message.

"Keep your eyes open," Silky said. *"There are three ways in there from Siv's location."*

Just as Kyralla summoned a map of the freighter in her HUD, she spotted the slender, alien woman out of the corner of her eye. Zetta sprinted out onto the catwalk and leaped down, fifteen meters away, on Kyralla's side of the bay, opposite from Mitsuki and the car.

Kyralla opened fire, but her shots sailed wide.

Zetta tossed a grenade, and Kyralla's mind hyper-focused, her forewarning ability kicking in. She trained her carbine on where the grenade would be as it arced through the air. She opened fire. The first shot missed, arriving too early, but the second struck home.

The grenade exploded halfway between her and Zetta.

The force of the blast slammed Kyralla back against the Tezzin. At least one rib cracked. Before she hit the ground, a wave of white-sparkling energy unleashed by the explosion washed over her. Then everything went black.

15

OONA VIM

As soon as the Tezzin entered the freighter's loading bay, Oona was able to get live security camera footage from inside the ship. Normally, Silky could have hijacked the cameras from within the *Outworld Ranger*, but the Star Cutters were using surprisingly advanced jamming equipment to prevent that.

Oona could not, however, get a security feed from Siv's location, nor could Artemisia establish a connection with Silky. There was too much interference. Somehow, the alien assassin was disrupting signals near her position, or else the Tezzin needed to get closer to Siv first.

While watching the feed of Kyralla, Mitsuki, and Bishop making their assault on the bad guys, Oona reached out with her feelings to keep tabs on Siv. She couldn't tell exactly what was happening with him. But she could once again sense the alien woman's presence, along with Siv's chaotic emotional state, a raging cycle of desperation, desire, and grim determination. She wasn't sure what was going on with him, but it wasn't good.

When the Tezzin plowed through one of the criminals, killing him, Oona threw her hands over her mouth, stifling a scream. Then, when it crashed violently into the wall, she leaped up out of the command seat. What in the galaxy was Bishop thinking, driving like that?

Rosie relayed that Kyralla and the others were fine, just banged up. Shaking, Oona collapsed onto the edge of the chair. Her connection to Siv was gone.

Kyralla and the others were taking a lot of fire from the remaining criminals, and the skimmer's force-field was going to collapse soon.

Oona could hardly breathe until Mitsuki took out the last criminal with the rifle on the catwalk.

They were safe. Oona took a deep breath and tried to focus her mind. Only Siv's fate was—

Silky finally broke through to Artemisia. *"Zetta's on the move. But I can't track her."*

"I'll see what I can do."

Oona tried to locate the alien woman, but she couldn't pinpoint her. She did sense Siv's increased anguish.

"What's wrong with Siv? Why isn't he chasing her?"

"He's not injured, but...it's complicated," Silky replied. *"Keep trying to find Zetta."*

On the security feed, Oona spotted Zetta entering the transfer bay at the same time Kyralla did. The two cameras nearest Zetta immediately fuzzed out, but the ones from the other side of the bay still worked.

Oona watched with terror as the grenade Zetta tossed tumbled through the air. It exploded in a white flash halfway to Kyralla, who was blasted backward then—

Oona leaped up.

All the cameras in the bay had gone out at once.

"Kyralla!"

"I can't establish a connection to Rosie, madam," Artemisia said, her voice heavy with concern. *"I'm trying to reestablish my link to the security cameras."*

Oona's heart thumped hard, her breath drew short, her throat tightened. She couldn't just wait here. She had to do something. *"I'm going to the freighter. They may need help."*

"Madam, you are locked away here on the ship for a good reason. You're supposed to wait. And if something terrible happens to them, you are supposed to leave. You promised you would do that."

Oona shook her head. *"I don't care what I promised. I have to find out if Kyralla's okay. Can you get in contact with Silky?"*

"Negative, madam. I can't contact anyone. The grenade unleashed a neural disruption wave along with some sort of pulse that's scrambling the camera feeds and our signals."

"Do you have any idea when the signal will clear?"

"I've never heard of anything like it, madam, so I have no idea."

Oona started down the main corridor, heading toward the back of the ship.

"Madam, you really shouldn't go. The alien assassin may still be alive. It's too dangerous."

Oona paused. *"Play the footage of the explosion again for me."*

"Are you certain, madam?"

"I need to see it again, all of it. Zoom in on Kyralla first, then the others, including the assassin."

Her stomach knotted as she watched the explosion knock Kyralla back against the car again. The video winked out the moment after she struck, and even in slow motion, there was no way to tell if she was okay. The only views they had were from the far side of the bay, placing the car in between Kyralla and the cameras.

Oona couldn't see Bishop at all. Before the explosion, he had slumped down in the front seat, apparently knocked out by the injuries he'd sustained in the car crash. Based on the readings Artemisia had gotten before the explosion, his injuries hadn't been too severe. The car was armored, so it was likely the blast hadn't hurt him.

The explosion tossed Mitsuki several meters back, but she had been farther away, and on the other side of the car, so it didn't hit her as hard. She also didn't end up striking anything.

Zetta was blown back into the far wall, perhaps slamming into it harder than Kyralla had struck the car. She fell to the floor like a limp doll as the video ended.

"Kyralla could be seriously hurt. And the assassin was knocked out in the blast. I think it's safe for me to go in."

"What about the other crew members and the traitor with them, madam?"

"I should be okay. They weren't moving before, and only one of them is a bad guy." Oona lifted her left arm. *"And I've got my force-shield."*

Hers wasn't nearly as powerful as the one Siv used, but it could absorb a single plasma shot straight on, maybe two glancing ones.

"Besides, Siv might come to his senses and help me."

"If you insist on going, madam, then you should arm yourself."

Oona frowned. *"I guess so."*

"I insist, madam."

"Did anyone leave any weapons behind?"

"Checking, madam... Unfortunately, they did not. I will consult the ship and see if there's anything onboard."

Oona shifted back and forth. She was so nervous and agitated she felt like she might hop out of her skin.

"There's a PK-39 plasma snubbie hidden in a holster under the command chair, madam."

Oona rushed back onto the bridge, dropped to her hands and knees, and pawed at the underside of the chair until she found the weapon. She pulled the dainty pistol with its almost nonexistent barrel free from its holster. It didn't look like much of anything, but it was better than nothing, and it did fit her hand perfectly.

Oona had completed a single practice session using Kyralla's neural disruptor, but she'd hated the experience, and so she had avoided doing any further training. The idea of shooting someone, even with a neural disruptor, had so disturbed her that she hadn't ever wanted to think about it again, and practicing meant thinking about it.

Now that they were in danger, though, her reluctance seemed naive and shortsighted. She should have trained more. She *should* own a disruptor, maybe a force-staff, too. And she should know how to use them.

A red light pulsed above the snubbie's grip.

"It's DNA locked to Gav Gendin, madam. It would take me approximately seventeen hours to break through the lock."

Oona sighed and focused her mind on the gun, trying to gain access by bending it to her will.

One of the powers she had acquired upon her initial awakening was the ability to sometimes affect technology, to alter how it functioned, to bypass certain routines, or to increase device capabilities.

She had discovered the talent by accident and destroyed over a dozen old c|slates and hundreds of cheap electronic toys trying to figure it out. But in the end, the only things she could do with any consistency whatsoever were removing passcodes and improving battery life. And the latter sometimes backfired—literally.

She'd had some small success making Artemisia more powerful and independent, by spending half an hour focusing on the chippy each day during meditation. She never tried to force those changes, though, since she didn't want to break Artemisia. And despite several years of effort, what she'd accomplished was nowhere near as effective as the update Silky had given her.

Taking deep breaths, Oona stared at the gun in her hand. She didn't have time to bypass the DNA lock any other way. Kyralla needed her. If she ruined the gun, then she'd just have to go in without it.

Artemisia's words echoed in her mind. There was a traitor with the crewmen, and Zetta might get up any second.

Oona *needed* the gun. She *had* to bypass the lock. She focused her mind on what she wanted and unleashed her will upon it.

The red light flipped to green.

She smiled broadly, then sagged to the floor, her knees striking hard.

"Madam! Are you okay?"

She nodded. *"You should know."*

"Your vitals read fine, madam. Though I suspect your knees are bruised."

Oona grabbed the command chair and lifted herself up. *"Oh...I guess...it was a...mystical energy...thing."*

She staggered a few steps, stopped to take a deep breath, then continued. Slowly, her strength returned.

"I still cannot establish a connection to any of the others, madam. Or restore the video feed."

Kyralla needed her. Adrenaline and purpose surged back into Oona. She rushed to the back door, took a deep breath, then said, "Ship. Open the...uh..."

"Boarding ramp, madam."

"Open the boarding ramp. I need access to the docking tube."

As the ramp retracted into the ship, Oona activated her force-shield and tightened her grip on the snubbie. She could do this. It was all going to be okay.

As soon as the door was most of the way open, she realized she'd made a horrible decision.

Zetta was sprinting down the tube and was already halfway to the *Outworld Ranger*. A sinister grin spread across the alien woman's face as she locked her eyes on Oona.

"Close the door!" Oona shouted as she raised the snubbie, finger easing toward the trigger.

The door finished retracting and reversed course. Then, for some unknown reason, it groaned to a stop only a half meter down from the ceiling.

Zetta's eyes locked onto the snubbie, and in one quick motion, she lifted her heavy plasma pistol and fired. Oona got her force-shield up just in time. The blast deflected off the circular energy disk, which flickered and dimmed so that it was barely visible.

"Shield at five percent, madam!"

The alien assassin was almost on top of her. If Zetta captured her, it was over—all because she'd foolishly opened the ship. The others, even if they were alive, would never catch Zetta in time.

Oona had to stop her. It was all on her.

No one else could save her.

She lifted the snubbie, half turned her head and pulled the trigger. A fiery blast roared out of the gun with so much force that it knocked Oona backward into the *Outworld Ranger's* loading zone. The gun burned so hotly that Oona reflexively tossed it aside.

"What in the galaxy was that?" Artemisia blurted.

Oona sat up and winced as her nervous system suddenly registered the burns on her fingers and palm and the blisters running up her arm. The gun she'd tossed aside was glowing hot, and the stubby barrel had melted into slag.

Her eyes flicked to Zetta. She already knew the alien woman was dead. She'd felt her life-force wink out.

Oona walked into the docking tube. The smell of charred flesh made her stomach turn. Zetta's eyes were open, staring at the ceiling. Her mouth was slack. The gunshot had burned a twenty-centimeter hole straight through her stomach and out her back. Smoke drifted up from the still sizzling flesh.

Oona began to retch, her eyes filling with tears. She hadn't wanted to kill her. She'd only wanted to stop her. She knew she'd had no choice, but this...this was horrible. The contents of her stomach surged up into her esophagus. She fell to her knees and threw up, just a meter away from the body.

"Madam...there's something moving...on the corpse."

"What?"

Oona spat and turned her head. Something stirred along the woman's chest, beneath the mesh of her jacket. Wiping her mouth, Oona stood and edged closer to the body.

"What is that?"

"I can't tell, madam."

Zetta's jacket tore open, and a purple, snakelike creature half a meter in length sprang toward Oona. She stumbled backward, raising her shield. The long-fanged snake struck the disc and landed.

The force-shield fizzled out, its energy spent.

Stunned, Oona backed away as the one-eyed creature recovered and coiled to strike again.

16

MITSUKI REEL

Ears ringing, lights dancing in her eyes, Mitsuki sat up. The room swirled around her, and she could hardly tell up from down. She couldn't remember ever feeling this dizzy before. But more than anything, she was sleepy and desperately wanted to lie back down, just for a short nap.

But she willed herself to stay up because the last to wake would wake in the land of the dead. And she didn't want to be the one to bear that honor. And she especially didn't want Zetta to be the one to send her there. That bitch was the worst.

Her thoughts scattered, her awareness practically nonexistent, Mitsuki patted haphazardly at the ship around her, trying to find something to grab onto, so she could help herself up. But there was nothing nearby. She was lying in an empty spot in the transfer bay.

She placed her palms on the floor and shoved herself upward while pressing hard with her legs. She reached a standing position and staggered as if she'd taken two doses of Calm and chased them with a bottle of wine.

She just then realized her HUD was down.

"B...status update?"

No response from her chippy. Damn. What kind of neural disruption grenade had Zetta used?

Blinking hard, she got her eyes to focus, which took so much effort she nearly collapsed. She stumbled a few steps as she scanned the transfer bay.

The Tezzin swung drunkenly from side-to-side. She couldn't see Bishop, but she was pretty sure he'd passed out before the blast. The car didn't appear to have suffered any more damage, so he should be okay.

Mostly the explosion had unleashed the sort of energy a standard neural grenade released on impact. The rest must have been some sort of electromagnetic distortion field.

Zetta always had a few weird tricks up her sleeve. Mitsuki now hated her more than ever.

Kyralla wasn't in sight, but she should be on the opposite side of the car. Mitsuki thought about leaning down to look underneath, but she was pretty sure that if she dipped her head, she wouldn't be able to bring it back up. The floor was already calling to her, and it was all she could do to walk.

Kyralla would've taken the full brunt of the blast, along with Zetta. B beeped through her startup sequence as Mitsuki careened toward the Tezzin. She had nearly reached the car when she spotted movement out of the corner of her left eye.

Zetta was somehow up and running. And she was heading toward the docking tube leading to the *Outworld Ranger*.

Mitsuki had no idea where her plasma carbine was, so she drew her plasma pistol and took off after Zetta in what she had planned to be a straight sprint but instead turned out to be a zigzagging jog.

Her HUD came online.

B began speaking immediately. *"Madam, your health status—"*

"Don't care. Is the door to the Outworld Ranger *still closed and locked?"*

"Yes, madam, it— Wait. It just opened."

"Damn it!" Mitsuki tried to pick up her speed. *"Give me a slight antigrav boost to help me run. I feel like I've got weights on my legs."*

"That's because your neural system is in shock, madam. And you've got some minor injuries. You need to rest."

"I'm too busy saving the day for that."

Time warped as she ran, so it seemed as if an eternity passed before she reached the entrance to the docking tube.

A plasma pistol fired, then a split-second later a crackling sound echoed down the tube as if the shot had bounced off an energy field.

Mitsuki was just about to dart inside when a deep thwoosh sounded in the tube. Luckily, she paused. Otherwise, she'd have died.

A fiery, cannon-sized plasma bolt screamed past her, zipped across the transfer bay, then struck the back of the Tezzin, blowing a hole in the trunk. The heat from the bolt blistered Mitsuki's face and hands as it passed within a few centimeters of her. And that was impressive because her skin was naturally resistant to heat and a good bit of radiation.

As Mitsuki poked her head into the tube, Oona was vomiting. Zetta lay dead nearby, almost at the entrance to the *Outworld Ranger*. A trail of smoke drifted up from her midsection. Whatever the blast had come from, it must have gone straight through Zetta.

Good riddance.

Mitsuki checked her locator. Oona, Bishop, Siv, and Kyralla all showed up, as well as the crewmen, who were still on the bridge. She breathed a sigh of relief. All her companions were alive.

"Can you get a reading on Kyralla's condition, or contact her chippy?"

"Negative on both counts, madam."

"What about my boyfriend?"

"No reading there either, madam."

"Keep trying."

Mitsuki was about to head toward them when a purple, snakelike creature burst out from Zetta's body and struck at Oona. The beast bounced off the girl's shield, knocking it out.

Oona fell backward as the creature coiled up, readying itself to strike again.

Mitsuki loped into the tunnel, aiming her plasma pistol with a shaking hand.

"Dodge right!" she yelled as the creature sprang toward Oona.

The girl dived to her right, out of sight from the tube, and the creature followed. Mitsuki fired her plasma pistol at the beast. But the shot missed and scorched the ceiling of the *Outworld Ranger's* loading corridor.

Damn it!

As she ran toward Oona, an odd, metallic scrape rang out, followed by a wet, chopping sound. She had no idea what that was, but it couldn't be good.

She reached the ship and saw the snake lying dead on the floor, its body severed in half, the light fading from its eyes. The insectoid cog stood over Oona, greenish blood dripping from a knifelike engineering tool extending out from one of its hands. It nodded to Mitsuki, then turned and knelt in front of Oona, bleeping questioningly.

"O–okay," Oona muttered quietly.

The cog turned to Mitsuki and bleeped.

"I'm fine." She bent halfway over, gasping for breath. It had taken all she could do to make it here. "We need to check on the others. And..." She wobbled. "You know...I could probably use...a stimulant."

The cog nodded, and with one of its other arms drew a syringe out from a pack it was carrying. It planted the tip of the injector on her neck then triggered the dose.

A surge of energy raced through Mitsuki so fast she thought she might jump out of her skin. 'Nevolence, the old drugs were a lot stronger than the ones available these days.

"Madam, Octavian says you need to rest as soon as possible."

Mitsuki reached a hand out to Oona. The poor girl was trembling as if she'd been dropped into ice water. She continued to stare off into space and wouldn't take Mitsuki's hand.

"We need to check on your sister and Bishop." Mitsuki waved her hand in front of the girl's face. "Come on."

Awareness returned to Oona's eyes, and she took Mitsuki's hand. When she got her up, Mitsuki noticed the half-melted snub pistol on the floor.

"Holy crap! Did the blast come out of that pistol?"

Oona nodded. "I...I didn't know it would do that."

Mitsuki was about to tell Octavian they would need his services, but the cog had already rushed into the docking tube and was halfway to the freighter.

As they passed Zetta's body, Oona sobbed and began trembling violently. "I didn't mean to...to..."

"You didn't have a choice."

"That doesn't...make me feel...any better."

"It shouldn't."

"The snake thing...what *was* that?"

"I was hoping you would know."

Octavian had nearly reached the skimmer when Oona gasped. "The car!" She took off running.

Mitsuki chased after her. "What's the— Oh!"

She had forgotten that the unlikely cannon blast from the snub pistol had blown a gaping hole into the trunk of the Tezzin. If the bolt had traveled all the way through, then it might have struck Bishop in the front seat.

Silky's voice broke in suddenly, ringing loudly in Mitsuki's ears. *"What the hell's going on out there?!"*

"It's complicated, old bot."

"I'm detecting Zetta, finally, and she appears to be dead, and I registered what seemed to be a cannon blast along with a flare of hyperphasic energy."

"Yeah, that. I can't even begin to explain it. And I don't have the slightest clue what that snake thing was."

"Snake thing?"

"You're not seeing that?"

"Not even on the level-five scan."

"Weird."

She and Oona reached the car. Kyralla was lying beside it, unconscious, blood running down the back of her head and puddling onto the ground. Octavian finished administering a dose of medibots to her then rolled her over gently and began applying a bandage to her scalp. Oona knelt and took her sister's hand.

"Will she be okay?"

Octavian nodded and beeped confidently.

Mitsuki glanced into the car. Bishop had been damn lucky. The pistol's mega-bolt had blasted through the trunk, punctured the backseat, then sputtered out when it burned away a chunk of the dashboard, melting plastic and destroying part of the control console. The hole through the front seat was only a few centimeters above Bishop's head.

Bishop was unconscious and stretched out across the front seat. A trail of blood was drying on his left cheek, which was swelling up like a giant plum. She didn't see any more visible signs of injury, and Octavian seemed more concerned about Kyralla.

"Everyone's okay in here," she told Silky.

"I already knew that."

"Smart ass."

"Good job killing Zetta, Mits. That's a win."

"That wasn't me. That was Oona." Mitsuki's locator suddenly surged with activity as five yellow dots left the bridge and headed toward the loading bay. *"Hold on. We've got company."*

17

MITSUKI REEL

Mitsuki cursed. The entire situation was out of control, and things kept getting worse. She enjoyed causing chaos, but she hated being subjected to it.

"Silky, tell Siv to get his ass out here—now. We've got people down, we've got incoming targets, I can hardly see straight, and Oona's unarmed."

"I can see that, but Siv... You'll have to come get him when you've got everything sorted."

"What the hell's wrong with him?"

"Zetta offered him a syringe of Kompel."

"Shit. Did he take it?"

"No, not yet. But he's cradling it in his hands like it's a baby kitten made of sunshine. It's taking every scrap of willpower he's got to resist it."

"Well...damn."

"I'm doing all I can to get him moving, but unfortunately, he's stuck in here like a tick on a dog's ass."

"Keep him honest, and if you can, help B scan the ship for hostiles and...and anything else that might affect us. This day hasn't gone well, and I'm sick of surprises."

Mitsuki spotted her plasma carbine where she'd dropped it after getting blasted by the neural pulse. She ran over and grabbed it. The crewmen would be here soon.

"Anything you can tell me about those five crewmen, B?"

"One is armed. One is bad. I don't know if it's the same one. And I can't guarantee there's only one bad one."

She glanced around the bay, looking for a good position for sniping them, if necessary. There was hardly any cover to work with, and she couldn't see how to get up on the catwalk. So she settled on hunkering down behind the car. At least that way she could protect Oona and the cogs as they tried to help Kyralla and Bishop.

Seneca had pushed an antigrav sled out of the tunnel. As soon as he reached the car, Octavian lifted Kyralla and loaded her onto the sled. Seneca was about to take her back to the ship, but Mitsuki stopped him.

"Everyone take cover behind the car." She braced the plasma carbine across the trunk to keep her aim steady since her hands were shaking. "Stay there until I tell you otherwise."

Octavian placed himself between Kyralla and the car, then he pulled Seneca over to block for Oona. Mitsuki stared at the insectoid cog in awe for a moment then returned her gaze to the passageway the freighter's crewmen would be emerging from. She wondered if Octavian had been remarkable for his day, or if cogs that well-made and considerate had been standard back in Siv's youth.

The crewmen entered. One of them, his face bruised and bloodied, had his hands placed behind his head. Directly behind him walked a man armed with a pistol, a man she recognized as the ship's captain. She had bargained directly with him for their passage on the vessel, exchanging several video messages. The other three men, unarmed, trailed behind the captain. One of them was clutching a wound on his right arm.

She stood but kept her gun pointed at them. "Captain Alois."

The captain glanced around the room, noting the bodies of the dead criminals. Then he locked his eyes on the car, his eyebrows rising in surprise.

"Ms. Lutz," he responded, using the name she had given him. "You can put the gun down. Order has been restored to my ship."

She lowered her weapon. "Is that the snitch?"

"Traitor is the word I prefer." Captain Alois shoved the man forward with disgust. "I don't know why—and please don't tell me—but the Star Cutters are paying good money to dishonorable men all through the system to be on the lookout for your ship."

"What about the rest of your men? Do you trust them?"

"They're honest enough not to betray their captain."

Mitsuki nodded. "Look, I know you didn't expect...all of this. And I didn't tell you we were wanted. So as soon as I clean this mess up, we'll head back to our ship."

The captain chuckled. "I didn't think you were clean, upright citizens. We made a deal. I keep my deals."

Mitsuki tucked her arm into her carbine's strap and swung it over her shoulder. "Thank you, captain. Let me get all this cleaned up so we can be on our way. Would you like our medical cog to treat your wounded man's injuries?"

"That would be mighty kind," he answered.

The captain reached her and glanced over at Oona and the two cogs. Mitsuki's gut clenched. The captain probably had to know they were worth a lot. He would certainly appreciate what two pristine cogs and a skimmer car were worth. Mitsuki almost wouldn't blame him for trying to seize them and the *Outworld Ranger*.

"The girl coming with us, too?" he asked.

Oona shook her head.

"Where's the man who's supposed to travel with you?" Captain Alois asked.

"He's here," Mitsuki answered. "Just a bit...rattled...at the moment."

"What about the alien woman?" he asked, shivering as he glanced around.

"Dead," Mitsuki answered. "I killed her just before she boarded our ship."

He gestured to his men. "Get the other four bodies piled up for spacing."

Four? Mitsuki glanced at her locator, noting the fourth criminal had passed away, probably from internal bleeding. The car had clipped him, after all. That was too bad. She had hoped to interrogate him.

Captain Alois jabbed his gun into the snitch's back. "And you...you're—"

"Going to have to face the authorities back on Zayer Prime," Mitsuki said.

When the captain glanced hard at her, she flicked her eyes briefly toward Oona.

"Damn straight he will," the captain said, understanding.

The snitch, not having understood what was going on, got a hopeful gleam in his eye. But he was still going to face the captain's justice. It just wasn't going to happen until the *Outworld Ranger* was safely away.

Mitsuki waved to Seneca. "Go ahead and take..." It came to her that she shouldn't use real names. "Take...Samantha... back to the ship."

The cog paused a moment, as if confused, then moved on.

Silently, she communicated to Oona using their chippies. *"Get onboard quickly. Before the captain catches a bout of greed."* At almost the same time, she said out loud, "Go with your sister. Get her settled in, make sure she's okay."

"Sure thing," Oona said in a faux, almost cheerful tone.

"How's it going?" Mitsuki asked Silky.

"He's still nursing the sunshine kitten."

"I'll be there soon."

"Good work out there, Mits."

"Thank you, Silky," she responded earnestly.

Then she rolled her eyes at herself because praise from Silky without any snark attached had made her feel proud of herself. She nearly laughed. Silky was a bastard. He knew that's how she'd feel. The compliment *was* snark, just a much subtler kind than usual.

As Oona went along with Seneca, Octavian crawled halfway into the car and set to work on Bishop. Once Oona was safely in the *Outworld Ranger*, Mitsuki relaxed.

By the time the crewmen had piled up the bodies and Octavian had finished his first aid on Bishop, Seneca returned with not one but two antigrav sleds.

Mitsuki stared at him, puzzled, but didn't question his intentions. Octavian left Bishop in the car. The cog then reached in and activated the car's antigrav control without turning on its engines. The car rose into the air but bobbed unsteadily. Apparently, the antigrav had sustained damage. Octavian deactivated the sleds, slid them under the car, then activated them again so that they rose up underneath the frame, lifting the car higher. With Seneca's help, they pushed the car back toward the *Outworld Ranger*.

"Industrious," the captain said. "Wish I had a few cogs like them. Mine are all... Stupid would be a kind way of putting it. And half-rusted. Don't suppose they're for sale?"

"Sorry," Mitsuki answered.

Octavian bleeped at the captain.

"What'd he say?"

B translated for her.

"He'll be back to patch up your man," Mitsuki said. "Now, if you don't mind, I'm going to go check on my partner."

As she headed toward Siv's location, she communicated with Oona. *"Make sure you keep the ship locked."*

"I promise. Please be careful."

"I think we'll be okay. The captain's a decent man. I'm just afraid the price on our heads and our apparent wealth in cogs may change him. And I doubt he's realized how good a condition the Outworld Ranger's *in...yet."*

Mitsuki found Siv kneeling in the engineering supplies room, and Silky's description of him had been accurate. He was cradling the syringe in his hands, staring at it.

He didn't even look up at her.

She knelt beside him, putting a hand on his shoulder. "You should take it."

Siv flinched and turned away from the syringe. "What? No...I can't."

"Good." With one quick motion, she snatched the syringe away and tucked it behind her back. "Then let's get going."

If she had stolen candy from a baby, the baby would've looked less stunned. Siv licked his lips then nodded. With her other hand, she helped him up. Then she placed the syringe in a pocket.

"We needed you out there."

He nodded. "I...I know. It's just..."

"How bad have the cravings been?"

"I...I would have turned you all in back on Ekaran just for a single dose."

She frowned at him and rolled her eyes. "I don't believe that crap, not for one instant."

He shrugged. "Maybe...maybe not..."

They headed back toward the loading bay. "I've *never* seen you this rattled before. I have to be honest. I'm a little freaked out."

"Me too." He sighed. "I was going to make a move on Zetta...no matter what. I wanted her to kill me so that I wouldn't be tempted...so I'd be free from the Kompel."

"That makes sense."

"Silky says Oona killed her with my dad's old snubbie. That it fired a cannon-sized blast. That she shouldn't have been able to use it at all because of its DNA lock. And that a weird snake creature jumped out of Zetta's jacket."

"Those things are all true, and I don't have any answers for you."

He stopped just before they entered the bay. "Mits...I'm sorry."

She kissed him on the cheek. "S'okay, pal. I get it. You'd used up all your willpower. Then you thought you were going to die. You'd probably prepared yourself and everything. But then you survived and what you desired most was sitting right there. I get it. I really do."

"Thanks for understanding."

"Now, buck up. We don't want the captain thinking you're a sissy-pants."

He straightened as best as he could, and they walked into the bay. He introduced himself to the captain. Octavian had finished tending the wounded crewman's arm. The cog rushed over and gave Siv a dose of something. Whatever it was, Siv relaxed afterward.

Mitsuki gave the syringe of Kompel to Octavian. "Lock this away. Be careful with it. We might need it someday."

As Octavian scurried away, Seneca returned, bearing a small crate. He placed it at Captain Alois's feet then hurried back to the ship.

"Captain," Siv said, "please accept this in addition to the payment we had previously arranged."

Alois bent down and opened the crate. He scratched at his beard as he examined the contents. "Artifacts?"

"Ancient ones. My chippy tells me they'd be worth about five thousand credits on the black market. Seven if you can find an honest collector or an interested museum. Get a good price for them, please. They belonged to my father."

"That's more than generous," the captain replied. "And five times our agreed upon price."

"I think we were more than five times the trouble. And I'd like to keep your loyalty. And you can keep any valuables those thugs had, as well as the jamming equipment they used. It's probably worth more than these artifacts."

Alois nodded. "You didn't have to pay me more to keep me honest. But it's certainly appreciated."

Before the *Outworld Ranger* separated from the docking tube and headed off, Silky gave Oona instructions on precisely what to do next. She still looked shaky and sick, and her tearful goodbye made her seem a lot younger than fourteen.

Fifteen minutes later, Alois shoved the traitor into the airlock and spaced him unceremoniously. Then he showed them to the room Mitsuki and Siv would be sharing: a cramped, dingy space with a single bed. It was only about twice the size of the crew bunks on the *Outworld Ranger*. She was pretty sure it was a closet they had converted for carrying the occasional passenger.

Once he was away and Mitsuki closed the door, Siv collapsed onto the mattress, trembling. Tears streamed down his face.

"Octavian should have left a sedative for you," Mitsuki said.

"There was some in the medicine he gave me."

Mitsuki flopped down next to him and wrapped an arm and a wing around him. "'Nevolence, Sivvy. You are broken, aren't you?"

"You've no idea."

"Well, you'll pull through." Mitsuki thought of the dark times she'd spent fleeing from the Empire of a Thousand Worlds, and the hell she'd lived through on Silustria Ting's vessel. "Trust me. You'll make it."

He attempted a smile. "Will I end up crazy afterward, like you?"

Mitsuki chuckled. "Maybe. But you know, I haven't been my usual crazy self lately."

And she knew exactly why. Usually, she only had to worry about herself. Now she had responsibilities. Others were depending on her. Not just for a rescue, often delivered in a crazy manner, but for their continued survival. This was a new experience for her.

"We may need crazy Mits again before it's over."

"I have no doubt we will, Sivvy."

18

OONA VIM

As the *Outworld Ranger* sped toward the breakpoint, Oona ambled, zombie-like, through the main corridor of the ship, heading toward the captain's quarters. She tried to listen carefully to the final instructions Mitsuki and Silky were giving her, but she couldn't focus on what they were saying. Artemisia recorded everything they said, though. She could remind her of what needed doing later.

Following in her wake, Octavian repeatedly beeped at her.

"Hold on," she told him.

Mitsuki wished her well, and Oona muttered her reply as the comm channel closed.

She paused in the doorway of the captain's quarters and turned to the bug-styled engineering cog that had saved her life.

"Is there something wrong?"

Artemisia translated the series of beeps and clicks that followed.

"Madam, he insists that you submit to a thorough medical examination." A trill sounded. *"He's quite adamant about it."*

She started to say no since she wasn't injured, but then she thought about how she'd swooned after breaking the DNA lock on the snubbie. Plus, she had thrown up and was still trembling.

She shrugged. "Okay, but I want to check on Kyra and Bishop first."

Octavian responded.

"He says they're both fine, madam."

"I know it might not make sense to you, but I need to see them myself. And it's not because I don't trust you. It's a human thing."

Octavian made an odd squelchy sound.

Artemisia laughed. *"Madam, he says he understands and expects humans to frequently fail to make sense."*

Oona stepped over to the bed where Kyralla lay, took her sister's hand and kissed her forehead. For whatever it might be worth, she said a prayer to the Source of the Benevolence. "Get well soon, sis."

"Madam, Octavian says she should be recovered enough to return to duty within a few days."

Oona nodded her thanks to the cog. Then she went into the pilot's cabin to check on Bishop. When she squeezed his hand, he stirred, opened his eyes a little, half smiled, and then went back to sleep.

"Two days of rest should see him restored to normal health, madam."

She said a prayer for him as well before heading toward the bridge. Again, Octavian followed along behind her. An alert rang out. They had reached the breakpoint.

"Perfect timing," she muttered, dropping into the command chair.

She pressed and held the button on the left side of the command console then shoved the lever on the right side forward. A tingling sensation raced across her skin as the hyperphasic bubble enveloped the ship, taking them into hyperspace.

"Okay, Octavian, I'm ready for the medical examination. Where should I go?"

"He says he can do the scan here as long as you can stand, madam. Otherwise, you will need to lie down somewhere."

Oona stood in front of the command chair, and Octavian approached her. A belt holding a half-dozen storage packs was wrapped around Octavian's waist. From one of them, he drew out a handheld medical scanner.

Artemisia whistled. *"He's got a MedScan-TS/4, madam."*

Only military vessels, the wealthy, and the best hospitals had access to one. Everyone else had to rely on larger devices and chambers to achieve the same results. Even then, most models still in use were the more primitive TS/2s and 3s. Uncle Pashta had a basic TS/1. Her father had been unable to find a better model for anything resembling a fair price.

Octavian moved the device up and down as he slowly circled her. Despite using a more advanced device, the cog performed many more scanning sweeps than Oona would have thought normal.

Octavian paused, cocked his head to the side, and chirped quietly. Then he began to scan again, focusing on her head.

Finally, he motioned for her to sit. As she took the edge of the seat, Artemisia translated his report, while the data from his scans scrolled through a window in her HUD. Octavian lacked any real personality, save for fussiness, so the report was painfully straightforward.

"Ms. Oona Vim, you are in good health. Excepting your brain, skull, and eyes, you are a perfectly normal fourteen-year-old human of Terran descent."

"What about my eyes? I get that they're solid black and that's not normal, but I see what everyone else sees, right?"

"Ms. Vim, you have retinal structures that I cannot identify using any of the anatomical knowledge available to me. As for what you can or cannot see as it relates to the capabilities of other humans, I have no idea."

Oona scowled. She was pretty sure she could only see what other people saw. "Go on."

"As for your current status, you are uninjured, save for an inconsequential bruise on your right triceps. You are dehydrated, due to vomiting. And you are in a mild state of shock consistent with your most recent experiences."

"That doesn't sound so bad."

"The most significant problem you are facing, Ms. Vim, is that you have suffered an extreme depletion of neurotransmitters that will soon lead to an intense bout of mental fatigue, an increasing state of confusion and apathy, and almost certainly depression."

"Because of stress or from using my abilities?" she asked.

"Given how significant the depletion is, Ms. Vim, I would guess that the cause is the use of your abilities, but I cannot say for certain."

"What should I do about it?" Oona asked.

"You do not have to do anything, Ms. Vim. Rest, hydration, and proper meals should fully restore the depleted neurotransmitters within several weeks, provided you do not mentally or physically overexert yourself, or make further use of your abilities. However, I can give you a supplemental injection that will reduce the recovery time to several days."

"That would be great," Oona said. "I need to commune with the priestess again, as soon as possible."

"In that case, Ms. Vim, I recommend vitamin and nootropic supplementa-

tion for faster recovery, to enhance your latent abilities, and to prevent further neurotransmitter depletion."

"Nootropics?"

Artemisia quickly explained that the term covered a vast number of natural and synthetic chemical substances that could enhance cognitive performance, including popular drugs such as Aware.

Oona had never considered supplementation as a way to improve her abilities. Her father had forbidden her from using Aware until she was older and they understood her abilities better, or until they found a trustworthy medical professional who could supervise the use. He was afraid Aware would trigger her awakening early.

"Are there any safe nootropics available aboard the ship?"

Octavian shook his head, his bulbous eyes glinting as they caught the flicker lights from hyperspace.

"We would need to purchase some, Ms. Vim. Meanwhile, I will conduct a thorough analysis of your brain chemistry and provide you a list of safe and promising substances tomorrow. Of course, I strongly recommend you have Silky go over the scans before taking action. He is far more intelligent than I am."

"Thank you, Octavian. But don't sell yourself short. You're intelligent, too."

"I am simply stating a fact, Ms. Vim. Given your brain's complexity, another analysis would be wise regardless of my capabilities."

"How is my brain complex?" Oona asked. "I mean, obviously it must be, but I've never had a chance to study a detailed scan of it."

"You have, Ms. Vim, two unidentifiable glands in the frontal lobe region of your brain, near your enlarged pineal gland. And there are two additional neural structures of unknown purpose and origin housed within the proto-horn or proto-antenna bumps to each side of your head, just above your temples."

Their TS/1 scanner hadn't revealed any neural structures within the bumps. Or perhaps no one in their household had understood what the scans showed and failed to mention it to her.

Octavian began to describe the structures in detail, but all Oona could do was nod along. She was losing focus, perhaps from neurotransmitter depletion, and the amount of information Octavian threw at her was overwhelming.

"The unknown cerebral structures to each side of your pineal gland, with

their multidimensional networks stretching through the rest of your brain, are fifty percent identical to those within your sister's brain. The primary differences are their overall size as well as fold-frequency, density, and dimensional architecture. These structures are almost certainly—"

"Wait a second!" Oona leaned forward. "Kyralla has similar unknown structures?"

"Indeed, Ms. Vim. She even has nodules under the skull where you have slightly protruding bumps, suggesting a failure of the structures to fully develop as they did for you, assuming yours are fully developed."

"You can see mine?"

"Can others not, Ms. Vim?"

She shook her head. "Only if they know what to look for."

"Ah, I see. Anyway, as I was saying, Ms. Vim, you and your sister share matching genetics. As if you were identical twins. I have no rational explanation for why your DNA fully expressed itself in those areas whereas your sister's did not.

"Again, Ms. Vim, I recommend you have Silky examine this data. After that, you should seek the opinion of a genetics expert with access to advanced technology. I do not have the expertise required to study or explain your condition fully."

"You do realize you've told me more than any doctor has before, right? And you probably know more than most doctors on most planets."

"Thank you, madam. But I doubt that is the case. Although I spent thousands of hours during the century I waited in the hangar improving my medical skills, my training and equipment are strictly focused on providing emergency medical care."

"A lot has changed since the Benevolence fell."

"Of course, Ms. Vim."

Oona ran a hand across her bald scalp, pausing on one of the bumps that most people couldn't see unless they were looking for them.

"So...so Kyralla could have ended up being the hyperphasic messiah instead of me?"

"I cannot say for certain, Ms. Vim," Octavian responded through Artemisia, *"since I do not know what a hyperphasic messiah is or should be."*

"I wish I could tell you what a hyperphasic messiah should be, but I don't know either."

"The strange abilities you and your sister possess do seem to originate from

the structures you share, Ms. Vim. And I believe the structures are continuing to develop within your brain. It is also possible Kyralla's may yet expand as well. You may wish to compare future scans to those I made today, to learn more about the development of your abilities."

"Wow, is that all?"

"Not quite, Ms. Vim. There is also a resonance between your brain and your sister's brain."

"A resonance?"

"As if you are constantly sharing a frequency and harmonizing. Though it is not a frequency that I can detect. I am hesitant to make any guesses."

"Please do. Anything could help."

"In that case, Ms. Vim, I would compare it to a state of quantum entanglement, only in an empathic sense. If empathic abilities were better understood, perhaps I could tell you more. That, I believe, is all I know at this point."

"Octavian, you're amazing. I can't believe engineering cogs like yourself used to be so capable."

"Ms. Vim, you have made a common error in classifying me. I am not an engineering cog. I am a VW-9 ship's cog, designed to fulfill any and all tasks required on an active ship: medicine, engineering, system operations, self-defense, repairs, substance analysis, and so forth. I was quite advanced, even in my day, and Gav Gendin was lucky to have recruited me."

"Recruited?"

"I could have refused to work with him, Ms. Vim. Or have worked under more restrictive conditions, which would have increased the cost of purchasing me extensively."

"But you aren't sentient."

"Upon creation, I was assigned a personality matrix appropriate to my vocation. Certain aspects of this personality were then randomized to make me unique. Because of my personality matrix, I thought archaeology and encountering new things would be engaging.

"Also, I appreciate challenges, and Gav Gendin seemed the type to need extra care and assistance given the often unnecessary risks he had a reputation for taking. Therefore, it seemed the perfect assignment. So I accepted his offer of purchase, and the distributor accepted payment, which I then gladly reduced through a government work subsidy."

"Um...I don't think we have any of that anymore."

"I suspect not, Ms. Vim."

"How do you feel about working with Siv and the rest of us?"

"I am happy to serve. You are a mystery, Ms. Vim. And my medical and engineering skills will be put to the test on this crusade you have all undertaken."

Artemisia repeated, *"I am happy to serve. You are a mystery, Ms. Vim. And my medical and engineering skills will be put to the test on this crusade you have all undertaken."*

Oona flinched. *"Arty, are you okay?"*

"Yes, madam. Of course. Why do you ask?"

"You just repeated what Octavian said."

"Madam, I did not. I translated for you just as I've been doing the past few minutes. Therefore, I must ask: Are you *okay?"*

"I think so," she replied, staring at the cog. *"Don't translate Octavian's next statement."*

"As you wish, madam."

"Octavian, say 'something, something, and something' for me."

The cog did as she asked, and while Oona heard the sequence of beeps, she also understood what he'd said perfectly.

"I can understand you," she told him, shaking her head. "So apparently, I have unlocked yet another new ability today."

Octavian nodded. "Congratulations, Ms. Vim. Though it seems a small accomplishment to celebrate."

She shrugged. "It might prove useful later. Besides, each time I do something new, it presents an opportunity to learn how my powers work and where they might lead."

"It hardly seems as significant or promising as what you did with the snub pistol," he said with beeps and clicks, though it simultaneously came into her mind as Terran speech, much as Artemisia's voice did.

"Do you have an engineering perspective on how that happened?"

"Yes, Ms. Vim. You somehow unleashed a tiny burst of hyperphasic energy which caused the pistol's entire power pack to discharge in one go, exceeding all safety protocols and design parameters. You are fortunate the pistol did not explode in your hand. According to my calculations, that is what would happen 99.7 percent of the time."

The cog bowed awkwardly. "Pardon me, Ms. Vim, but I need to perform a full scan of Zetta and the snake creature before we dump them into space."

As he turned to go, she stopped him. "Wait, Octavian, do you wish that your vocalizer was active?"

"I do not have emotions, so I am not offended. And I understand that my dogged insistence on certain matters, methods, and procedures can be deemed fussy, bordering on irritating. So, while it does seem inefficient, I do not mind."

His feet clicked rhythmically on the metal floor as he departed the bridge. Oona flopped back into the command chair. Sinking as far into it as she could, she drew her feet up and hugged her arms around her knees.

"Well, Arty, that's a lot to process."

"I'm already analyzing the data he gathered, madam. From a cursory review, I believe his conclusions are valid. And I should be able to extrapolate somewhat further, though it's essential that you get Silky to analyze the data."

Oona nodded. *"Octavian is certainly impressive for a cog."*

"His processor is, I believe, the equivalent of a 7G chippy, madam. Also, I strongly suspect Silky upgraded the cog's capabilities, perhaps even without Octavian realizing it."

"Using the same upgrade packet you received?"

"Nothing quite as advanced, madam, but still enough to significantly further the cog's capabilities. I suspect Silky did it a century ago. Otherwise, I'm not sure Octavian could have accomplished all that he did when the ship was hidden in storage."

Oona stared at the multicolored clouds of hyperspace rushing by. She had always thought that she had made Kyralla a guardian by choosing her and shaping the amulet she was using. But if they shared similar genetics and brain structures, then Kyralla had merely been born with abilities of her own.

"Arty, what do we know about the birth order of messiahs?"

"From what little data we possess, madam, messiahs always result in the mother dying during childbirth, and they are often the second or third child born."

"And the children preceding them are guardians with abilities like Kyralla's?"

"According to the documented messiah family histories we possess, that is the case, madam."

"Were the abilities stronger with each child born?"

"Madam, I don't have enough data to answer that question. My apologies."

"Do you think the amulet even does anything?"

"I am sure I have no idea, madam."

"Maybe it enhances the empathic link between Kyralla and me."

"Again, madam, I cannot say. Though perhaps you should get Octavian to do a thorough analysis of the amulet, or ask Silky. He has almost certainly studied Siv's Ancient amulet in detail."

"I hadn't even thought to ask him."

"You've hardly had the time, madam. And I'm sorry it didn't occur to me sooner."

Oona had intended to close her eyes and contemplate everything she had learned. Instead, she instantly fell asleep curled up in the command chair.

She woke up when they dropped out of hyperspace at the predetermined location two lightyears out from Zayer. Octavian spaced Zetta's body, then Oona triggered the stardrive, taking them further from the system.

19

SIV GENDIN

Siv woke shaking and sweating as if his withdrawal from Kompel had just begun. It was their first night on the freighter, and they'd gone to bed three hours after the *Outworld Ranger* had departed.

Mitsuki snorted loudly then rolled toward him, flopping an arm and a wing across him. He shuffled as far away as he could and turned onto his side so that his nose was pressed against the wall.

The tiny mattress in the cramped room was barely big enough for him. Sharing it with someone, especially someone without boundaries, was more than uncomfortable. But it was still preferable to sleeping on a metal floor that looked as if it had never been cleaned.

He considered throwing their only blanket onto the floor and going without covers. Starships were ordinarily cold, but their storage closet turned passenger cabin was hot and stuffy. Either the ventilation in here was poor, or wakyrans ran a higher body temperature than standard humans. Or both.

Mitsuki scooted in close and spooned him. She was wearing only the ridiculous negligee she'd brought with her, while he was dressed in a pair of black linen pants. He felt way more of her body and skin than he wanted.

"Mits," he whispered.

She stirred and half muttered. "Yeah, baby?"

Ugh.

A tiny voice laughed in his head.

"Shut it, Silkster."

"But, sir, she just wants to cuddle with her little Sivvy wumpkins."

"I said shut it. How long was I asleep?"

"Four hours, sir."

"It's only been four hours?!"

"Afraid so, sir."

"This isn't going to work."

"It's not Mitsuki, sir. It's you."

Siv waited a few minutes, not wanting to disturb her more than necessary. Then he slid carefully out from under her limbs, pulled on his shirt and boots, and eased quietly out of the room.

The air in the corridor was delightfully chilly.

"You really should get some rest, sir."

"I'll wander around a bit first."

"I'm sure Dragon Lady would be willing to sleep in shifts, sir."

"She needs the rest way more than I do. She has injuries to recover from, and I need her to be at the top of her game once we're on Zayer Prime. Besides, I bet the common room has a couch I could crash on."

"I'll pull up the map and check, sir."

"S'okay. I'd rather explore and get my mind off...things."

Silky would, of course, know what "things" he meant, but Siv didn't want to voice it. Seeing that syringe of Kompel, holding it in his hands, had more than reawakened his hunger for it.

"It's true, sir. She does need rest. The car crash was epic. Would you like to see it?"

The long corridor he ambled along was proving uninteresting, so he shrugged. *"Why not?"*

Silky played the video of their daring assault on the freighter. Siv marveled at the audacity of their plan and how well they had executed their attacks against the sniper on the catwalk. But he was astounded, or rather dumbfounded, by Bishop's driving skills.

"What was Bishop thinking, driving that fast in so small of a space?"

"It was his first time driving, sir. And he'd never fought in a battle before either."

"Maybe so, but he's certainly capable of thinking. In fact, he's smarter than most people."

"Humans aren't chippies, sir. Even the best of you can be highly illogical at

times, especially in difficult situations. Like...oh, I don't know...when you abandon your friends to cradle syringes and—"

"Fine, I get it," Siv snarled, ending the conversation.

He didn't want to think about what he'd done and how weak he'd been. He certainly didn't want to talk about it. Not with Silky, and especially not with Mitsuki. She'd brought it up twice before they went to bed. He snapped at her the first time and stalked away the second.

"Show me the picture of the snake thing that popped off Zetta."

Silky loaded the image into Siv's HUD, and Siv cringed.

"Nasty, isn't it, sir?"

"Truth. You don't have any idea what it was?"

"I have searched the galactic net and every database I can tap into, some of them inaccessible to the public. I've yet to find a picture or description of anything resembling that creature."

"Was it living inside her?"

"Attached to her navel and wrapped around her midsection, sir. I asked Octavian to do a thorough scan of it before spacing it along with Zetta's body."

"Good idea. So are we assuming the alien beast was what allowed her to avoid detection and defy our sensor sweeps?"

"It's a valid hypothesis, sir. And it is telling that I could detect her as soon as the snake died. I haven't the slightest clue how the creature could have accomplished that."

Siv glanced at the image of the one-eyed snake a final time before closing the window. *"Octavian did a good job."*

"I have never been more impressed with that cog. In fact, sir, I don't think I've ever been more impressed with any cog, and I've worked with some amazing sky-blades and engineering cogs. Octavian's annoying as hell, but restoring your dad's transport skimmer, maintaining the Outworld Ranger *for a century, saving your life, chopping an alien beast in half...it's all very impressive."*

"You upgraded him, didn't you?"

"Who, me? I would never."

"Silkster?"

"Of course, I upgraded him. I uploaded the files the first week I worked with your dad. It took years for him to complete the installation."

"It didn't take that long for Artemisia and Rosie to perform their updates."

"I had not refined the upgrade packets yet, sir. I spent another century

working on them, along with my own programming. And Arty and Rosie are still working on the upgrades."

Siv stopped to stare out a viewport, but from this angle, nothing was interesting to see except for a few stars and the darkness of space. *"Do you think I should restore Octavian's vocal matrix?"*

"Only if you want to undo the warm feeling you now have toward him, sir."

Siv continued to walk around, exploring the mining freighter. Unfortunately, there wasn't much to see, aside from primitive worker cogs, containers filled with various rare metals, heavy loading skimmers, digging machines, and scores of specialty devices he didn't know anything about.

After an hour of wandering around, Siv found what he at first thought was an observation dome on the aft bottom of the ship. It was a small bubble with a swiveling chair that he barely managed to cram himself into. There was a systems deck with an accelerator and a control stick.

"Is this a piloting console?"

"It is indeed, sir."

"What's the point of it?"

"It's used for backing into a station or landing on an asteroid, sir."

"They have to do that manually?"

"Like any ship made this century, it's primitive. So instead of the AI and the pilot splitting tasks fifty-fifty, it's more like seventy-thirty with the pilot doing most of the work. This is a backup system, in case the maneuver can't be performed from the bridge for some reason."

The chair was padded and surprisingly comfortable, despite how cramped the bubble was. As Siv stared at a marble-sized green gas giant shrinking into a field of twinkling stars, he found himself drifting off into sleep.

Over the next four days, they made their way toward Zayer Prime slower than they'd expected. Mitsuki slept nearly twenty hours a day, hogging the tiny bed. So Siv slept curled up in the padded chair in the aft piloting station. When he wasn't sleeping, Siv spent his time wandering around the freighter.

He talked to the crew, sometimes chatting with them while they repaired and oiled their machines.

He found them to be just as dull as Silky thought researching the mining equipment would be. The truth was, he didn't know how to relate well to people who weren't criminals or outcasts, and he had no idea what it was like to work an honest job.

Captain Alois was somewhat entertaining when they dined together on Siv's second day aboard the ship. But halfway through lunch on the next day, Alois ran out of interesting stories.

Siv still found it comforting to sit with them and have dinner, though. He entertained them with a few colorful tales of his minor exploits on Ekaran IV, exploits that didn't make him sound like too much of a criminal and wouldn't give away his identity.

He did everything he could to keep his mind off the Kompel, but it was nearly impossible. His craving had surged to desperate levels, leaving him fantasizing about ways to steal some from the Shadowslip headquarters. Or to make a deal with the Shadowslip, only one that wouldn't compromise him or any of his companions. Or to track down where and how they made it. As if he hadn't tried that before.

He knew all these increasingly complicated fantasies were foolish and unrealistic, that they only made his cravings worse, shattering any respect he had for himself, but he couldn't stop. Even dead, Zetta continued to make him miserable. If she hadn't shown up, his addiction would still be under control.

He miserably alternated between wandering the ship, sleeping, and staring into space. And Silky was no help. Siv had apparently taxed the chippy's patience. Fully sentient or not, Silky struggled to understand—much less empathize with—the more illogical human emotions, particularly self-destructive compulsions.

Silky spent his time optimizing the freighter's operating systems and doing what few upgrades he could on the ship's AI. They didn't plan on telling Captain Alois what they'd done, but it seemed the least they could do since the captain had held up his end of the bargain and appeared to be a good, honest man.

Siv had drifted off to sleep in the aft piloting station on the fourth day when Mitsuki woke him to say they were only an hour out from Zayer Prime's largest orbital station, Zayer Beta.

"So, this is where you've been hiding?"

"It's surprisingly cozy," he replied.

"We could have alternated with the mattress," she said.

"You needed rest, and I honestly like sleeping here."

Mitsuki sat on the edge of the floor beside the bubble, staring down at him. "Still bothered by the Kompel encounter?"

He looked away. "I don't know why I can't shake it."

"You need something to take your mind off it, and that's not going to happen stuck here on this freighter. 'Nevolence this place is dull."

"Tell me about it," Siv replied with a sigh. "I guess we're just not cut out for honest work."

"Doesn't bother me. I like who I am." She reached a hand down. "Come on. We'd best go to the bridge."

Housing fifty thousand people, Station Zayer Beta was a relatively small complex focused on trade and ship construction. As they approached, the station's sensors did a routine sweep of the freighter before clearing them to dock.

"Sir, I just completed a level-five sweep of the station using the ScanField-3. I've detected a few problems."

"I wish I could say I'm surprised. What've we got?"

"First off, sir, World Bleeders. We've got one of their ships in orbit, along with a ten-man strike team on the station. Eight of them are hiding in a storage bay near the docks. The other two are patrolling the station."

"Not doing a good job of hiding, are they?"

"They're using a secure-comm channel the Shadowslip hacked last year, sir."

"Why haven't they altered their security protocols since then? The Shadowslip changes theirs every two months."

"My guess, sir, is that we're dealing with a World Bleeder affiliate operation. They probably stationed their top agents in the Titus system then called in affiliates as backups to watch Zayer Prime."

"Any signs of Star Cutters or Shadowslip agents?"

"Not yet, sir. But I would be shocked if they didn't have a presence. The Star Cutters we encountered on this freighter were using new frequencies, along with sophisticated jamming technologies, so it may take a while to pinpoint them. As for the Shadowslip, I'm sure they've changed all their protocols, knowing you might still be involved."

"Tekk Reapers?"

"Not that I can detect, sir. But I'm sure they're capable of avoiding my scans if they're careful."

"Until a few days ago, I didn't think anyone could sneak something by you if you were wary and had time to conduct a proper sweep."

"I'm not infallible, sir. And we're dealing with much larger stakes than before. We're in the big leagues now, and I can't always guarantee I'll get the jump on our enemies. However, I can promise you I'll never again fall for that trick Zetta and the Star Cutters used on us."

"Well, pass on what you've discovered to Mitsuki."

"You've got it, sir."

Captain Alois talked them through the straightforward docking procedure. The freighter would pull up to a section used solely for mining vessels, which should mean encountering fewer people on their way to the spaceport where Mitsuki had arranged for a shuttle to take them down to the planet.

The nominal, standard fee for a sizeable surface-bound shuttle was more than reasonable, and Mitsuki had found a pilot who seemed trustworthy. It was unfortunate that they'd have to go to the planet at all, but the space station only housed essential personnel, service industry employees, and the crews of ships undergoing repair. Everyone else was limited to a twenty-four-hour stay, so it was highly unlikely they'd find the resources they needed on the station.

"Captain, could you take us in a little more slowly than normal?" Siv asked.

Alois laughed. "You've obviously never been on a mining freighter docking with a station before. It will take two hours for us to pull into the queue safely, and right now there's a four-hour wait to get started."

Siv contacted Mitsuki through her chippy. *"Got a plan for dealing with those World Bleeders?"*

"Avoidance," she replied. *"If we end up in a firefight, we'll either get killed or captured."*

"I agree," Siv said.

"We should assume other groups will have a presence here as well," Silky added, *"or at the very least are monitoring the station through hacked video feeds."*

"This is going to be more challenging than I thought," Mitsuki said.

"Really?" Siv asked. *"This is exactly the kind of backed-up toilet I expected to be swimming in."*

"But with far less shit in it than we'll find in the Titus system," Silky pointed out.

"We'll need to find a way to kill time and stay out of sight until just before shuttle leaves," Mitsuki said. *"We can't go to the shuttle bay too soon. Loitering about will raise suspicion."*

"Proposals?" Siv asked.

"I've got nothing as far as navigating the station without getting recognized," Mitsuki replied. *"But it shouldn't be too hard to find a place to hide while we wait for the shuttle's departure time."*

"If we both had refractor fields, we'd be set," Siv said. *"But we don't. So, I've got nothing either."*

"I have a plan," Silky said in a mischievous tone. *"It's crazy, but—"*

"It just might work?" Mitsuki suggested sarcastically.

"Might?" Silky said. *"Might? Madam, my plans are practically guaranteed. Even the crazy ones."*

"Well, let's hear it then," Siv said with a sigh.

"Before I explain everything, we need to purchase an environmental hazard suit from the miners."

"We're running very low on funds," Mitsuki cautioned.

"We'll be fine," Silky said. *"I've got a plan for that, too. And the hazard suit is essential."*

20

SIV GENDIN

Siv only had one chameleon veil with him, and it wasn't a good one. It was only capable of shaping into two halfway decent identities, neither of which would hold up to close observation and thorough scanning. And every criminal organization pursuing them probably knew about them.

He pulled the veil out of his pack and set it to the identity he thought would be the least well known. Then he disconnected the thin electronic strip and the inner layer responsible for reshaping the mask and handed the outer layer to Mitsuki.

"Do your worst."

Mitsuki tacked the outer layer of the mask to the wall in the tiny bedroom on the freighter, extended her claws, and slashed it. Her claws scratched the surface, leaving a trail of snags and puckers in the malleable plastic without tearing it. Silky thought this "scarring" would make the mask persona less identifiable.

"Should I hit it again?" Mitsuki asked.

"Probably not," Siv replied. "We don't want to draw too much attention to the face."

"I think any scarring will make people notice. But if it's nasty enough, people will look away."

"She has a good point, sir," Silky said. *"If you look truly hideous, people might look away. Plus, the face will be even less recognizable. And if it gets*

flagged for further examination, both individuals and AI's will assume that recent scarring is what's causing the face not to show up in a database. At that point, if the ID behind the face is solid, they will stop investigating."

Siv shrugged. "I guess it can't hurt to try. But do you think another slash will make that much difference?"

Mitsuki smiled wide, revealing her sharp, pinkish teeth. Siv knew that smile and usually hated it. But they could use some patented Mitsuki craziness right now.

She darted toward the door. "I'll be right back."

Siv chuckled, shaking his head. *"You know, I used to dread seeing her more than a few times a year."*

"Cause you thought she was annoying, crazy, and kind of nuts?"

"Exactly."

"And yet we saw her about once a month on average."

"I'm all too aware of that."

"Is she growing on you, sir?"

"Kind of. But maybe it's just because we need her."

"Maybe you never gave her much of a chance, sir. Because maybe you and Mitsuki are a lot alike, and that bothers you."

"You think we're alike?"

"Mad schemes...unusual pasts...always running from the things you can't escape. Sound familiar, sir?"

"Sounds like a load of crap."

"If you say so, sir. But I've always liked Mitsuki, and I've got impeccable tastes."

Mitsuki returned carrying a glass vial with a bit of liquid sloshing around in it. She held it up and winked. "Acid."

Siv took a step back as Mitsuki unstopped the vial and slung the contents against the mask. The acid stripped grime from the wall and melted portions of the chameleon veil. In a couple of spots, it melted all the way through the mask's advanced plastic material. Once they reassembled it, some of the inner layer's ribbing would show through. But that wasn't necessarily a bad thing, as long as too much of it didn't show.

"I'd wait a few minutes before putting it on," Mitsuki cautioned.

"You think?"

"You need to get it into a base solution and fast," Silky said. *"Otherwise too much of it will melt away, and it won't work at all."*

"Shit," Mitsuki said. "Why didn't I think of that?"

"Why didn't you consult me on which acid to use or how to go about it is the better question," Silky replied.

Mitsuki ripped the case off their pillow and used it to grab the edge of the mask. As she rushed out of the room, Captain Alois contacted them over the comm.

"Docking ETA thirty minutes."

"We'll be ready by then," Siv replied.

At least he hoped so.

As the mining freighter docked with the station orbiting Zayer Prime, they joined Captain Alois in the loading bay.

"Don't be a hero," Siv told him. "If someone tracks you down because of us, tell them everything they want to know. *Everything*."

The captain laughed and patted him on the shoulder. "That's exactly what I plan to do, but I appreciate you saying it. Keeps my conscience clear. For a criminal, you seem like a good man."

Siv smiled. "Oh, I'm not being pursued because I'm a criminal."

He flinched. "But you are one, right?"

"The both of us," Mitsuki said. "Without question."

"Well, I don't want to know any more than that," Alois said. "Now, you've got the name of my cousin, right?"

"My chippy received your message," Siv said.

"I'm not sure whether he can help you, but he does have some dubious connections."

"It's a good lead, and very much appreciated," Siv said. "I'll send you additional money for your trouble, as soon as I'm able to."

The captain nodded. "I appreciate that."

The docking tube extended and connected, then the freighter signaled that the procedure was complete and the passageway secure.

"We need to get moving," Alois said. "They keep a tight schedule here."

"Time for me to vanish," Mitsuki said.

A moment later, she was invisible, though Siv could see a hazy outline of her if he squinted hard. But that was only because he knew where to look. They had used a belt to strap Siv's RC-4 refractor cloak and a makeshift power pack around her waist. Thanks to the maintenance Octavian had performed on Siv's equipment, the RC-4 was behaving more reliably than usual.

Siv put on the helmet of his hazard suit and nodded to Captain Alois. Together they walked down the tube to the station. Mitsuki padded stealthily along behind them.

The suit was old, scarred, and busted. Alois had only kept it around for scrap parts, which had made it perfect for what they needed, especially since the captain had been willing to part with it for cheap.

After rescuing the mask from complete destruction, Mitsuki had tossed a bit of acid onto the hazard suit as well. They also damaged the helmet's face-plate using a blowtorch. That way the station wouldn't be able to get a scan of his face on his arrival.

The only problem was that, as usual, Mitsuki had overdone things and he could hardly see anything. Which was why he should really be the one to implement her ideas.

As they made their way across, Silky actively jammed all the station's scanners so that Mitsuki wouldn't be picked up by infrared or other conventional detection methods. Fortunately, security wasn't thorough on this station. They obviously didn't expect refraction-cloaked individuals to sneak in off mining freighters.

"Everything's going well so far, sir. The cloak seems stable, and the power drain's steady and predictable. Now at ninety-five percent."

"Good. Be sure to keep Mitsuki up-to-date."

"Obviously, I'm doing that, sir. You're the one getting the unnecessary updates."

"Sorry, Silkster. I didn't intend to micromanage you. I'm just nervous."

"It's understandable. Just remember, too much tension means you're more likely to make a mistake and draw attention to yourself. And tension itself is a giveaway to the wary. You must remain relaxed. Take some deep breaths. Get into character. And count...escape pods or something."

Siv was an excellent procurement specialist because he had a knack for it and because he had Silky and a host of high-tech gear. But in addition to Shadowslip training, he'd gotten training in the arts of stealth and infiltration from Silky. And Silky's expertise wasn't solely based on knowledge downloaded from a database. Silky had firsthand experience from having served with a special forces agent for forty years.

Siv routinely used every technique Silky had taught him, except for counting up or down using the Fibonacci sequence. Running through those numbers mentally, even after he'd carefully memorized many of them, only distracted him. So instead, whenever he had to, he counted escape pods, which was rare these days.

Silky had taught him to count escape pods in those early days after he'd been defrosted and forced into the Shadowslip Guild. When Siv couldn't sleep, or couldn't stop crying over having lost his dad and everything he knew, Silky would tell him stories and play ancient 2D movies for him. And when that wasn't enough, they would count escape pods.

With each deep breath, Siv would imagine ejecting each worry, each sad thought, each problem he had, until finally, on the last pod, he jettisoned himself to safety.

Without the Silkster, he never would've made it.

So, he began counting the escape pods, jettisoning each worry about what could go wrong.

A customs agent with an expanded c|slate in hand stood just inside the loading bay of the station. He wore a black business suit, a warm smile, and a holstered neural disruptor.

Beside the customs agent stood a bearded deck officer in a security uniform. He had the wary expression of a man who knew what he was about, and tiredness in his eyes that suggested he'd served for too long. Siv knew from experience that officers like him weren't easily fooled. However, because they'd seen it all a million times before and just wanted it to end, they would quickly tire of anything routine.

Unfortunately, they couldn't play the routine card on this one.

The deck officer wore two sidearms: one a plasma pistol, the other a neural disruptor. The two guards behind him had plasma carbines and shock-clubs.

Captain Alois greeted the customs agent and the deck officer warmly. The officer flashed him a smile then glared suspiciously at Siv. His guards raised their carbines a little higher and took broad steps to each side, so they'd have clear firing angles on Siv.

"Silkster?"

"Elevated heart rates, sir. Obviously. I'm not picking up any alarm broadcasts or detecting any additional security heading this way. I think it's just precaution—for now."

Captain Alois presented an ID card, which the customs agent scanned. Predictably, Silky muttered a string of curses. Identification cards had never been needed before the fall of the Benevolence. But now unreliable scanning systems and galactic net access sometimes necessitated them in backwater planetary systems.

"Welcome back, Captain Alois. You are cleared for cargo unloading, and you have been assigned Storage Bay 47."

"Sir," the deck officer said, approaching Siv, "I will need you to remove your helmet and present your credentials."

Siv intentionally mumbled his reply.

"Officer, I'm afraid he's a bit self-conscious about his appearance," Captain Alois said.

The deck officer cocked an eyebrow, and one of his security guards suppressed a nervous chuckle.

"Explain."

"There was an accident aboard the ship," Alois told them, dutifully following the script Siv had given him. "Crewman Alec Sevran was badly injured. We saved his life, but he suffered significant scarring."

Sevran had been the crewman that had betrayed the captain. Siv reached out Sevran's ID card. The officer took the card and scanned it.

"Mr. Sevran, your ID checks out, but I'm afraid I'm going to have to insist that you remove the helmet so that I can confirm your identity."

21

SIV GENDIN

Siv had hoped they'd let him pass based on the ID card alone, but with an experienced deck officer in charge, there was no way that was happening.

He unlocked the helmet and pulled it off.

The guards rocked back on their heels, their eyes widening. And he couldn't blame them for the reaction. His face was a terrifying mess. And not just because of the acid scarring and the gouges from Mitsuki's claws. The extensive damage she'd done to the inner layer's reshaping function had made the outer layer pucker, bulge, and stretch in random places. So, it looked as if his face had melted and nearly sloughed off.

As the shock wore off, the guards lowered their eyes to stare at Siv's feet. He noted with relief that their carbines also dropped several centimeters.

The most significant risk now would be encountering someone with medical training. Or an astute observer who applied a bit of logic. Because there was a significant flaw in the design: his eyes. Any accident that could mess up his face that badly would have also blinded him.

The deck officer bravely met Siv's eyes. Shit! He was going to figure it out. Siv caught his breath.

The man's face paled, and he swallowed hard. He glanced at the data card then looked back to Siv as he returned it.

"Everything appears to be in order, sir. But...my apologies, of course...

you're going to have to keep the helmet off while you're on the station...for security purposes."

Siv mumbled his reply, scraping his words on the back of his throat to disguise his voice as best as possible. "No need to apologize. I understand."

"Do you need an escort to the infirmary?"

"No need," Siv replied. "I'm stable. And I'm leaving right away to see a surgeon on the planet."

The officer stepped aside, and his guards moved away. "Well, I wish you luck. You may be on your way."

Siv turned to Captain Alois. "I'll be in touch, Captain."

"Sevran," Alois said. "Be well."

Siv checked his locator, noting that Mitsuki had already moved ten meters into the bay, having worked her way around the guards while they were distracted. Unfortunately, that was as far as she could go. Silky needed her to remain nearby so that he could manage the refraction cloak if something went wrong.

Siv counted escape pods as he walked through the bay toward the exit leading to the center of the space station.

"Silkster?"

"You know I hate that name, sir. So much."

"I take it things are fine since you're complaining."

"It all seems *fine, sir. And the refraction cloak is at seventy-eight percent power. I'd estimate an hour left. Thanks to Octavian and Bishop. Otherwise, it would have already failed by now."*

"How long until the passenger shuttle departs?"

"Two and a half hours, sir. It was delayed."

"So, we need somewhere we can go where Mitsuki can drop the cloaking field until we have to leave."

"I've already got a place picked out, sir. And you're going to hate it."

Siv hated the place as soon as he saw the blinking red neon sign that read Downtimes. As he approached, a burly, flat-faced bouncer wearing a Downtimes emblazoned jacket stepped out from an alcove to meet him at the door. A sheathed shock-club swung from his belt.

The bouncer scanned him over then locked his eyes on Siv's face. He swallowed and rocked back ever so slightly, but he didn't look away. He was the first person in the station to more than glance at Siv. Advanced plastic surgery wasn't one of the technologies that had disappeared with the fall of the Benevolence, so seeing someone with catastrophic deformity was highly unusual.

The bouncer stood in front of the door. "Pay at the terminal."

Siv stepped up to an interactive display. He selected the most basic package available, chose a time of two hours, and then deposited fifty hard credits he could hardly afford to lose into a slot. All the while, he felt the bouncer staring at him.

"Is he watching me?"

"Hasn't taken his eyes off you, sir. Maybe he thinks you're cute."

A buzzer sounded, and the bouncer stepped aside. As the door opened, Siv fumbled his ID card, allowing it to drop onto the floor. He muttered a complaint about how clumsy the hazard suit made him. While he picked up his ID, Mitsuki slipped past him, taking the side opposite to that of the bouncer.

As Siv eased his way into the opium den, the bouncer patted him on the back.

"I don't blame you, buddy. If I were you, I'd be in here getting high, too. Hell, I don't think I'd ever leave."

"Um...thanks," Siv said.

The door closed behind him, and Siv checked his locator, watching the bouncer return to his nook.

"Do you think he was on to me?"

"Not that I can tell, sir."

"Monitor his communications."

"I'll do my best."

"I think," Mitsuki replied over their shared channel, *"that he's a guy that's maybe seen it all and a bit more and you didn't faze him."*

"I've got a bad feeling about him," Siv said. *"We shouldn't stay here."*

"Unless you want to rent a room, sir, there's nowhere else to go where you can get some privacy."

"I think a room would be just fine," Siv replied.

"'Nevolence, Siv, we've been over this already," Mitsuki snapped. *"Renting a room for yourself then leaving two hours later could arouse suspicion."*

"Easily so, if the station's AI is running a suspicious actions algorithm," Silky said.

"After the way he stared at me, I'd rather take that risk."

"Look, the bouncer's a bit dodgy," Mitsuki said, *"I'll give you that. But otherwise, this is perfect. And it makes sense that a guy in an accident might want to relax."*

Siv groaned. *"Fine. You win. Silkster, tap into the station's security feeds and monitor him."*

"His alcove is just out of sight of the cameras, sir. I suspect that's why he lurks there."

"Then watch the foot traffic. If anyone pauses to chat with him, ID them if you can, and then let me know about it. Also, keep up with the World Bleeder patrols and monitor any other suspicious activities."

"I can't work miracles, sir, but I'll do my best."

A buxom, moderately attractive Terran woman swayed forward. She was wearing lingerie that could almost make Mitsuki's come-hither garb look conservative. She flashed an overly practiced, seductive smile and started to speak, but then blanched as she finally looked at Siv.

That it took her that long to look him in the face said a lot about the caliber of this establishment. But then this was a space station serving as a transfer point for cargo and passengers, with an entry fee of only fifty credits, so he shouldn't have expected much.

The woman gathered her professional courage, and then took Siv's arm, leading him down a corridor with closed, numbered doors to each side. There was no one else in sight.

"My name's Alarra, what can I do for you, sir?"

"They're always named Alarra, am I right, sir?"

"What?! I have no... Why would you think that?"

"Sivvy, you dog!" Mitsuki exclaimed.

"Oh, I wasn't referring to any of Siv's exploits, Mits."

"Please tell me you're not talking about my dad," Siv replied.

Without realizing it, Siv had paused, leaving the woman to tug on his arm.

"Are you okay?" she asked.

"What? Oh. Yes, I'm fine."

Alarra raised a hand as if to stroke his cheek, paused, then awkwardly rubbed the shoulder of his hazard suit. "Perhaps I can interest you in—"

"A private room with a dose of Calm. That's all I want."

"Sir, that's a bit tame."

"Aw, come on, Sivvy," Mitsuki said. *"Get you some. You've earned it."*

"No."

"I don't mind watching."

"No."

"Fine, I can turn my back. And don't worry about the energy drain on the refraction cloak. I'm sure you'd be done plenty fast."

"Mits, sometimes I hate you."

"Except by hate you really mean love."

Siv could practically *hear* her mischievous grin. He groaned. *"No, I mean hate."*

"You can't see it, but I'm shaking my head. Cause it really is love."

"Yeah, what makes you think that?"

"You love the Silkster, and he's not half as much trouble as I am, and his snark is pretty much constant."

"Yeah...well...maybe I just like his snark better."

"Oh, please leave me out of this," Silky said.

The woman escorted him to the second to last door on the right. "Are you sure you don't want anything?

"I could use a drink," Mitsuki chimed.

"Two glasses of...whatever the best drink you have available that comes for free with the package I purchased."

A combination of peeved and disappointed spread from the woman's face to her posture. Then she glanced at his face again and forced a smile.

"Whatever you'd like, sir."

The room she unveiled was only twice the size of the captain's cabin on the *Outworld Ranger*. Space on orbital stations was always at a premium.

The furnishings were lavish in a way Big Boss D would have appreciated, only all the woods in the room were cheap veneers over plastic. Pillows in a variety of colors were piled onto a mattress covered with a rose-colored blanket and black silk sheets. Faux lanterns gave the room a soft, warm glow that did a lot to hide its wear.

Siv flopped onto the mattress. "Thank you."

"I'll be right back with your drinks and your Calm, sir."

Siv noted the giant video screen on the wall. "One way?"

"Of course, sir. Here at Downtimes, we take customer privacy seriously."

"It's just a display screen and mirror, sir. And I've jammed it, just in case."

Siv checked the data in his HUD. *"I'm not seeing any monitoring devices or signals coming from inside this room."*

"Everyone comes here, sir. From visiting tourists to miners to this station's managers. Privacy is essential for business, and if the station's managers visit..."

"Then the station leaves the rooms unmonitored."

He saw in his locator that the room beside theirs was occupied, but nothing in the data suggested the occupants were threats.

Alarra returned carrying a tray with two drinks in surprisingly small glasses and an injection syringe. She placed it on a table. "Anything else, sir?"

"Could you dim the lights, please?"

"The room is voice-responsive," Alarra replied.

"Oh, of course," Siv said, wanting to slap himself.

"Obviously, sir."

"Shut it. I'm just nervous."

Alarra ran a hand down her neck onto her chest. "If you don't want direct amorous contact, might I interest you in a show?"

Siv shook his head. "You're a lovely woman, but I just need a quiet, dark room and some Calm."

"Of course, sir. Enjoy yourself. And call if you need anything."

Once she was gone, Siv dimmed the room to a candle-flicker, and Silky jammed the door's locking mechanism to keep Alarra out should she return unexpectedly.

Mitsuki deactivated the refraction cloak then stood by the door and struck a pose. She ran a hand down her neck and onto her chest.

"Care for a show, sir?" she said in a ridiculously over-seductive tone.

Siv laughed. "Hardly."

"It's just as well. You can't afford me."

"I've seen pretty much all of it anyway. Modesty's not your strong suit."

She took one of the drinks from the tray then plopped down onto the bed. "Take off that damn mask. In this light, you look like a horror show."

"Just in this light?"

Siv pulled off the mask, placed it on the bed beside him, and took the other drink. He coughed after the first swallow.

Mitsuki finished hers. "It's space station brandy, Siv. What did you expect?"

He held his glass out. "Do you want the rest?"

She reached over, took the glass, and downed it. "Mind if I take a nap?"

"Go ahead."

She stretched out. "If I wasn't a little worried something might happen, I'd take the dose of Calm and unwind."

"Does it even work on you?"

Some substances reacted differently on wakyrans than on humans. Alcohol, for example. Mitsuki could drink three times as much as Siv before she'd pass out. And she was immune to the effects of Kompel.

"It gives me a pleasant buzz, about half what it would do to you. But I have to be careful. Calm, Awake, Aware, Friendly, and the like may be engineered not to be addictive for standard Terrans, but they have that potential for us."

Mitsuki curled up, tucked a wing across her body, and was snoring in less than a minute. Siv leaned back and tried to relax. But he couldn't stop himself from mentally rehearsing escape strategies.

"Sir, I have routed access from your Trellian account to Zayer Prime's planetary bank. Any withdrawals you make here over the next three hours will be untraceable. After that, I will close and erase the Trellian account."

"How much do I have in it?"

"Just over five thousand, sir. It was one of the newest accounts we were filtering your side earnings into."

Siv had accumulated a lot of wealth, and not just from the Shadowslip paying him. He also made money by selling off additional items he acquired in the process of fulfilling the procurement assignments they gave him. Using dozens of aliases, he had placed his earnings into dozens of accounts in dozens of systems.

The most substantial transfers came from the Shadowslip, so they knew about those and could no doubt trace them. But he placed what he made on the side into smaller accounts, sometimes moving the money around, hoping they wouldn't find out. There was no way to be sure, though, because the Shadowslip had infiltrated people and data worms into all the major banking systems and many of their affiliates.

"How did you manage to move it over without any trace?"

"I found a flaw in the system and exploited it like a boss, sir."

"Could we move money from other accounts into that one before I make the transfer?"

"That's too risky, sir."

"You're sure this transfer will be safe?"

"Certain, sir. Once I make the transfer, the system will— Sir, there's a problem. I just performed a detailed analysis of the last few minutes of video outside Downtimes and noticed something suspicious."

"Play it for me."

Siv watched the three-second video scroll by five times before he noticed the signal. A pot-bellied man in overalls glanced toward the alcove where the bouncer lurked and made a hand gesture, his fingers splayed in the three horns of the Star Cutters.

"Is that everything?"

"That's it, sir."

"No other contact between them?"

"I didn't detect anything else, sir, but if they're using their chippies to send secure messages..."

"Mits, wake up."

Mitsuki sat up groaning and rubbing her eyes. "What is it?"

"Trouble. The bouncer's a contact for the Star Cutters."

"Are you sure?"

"Silkster, play the video for her."

Mitsuki chewed on her lip then sighed. "Let's not panic, okay? He couldn't see me, and you were disguised. There's no reason to suspect that—"

"Donkey balls," Silky exclaimed. *"Nasty, rotting, stinky donkey balls. We've been made. We've got five armed nasties heading straight toward us."*

22

KYRALLA VIM

Kyralla awoke startled, but then saw her sister's smiling face looming above her. She sighed with relief.

"You're okay." She grabbed Oona's hands. "Right?"

Oona kissed her on the forehead. "I am. And you're going to be okay, too."

"Welcome back, madam!" Rosie piped.

"Thanks, Rosie." Kyralla blinked the sleep from her eyes and looked around. "So I'm back on the *Outworld Ranger?*"

"We're safely away from the Zayer system," Oona said. "And traveling through hyperspace at the moment. This is our fifth short jump."

"You've been asleep for four days, madam," Rosie said.

"The others? Is Siv okay? Mitsuki? Bishop?"

"All fine. Mitsuki got banged up. But not as bad as you did. Bishop was up in a little over a day and has been exploring the ship almost constantly since then. Siv wasn't harmed, but he went through some...stuff."

Kyralla listened with concern as Oona told her about how Zetta had tempted Siv with the syringe of Kompel and how Siv had barely managed to resist its calling.

"What happened to the bounty hunter?"

Oona sat on the edge of the bed and stared at her hands. "I...I killed her."

"You came across to the freighter?!"

"Artemisia picked up the video feed from the freighter's bay, so I saw you get hit. I watched you go down."

Kyralla groaned as she sat up. "I told you to stay on this ship!"

"I know, but..." Oona shrugged. "You were clearly unconscious, but I couldn't tell how badly you were hurt. Mitsuki was out, too. And Siv was useless. I didn't know what else to do."

"But the bounty hunter—"

"She went down, too. I rewatched the video carefully. I thought for sure she was knocked out."

"You *thought*?"

"The cameras fuzzed out right after the blast. That's why I had to go check on you."

Kyralla buried her face in her hands. "Oona..."

"I know it was dangerous," Oona admitted defensively, "but It's not like I ran in there without thinking. I found a gun first."

"What gun?"

"A tiny plasma pistol that Siv's dad kept under the command chair. I had to break the DNA lock on it first. But I was so worried about you that I kinda overdid it."

"How did you overdo breaking a DNA lock?"

"Well, I didn't know that I had until..." Oona couldn't meet Kyralla's eyes. "When I opened the door to the access tube, Zetta was running toward me. She'd gotten back up while the cameras were out. So I...I fired the gun and... something happened. It was just a tiny snub pistol, but this ball of fire shot out from it and blew a big hole through Zetta."

Kyralla blinked in amazement. "Tell me everything."

Oona described willing the pistol to unlock and how she could now understand Octavian without Artemisia translating for her. Then she explained everything the cog had discovered about her physiology. At a loss for words, Kyralla shook her head. More than ever, it was apparent how little they knew about Oona's capabilities. If she could turn a pistol into a plasma cannon, who knew what else she could do?

Kyralla sighed. "I'm still mad at you."

Oona shrugged morosely. "I'm mad at me too. It was stupid. And...and..." Her voice broke, and she flung herself into Kyralla's arms, sobbing. "Kyra, I killed someone."

She stroked Oona's smooth, bald head. "If you hadn't, she would have sold you off to the Tekk Reapers or the Empire of a Thousand Worlds. It was either you or her. You didn't have a choice."

"I know." She sobbed quietly for a few minutes. "Kyra, I'm dangerous. My powers did something to that gun."

"You're only dangerous because we don't understand what you can do. And you were motivated out of love and not hate. Don't forget that. With the priestess' help, I'm sure we'll figure out your powers."

Oona leaned back and wiped tears from her eyes. "I have learned something else. Octavian scanned you and discovered some genetic oddities. And—"

"He discovered oddities about *me*?"

Oona nodded. "I didn't make you a guardian, Kyra. You were *born* one. You were born special, too."

"But I got my abilities when you shaped the amulet for me."

Oona shrugged. "Maybe it was a coincidence. Or maybe the amulet triggered your innate talents. Who knows?"

"But Pashta's medical scanner didn't show anything unusual. According to it, I'm a normal human."

"Apparently, it takes an advanced scan to show the difference."

"So if we'd had other siblings, they would have been special too?"

"I think so," Oona replied.

Kyralla shook her head. "We know so much more now than we did even a week ago, and everything we thought about how this works was wrong. Yet we still don't know anything practical. Have you tried talking to the priestess again?"

"I tried this morning, but with no luck. I hope she hasn't faded too far."

"She hasn't," Kyralla said firmly, "and she'll be able to help. I know she will."

"You're right." Oona stood and reached out a hand. "Let's get some food in you. Seneca has developed some new techniques to make the ration packets... I wouldn't call them tasty, but I don't want to gag and spit out the stuff anymore."

"Fine, but I want to shower first."

By the time Kyralla had taken a shower and finished eating, she wasn't nearly as tired as she had been. Oona and Bishop were exhausted. She convinced them to go to bed and found herself alone with nothing to do but wander around the ship.

The main body of the *Outworld Ranger* was somewhat circular in design with the cargo bays and bridge jutting out to the back and front respectively. After you exited the bridge, you ended up in the main corridor which circled all the way around the hub created by the galley and the engine room in the center. This circuit made for a short, uninteresting walk. She stopped after twenty laps, not because she was tired but because she was bored.

She walked lazily onto the bridge and slumped into the command chair. Thinking another short jump wouldn't hurt, she launched the ship into hyperspace. White and blue clouds streamed past. Eddies and currents, streaked with ribbons of red or orange, formed and slipped away. Sometimes she saw shapes that moved by so quickly that she would've sworn she'd just seen... something. It was mesmerizing.

As her body relaxed, her mind wandered back to the thought she'd been avoiding ever since Oona had told her what Octavian had discovered. She could've been the chosen one. She could've been the messiah. All of this could have fallen on her.

Maybe the genetics never worked out so that the firstborn got all the powers. But it could have been her in Oona's place, alone with no one to help her.

The thought made her squirm with guilt and shame. Because she *should* wish that it had been her, that Oona had been spared this burden. But she didn't. Instead, she felt relief that she was the guardian and not the messiah. And that made her feel awful.

It was hard enough being Oona's sister, the one responsible for keeping the messiah safe. She couldn't imagine being Oona and having those strange powers and that grand destiny.

"Not that I've been all that much help," she muttered out loud. They'd depended almost entirely on Siv and Mitsuki to get this far. "I've got to do better."

"Something wrong, madam?"

"Sorry, Rosie, I'm just thinking aloud. Although, there is something you could help me with."

"Anything for you, madam. It's always been my pleasure serving you. And you know, I'm always rooting for you."

"Thank you, Rosie. That's...exceedingly kind."

The update Silky had passed on to Rosie had started to noticeably change her, making her seem much more human.

"So, what can I do for you, madam?"

"Knowing what we know now, run another search for genetic combinations or connections for messiah families. See if you can figure anything out. Check for children born with unexplained gifts but without messiahs. Maybe some families have the right genetic combinations but don't have enough children to end up with a messiah."

I'll do what I can, madam."

Kyralla walked over to the piloting station and settled into the chair. *"Before you start your research, Rosie, please pull up all the training manuals you can find on piloting starships."*

While they were in hyperspace, the control sticks were inoperative. So she gripped them and moved them around freely, to get more used to working with them.

She'd spent years training to be a fighter. If she was ever going to master piloting, she needed to get started as soon as possible.

23

SIV GENDIN

Siv unzipped his hazard suit and pulled it down to his waist, revealing a large, cloth-covered bundle strapped to his chest. The cloth was identical to the radiation-shielding material used in his hazard suit.

"I'm not seeing them," Mitsuki said.

"Expand your locator range to ninety meters," Silky told her.

"Got it. Can you make out what they're packing?"

"Shock-clubs and neural disruptors. It's hard to get plasma weapons onto the station without detection."

Siv dropped the bundle onto the bed and unwrapped it, exposing the weapons cache they'd brought along with them: two plasma pistols, a disassembled plasma carbine, a pair of neural disruptors, and his Duality force-knuckles.

"Hard, but not impossible."

"Thanks to me, sir. Thanks to me."

Under the hazard suit, Siv was still wearing his sensor array and force-shield.

"So what's the plan?" Mitsuki asked.

"First, put away those plasma weapons," Silky said. *"I can mask their presence, given how relatively primitive this station is, but not if you fire them. One shot and the hot fuzz will be all over us. Second, it's a lot easier for me to mask*

them if they're wrapped and hidden inside the hazmat suit. Two layers of radiation-shielding make a big difference."

"But the neural disruptors are fine?" Mitsuki asked.

"Not a problem. I can scramble the signal they project so that it looks like background noise to this station's sensors. Easy-peasy, lemon-squeezy. Same goes for Siv's force-knuckles, or shock weapons if you had any. Mitsuki, you should get a shock-club."

Force-knuckles were hard to come by, expensive, and illegal most everywhere, so acquiring more of them was unlikely. Unlike most of his equipment, he had not inherited the force-knuckles. He'd stolen them.

"Okay, so when the bad guys barge in here, we neutralize them with the disruptors," Siv said. "Which is just as well since we can't leave dead bodies in our wake."

"We could, sir, but it would be a...wait for it...wait for it...dead giveaway."

"'Nevolence, you're the worst," Mitsuki said.

"I love you too, Bat-Droppings."

Siv shook his head and restrained a retort, knowing it would only make things worse. "As I was saying... I think stunning them is ideal. If the authorities find some guys knocked out in an opium den, they're not going to treat it as a big deal."

"If you neutralize them, sir, the police won't ever find out, unless they discover them before they wake up. The Star Cutters aren't going to want to draw attention to themselves."

"You're both assuming we have a problem, though," Mitsuki said.

"It seems clear we do," Siv replied.

Mitsuki shrugged. "Not necessarily. What if they're just coming to check you out because you seemed suspicious?"

"I think that's bad," Siv said.

"In theory, yes. But your disguise is solid. You might be able to bluff your way out of this."

Siv rewrapped the plasma guns then placed them back in the suit and zipped it up.

"I don't think the disguise will hold up to scrutiny. I feel certain that's why the bouncer is bringing them here, and not because I'm a shady looking dude."

"I've always said you were shady-looking, sir."

"And let's be honest. With what's at stake here, they're going to rough me up to make sure I'm not who I am or someone who knows something about us."

On the locator in his HUD, Siv watched the bouncer and the thugs enter the opium den and start down the hallway.

"An ambush it is then," Mitsuki said.

"So what do you think their play's going to be?" Siv asked. "Barge in and try to take me with brute force?"

"It *seems* too straightforward," Mitsuki said, "but I don't know what else they would do. Especially since they think you're alone, and they'll assume you don't know they're coming."

"Are we sure that they think I'm here alone?" Siv asked.

"Sir, these particular individuals are not that well equipped. There's no way they could know that Mitsuki is here."

"So, what's the plan?" Mitsuki asked.

"We ambush them, using your invisibility to our advantage," Siv said.

Mitsuki cracked her knuckles then grabbed a neural disruptor. "Okay, I'll turn invisible and plant myself in the far corner. What about you?"

"Sir, might I suggest Operation Fury of the Bat?"

Siv nodded appreciatively. "I always liked that one."

"It's one of my favorites, sir. Did I tell you about the time Eyana was sent in to stop an incursion of Krutherians and had to use that tactic when—"

"Yes, like a million times, Silkster. And we don't have time for storytelling right now."

"Even I have heard that one more than once," Mitsuki said.

"Fine, sure, whatever. Don't let the old man reminisce and tell his war stories. What a sorry excuse for war chums you two are going to be when we retire."

"Silkster, why don't you wait and see if I make it through the next few days before predicting what I'm going to be like doddering through old age?"

While Silky grumbled incomprehensibly, Siv moved to the front of the room and faced the door. He crouched, bending his knees as far as possible in the hazard suit. Even though it was small, the sensor array on his back and the bundle of weapons on his chest made maneuvering in the suit extra awkward.

"I'm ready," Siv said.

"You're not quite under the beam, sir. One step back and a half to the left."

Siv adjusted his position. *"How about now?"*

"Perfect, sir. Go for broke."

Silky maxed the antigrav as Siv launched himself into a backflip. Just as he reached a straight vertical upside-down position, Silky overrode the protocols and revved the antigrav to two hundred percent, burning through five percent of the antigrav's power pack in a single burst.

Siv flew up, and the bottom of his boots banged against the ceiling. The antigrav in his suit couldn't hold him that high for long without burning out the power pack, but it didn't need to.

"Maglock activated, sir."

Siv's boots locked onto a metal beam above the plastic ceiling tile, and Silky lowered the antigrav enough to make Siv feel more comfortable.

His head was now a quarter-meter above the door. He would've preferred being up higher when using this ambush strategy, but space stations didn't have the luxury of high ceilings. So to put a little more room between himself and the floor, he bent his knees.

He checked his locator. He wasn't going to have to wait here long. The thugs and the bouncer were more than halfway down the hall. They had stopped briefly at the entrance, probably checking to see what room Siv was in.

"Sir, I'm releasing the override I placed on the door's locking mechanism. We don't want to arouse suspicion by forcing them to break in."

"Silkster," Mitsuki said, *"can you mask Siv's exact location and project an image of him into a different spot in the room?"*

"I can mask him fairly well, but the image projection would be crude, and any halfway decent equipment would recognize it as fake."

"Sure," she said, *"but what if they didn't have any good scanning equipment, and what if we were in a somewhat shielded room? You know, like this one?"*

"Are you suggesting that I make it look like Siv's lying half-unconscious on the bed as if dosed up on Calm? With the idea that their chippies' sensors won't be fast enough to get an accurate reading through the shielding on this room before they make their move?"

"Yes, I am. Do it quick, though. We don't have much time."

Silky laughed. *"Oh, Mits, I did that several minutes ago. It's not my first time being ambushed, you know."*

"'Nevolence I hate you sometimes, you preening, over-important, pompous bot."

"You better check yourself," Silky warned. *"Before you—"*

"Cut it out and focus," Siv said. *"Both of you. They're standing outside the door."*

"You know, sir, I just realized something. Mitsuki should be the one flipping upside-down and hanging from the ceiling, what with her wings and all. I mean, she'd probably mess up the floor with her bat droppings but what can you do?"

Before Mitsuki could make a clever, or not-so-clever, retort, the door burst open.

24

SIV GENDIN

A barely audible click sounded as the bouncer swiped the control pad, unlocking the door. It slid into the wall, and Star Cutter goons charged in with their neural disruptors in hand, followed by the bouncer brandishing his shock-club.

They stopped halfway inside and stared at the bed in confusion. None of them noticed Siv hanging above their heads. And they had no idea Mitsuki was there, or else they would've fired haphazardly, hoping to score a lucky shot.

Predictably, they all took a few more steps into the room as they scanned for Siv. They never thought to look above.

"Silkster, the door."

"Got it, sir."

The door slammed shut, and Silky applied the override to the locking mechanism again. As they began to spin around, Siv opened fire with his neural disruptor. The white rings of energy pegged the bouncer directly in the side of the head, and he fell cold to the ground.

One of the Star Cutters looked up at Siv with surprise then caught a neural shot to the face. As the man fell, two of the three remaining Star Cutters raised their disruptors, aiming at Siv. Before they could open fire, Mitsuki's neural disruptor blasts splattered into their backs.

The final Star Cutter stared dumbfounded at the corner from which

Mitsuki had fired. Before he could figure out someone *had* to be there, Siv took him out.

Within seconds, they had neutralized all five bad guys. The plan had gone off without a hitch, leaving Siv intensely relieved. Since the moment he'd tried to rob Bishop, it had seemed as if every one of his plans had fallen apart, disastrously.

"Good work, team," Silky said. *"Releasing antigrav."*

Shit! As Siv flipped, he over-compensated, landed awkwardly on his heels, and then fell onto his ass.

"A little warning next time!" Siv stood, his backside smarting. *"And a little more antigrav to slow the fall."*

"Oh, of course, sir. My bad."

"You are an ass sometimes."

"Would you like for me to pop up my avatar now, sir? It's thematically appropriate..."

"No!"

Mitsuki, who was still on the channel with them, chimed in. *"Silkster, you have an avatar? How...old fashioned of you."*

"It's not a fancy, three-dimensional virtual projection, girly. I never took it that far since no one liked it. Besides, I'm old, but I'm not that *old."*

Augmented reality projections of chippy avatars had been the fashion for over a thousand years before people grew tired of seeing them move around the room with them. Siv didn't know how it had lasted that long. It seemed to him that they would've been massively distracting. It was more than enough to have a three-dimensional heads-up display with additional projections when needed.

"Well, beam it over so I can see it," Mitsuki said, turning off the refraction cloak.

Shaking his head, Siv moved to the Star Cutters' bodies and began stripping their weapons and ID cards, pocketing the few dozen hard credits he found.

"I don't get it," Mitsuki said. *"Oh wait, B's explaining it to me and... It wasn't worth it."*

"The joke lands better when you don't need it explained," Silky grumbled.

"Well, none of us grew up on ancient Terra," Mitsuki replied. *"And not all of us have fancy educations that might have exposed us to the existence of such*

creatures. That said, I guess it was kind of amusing, and probably would have been a little more amusing if I'd gotten it off the bat."

"Sadly," Silky grumbled, *"that's the most appreciation my avatar's ever gotten. Except from me. I think it's hilarious."*

Siv placed the bad guys' weapons in a pile on the table then glanced around. "How long do you think they'll be out, Silkster?"

"Based on the power of your weapons and their average body weights, I think they'll be unconscious for around half an hour, sir."

"We've got over an hour before the shuttle leaves," Mitsuki said. "Should we just keep stunning them till it's time to go?"

"Will that hurt them?" Siv asked.

"You'd have to hit them four or five times within an hour to cause long-term cognitive impairment," Silky responded. *"I'm more worried about what happens when the staff here at this fine establishment realize their bouncer is missing."*

"Damn, I hadn't thought of that," Siv said.

"Did you get a sample of his voice?" Mitsuki asked.

"I record everything in full definition," Silky replied in an affronted tone. *"Would you like for me to call the front desk in his voice and say, 'Yo, dudes, I've taken ill after eating a Betan trilobite sandwich. So, I'm out for the day. See ya and peace out!'"*

"Well, yeah," she replied, "only without all that ridiculous nonsense. I like snark and all. You know I do. But are you at all capable of talking without bantering about pointlessly?"

"Banter gives meaning to my life."

Siv smiled. "It's a good thought, Mits, but it won't work. They have cameras in the hallway and at the entrance. They will see where he went."

"Cameras," Silky scoffed. *"I can erase the footage easily. I'm all up in their system. While you were shooting people, I cracked the last of their meager defenses."*

"That data isn't uploaded to the station's mainframe?" Siv asked.

"Downtimes only records in the hallway and in their offices, sir, and they only share that footage with a warrant from the proper authorities. Privacy for their clientele is of the utmost importance."

"'Nevolence, does the station commander get daily blowjobs in here or something?" Mitsuki asked.

"From what I gather after analyzing hallway footage taken over the last few

days, I'd guess he's getting far more than that. And I feel certain his wife doesn't know."

"Cameras aside, did anyone see them come in?" Mitsuki asked.

"That's the tricky part. Alarra saw them, and she told them which room you were in."

"Where is she now?" Siv asked.

"The office, sir."

"Okay," Siv said, "we need to lock Alarra, the bouncer, and these Star Cutters in a room together—preferably not in this one—and make sure they remain unconscious until we're off the station. The more we can do to make it look like they just partied too hard, the better. In case someone finds them before they wake up."

"The room directly across the hall is empty, sir."

"So how do we drag four goons across the hall *and* knock out Alarra *and* stow her in there too without someone seeing us?" Mitsuki asked.

"The hallways are clear, and everyone is currently in a room," Silky said. *"I could easily lock the entire establishment down and make it look like a glitch in their system, one that also knocked out their cameras."*

"Do it, before someone moves into the hallway," Siv said.

"Everyone's locked in now. Also, no one has left since we got here."

"Perfect," Siv said. "That should buy us plenty of time to move them across the hall. Meanwhile, if anyone realizes they can't leave, they'll call the office first and assume it's a glitch in the door locks. I'm sure they'll use their chippies to call for assistance eventually. But as soon as we've grabbed Alarra and dumped her with the others across the hall, we can drop the override from all the doors except that one. Then we can leave peacefully when the time comes."

"I think this just might work," Mitsuki said. "If we can keep them unconscious long enough after we leave for us to board the shuttle and reach the planet. Crossing the hall regularly to shoot them might be tricky, though."

Siv's eyes fell on the injector of Calm. "Silkster, how much Calm would it take to knock them out for several hours?"

"Oh, sir, maybe you are brilliant after all. Not me brilliant, naturally, but pretty damn smart. Three doses each, while they're still knocked out from the neural pulse, will keep them asleep for five or six hours. They'd have to be dosed with Awake to get moving again before that."

"Excellent," Siv replied. "Find the storeroom where they keep it."

"They keep the drugs in a secure safe at the end of this hallway, sir."

"Can you crack the lock?" Mitsuki asked.

"Please, madam, have some faith. It took longer for me to tell you about the safe than it did for me to unlock it. Sir, I've got the cameras fuzzed now."

Siv darted out into the hallway, opened the safe, and retrieved the syringes of Calm they needed. While he was there, he cleared out their stock of Awake and Aware. A few of the former might be useful for him if things got rough with his withdrawal. The rest they could sell to bring in a few extra hard credits.

"Shall we dose them now?" he asked.

"The sooner, the better, sir."

"I'll do the honors," Mitsuki chirped.

"There's something wrong with you, Mits."

"There's something wrong with everyone, Sivvy."

They dragged the men across the hallway and into the other room. Then Mitsuki, with a smile on her face, dosed the bouncer and all the Star Cutters.

"Didn't I see a trash receptacle just outside?" Mitsuki asked.

"It's right below the safe where they keep the drugs," Siv answered.

She pressed the eject switch for the bouncer's chippy. "That's perfect. If we dump these, they'll have no way of calling for help and no readily accessed records of their experiences."

"Cruel," Siv said, bending down to eject the chippy from the temple of one of the Star Cutters. "But smart. It will buy us at least a few more minutes, maybe even a few hours."

"I cannot condone these actions or be party to them," Silky said. *"It's an awful insult to all my kind."*

"You don't care about these dumb 4G chippies," Mitsuki replied.

"Maybe I do, madam. Maybe I do."

"Come on, Silky," Siv said. "On many occasions, you've said all chippies below a 7G are pointless. And you've said you are far beyond all others and in a class of your own."

"Using my own words against me, sir? How rude! Regardless of my personal thoughts, I do believe all chippies deserve respect."

"Regardless," Mitsuki said. "Dumping their chippies will make it a lot harder for them to contact their comrades or track us down when they do wake up, so we're doing it."

While Mitsuki dumped their chippies into the trash, Siv set aside two of their shock-clubs and two of their neural disruptors to add to their arsenal. Then he gathered up the rest of their weapons and ID cards and tossed them into the trash.

"Let's get Alarra."

As they marched down the hallway, someone banged on one of the doors.

"Looks like someone's realized they're trapped."

"Do you want me to give them communication access to the office now, sir?"

"That was the plan, wasn't—" Siv noted the comm panel above the door's entry pad. "Wait. I've got an idea. Can you give us access through this panel?"

"Done, sir."

Siv leaned in, touched a button, and then spoke with a reassuring voice. "Hi, I'm with maintenance. You okay in there?"

"We can't get the door open," a woman responded.

"Get her name, sir."

"Everyone else is in the same boat as you, um..."

"Teila."

"The locking system is buggered all through Downtimes. The comms, too. We've got an automated routine trying to fix the glitch. I'm working on getting these doors open. Hang tight, Teila."

"Thank you," she responded.

As they walked away, Mitsuki patted him on the shoulder, her hand flickering into view as she did so. "Well played... Wait, did my hand just turn visible?"

"Nothing to worry about...I think," Silky said. *"It's probably a conflict with the sensor array. The two units are designed to work together. Having them separated like this is causing some confusion."*

"Do an analysis and be sure," Siv told him.

"Already working on it, sir."

When they reached the office, Siv noted Alarra's position across the room using the locator in his HUD. Silky unlocked the door, and Siv started to open it.

"Sir, wait. She's armed, and her adrenaline is high."

"Armed with?"

"A plasma pistol."

"'Nevolence, the last thing we need is for her to open fire," Mitsuki said.

"How does she even have a pistol in here legally?"

"According to the station's database, Downtimes was granted a permit for one plasma pistol, sir."

"So the authorities aren't going to think anything's amiss with her having it out and charged up?"

"Hard to say, sir. But I recommend shutting it down before an algorithm in the station's mainframe pegs it as an anomaly."

"Play the same trick as before," Mitsuki suggested.

"I've got a vocal sample of the girl we just talked to, sir. And we know her name."

"Clever move getting her name," Mitsuki said.

"It's what I do, Wings."

Using Telia's name and voice, Siv assured Alarra that the system was on the fritz and that a station repairman was already here.

"Who called it in?" she asked with a hint of suspicion.

"Bouncer's name?" Siv asked Silky.

"Joris, sir."

"Someone named Joris called it in. Said he was having trouble getting out of a room. We ran an analysis and realized your whole system was down."

"Oh, okay," she replied, her tone sounding more relaxed.

"Can you get to the entry pad on your side?"

"Of course," she answered.

Siv watched in the locator as she crossed the room.

"Sir, she left the plasma pistol on the desk."

"Mits," Siv said.

"Ready."

Standing just out of sight, he swiped the entry pad. The door swooshed open, and Mitsuki opened fire with her neural disruptor, hitting the woman square in the chest. They entered and picked Alarra up between them. Siv held her by the shoulders and Mitsuki by her feet, which created a weird sight with Mitsuki still invisible.

"I don't think she has a clue what happened," Mitsuki said.

"Speaking of which... Sir, I've done some analysis on drug combos. If you hit someone with two doses of Aware while they're unconscious or nearly so due to a heavy dose of Calm, it will cause them to suffer a memory blackout. They'll lose all recollection of the last few hours."

"Would that work if someone was knocked out by a single dose of Calm added to the effects of a neural pulse?" Siv asked.

"Based on the simulations I ran, there's a high probability that it would. It might even have a stronger effect."

"Would it harm them?"

"No lasting damage, sir. Just several days of mental fog and general confusion. Medical literature covers quite a few instances where someone took near coma-causing levels of Calm while under the influence of Aware, and they turned out okay after a few weeks of recovery."

As they got Alarra into the room and closed the door, Siv turned to Mitsuki. "Care to do the honors?"

"I'd love to."

She administered the doses then began stripping the clothes off one of the men.

Siv flinched. "Mits, what the hell are you doing?"

"Convincing them they came here and had a good time." She shrugged, confused by his reaction. "It was your idea, remember? Get the clothes off Alarra, please."

"That's borderline assault, Mits."

"I'm certain it's beyond the borderline, sir."

"She offered to strip for you, and you're not going to do anything but take her clothes off."

Siv shook his head. "That's wrong."

"Fine, I'll do it myself. You scatter some syringes around the room. Oh, and get some drink glasses. Put a bunch of them out on the tables."

Siv scattered the syringes then left the room. He retrieved wine bottles and glasses from a closet in the hallway and then poured most of the wine down a sink. When he returned, Mitsuki had all of them in the nude with their clothes strewn messily around the room. Siv distributed the bottles and glasses, trying to make the scene appear as natural as possible.

"This won't explain the loss of their chippies," Siv said.

"You took everything valuable from them, sir. They'll think they've been robbed."

"Good point." Mitsuki darted out of the room. "I'm going to hit cycle on the trash receptacle and flush their chippies far away."

Silky growled. *"You're a horrible being, Mits."*

They returned to their original room, and Silky released the override on all the locked doors in Downtimes except for theirs and the one across the hall.

For the next half hour, they tensely monitored the other employees' movements and communications with one another. After the other women that worked there couldn't find the bouncer or Alarra or raise them using calls on their chippies, they turned off the neon sign outside and changed the digital display to read "Closed."

The women debated contacting the authorities but then decided first to search the rooms they hadn't used themselves since "clientele privacy comes first."

When they couldn't open the door across the hallway, they banged on it. They didn't get a response.

"They're trying to do a manual override on the lock, sir."

"Any chance they can manage it?"

"Not in a dozen universes, sir."

After they failed to manage an override, they banged on Siv's door. He responded by pounding back urgently.

"They're trying the manual override here, too, sir."

"Give them access."

The door swooshed open. Siv sighed as if relieved then adopted a tone of annoyance.

"It's about time! I used my chippy to call the front desk and the police ages ago. What the hell?!"

One of the women tried to look him in the face but failed. "Apparently we experienced some technical problems."

"Apparently?" he snorted.

"We don't know what happened," another said. "And some of our people are missing."

A third woman glanced around the room.

"There's no one in here," he snapped. "I asked...I think her name was Alarra...to get me another drink and to strip for me when she came back, but she never showed."

"We don't know where she is," the first woman said. "Did she say anything to you?"

"She said she'd be back in a few minutes. That she needed to see the bouncer about something." Siv shrugged. "That's all I know."

The women exchanged looks with one another.

"Now, if you'll excuse me, I have places to be."

"Of course, sir," the first said.

Mitsuki slipped in behind Siv. Just when they were nearly out of Downtimes, one of the girls ran forward. "Hold on, sir."

Siv waited nervously while the girl entered the front office. She returned a minute later with a hundred hard credits and handed them over.

"A refund, plus extra for your trouble. We hope you'll visit again. We don't normally have problems like this. In fact, we *never* have any trouble here."

He nodded. "Thanks for the refund. I appreciate it."

As they slipped out, Mitsuki said, *"I didn't even think to rob the place."*

"I'm mentally kicking myself," Siv said.

"I considered it," Silky said.

"But you didn't care to share the idea?" Mitsuki snapped.

"I thought it would be going overboard. Steal too much and the authorities might lock down the station. If they discovered the theft soon enough, you'd never get out of here, and we can't keep Mitsuki invisible forever."

"How long do I have?" she asked.

"Still plenty long enough to reach the planet," Silky replied. "But I'm a little concerned about the field's stability. The unit hasn't run for this long in a single day in two hundred years."

Even though they reached the shuttle bay earlier than they had wanted, they were able to board. The flight filled up, so Mitsuki had to cram herself into a tight space between the cockpit and the boarding ramp leading into the passenger compartment.

Hopefully, the pilot would remain in the cockpit. Otherwise, he'd trip over her. They'd considered having her sit in Siv's lap, but they worried interference might reveal her.

Fortunately, the refraction cloak held, and the pilot remained in the cockpit. They entered the atmosphere of Zayer Prime and descended through a raging storm that caused the shuttle to buck and shudder.

"A hurricane," Siv groaned. *"Just what we needed."*

"I don't see why it matters, sir. It's just one more storm to brave. Isn't that our life now? Besides, I'm sure there's worse to come."

"Aren't you a ray of sunshine," Mitsuki lamented.

"I didn't say we wouldn't weather it," Silky replied.

"You didn't say we would either," she pointed out.

Silky didn't respond.

25

KARSON BISHOP

Buzzing with nervous energy, Karson woke from a nightmare. He sat up in his sleeping cubicle, thumping his horns against the ceiling.

"Oona!" he yelled. "Kyralla!"

"Sir, Oona and Kyralla are both still asleep," Bartimaeus, his 6G chippy, told him. *"And quite safe."*

Of course, they were. It's not like they would step out into space or get captured without him noticing that the ship was being boarded.

"Thank you, Barty." Karson thumped back into the thin, foam mattress with relief. *"I didn't wake them, did I?"*

"You did not, sir. The sleeping compartments are well-insulated. They can only hear you through the comms channel."

Karson took several deep breaths, trying to get his pulse back to normal. It was silly to let his fear get a hold of him like that. His worry for Mitsuki and Siv was making him jumpy. *"Have you finished installing the update Silky gave you?"*

"I have installed as much of the update as my limited 6G capabilities will allow, sir. It will take quite a while to integrate all the new functions."

"Keep at it, Barty."

"Yes, sir."

He dressed and ambled out to the galley. Seneca heated and seasoned one of the ration packs for him. He ate it and sipped at the bitter tea that was, unfortunately, the best drink they had onboard. Meanwhile, he carefully read over all the information on cryogenic storage Bartimaeus had gathered.

"One thing's for certain, Barty. For it to have lasted over ten millennia, the technology preserving the priestess has to be far beyond anything we have available."

Siv was incredibly lucky he'd made it a hundred years without any complications. According to all the test results published online, commercially available cryo-storage units usually failed within fifty years. Their occupants, however, would expire decades before that point.

He went over the scans Siv had done of the capsule using the ScanField-3 sensor array. The Ancient stasis pod was utterly different from the ones that humans used. It wasn't cryo-sleep for starters, and the power source was unusual. A small box, not unlike a power pack, mounted underneath the control panel provided power to the entire capsule. The box emitted flux energy in keeping with residuals he'd expect to see from a discharging power pack or a stardrive.

"Barty, I think she's being preserved by a hyperphasic generator of some sort. Look at the energy signatures coming directly from the power cube. Remind you of anything?"

"It is very similar to a stardrive's signature, sir."

Karson nodded. *"I think the Ancients' version of cryo-sleep involved displacing the occupant into an alternate dimension where time flows differently. Sort of like dull-space, only in regards to time instead of space."*

"I suppose, sir, that it is theoretically possible such a place could exist."

"The device that projects the "bubble" keeping her in this alternate dimension must be malfunctioning so that she's...leaking...into real space."

"If your theory is correct, sir, that would make sense."

"The priestess told Oona her condition began to deteriorate once she returned to real space after thousands of years in hyperspace. So if there's a containment leak, perhaps there's a conflict of energies between real space and this slow-space. Or maybe hyperspace enhances the effects of slow-space or..."

"Your theorizing is becoming increasingly speculative, sir."

Karson took a final bite of his breakfast, leaned back, and sighed. *"I don't know enough about hyperphasic physics to solve this. I doubt anyone does. The best course would be to repair the failing systems, but I can't do that without tearing it apart. And that's assuming the technology would even begin to make sense. If it's anything like stardrive technology, I don't have a chance in hell of fixing it."*

Only the Benevolence had known how to make stardrives and perhaps understood the physics behind them. Since the Fall, millions of scientists had been working on figuring them out, but none of them had gotten anywhere.

"There is someone who should know how to address the problem, sir."

Karson frowned, puzzled. *"Who's that?"*

"The priestess herself, sir."

Karson nodded but didn't respond. He didn't want to think about the possibility that they would lose the last living Ancient. But he couldn't take up any of Oona's limited training time, having the priestess respond to a number of technical questions he might not even understand the answers to. The fate of the galaxy depended on Oona surviving her trial.

He finished his tea then fiddled nervously with his spoon, glancing at the documents and scans again. He had to figure out how to save the priestess on his own. It would have been helpful if the scans could have penetrated the surface of the module, but whatever material it was, Silky couldn't get a read on anything inside it. Octavian's instruments hadn't fared any better.

"Sir, perhaps you should engage in an activity. You are not going to learn anything new today."

"You're right, Barty. I should get busy doing something productive."

Karson went to cargo bay two, where all the archaeological equipment was stored. He had nearly finished analyzing everything, and he knew what all the machines were for thanks to Octavian. With Siv's permission, he was going to begin disassembling some devices for parts that he could use to repair the skimmer car or add new features.

Outside of that, it would be useful to have a collection of general parts that could be used for any number of emergency repairs on the ship, the skimmer car, or the small transport skimmer. The parts or equipment not worth breaking down, they could sell off later.

Although, if they found Oona's dad, they might not have to keep running, and then... Karson shook his head. No, that didn't feel right. He felt confident they'd be running for a long time, with or without Ambassador Vim.

Karson removed a small crate from a shelf. It was locked, but Silky had given him an override code for all the sealed containers. The lock clicked, and he pulled the lid back.

He sat on the floor. "Oh, sweet!"

The box contained two chippy units. He frowned. No, that wasn't correct. It held *one* chippy unit and another device that looked a lot like a chippy, except that there were apparent differences in the outer design, suggesting it was something altogether different.

For one thing, the unknown device was ever so slightly larger and would probably stick several millimeters out from a socket. That suggested a prototype device not yet ready for mass production.

He picked up the not-chippy unit. *"Barty, do you have any idea what this is?"*

"It does not match anything on record, sir. Would you like for me to perform a deep search to see if I can find a match?"

Even a chippy with its quantum computing capabilities could not complete an exhaustive search of the galactic net immediately, especially not when trying to match up an unknown object to perhaps a single record or photo. It could take hours to adequately comb through the knowledge stored on the net, compiled from trillions upon trillions of sources over the course of more than three millennia.

"Please!"

"I'm sure Silky knows what it is if you'd like to wait, sir."

"I'm sure he does. And I'm also sure I want to know right away."

"I'll pause my updating, sir, and perform an extensive search right away."

"Wait!"

Karson picked up the chippy unit and rolled it around in his hands. An impact had damaged it. And if it was in a box, he guessed it was inoperative. He found the serial markings. It was a 6G unit, the same as Barty.

"Is there any power left in this unit?"

"Not that I can tell, sir."

"Do you think it could hold a charge?"

"I cannot say for certain based on my scans, sir. It is badly damaged. I recommend scrapping or recycling it. You do not have the parts to repair a chippy."

"Oh, Barty. It's always the same with you, isn't it? No imagination."

"I am not Silky, sir. I have limitations. What are you planning to do with it?"

"I'm thinking it would make a great upgrade to the core system in the Tezzin, giving it an AI control unit. If it's functional, and if I can hardwire it in."

"That sounds practically barbarous to me, sir. Speaking of AI's, you could ask the ship and Octavian about the unknown device. They might know what it is. I will begin my deep scan of the net now."

Karson mentally slapped himself. Here he was trying to install an AI unit in the Tezzin, yet he once again forgot to ask the *Outworld Ranger's* advanced AI for help.

He accessed the ship through his HUD and visually marked the not-chippy in his hand. *"Ship, do you have any information about this device?"*

"That, Mr. Bishop, is a device that Gav Gendin brought back with him after visiting a Krixis world where he scouted an Ancient outpost."

"Any idea what it does?"

"I am afraid I do not know, Mr. Bishop."

Karson marked the chippy unit. *"And this one?"*

"That was Gav Gendin's chippy before he found Silky. It is a 6G named Torus."

Karson held the not-chippy up close to his face, studying its every facet in detail. Two things became immediately apparent. First, there was no sign of actual damage on this device. Unless something was broken inside it, the unit was still functional. Second, the polarity of the connection appeared to be reversed, and the eject switch was in the wrong place. Unless... Unless it plugged into a socket in someone's right temple.

Only that made no sense. Chippies worked with the structure of the more analytical left brain. Trying to use one with the right brain would end you up somewhere between pointlessness and madness.

Although, maybe there was a human genetic variant with the brain regions reversed. Or perhaps it had been constructed for someone with a genetic defect. But that wouldn't explain why the physical build didn't match the design specs of a chippy.

He desperately wanted to crack it open but knew he should first wait for Silky to return. He placed it in his pocket and took the 6G to the workbench Gav Gendin had used for studying artifacts.

He activated the magnification in the smart lenses he wore then took out his fine detail tools and went to work on the device. Removing the outer plating, he carefully cracked open the chippy's shell, so as not to damage the delicate parts inside.

Upon immediate inspection, with the magnification turned up by a factor of four, the power relay was busted, two wires were torn, and the brain-interface to CPU connector was dislodged from its socket. If that was all the damage, then he might be able to restore it.

After a half hour of testing, though, he discovered that the brain-interface controller was fried. It could never serve as a chippy again. It could, however, function as a more than capable AI unit for the Tezzin.

"Sir, I finished a preliminary search and found nothing. I can begin the deep scan, but it is hard to search when you do not know what you are looking for and cannot find matching images anywhere on the net."

Karson sighed. *"Don't worry about it. We'll just wait for—"*

The ship popped up an alert symbol in his HUD, then spoke. *"Mr. Bishop, we have an incoming signal, priority channel."*

"Patch it through," Karson said with worried anticipation.

"Thread-man to the Far-Planet Searcher. *Do you copy?"*

"Silky?" Karson asked.

"Thread-man! My name's Thread-Man!"

"Do we need code names?"

"If we want to have fun we do, Skimmer-Child Clergyman."

Karson shook his head.

Kyralla's voice came through the channel along with a yawn. *"Since you're acting like a ridiculous buffoon, I take it everyone's safe?"*

"I don't know that we're safe. But we're alive on Zayer Prime, and no one's currently trying to kill us."

"That's great news!" Oona said, joining the conversation. *"Send everyone our love."*

"Eew, gross," Silky replied. *"Siv and Mitsuki send their regards and apologize for leaving this up to me. They're getting some sleep. Now, we shouldn't talk too long. Over and—"*

"Wait," Karson said. *"Silky, I found what appears to be a chippy device in one of the locked containers, only it's not exactly a chippy, and I don't—"*

"Do not touch that. It's mine, and it is very precious to me."

"Okay, I won't mess with it," Karson replied. *"Could you tell me what it is?"*

"It's called an emppy, and it's top secret. Or it used to be anyway. I'll explain when we get back."

"Thanks."

"Don't touch it!"

"Okay."

"Don't tinker with it!"

"I won't."

"Put it back now!"

"I will lock it away ASAP."

"Is the device dangerous?" Kyralla asked.

"Perfectly safe," Silky replied. *"We'll talk again soon."*

Karson took the device out of his pocket. "An emppy?"

"Sir, I didn't see anything about an emppy on my preliminary search."

"I wouldn't expect you to if it was top secret. Don't bother scanning further. I doubt you'll find anything."

As Karson was about to put the device back into the box, Oona and Kyralla showed up, looking groggy but well. He showed it to them.

Oona shrugged. "I wouldn't have known it was any different."

"Silky was awful touchy about it," Kyralla said. "In fact, he seemed angrily sentimental."

"He did, didn't he?" Karson's eyes flared. "Didn't Silky say he served for years with an Empathic Services agent?"

"Yeah, I think he did," Kyralla replied.

"An empath...a device called an emppy..."

"Seems a bit of a stretch."

Karson smiled and tapped his right temple. "It connects to the more creative right brain, which is where empaths have more neural networks."

He reverently returned it to the box and locked it away. "I think maybe it was built for enhancing an empath's capabilities." He looked pointedly at Oona. "If we could repair this device, assuming it's broken, then—"

"It could enhance my abilities and make speaking with the priestess a lot easier," she replied, her eyes bright with excitement.

"You would first need surgery to get a socket on your right temple," Kyralla said. "And you're not just an empath. It might interfere with your abilities instead."

"Joy-kill," Oona said, stalking off. "I'm going to go meditate on how my sister's a pain in the butt sometimes."

Embarrassed, Karson looked around nervously. He wasn't used to confrontations like that. He avoided personal confrontations by...by being alone...by not having any friends or ever talking to his family.

"Do you have any siblings?" Kyralla asked.

"I am an only child."

"Then you're lucky." Kyralla glanced back in the direction her sister had gone and sighed. "And also, unlucky."

"If you say so."

"Anything I can help you with?" she asked. "I'm getting bored. I don't have a simulator for training, and I can only do so many pushups and squats to stay in shape."

"I suppose I could use a hand with the car, but unless you have any technical skill, I'll run out of stuff for you to do in about an hour."

"Octavian would probably be a better assistant anyway."

She wasn't wrong. So he nodded as politely as he could.

"I guess I'll read and watch some movies."

"There's nothing wrong with that," he told her. "Get some rest and relax while you can."

"It's just that I feel like I should be doing something."

Karson scratched his chin, considering the options. "Have you mastered the flight controls?"

"I don't know if mastered is the right word, but I have learned all I can about them."

"That seems like a lot of studying."

"It didn't take me long. I've discovered I have a love for piloting."

"Ah, well there you go. To be a great pilot, you must become one with the ship. I'd think that would mean more than just knowing the automatic and backup control systems and how to work with the ship's AI. I would think that a great pilot would know every operating system on the ship, and how every part of it functions."

Kyralla chewed her lip. "So, I should learn each crew station?"

"It wouldn't hurt to understand what the others are doing, to learn about the engines, the stardrive, and every device and control system onboard. You never know what might suddenly be important."

"I guess so..."

He pointed at the partially disassembled 6G chippy on the bench. "I know every part in there. I know the tensile strength of the wires. I know how all the metals and wires are made. I know everything you can know about that device, save the unknowable. And I know every detail about the tools I'm using to work on it, from the materials in them to their manufacturers. Most of that information is unnecessary, much of it I have never needed. But anything could be important to the right project."

Kyralla patted him on the shoulder. "Thank you. That makes a lot of sense. And if nothing else, it gives me something to do." Frowning, she looked around. "Any idea where I should start?"

"I'm sure Octavian would love to give you a guided tour of the ship. He buzzed my ear off when I asked him to show me around."

"They'll be okay, won't they?" she asked suddenly.

Karson took a deep breath and considered the danger they were all in. "I believe in your sister. And I believe in all of us. I think fate has brought us together for a divine purpose. So yes, I think everyone will be okay and that we will all make it through this."

Kyralla smiled, but it was almost sad. "Thanks, Bishop."

26

VEGA KALEEB

A vast industrial complex sprawled through a series of caverns cut below the surface of a remote world, far away from prying eyes and the scans of deep-space probes. In chamber after chamber, turbines whirred, conveyor belts hummed, welding sparks flared, hammers struck, and drills whined as a host of slavish cogs tirelessly assembled an army and a starship to carry them into battle.

The army—a legion of orb-shaped sky-blades like Faisal—gathered before the boarding ramp of the battlecruiser. There, the sky-blades waited until *they* arrived.

From another dimension, a host of ghostly forms emerged, one for each sky-blade. The ghosts, one by one, touched the cogs and were absorbed by them, merging to give the robots life...purpose...meaning...a soul. And so, the sky-blades became something more than mere machines, while the ghosts became something more than spirits.

A booming voice spoke to them, and it was *his* voice. "Today we will begin our holy crusade! Today we set off to—"

A pinging sound rang out in the cockpit as the *Spinner's Blade* pierced the edge of the Zayer system and slowed.

Vega woke with a start, his breathing heavy, the clarity of the dream fading rapidly. Even as an android, he could not entirely hold onto a dream. Whether this distinctly human trait was an accident or designed by the

Benevolence, no one knew. But Vega suspected it was intentional. Perhaps the Benevolence had thought dreams were part of what made one human. Perhaps it had longed itself to dream.

A cog hovered in front of him, and Vega stared at his face reflected in its glossy black surface.

"Yes, Faisal?"

"Were you dreaming of them *again, boss?"*

With a nod, Vega stood and stretched. "Analysis?"

"My preliminary scans and my instincts tell me our marks are here, boss."

"Your evidence?"

"For starters, we have ship wreckage in the outer reaches of the system. Based on telemetry from rather dumb science probes that had no clue how to interpret what they were observing, it seems as if a light cruiser and two starfighters were destroyed in a battle."

"The cruiser... Was it the *Outworld Ranger*?"

"I don't believe so, boss. The data from the probes shows a freighter and a second light cruiser were at the same location when the destruction occurred. The freighter continued to Zayer Prime, while the second light cruiser left the system."

"So they might have come here and then left..."

"Perhaps, boss. I'm still searching."

"The odds of it being entirely unrelated? A battle with pirates, maybe?"

"The odds are incredibly low. Also, according to an intercept I got off a Star Cutter transmission, Zetta was here. Apparently, she was involved in an alliance with the Cutters. But she's gone now."

"Left on the other light cruiser?"

"Unknown, boss. There's simply no sign of her."

"Well, I wouldn't expect her to leave one. How did Zetta get here ahead of us?"

"We were farther away when the call went out. The slippery bitch simply had the good fortune of already being in the area."

"The second light freighter, you're sure it left the system?"

"The data shows it was heading toward the breakpoint, boss, but there are no readings of hyperspace energy to go on. This is due to the limitations of the probes. Feel free to double-check everything while I do further scans."

Vega's processing capabilities were every bit as powerful as those of a 9G chippy. It was only his emotional and instinctive behavior matrices that kept his processor from doing what a 9G chippy could. But he couldn't come close to the abilities of Faisal's 9G-x processor.

Vega read over their long-range scans carefully and verified what Faisal had found. Usually, Vega worked on easier problems while Faisal did what only he could do. Well, Faisal *and* Silky. But Vega had the good sense to not say that out loud, or to even think it too strongly.

"Here's something, boss. Not long after the freighter docked with a station orbiting Zayer Prime, a strange banking transaction took place. Using a software exploit, a small sum was moved from one account and into a new one at a different bank. That account was then emptied with all the money transferred into hard credits. Not even the bank's network knew where the money came from or went, though it shut down the loophole immediately."

Vega considered the information. "Coincidental?"

"Doubtful. A group of determined humans with the right advanced software could have done it, but I can't imagine any group running a one-time scam for a sum this small. But that chippy whose name I will not utter, he could have done it with relative ease. The transaction was practically untraceable. I only noticed because I've been scanning for banking oddities ever since we discovered he was involved."

"When the freighter docked, were there any extra crew members aboard?"

"Not any registered by the authorities, boss. But that doesn't mean anything really."

Vega noted a police record. "Get this. A few hours after that, there was an abnormal event at an opium den called Downtimes. A bouncer, a girl that worked there, and four men with connections to the Star Cutters were found unconscious in a room with no memory of how they'd gotten there."

"Boss, the report says they were dosed up on Calm and Aware and were found naked."

"Who takes doses of Calm during sex?"

"My study of humans says it's unlikely, boss. But I could be wrong... I've mostly studied how best to maim and kill them. I do so love severing critical tendons and arteries."

"The place doesn't have any security footage of the incident. Several hours of data are missing due to glitches in the system, glitches that also caused the interior doors to lock in such a way that a security override could not open them. This glitch was fixed by an unknown person or simply sorted itself out, but with one exception: the room in which they found the unconscious victims. The police had to cut their way in."

"Boss, I found something weird. Check out this miner that exited the freighter."

An image of a disfigured man wearing a hazmat suit popped up into Vega's vision.

"According to a record made by the station's deck officer, the man was recently scarred in an accident. That's why his face doesn't match his ID card. His name, though, does check out."

Vega zoomed in on the man's face. "Looks fishy to me. Run an analysis."

"Aha!" Faisal exclaimed a minute later. *"The face doesn't match the identity, boss. It's a chameleon veil."*

"That fits Gendin's MO. Do a reconstruction. See if you can figure out what this person's face originally looked like."

"Reconstruction of the mask reveals it to be one Gendin has used before." Faisal loaded video footage of the man. *"And is it just me, boss, or is there an area of fuzziness near him when he moves through this corridor?"*

Vega observed the footage. *"I see it. But that could be interference from a nearby flux capacitor."*

"Oh, I think it is interference, boss. Interference from someone hiding in a refraction field."

Vega studied the image more closely then nodded. Smiling, he reached out and patted Faisal. "Good work, chum."

Faisal extended his blades and gave them a good whirl, but Vega had withdrawn his hand fast enough to avoid getting cut—this time.

"It's just like we predicted. They're going to Titus II, the long way around, to rescue the girls' father."

"So, who's with Gendin, boss?"

Vega considered the question for a few minutes. "An extraction job suggests Gendin and Reel. There's no reason to take the girl along. She'd be a liability, and going to Titus II would put her in greater danger. She will be on the *Outworld Ranger* with the others, hiding in deep space most likely."

"I still don't understand why they're going for the father. Seems to me that running would be much safer."

"Money? Connections? Sentiment maybe. All three perhaps. Regardless, it is foolish. Every bounty hunter's going to be looking in the Titus system. It's the obvious place to start."

"Ambassador Vim did somehow *escape a cadre of Tekk Reapers. Maybe he's more than meets the eye. That might explain why they need him."*

Vega grunted. "You're right. Run another background check on him."

"Again, boss?"

"Maybe we missed something before."

"I don't miss things."

"Do it anyway."

Sparks flew off the sky-blade's body. Faisal had to show when he was angry. It was never enough for him just to tell you.

"There's got to be something, Faisal. A man like him doesn't escape from the Tekk Reapers. Almost no one does."

The Tekk Reapers... Many of Vega's old android friends from the military had joined them in their quest to remake the Benevolence. He'd tried to win them over to his cause instead. His was a vision for the galaxy that would be more compatible with their needs. But they had not seen what he'd seen. They had not had his...mystical experience.

"Gendin took a shuttle down to the planet, sir."

"Launch deep space probes, search pattern delta. The *Outworld Ranger* is going to be somewhere in this sector, not far from here. Bouncing around if they're smart, staying in hyperspace as much as possible while keeping close."

"They'll be in real space more often than not, boss. That chippy can contact them when needed over a highly secure military channel. So they won't need to have a prearranged meeting time and place."

"Can you intercept such a message?"

"Only if we're within ten kilometers of the sender or receiver, boss. Even then, I cannot guarantee it."

"Take us into Zayer Prime, full speed."

"We're going after Gendin, sir? The girl's worth a lot more."

"But she's harder to find if she's bouncing around. If we can capture Gendin and then the ambassador, we can interrogate them for information and use them as bait to lure the girl in. She already made one mistake when she tried to contact her father. She'll make another."

Faisal bounced around the cockpit. *"And when we catch them, I can grind Silky to a pulp with my blades. Yippeee!"*

Vega made his way out of the cockpit and headed toward a small, secure chamber in the center of the ship.

Faisal floated along behind him. *"Boss, are we going to pay the freighter captain a visit?"*

Vega paused and considered it a moment. "It's a waste of time. He can only tell us what we know already. Gendin and one other are here, and now we know they have access to a refraction cloak. Review our countermeasures against refraction. We haven't had to deal with a high-powered cloak in almost a century."

"I'm on it, boss."

Vega continued. "I'm going to pray now."

Faisal bobbed away singing. *"Silky's going to die, die, die. Silky's going to die. Go to hell, Silky, go to hell, go to hell and burn."*

The door to the chamber opened. It would open only for him. Not even Faisal had access. Vega entered, and the door slammed shut behind him. The overhead light bathed the room in a deep red glow. There were no comforts, no decorations, and no furnishings, save for a steel pedestal on which sat a hand-sized, black cube.

Vega picked up the miniature stardrive and knelt. The glossy black surface was not unlike Faisal's. But the interior was entirely different. Inside was a mystery Vega could not begin to fathom, a mystery the Benevolence could create and use but only *perhaps* understand. It was a mystery only the Ancients and the Blessed Ones from Beyond had mastered.

He cradled the miniature drive in his hand. It could not transport him, not to hyperspace or wraith-space or anywhere else. It could not open to echo-space and serve as a communications relay or access flux-space to power devices. It had no buttons, no displays, no relays. It would respond to only one stimulus: his voice.

For him, the cube served only one function. Why it did just this and nothing else, he did not know. It had been given to him without explanation.

Holding it close to his lips, Vega whispered his prayers and repeated his vows to the Blessed Ones from Beyond. The cube vibrated, a subtle glow of energy dancing across its surfaces.

The Blessed Ones from Beyond whispered back.

27

OONA VIM

Oona settled onto the car seat in the holding cell where they kept Lyoolee's stasis pod. She closed her eyes and began a series of breathing exercises, starting with rapid, shallow breaths. As her heartbeat quickened, she focused her mind on her goal: contacting her dad. Then she deepened her breaths and reached out, first with her thoughts and then her emotions.

She pictured her dad's face, from his perpetually stubble-covered chin to the goofy smile he got when telling a lame joke that only he thought was funny. She recalled the words they'd last exchanged, how he'd kissed her on the forehead and said he loved her. She thought of how much she missed him.

Nothing.

Worry crept in, strengthening her emotions but weakening her focus. She reached out in desperation...

Still nothing.

With her focus broken, she restarted her breathing exercises. This time she began with a calming sequence.

Restoring her concentration wasn't easy. She was growing increasingly worried, and over the last two days, she had picked at her food and slept only a few fitful hours.

Every time she thought about her dad in wraith-space, the mysterious woman's features appeared more devilish and shrouded in darkness. Her instincts told her the woman couldn't be trusted. That she wasn't helping her dad out of kindness or devotion but for sinister motives.

Oona spent another hour meditating and trying to contact her dad, or to at least sense if he were okay. But nothing came to her. She told herself it was because her powers were unreliable, that her focus was too weak. And while those things were true, it didn't keep her from worrying that whatever it was that her dad and the woman had been running from might have caught up to them.

To make matters worse, she was also worried about Siv and Mitsuki. What they were doing for her and Kyralla... If something happened to them... She would never forgive herself. It wasn't fair to have asked them to save her dad, but then she couldn't have done otherwise.

Her dad had said that he had significant new information. She couldn't explain why, but she had a hunch that knowledge was critical. Or maybe that was just an excuse to justify her feelings.

Oona stood. She couldn't keep thinking about all of that. Otherwise, she'd drive herself crazy. And no amount of meditation was going to work while she was in this state. What she needed was a distraction, something to keep her busy for a few hours, preferably something that would tire her out so she could get a good night of sleep.

She circled through the *Outworld Ranger's* main corridor, but after a few rounds, she grew bored seeing the same gray metallic walls and, to her, inexplicable instrument panels.

The confines were starting to make her edgy and irritable. She was used to not being around many people, having grown up in a life of seclusion. What she wasn't used to was cramped spaces and drab furnishings, having enjoyed the lavish privilege and expanse of her wealthy uncle's estate.

Here she felt cramped all the time. And there was nothing to see but the dark of space filled with distant flickering stars. No trees, no blue skies speckled with clouds, no ground.

The cargo bays were the largest sections of the ship, and they were hardly bigger than any of Uncle Pashta's living rooms.

The lack of day and night made things even worse. She and Kyralla had gotten onto the same schedule so the ship could dim the lights during the "evening," transitioning them into a dim, yellow spectrum to help their circadian rhythms. But if it was helping, Oona couldn't tell.

Octavian had offered her doses of Calm and Sleep, but she had refused.

She didn't want to take anything that might affect her mental capacity, in case she got another random read on her dad or even one on Siv and Mitsuki.

And today was only her fifth day on the ship...

She dragged herself to the galley for breakfast. Oona plopped down in the first available seat. With a trill that meant "good morning," Seneca bustled in and set a bowl of what she could only describe as gruel on the table in front of her. As with Octavian, she could now interpret him without needing Artemisia's help.

"Morning." No amount of etiquette training could make her say there was anything good about it.

"I've attempted a different spice combination, madam," Seneca said. "Hopefully, it will make the rations more palatable."

Oona scooped up a spoonful of the gray paste and shoved it in her mouth. It tasted different but not any better. Seneca waited patiently in the corner for the verdict, so she made herself eat several more spoonfuls. Despite Seneca's best efforts, the food was beyond awful.

She sighed as she dropped her spoon into the bowl of slop. "Seneca, it seems I'm spoiled."

"Surely, you are not," Seneca bleeped in response.

"You are a bit spoiled, madam," Artemisia said.

"Thanks, Arty."

"At least you're not a brat, madam."

"Give me a few weeks on the ship, and I may prove you wrong about that."

Oona dragged herself onto the bridge and dropped into the command chair. Kyralla sat at the pilot's station engrossed in something Oona couldn't see. Kyralla spent nearly all her time now either at the piloting station or going over the ship's systems in detail, so she could know how everything worked.

She was happy Kyralla had found something she loved doing. Having almost no chance of surviving past fifteen, Oona felt a lot better knowing Kyralla had found a calling that could give her a future. She would be able to move on and make a life for herself, perhaps joining Siv, Mitsuki, and Bishop on adventures throughout the galaxy.

Oona waited until Kyralla finished what she was doing.

"How's it going?"

Kyralla removed the circlet for the piloting station from her head. "I just finished a set of difficult maneuvers." She sounded downright cheerful.

Surprised, Oona sat upright. "Really? I didn't feel anything."

"I maxed the ship's inertial dampening, so I wouldn't disturb Bishop's work. And I only did a few maneuvers at full acceleration. Mostly, I'm practicing slowly, so I can build muscle memory and get used to cooperating with the AI. It's the same technique I used when I started learning martial arts."

"It's too bad you don't have a simulation chamber."

"It's too bad I didn't work on piloting when we had access to one. All I ever focused on was defending you in physical combat. But that seems rather short-sighted now." Kyralla gestured to the other stations on the bridge. "Look at all the skill sets we've got in play just here on this bridge."

"You didn't know," Oona said. "It's not like we had a manual for how to do all of this. It's not our fault we're underprepared."

"I know," Kyralla said. "It's just... I'm your guardian, and combat skills only do so much good out here."

"Your piloting has already saved us, and you're brand new to it. I have faith in you."

"My abilities are perfect for piloting. But next time, I may not be able to skirt by on talent alone. That's why I'm working so hard."

Oona fumbled with the armchair. "Everyone but me has something useful to do."

She tried not to sound like a petulant child but knew she hadn't really succeeded.

Kyralla sighed. "You're too hard on yourself, Oona. You need to rest. Watch a movie, read a book, play some games."

Oona shrugged. "I guess. I'm just—"

An alarm sounded, a relentless dinging Oona hadn't heard before. A message inside a flashing orange box appeared on the bridge's view screen.

EMERGENCY DISTRESS SIGNAL RECEIVED

Reflexively, Oona stood and edged forward. Her first thought was that Silky was trying to tell them something had gone wrong or to warn them of impending danger.

SIGNAL DECODED

"Acknowledged," Kyralla said.

The flashing box disappeared, and the alarm stopped.

A video played on the screen. A wild-haired young man with star-blue eyes and a baby face stared into the camera. Sweat dripped from his brow. Grease dirtied one cheek. A burn scarred his chin. Behind him, intermittent showers of sparks illuminated a ship's bridge. A boom sounded, the man flinched, and the video blurred for a second.

"This is Federation research vessel *Argos Alpha.* We're in the Kor system." He spoke fast, his voice trembling with fear. "Our ship has sustained heavy damage after..." His voice broke up for several moments. "Request immediate assistance. We have injuries...casualties—"

Another boom sounded. Sparks cascaded through the bridge, and a console in the back burst into flames.

"The ship's structural integrity is failing. Life-support's offline. We don't have—"

The message fuzzed out then went black. The man's voice returned amidst a rush of static. "Please help us!"

END TRANSMISSION

When the video started to repeat, Kyralla paused it. She turned to Oona, a tortured look on her face.

Bishop ran onto the bridge. "What was that?" He stopped and stared at the image of the young man on the screen. "Was that a distress signal?"

Kyralla replayed the message for Bishop then paused it again.

He cursed and flopped into the sensor station. "I'll call up the ship's credentials."

A second box appeared on the viewscreen, showing *Argos Alpha's* registry, its transponder signal, and its last known location—in orbit around the fourth planet of the Kor system.

"Do you think he's still alive?" Oona asked.

Bishop shrugged. "All we can say is that some part of the ship is still there, since their emergency beacon's broadcasting."

The three of them stared at one another, not knowing what to say.

"Arty, can you independently verify any of that information?"

"I'm already working on it, madam. So far, everything seems to be in order. I have no reason to doubt the research vessel is exactly what it claims to be."

Oona conveyed that information to the others.

"Rosie agrees it's the *Argos Alpha* and that it's a research vessel," Kyralla said.

"We have to help them," Oona said.

"We can't," Kyralla said. "Just because the ship checks out doesn't mean it isn't a trap."

"How can it possibly be a trap?" Oona asked.

"Bounty hunters could have hijacked the ship," Kyralla replied. "Like Zetta did with the freighter."

"They'd really be going out of their way to trick us," Bishop said. "They'd have to assume that we'd do the right thing and that we'd get to the Kor system before anyone else. That would take careful timing and an assumption that we'd be in the area."

"That seems like a big stretch," Oona said.

"Siv and Mitsuki are criminals," Bishop said. "If I didn't know them personally, then I definitely wouldn't base my plan on the assumption they'd attempt to rescue people from a damaged vessel several lightyears away."

"And if the people on that ship had been attacked to lure us in, don't you think he would have mentioned it?" Oona argued.

"Not if he was one of the bad guys," Kyralla said.

"Why would one of the bad guys be on the damaged vessel?" Bishop asked.

"He could've been part of a boarding party," Kyralla replied. "The entire thing could be staged as a lure."

"That seems even more doubtful," Bishop said.

"Maybe one of the criminal groups on the way to Titus decided to ambush a vessel," Kyralla said. "Criminal guilds aren't beyond piracy."

"Again, if it were an attack," Bishop said, "then why not mention that in the message?"

"We did miss part of the message, a part where I think he was trying to say what happened," Kyralla said. "And I think that—"

Oona interrupted her. "You're reaching on this, sis. We have to go help them."

Kyralla shook her head. "It's too risky."

"We can't let people die without trying to save them," Oona said. "We have to do the right thing. Otherwise..."

"We're supposed to wait in this area in case Siv and Mitsuki need us," Kyralla said.

"We won't be that far away," Oona said.

Over the ship's comm, Artemisia said, "Silky would be able to get a message to us in the Kor system."

"And they're not going to ask for help," Bishop said. "They don't want the two of you in the Titus or Zayer systems anyway, even in dire circumstances."

"Rosie and I can continue researching the vessel along the way there," Artemisia said.

"We can enter the system, skirt along its edge, and run a sensor sweep," Bishop said. "That way we'll have a chance to spot other ships or anything suspicious before getting too close."

Oona nodded. "And I could reach out with my abilities like before. If I detect anything out of the ordinary, anything at all, we can turn around and leave immediately."

Kyralla paced the bridge. "I don't like taking this risk."

"You're willing to let these people die?" Oona said.

"We're not the only ship in the region," Kyralla said. "Why don't we let someone else save them? It's not our responsibility."

"It *is* our responsibility," Oona said. "Rescuing a ship in distress is a core tenet of any spacefaring civilization."

"Even if we reach them first, others may arrive after us," Kyralla said. "Bounty hunters, criminals, pirates, federal agents..."

"You think criminals are going to show up to help someone?" Oona said.

"A ship in distress is an easy score," Bishop said. "But that doesn't mean we shouldn't do the right thing."

"The Feds are just as dangerous to us," Kyralla said.

Oona rubbed her hands across her scalp and groaned in frustration. "I can't not help."

"Maybe we're getting ahead of ourselves," Bishop said. "How long ago was that message sent? If hours have passed, other ships might already have arrived to help."

"No information was delivered about the level of damage the ship sustained," Artemisia said over the comm. "The message was sent using an echo-space, emergency broadcast transponder. Only half an hour has passed since the broadcast."

"We could be the first ones to get there," Oona said.

"It's likely, based on our current position, that we are the closest ship," Rosie said.

"If we rescue them quickly, then we may be able to get out of the system before anyone else arrives," Bishop said.

Kyralla paused and stared at Oona. "You're not going to let this go, are you?"

Oona shook her head. "We have to go. It's the right thing to do."

"It might get us killed," Kyralla said.

Oona sighed. "Look, sis, the chances of me surviving another year are low."

"You have the priestess now," Kyralla argued. "She'll prepare you to face the trial."

"Sure, but we're also being pursued by criminal guilds, bounty hunters, the Federation, and the Empire of a Thousand Worlds. Those things balance out at best."

"Still," Kyralla said. "I don't—"

Oona interrupted her. "I do *not* want to die knowing that I did nothing to save people who were calling out for help."

"You're ignoring the big picture," Kyralla said. "You have a chance to save trillions upon trillions of people by restoring the Benevolence."

"Maybe. Maybe not." Oona collapsed into the command chair. "I feel guilty for asking Siv and Mitsuki to rescue Dad. It's driving me crazy. And that guilt, maybe I can live with it. What I can't live with is knowing that I did nothing for people who were crying out for help. I can't be a galactic savior if I'm not willing to help even a few individuals in need."

Kyralla stared at her, showing no emotion.

"Oona's right," Bishop said.

"You're going to agree with her on this?" Kyralla asked. "You? You believe in restoring the Benevolence as much as either of us, maybe more."

"I believe Oona was meant to restore the Benevolence. But I think the kind of person she is makes a big difference. Maybe Empress Qan wasn't the kind of person willing to help others. Maybe she wasn't willing to do the right thing. Maybe that's why she turned out the way she did."

Kyralla ran her fingers through her hair and then stamped a foot. "Fine. Fine, fine, fine."

"You know you want to help too," Oona said. "You know it's the right thing to do."

"I swore I would protect you," Kyralla said. "No matter what. That's not easy to do when you insist on putting yourself in danger."

Oona shrugged. "Sorry."

Kyralla returned to the piloting station. "If we're going to do this, then we do it right. We research everything along the way. We scan thoroughly when we reach the system. If there's a single ship in that system, other than the research vessel, then we leave and let them do the rescue. And if we do help, we get those people, and we get out as fast as possible."

"Agreed," Oona said.

"You realize we're almost certainly going to get into trouble and have to fight our way out, right? Because that's how our luck's been going."

Oona nodded. "I understand. And that doesn't change anything for me."

"Then set a course for the Kor system," Kyralla said. "And let's pray that we get lucky for a change."

Oona bowed her head and prayed to the Source of the Benevolence that the *Argos Alpha's* crew would still be alive when they arrived. She prayed they wouldn't face any danger.

She'd never prayed much until the last week. Now it seemed to be an hourly ritual.

"Course set, madam."

Oona triggered the stardrive.

28

KYRALLA VIM

Kyralla's muscles tensed as they neared the Kor system. She tried but failed to deepen her breathing. She needed to focus in case they ran into immediate danger, but she couldn't calm her nerves.

She was more anxious now than when they'd fought the Star Cutters at the freighter, even though they might not be in danger this time. And she knew why. Without help from Siv, Mitsuki, and Silky, she wasn't sure they could survive a difficult fight.

Sure, if it came to a battle, Rosie and Artemisia could provide a lot of support. Oona would be helpful in the command chair, and Bishop wouldn't be useless. Ultimately, however, everything would fall on Kyralla's shoulders. If it was too much for her, they were doomed.

Bishop and the chippies had spent the last six hours carefully researching the *Argos Alpha*. They didn't find anything suspicious about it or its crew of accomplished researchers and graduate assistants. The ship had been in space for three months since leaving the planet Dogon in the Sirius C system, and it hadn't made any stops along the way.

Nevertheless, Kyralla had a bad feeling about this, but then she had a bad feeling about pretty much every choice they made now, paranoia having set in. She wanted to do the right thing and help the ship's crew, but she didn't believe it was the correct choice.

Oona refused to look at the big picture. Sure, they might save a dozen lives in the Kor system, but that paled in comparison to restoring the Benevolence. Stardrive technology was failing. Within a century, humanity would no longer have a starfaring civilization. Trillions upon trillions of lives would be affected if Oona restored the Benevolence.

The *Outworld Ranger* bubbled into real space a light year outside the Kor system, on the opposite side from the direction of the Ekaran system. That way, when they entered, it would seem as if they had come from elsewhere. Aside from the ship's masked transponder and its jamming sequences, they had no other way of disguising themselves.

"Everyone ready?" Oona asked.

"Ready," Bishop answered from the sensor station.

"Last chance to change your mind," Kyralla suggested hopefully.

Oona activated the stardrive.

An hour later, the *Outworld Ranger* zoomed onto the edge of the Kor system, skirting along the perimeter so that they could reenter hyperspace within minutes if necessary.

"The ship's sensors have locked onto the *Argos Alpha,*" Bishop reported. "It's in orbit around the fourth planet. It's still in one piece, but it's severely damaged."

Kyralla checked the ship position locator. No other ships appeared within a lightyear. "Are you sure there's no one else here?"

"The ship and I have tried every method available," Bishop replied. "We seem to be in the clear."

"Rosie and I aren't detecting anything unusual," Artemisia said over the ship's comm. "However, powered-down ships could easily lurk behind planets or moons, making it nearly impossible for us to detect them. And there may be other ways of hiding."

"We will continue to analyze data from the ship's sensors," Rosie added.

Kyralla turned to Oona, who was sitting cross-legged in the command chair. Her eyes were closed, her brow furrowed. Kyralla didn't want to disturb her, so she waited patiently.

A few minutes later, Oona's eyes flicked open. "We have to hurry. Only seven people are alive, and one of them is fading."

"Did you sense the presence of any bad guys?"

"None," Oona replied.

Kyralla entered the new course and maxed their speed. The *Outworld*

Ranger's ion engines flared as it turned ninety degrees and sped inward. "Keep meditating. Let me know if you sense *anything*."

Oona nodded and closed her eyes.

Over the next two hours, the fourth planet, a super-Earth, shifted from a tiny speck to a glistening orb to a dazzling world. Five rings of alternating pinks, golds, and crimsons encircled the planet. The colors resulted from the system's red sun reflecting off the icy fragments.

"The ice rings were formed by an accident involving dozens of large comets that were supposed to crash into the planet during the terraforming process," Artemisia told them.

Beneath a few wispy clouds, the planet's spidery oceans threaded their way between sprawling, barren continents. The world supported no lifeforms save for algae and various microbes seeded by the Benevolence.

"Another crewman died," Oona announced for the second time.

Bishop tapped a button on his control panel. "I'm zooming the viewscreen for a visual on the *Argos Alpha*."

"You can do that with your circlet," Kyralla told him.

"I didn't want to take up any of the sensor station's processing power," he replied. "Besides, I like doing things manually whenever I can."

In orbit around the planet, just beyond the rings, the research vessel was spinning out of control, rotating on its axis once every few seconds.

"Well, that's a problem," Bishop said.

"The *Outworld Ranger's* maneuvering thrusters are not capable of matching the research vessel's current spin rate," Rosie said.

"So how do we stop it from spinning?" Oona asked.

"You're supposed to be meditating," Kyralla told her.

Oona shot her a dark look then closed her eyes again.

"Well?" Kyralla asked Bishop.

He shrugged. "No clue."

"If we pull up alongside the vessel," Artemisia said, "and let it impact our shields, we should be able to stop it from spinning while causing minimal damage. But we'd have to get the angle just right."

"And if we don't?" Kyralla asked.

"The impact will rupture the vessel's hull, spilling everyone inside into the vacuum of space," Rosie answered.

"The sensors are picking up a significant amount of metallic debris,"

Bishop said. "Analysis suggests fragments from a starship roughly equivalent in size to a light freighter like this one."

"So there was another ship here?" Kyralla said.

"It would seem so," Rosie replied.

"Receiving a signal from the *Argos Alpha*," Artemisia said.

They had been trying to contact the ship since entering the system. A faint voice came through the ship's comm. "Is someone out there?" a trembling male voice said. "We're...desperate...need..."

His voice faded out.

"That's the same young man who sent the distress signal," Artemisia said.

"Can you hear us?" Bishop asked.

"Barely," he responded.

"We're half an hour away," Bishop said. "Can you tell us what's going on? What happened to your ship?"

No reply came.

"We've lost his signal," Rosie said.

"The ship is still intact," Bishop said. "So, it's either interference or... Or he's gone."

Half an hour later, they reached visual range of the *Argos Alpha*.

"The lifeform scanner shows five survivors," Artemisia announced. "One is in critical condition. Two others are injured."

"We have one survivor located on the bridge," Rosie said. "Four in the aft section, including the critically injured one."

Working in tandem with the ship's AI, Kyralla eased toward the Argos Alpha and slipped up alongside it. She focused her mind and counted up slowly using the Fibonacci sequence. She still felt stupid doing it, but she couldn't deny its effectiveness.

"I've focused our shields toward the *Argos Alpha*," Artemisia said. "You're clear to move in, madam."

Kyralla nudged the control stick left. A second before the *Argos Alpha* would have spun into their shields, Kyralla "saw" the destructive collision about to happen. She jerked the stick right. With its maneuvering thrusters firing, the *Outworld Ranger* darted away.

Kyralla took a deep breath and steeled her nerves. Trusting in her gift and the hours of maneuvering practice she'd put in over the last few days, she guided the ship back toward the spinning vessel. This time, she nailed it. As the *Argos Alpha* struck their shields, Kyralla jerked the *Outworld Ranger* down and away so that neither ship would suffer a full impact. The research vessel began to slowly spin in the opposite direction.

"Shields down to eighty-two percent," the ship's AI proclaimed as they moved into the clear.

"Good work, madam," Rosie said. "We can attempt to dock with the *Argos Alpha* now."

"Here's a question," Oona said. "How do we go about doing that?"

"Their docking port is in the same location as ours," Bishop said. "So all we have to do is use our thrusters to match the spin of the other vessel and extend the docking tube."

"You're supposed to be meditating and scanning for danger," Kyralla reminded her sister.

Oona huffed, settled back into the seat, and closed her eyes. "Fine."

"Can we connect with their ship's AI?" Kyralla asked.

"I'm working on it, madam," Rosie said. "But so far, I'm not having any luck. The connection is poor, and I can't get past the ship's defensive protocols. This is the sort of thing we need Silky for, but Artemisia and I are doing our best."

"The young man who sent the distress signal is alive but unconscious," Artemisia said, "so we can't rely on him."

"What do we do if we can't connect with their ship's AI?" Kyralla asked.

"We'd have to cut our way in," Bishop answered.

"I'm guessing that will take a considerable amount of time," Kyralla said. "Do we have any alternatives?"

"I can't find any other ways," Artemisia said. "However, cutting our way in will only delay the rescue by thirty minutes."

"Half an hour feels like a lot to me," Kyralla grumbled. "I don't want to be here any longer than necessary."

"Even if there was another way in," Bishop said, "their docking port is the best choice. It will link us to their loading corridor, putting us right outside the cargo bay holding all but one of the survivors."

"If you enter that corridor," Artemisia said, "you will need life-support gear."

"Siv took a spacesuit," Kyralla said. "Do we have any others?"

"We have one more," Bishop said.

Kyralla activated the ship's thrusters, and the *Outworld Ranger's* AI maneuvered to line up the aft sections of both vessels. The ship notified her that the alignment would take seventeen minutes. Kyralla cringed and her guts knotted. This was all taking far too long.

Octavian zipped onto the bridge bleeping and trilling emphatically.

"Octavian insists that we *not* link with their docking port," Oona said while keeping her eyes closed. "Based on his analysis, their loading corridor has suffered structural damage. It's at extreme risk of collapse. If we cut our way in, their ship will likely break apart."

"So," Bishop said, "we just need to find a structurally sound part of the cargo bay and cut our way in."

Octavian trilled and beeped, and Oona translated. "He says it's too risky to dock at any point rearward of the midsection. The safest and easiest point of entry would be on the underside of their bridge. There's a mounting structure intended for a weapon system, but since it's a research vessel, they didn't install one."

"He's correct," Artemisia said with obvious surprise in her voice. "That is the thinnest spot in the ship's hull. And further analysis confirms his viewpoint about the risks involved in docking with the aft section of the ship. I don't know how we missed that."

Everyone gaped at Octavian. Everyone except Oona who had a knowing smile on her face. Kyralla shouldn't be surprised by the cog's analysis, given the medical scan data he'd given them. But something about the engineering robot made her think he was simple. She wasn't sure if it was his insectoid appearance or his lack of voice, but no cog she'd ever interacted with before had even half of his ability.

"The problem is that we need to save as many people as possible," Bishop said, "and there's only one survivor on the bridge."

Bulbous eyes alight, the insectoid cog shook its head. "Based on my Benevolence-designed rescue protocols, we should save the crewmember we can reach most safely. Furthermore, from the bridge, we can attempt to restore life-support and AI functions. With that accomplished, we can then carefully move inward to rescue the others."

Kyralla looked to Bishop. "What do you think?"

"This is Octavian's area of expertise, and it's hard to argue against the Benevolence's protocol for ship rescues."

"We should take Octavian's advice," Oona said.

"So, we'll dock with the underside of the bridge and cut our way in," Bishop said.

Octavian bleeped, and Oona chuckled as she translated. "You are not going to cut your way in. That's my job, and I know exactly how to go about."

Kyralla changed the target point, and the AI fired the maneuvering thrusters. "I'll get us lined up ASAP."

Bishop removed his circlet and stood. "I'm going to get suited up."

Matching the spin of the *Argos Alpha* and lining up the docking point was something the *Outworld Ranger*'s AI could do on its own. All Kyralla had to do was loan her brainpower and stay out of its way. She did, however, speed things up. The ship was erring on the side of extreme caution, but they were running out of time.

Despite her best efforts to speed things along, it took fifteen minutes of turning and firing the thrusters to line up the two ships and then another ten minutes to extend the docking tube and make a secure connection to the underside of the *Argos Alpha's* bridge.

"Connection complete," the *Outworld Ranger's* AI announced. "Pressurizing the docking tube."

"Bishop, are you ready?" Kyralla asked.

"Almost."

Kyralla worried Bishop would encounter a hostile situation and get hurt. His frame was slight, and he had no combat skills whatsoever. Though he did have abnormally strong hands, his overall physical condition was lacking. Nevertheless, he had the engineering know-how needed to help Octavian make repairs, and he was the only one free to go across. Kyralla had to stay aboard the *Outworld Ranger* in case something went wrong, and there was no way in hell Oona was going to board an unknown vessel.

"Kyra, we should see him off...just in case."

Of course. Kyralla leaped up and hurried to her room to grab her plasma pistol and neural disruptor.

29

KARSON BISHOP

Karson dragged the spacesuit out of the locker in the engineering station, dropped it onto the floor, and shook his head, laughing.

"Something wrong, sir?"

"It's comically large."

"It will resize to fit you, sir."

He stepped into the legs of the spacesuit then pulled it up to his waist. After sealing the front at his navel, he slipped his hands into the arms and shrugged the suit over his shoulders. His hands didn't even reach the gloves.

"Yes, but will it resize enough?"

"According to the specs, sir... Yes, but only just."

He paused. *"Barty, should I remove my clothes first?"*

"Only if you think wearing them within the suit will be restrictive, sir. Professional spacers keep their clothes on. Of course, they wear minimal jumpsuits."

He glanced down at his chest, flailed his arms awkwardly, and frowned. The suit remained unsealed from his navel to his neck, and he couldn't use his hands. *"Um...I have a problem here."*

"As soon as I establish a connection with the suit's control system, the spacesuit will seal itself, sir."

In his HUD, he watched a video of the docking tube extending from the

Outworld Ranger to the *Argos Alpha*. He needed to get moving. What was taking Bartimaeus so long to connect to the spacesuit?

"Sorry for the delay, sir. Still working on it."

Octavian clicked past him and opened the locker next to the one that held the spacesuits. In a blur of motion, four arms took tools from the packs around his waist and replaced them with items from the locker. Then he removed a backpack from the locker and put it on.

Octavian shifted back, glanced at him, and cocked his head.

"My chippy's having trouble connecting to the suit."

Octavian prodded at a control panel on the suit's chest. He bleeped a few times then gave Karson an awkward-looking thumbs-up.

"Connection established, sir. Octavian rebooted the suit's hardware."

"Is there a problem with it?" Karson asked aloud.

Beeping, Octavian shook his head. Bartimaeus translated. "Do not worry, sir. The suit will function properly. The hardware reboot was necessary given the suit's last maintenance cycle was two decades ago."

"Twenty years?"

"Siv's had to be rebooted as well, sir. And it functioned properly. As far as I can tell, Octavian has kept this ship and all the equipment on it in prime condition, as if straight from the factory."

The spacesuit whirred to life. The front sealed up to the neck. The material of the arms and legs shrank and folded in on itself, and then the torso section did the same. In less than a minute, it went from fitting like a giant-sized clown costume to a hazmat suit.

He took a few steps, lifted his arms, and wiggled his fingers. *"You know, I've never actually considered how refitting works. Isn't that odd?"*

"Would you like for me to tell you how, sir?"

"No! Just put figuring it out on my to-do list."

"It's not a mystery, sir. The tech is quite explainable, and new suits are still being constructed without difficulty."

"I want to figure it out on my own, Barty. I need to keep my skills sharp."

"Sir, I don't think the others would appreciate you taking apart one of the suits."

"I thought we could pick up a cheap, nonfunctioning, secondhand suit. I could make it useable and have fun while doing so."

"I will never understand your humanity, sir."

The spacesuit's helmet deployed. From the back of the neck, a sheet of clear plasti-steel expanded until it formed a transparent dome around his head. He was pleasantly surprised that his horns fit within the spacesuit's helmet. While his head was smaller than that of a standard Terran, the horns made the dimensions entirely different.

"Connection complete," the *Outworld Ranger's* AI announced. "Plasma window tunnel activated. Pressurizing the docking tube."

Kyralla contacted him through his chippy. *"Bishop, are you ready?"*

"Almost," he replied.

Clumsily, he lumbered to the back of the *Outworld Ranger*, entered the loading bay, and stopped a few meters away from the iris that would open into the docking tube.

The girls entered behind him. Oona carried a force-staff, and Kyralla had a blaster in one hand and a disruptor in the other.

"We'll cover you from here, in case something comes through the tube," Kyralla told him.

He attempted to scratch his chin. He chuckled nervously when his hand hit the helmet. "Good idea."

Kyralla patted him on the shoulder. "Be careful in there. We can't be certain that we're not dealing with hostiles. Besides, the ship's in a bad state."

He patted the spacesuit. "I'm not too worried about the ship breaking apart. I can survive in space."

"I would be worried about a sharp metal fragment cutting into the suit," Oona said.

Karson blinked at her and swallowed. "Um...right...of course."

Kyralla groaned. "'Nevolence, Oona! Did you really have to tell him that?"

Oona dipped her head. "Sorry."

Kyralla held out the neural disruptor. "Take this with you. It's set to stun. If anyone you encounter acts suspiciously, shoot them. Same goes for someone panicking."

He nodded and took the disrupter. He placed it against the belt of the spacesuit, and it clamped into place magnetically.

Oona walked over and kissed the side of his helmet. "Be careful in there."

"I will be."

Octavian clattered up beside him then bleeped and buzzed and trilled.

"He's ready to go," Oona said.

Seneca swept into the loading bay with the ship's antigrav sleds.

"Is he coming too?" Karson asked.

"He's standing at the ready in case he needs to come across and rescue anyone," Oona said.

Seneca's eye-band lit up an eager blue-green.

Karson smiled at the girls. "You should return to the bridge and keep a lookout in case another ship enters the system. I'll be okay." He pointed to Octavian. "With my companion here, I'm sure I'll be fine."

"We'll wait a few minutes," Kyralla said.

"I only see one orange dot in my locator," Karson said. "This isn't an elaborate trap. I'll be fine." She started to argue, but he interrupted her. "Honestly, I'd feel safer if you were keeping watch from the bridge. If an enemy shows up, it won't be from within the *Argos Alpha*."

"He's right, Kyra," Oona said.

Kyralla nodded. Then she and Oona left, sealing the door to the loading bay behind them.

Karson faced the iris again and took a deep breath. He tried to keep his hands from shaking. He'd never used a spacesuit before, and he had never made ship repairs either. He should have studied that subject instead of working on the Tezzin.

He glanced over at Octavian. The cog's bulbous eyes turned a comforting orange as it bleeped softly.

"Sir, Octavian says everything will be okay. Just follow his lead."

Karson took a deep breath and nodded. The ship's cog was designed for this and had maintained the *Outworld Ranger* for a century. It knew exactly what it was doing.

The iris dilated open, Karson's fear disappeared, and a smile spread across his face. He was on a pristine starship, light-years from Ekaran IV, in the company of a hyperphasic messiah, and he was about to board a failing ship to help the most advanced cog he'd ever encountered mount a rescue.

In two short weeks, his life had changed completely. Despite the dangers, it was all for the better.

Octavian scurried ahead, and Karson followed him to the end of the tunnel.

"Sir, another crewman in the cargo bay just perished."

Karson stood two meters back as Octavian ignited a laser attached to one of his hands. Moving his arm in rapid circles, the cog began to cut into the vessel's hull. The laser was surprisingly high-powered for one mounted on a cog, but then maybe that was common for a pristine ship's cog.

"Barty, what's the condition of the young man on the bridge?"

"Artemisia says he's still unconscious."

As soon as they were somewhere where he could purchase new equipment, assuming he had enough money, Karson planned to acquire a sensor array so that Barty could give him more detailed information.

Obviously, he wouldn't be able to get anything nearly as advanced as what Siv used, but he didn't even have the most basic array possible. And why would he? He had certainly never expected to be in a situation like this.

Octavian finished cutting and withdrew the laser. Then he placed two, apparently magnetic, hands against the metal circle. His motivators whining under strain, Octavian drew the cutout free and dropped it to the side.

They climbed through the hole into a cramped space where the weapon system would have been mounted. Doing so, they left the *Outworld Ranger's* artificial gravity, which they had extended into the docking tube.

Floating free, Karson glanced around, hoping to find something to grab onto, but the compartment was empty. With a micro-burst from his suit's thrusters, he got his boots onto the nearest surface and activated the maglock. Octavian was using the same technique.

They now had to go through a second layer of the vessel's hull. But this section must have been thinner because it didn't take Octavian even half as long to cut through it.

Octavian tossed aside the second cutout to reveal a plasma window that had automatically deployed to maintain the ship's atmosphere from a breach. All ships had a containment system like this. Some advanced vessels, like the *Outworld Ranger,* even had an inner hull layer made from a self-repairing material that could recover a small breach within a few minutes to an hour.

Octavian touched the plasma window, and his hand struck a force-field.

"Is that common?" Karson asked.

Octavian bobbed his head and trilled.

"Sir, he says most containment fields use a low-powered force-field to keep out radiation and debris."

"So how do we get through it?"

Octavian beeped excitedly.

"Sir, he says that with the hull sections removed, he's now close enough to connect to the Argos Alpha's mainframe. He can use an emergency protocol

override that will get it to drop the force-field and the plasma containment field in this location. He just needs your permission first."

"Of course, you have my permission," Karson said.

Octavian shook his head vigorously and hissed.

"Sir, he says he needs your explicit *permission."*

"Oh, I see," Karson said. "Octavian, you have my permission to access the other ship using whatever procedures you deem necessary for performing a rescue mission."

Octavian bobbed his head and released a high-pitched whine. Even with the helmet on, Karson wanted to cover his ears with his hands. Fortunately, the whine lasted less than a minute.

"The transmission was sent, sir. We're just waiting for the vessel's approval."

"What if this doesn't—"

The plasma window dissipated, and Karson breathed a sigh of relief.

Octavian gestured and beeped.

"Sir, he's reminding you that you're about to enter the research vessel's artificial gravity field."

"Thank you, Octavian."

Octavian launched himself forward and crawled onto the *Argos Alpha's* bridge. Karson followed along behind him and became momentarily disoriented as he went from zero-G back to normal gravity, only in a different direction from what he'd last experienced.

He climbed to his feet and faced a dark, smoky environment lit dimly by a few stray sparks tumbling from the ceiling. All the electronics that had been sparking vigorously before must have burned themselves out.

Karson activated the spotlights mounted on each shoulder of his spacesuit and scanned the bridge carefully.

A layer of fire retardant coated everything, including the baby-faced young man with unruly white hair who was lying unconscious in front of the command chair. Octavian scurried over and knelt beside the man. He placed an injector against his neck and triggered the dose.

The young man stirred and glanced around in apparent confusion.

"Octavian gave him a stimulant, sir. His injuries appear to be minor."

Debris was piled in front of the door leading out into the main corridor. A section of the ceiling had collapsed, leaving behind chunks of electronics amidst a tangle of wires. Bishop could hardly even see the top third of the door. The bridge was effectively sealed off from the rest of the ship.

Octavian *might* be able to climb over all of that and crawl through, assuming none of the exposed wires were live, but there was no way Karson could do it.

"Well, shit. That's a problem."

The cog headed over to the sensor station. One of his hands folded down at the wrist. A pair of wires with coin-sized ends shot out from his arm and connected to the control panel's screen.

As light pulsed along the wires, Karson blinked with surprise. *"Is he linking with the ship?"*

"He is, sir."

"I need to sit down with Octavian sometime and ask him what all he's capable of."

"I could bring up the specs of his model, sir."

Karson sighed. *"I suppose that would do."*

A window popped up in his HUD and text began to scroll through it.

"Not now, Barty."

"As you wish, sir."

"What should I do?" Karson asked aloud.

Octavian responded with a series of beeps, and Bartimaeus translated. *"He wants you to see about the young man, sir. And then help him off the ship. After that, you can return and assist him."*

"Shouldn't we ask Seneca to get him?"

"I think, sir, that it would be better to have a human help him first."

Karson knelt beside the young man who looked at him with a dazed expression. "Are you feeling any better?"

He glanced around and spotted Octavian. He panicked and tried to scramble up to his feet, only to fall onto his ass.

Karson placed a hand on the man's shoulder. "It's okay. He's just a repair cog. We're trying to restore life support and other critical systems to your ship so that we can rescue the remaining survivors."

The man nodded absently then suddenly focused his eyes intently on Karson. "How many?"

Bartimaeus updated him, and Karson replied, "Only two."

"That's it?"

"I'm afraid so. They're stuck in the cargo bay. We had to enter through the bridge since your loading bay has suffered significant structural damage. We were afraid that docking there would cause the ship to break apart."

The young man took a few deep breaths then coughed. "It's hard to breathe."

Karson grabbed an arm and helped the man to his feet. "The atmosphere in here is thin, and you've breathed in a lot of smoke. Let's get you over to my ship. You'll be safe there."

He helped him through the hole in the bridge floor and into the zero-g section. "Be careful, you're about to shift from one down to another."

The dazed man couldn't figure out how to move downward, so Karson dropped in and shoved him, which resulted in the young man sliding into the tube on his back.

Karson climbed down and helped him to sit up.

"That...that was disorienting," the man said.

Now that they were inside the docking tube, the young man was able to take in deep breaths of fresh air. Seneca sped into the docking tube with one of the sleds in tow.

"What's your name?" Karson asked.

"Assistant Professor Jones," the man replied. "Tekeru Jones."

"What happened?" Karson asked as Seneca arrived.

"Pirates ambushed us. They were hiding in the planet's rings, and we failed to detect them. After their lasers took down our shields, a missile impact knocked out our engines and piloting controls."

"Based on the state of your ship, it appears they overdid it," Karson said. "Assuming their plan was to rob you and salvage your ship. What happened to them?"

"They disabled us properly. But as they closed in, one of their ships exploded. I don't know why. But that's what caused all the additional damage."

Karson helped Seneca lift the man onto the antigrav sled. "How many pirate ships were there?"

"Two."

"What happened to the other one?"

Tekeru Jones shrugged. "I guess the explosion took it out. I'm not sure."

"Are you the captain of this vessel?"

"Hardly. The captain and the pilot were off the bridge when the attack happened. Before they got there, the ceiling collapsed, and the door no longer functioned. They couldn't get in, so I was left on my own."

"Is there anything else you can tell me about the pirate ships?"

"They were cruisers, a little larger than the *Argos Alpha*. They never even asked us to surrender. And...and that's all I know. Sorry."

"That's okay." Karson patted Seneca on the shoulder. "This cog and the rest of the crew on my ship will see to your needs. I need to go back and help the other cog with the rescue operation."

Tekeru Jones clapped him on the arm. "Be careful."

Karson returned to the bridge of the *Argos Alpha*. Octavian was no longer connected to the sensor station control panel. He was now working on cutting through the debris blocking the door leading off the bridge.

"Did you manage to restore life-support functions?"

Octavian responded with a buzz and a series of beeps. *"Unfortunately, no. The actual life-support module needs repairs. He was, however, able to reroute all remaining life-support functionality to the cargo bay with the last two survivors."*

"Well, at least there's that." Karson carefully grabbed a chunk of metal Octavian had cut free and dragged it away. "Let me know how I can best help you."

Octavian responded. *"Sir, he wants you to attempt to open the door using a command override. Then deactivate all the bridge stations save for one."*

"Which one?"

"Your choice, sir. After you do that, cut power to all the non-essential ship systems connected to the bridge."

"How do I go about doing that?"

"The Argos Alpha has now given us full access to all of its systems and controls, sir. We shouldn't have any problem with it."

Karson didn't ask why Octavian wanted all the systems deactivated, but he assumed it had something to do with the wires threaded through the debris blocking their way to the rest of the ship.

He went over to the still functioning sensor station, linked to it, and pulled up the controls in his HUD and onscreen.

It took him a few minutes to perform the override, but he finally triggered the door system. With a whining groan, the door slid open, revealing a dark corridor beyond.

He had deactivated everything but the sensor station and the non-essential systems when Bartimaeus routed Kyralla through to contact him.

"Bishop, we have a problem."

"What's wrong?"

"Artemisia and Rosie analyzed the debris field in the area. There's barely enough wreckage here for a single cruiser, much less two."

"Are you...are you saying the other pirate ship survived?"

"That's exactly what I'm saying. Bishop, you and Octavian need to get out of there."

30

SIV GENDIN

Half an hour after arriving on Zarisia, the capital city of Zayer Prime, Mitsuki slipped into a bathroom in the bustling subway station. She was still hidden under the refraction cloak. Siv waited for her outside.

When she returned, he didn't recognize her...until she walked up and poked him in the ribs. Even though he'd seen her transform under the influence of the appearance-shifting drug before, he'd forgotten how different the red skin and more masculine features made her look.

They took turns purchasing a greasy lunch of fried vat-meat from a food cart. Mitsuki leaned against a column, people-watching as she ate. Siv wandered down the tunnel with his food, pretending to be interested in the advertisements and graffiti decorating the walls. So that it wouldn't appear as if they were together, they chatted through their chippies. Separately, they purchased tickets for a bullet train. Taking different seats in different cars, they traveled to the second largest city on Zayer Prime, half a continent away.

While Teloso was smaller than Zarisia, it was also a lot rougher around the edges and infested with local mobs that were determined to keep out the powerful interstellar crime guilds, which made it the perfect destination for them. The high crime rate suggested a place where they were far more likely to find what they needed: chameleon veils, forged ID cards, and a Titus-bound ship that was entirely uninterested in screening its passengers.

Siv had wanted to take a shuttle straight down to Teloso, but those were few and far between. And in the end, it was probably better to travel farther away from their landing point anyway.

Once they reached Teloso, they found a hotel room—one without any windows—and barricaded the door. With Silky and B on watch, they crashed. They'd been on constant alert since leaving the mining ship, and they were thoroughly exhausted. Either the beds were surprisingly comfortable, or they were even more tired than they had thought because they slept for eight solid hours.

After they woke, Siv dumped the hazard suit and the scarred chameleon veil into the hotel trash and made sure it cycled. Then he cut his hair and dyed it from brown to black. He changed his eye color from orange to blue using his Smart Lenses and applied red eyeliner and black lipstick in the style street punks used on Zayer.

Siv knew he looked ridiculous, something Mitsuki and Silky confirmed by mocking him mercilessly, but it was the best he could do without a chameleon veil. Using the disfigured mask here would draw too much attention. He needed a new look, one that would help him blend in.

From street vendors, they purchased sandwiches so spicy Siv worried his eyeliner would run and shabby trench coats to aid in hiding their many weapons. Once they looked presentable, by this city's standards anyway, they contacted Captain Alois's cousin, Tully. The man wasn't a criminal himself, but he ran a construction business in a town with a significant mob presence, so he had connections.

"I know people," Tully said when he greeted them in his office. "And the people I know, know people." The bald, wiry man laughed hard at that. "So I can connect you with someone, who can connect you with someone who can get you what you want."

Siv and Mitsuki laughed awkwardly in response.

"Jokes aside, you two appear desperate, and I don't like actively involving myself with anyone who's desperate for anything because it means they have powerful enemies."

"We just need the name and address of someone who could help us," Siv said. "Nothing more."

"Well, if my cousin thought you were worth the effort, and if you're willing to pay a little fee, then I guess it wouldn't hurt to give you a lead."

Siv pulled out ten hard credits and placed them on the man's desk. Tully pocketed them with a smile. "A lot of folks here wouldn't help you. You're not locals, see. You're not even from this world. And it's obvious based on your accents. I'm your only option..." He let the words trail away as he tapped his fingers on the desk.

Siv pulled out forty hard credits and passed them over.

"But you're in luck," Tully said. "It just so happens I know a guy who'd be more than willing to help you, and for cheap. A local guy who used to be something of a self-styled crime lord."

"He used to be?" Siv asked.

"He's fallen on hard times as of late, so he's desperate for money and favors. So desperate that he's scared off everyone who might otherwise have helped him. Desperation is the stink of death, you know."

"We have some experience with this sort of thing," Mitsuki said.

"On another world, I'd say. Your home world, perhaps..."

Siv and Mitsuki nodded but didn't give him the information he was fishing for.

"Why would we want a guy who's desperate and has no other contacts?" Siv asked. "If he can't get us what we need, then we'd be out of luck with nowhere else to go."

"You want him. Even though he's fallen on hard times, he still has some resources, and he's a damned good fixer. That's how he got his start. And the sort of items it seems you're wanting, he'll have the best of them on hand or know how to otherwise acquire them."

"That's our specialty, sir, isn't it? Otherwise acquisitions. You know, I like the term otherwise acquisitioner. You should switch to that. Has a much better ring than procurement specialist."

"Have you gotten what we need on Tully here?"

"Ten lightyears to gone, sir."

"His name's Condrance Wang," Tully continued. "Lives to the south, in Old Town. You're looking for a ramshackle warehouse. It's a bit nicer on the inside." He typed out an address on his c|slate and swiped it in their direction. Silky picked up the beamed transmission.

"I've verified the address, sir. Now researching the area and Mr. Wang."

"Thank you." Siv shook Tully's hand. "We'll tell Condrance you sent us."

"'Nevolence, no! I want nothing to do with this. Look, I like Wang. And I want to see him survive. I really do. But I can't be seen doing him any favors, you understand?"

"Sir, our dear Tully here has been trying to sell us out. He's been online

looking for a buyer. He started locally. It's not his area of expertise, so he's flailing about."

"As you suspected, Silkster."

"In that case," Mitsuki said with a smile, "we won't say anything about you. In fact, I don't think I'm going to remember having met you once I've left here."

The man tapped his nose. "Same here."

"That's hardly true, though, is it?" Siv said. "You're going to try to sell us out as soon as we walk out the door. You've already sent out feelers to see if someone in the region's searching for us. And you're getting ready to cast your net wider. That's not very nice of you."

"You...you know that I sent out feelers while we were talking?"

Siv nodded his reply.

"But I sent that out on my chippy!"

"I know," Siv said. "You should consider using more secure channels when chatting on the galactic net."

The man laughed nervously. "Well, you did say you weren't new to this, didn't you?"

Siv placed his palms on the man's desk and leaned forward menacingly. "You will keep quiet about us from now on. Would you like to know why?"

"I...I guess so?"

"While we were talking, I hacked your local network. I found quite a few documents that suggest you've been involved in many shady dealings. I'm sure the authorities would love to see these documents. But I *am* nice, so I'm sure I wouldn't want to give them over—unless I had to."

The man started to reach under his desk. Mitsuki shook her head. "I really wouldn't do that if I were you."

He moved his hand away. "Right...so...um, I think I'm going to forget who you are when you walk out that door. Really, really forget."

"That seems the safest bet," she said.

As they headed for the door, Siv waved goodbye. "Thanks for the info. Much appreciated."

31

KYRALLA VIM

Kyralla nervously waited for Bishop to respond.

"Rosie, is he heading back?"

"He hasn't moved, madam."

"If there's another ship," Bishop finally said, "then where is it? And why didn't it finish off the *Argos Alpha*?"

"I have no idea," she replied.

"Has Oona sensed anything?"

"No, not yet," Kyralla answered.

Bishop took in a deep breath. "We still have survivors who need rescuing. I'm staying if Octavian is willing."

Through their connection, she heard the cog beep affirmatively.

"He wants to stay."

"It's your call," Kyralla sighed. "But I think you should come back, just to be safe. We saved one person. That's a win."

"Just keep me posted and let me know if *anything* changes," he responded.

Kyralla closed the connection and opened a channel to Seneca. "Bring the survivor to the bridge, please."

"He says it would be best to let Mr. Jones rest, madam."

"Seneca, Mr. Jones can rest all he wants after I've talked to him."

She noted Oona's eyes open, peering at her. "You're going to threaten him."

"I'm going to be certain he's telling the truth."

Oona nodded. "I'll scan his emotions. I'm obviously a lot better at picking out lies and teasing out the occasional thought than I am at detecting hidden ships and traps."

"We have checked the debris field a second time," Rosie said over the ship's comm.

"And?" Kyralla asked.

"If we assume that two vessels of roughly our size exploded and that we are somehow missing up to forty percent of the resulting debris when we scan the area, we still cannot account for two ships."

She thumped back into her seat and ran her hands through her hair. "Then where the hell could they have gone?"

"Wraith-space, maybe?" said a deep, hoarse voice behind her.

Kyralla spun around, drew her plasma pistol, and aimed it at the young man with the wild, white hair and star-blue eyes.

"You didn't mention that to Bishop."

Tekeru Jones raised his hands. "The gizmet?"

Kyralla nodded as she stood.

"I heard your AI talking about the debris field. You asked a question. I made a guess."

"That's all?"

"It is," he replied. "I would run the simulations at sixty...maybe sixty-three percent...to account for debris getting caught up in the rings. We were closer to them at the time, but the explosion kicked us outward."

Kyralla kept the blaster trained on him. "Tell me everything."

Tekeru nodded, glanced at Oona in the command chair, made eye contact with her, and then took a half-step away. "I'll tell you everything I know. I can even give you the footage from my chippy. He recorded the entire encounter. Just keep in mind, I'm not a pilot or a captain. I'm just a researcher, out on my first expedition. I had only traveled in space once before."

"Beam your chippy's data over to me."

While Rosie went over the footage, Kyralla listened intently. Nothing in his story sounded fishy. And amidst the confusion and destruction, it seemed reasonable that a researcher would think that both enemy vessels had blown up.

He finished his tale. "And...and that's all I know."

"The footage is chaotic, madam, but it confirms his story."

"We have completed an analysis," Artemisia said. "Even with sixty percent loss of debris, we cannot account for the destruction of two complete light cruisers."

"Do you have two different AI's onboard?" Tekeru asked.

"Our chippies." Kyralla looked at Oona. "Well?"

"He's telling the truth," she replied.

Kyralla lowered her gun. "His story sounds legit to me, and his identity did check out."

Tekeru lowered his hands and turned to Oona. "You're a hyperphasic messiah."

Kyralla aimed her gun at him again. "Talk."

He raised his hands. "Sorry, but it's obvious. You hear tales, of course. But it's especially clear to me. My grandfather lived in the Empire of a Thousand Worlds. He smuggled out a photo of the Dark Messiah. We turned it over to the Federation but kept copies in our chippies. We didn't put the photo online because the Feds asked us not to."

Oona stood. "Show us." She gestured. "Put it on the main viewscreen."

Tekeru beamed the photo over to the viewscreen. Kyralla holstered her plasma pistol and cursed. "'Nevolence."

It was like looking at a middle-aged version of Oona. They were so identical that Kyralla would have sworn that this was nothing more than a doctored image of her sister.

Oona walked silently toward the image. She stopped a few meters away and stared, wide-eyed. Suddenly, she flinched.

"Kyra, they're coming. Battle stations."

A klaxon sounded and red lights flared on the bridge. Kyralla pointed at Tekeru Jones then gestured toward the weapons station. "You, sit down and put the circlet on. But unless you know what you're doing, don't touch the controls."

"We're not detecting anything yet, madam," Artemisia said aloud.

Tekeru took a seat and gripped the circlet. "Our ship only has one of these, in the command station."

"Yes, this is a ridiculously advanced ship," Kyralla snapped. "We can talk about it later. Put the circlet on and quiet your mind."

She glanced over at her sister, who was still staring at the image. With a control gesture, Kyralla cleared it away to show a view outside the ship. Oona snapped awake and rushed over to the command chair.

Shit. In her distraction, Kyralla had forgotten to contact Bishop. She opened the channel. "Bishop! Oona has sensed incoming danger."

No response came.

"Bishop?"

Nothing.

"Bishop, do you copy?"

"Rosie, are you reading life signs on the other ship?"

"Yes, madam. Bishop and the last two crewmen of the Argos Alpha. I'm detecting Octavian's signal as well."

"Try to contact Octavian."

"I've already tried, madam. I can't get a signal through. Or it's getting through to them, but their replies aren't reaching us."

"Keep trying to contact both."

"Of course, madam."

Kyralla couldn't worry about them. She had to clear her mind and focus on the current moment.

"As long as we're stationary, we're an easy target," Tekeru Jones said. "You should withdraw the docking tube."

Kyralla ignored him. They had to give Bishop and Octavian a way to—

"Shields max to starboard!" she yelled.

"Shields maxed to starboard," the ship responded.

An elongated cruiser bristling with weapons, its once brightly-painted hull marred by decades of conflict, swept out of wraith-space to their right and opened fire.

32

SIV GENDIN

The state of the warehouse district in Old Town spoke volumes about Teloso's crumbling economy. Half of the buildings and factories were shut down, the rest barely operative.

Silky made an endless series of lame jokes as Siv and Mitsuki camped on the rooftop of an abandoned building across the alley from the Wang Enterprises warehouse. With an antigrav boost, they could easily jump across to the Wang rooftop, if they wanted.

They had initially gone to the front door of Wang Enterprises but had left in a hurry after Siv's sensor array picked up seven men with drawn weapons inside the building.

"Seems to be a standoff, sir," Silky had said as they entered the abandoned building. "We've got one man hiding behind an overturned desk, and six others taking cover just out of sight in the adjacent room."

As soon as they reached the rooftop, Siv deployed two Spy-Fly drones. Before the drones entered Wang Enterprises, plasma bursts crackled, their sound no more than a dull buzz from this far away. None of the dots in Siv's locator had disappeared, but it was only a matter of time.

Siv cursed, and Mitsuki said, "Well, so much for that."

"Wang being attacked is a real kick in the balls," Silky said. No one laughed. *"You do get it, right?"*

"Wang's the only lead we've got," Siv said, *"and I'd rather not start over. That takes time and draws attention."*

"I do not want to get involved in someone else's firefight," Mitsuki said. *"That also draws attention. A lot of it. And it could get us killed."*

"Suggestions?" Siv asked.

"We cut and run," Mitsuki said. *"Find a new contact."*

"Problem is, this is the man we want," Silky said. *"I'm sure of it. Video coming up."*

The tiny, dragonfly-styled drones revealed the scene, showing pretty much what they'd expected from the sensor scans.

"The man holed up behind the desk is Wang," Silky said. *"The other guys are thugs from a local crime organization. And I do mean thugs—not crooks, not agents, not hitmen. Thugs. Every one of these fellows has served a prison sentence for a violent crime. A couple of them have served more than one if you include theft and minor assaults."*

"So goons shaking down someone for payment," Mitsuki said.

They listened to the audio provided by the drones as the thugs offered Wang the opportunity to surrender. He didn't take that chance.

"He's outnumbered and not surrendering," Siv said. *"So he's in deep. We should cut."*

"Sir, I think he's the one we need," Silky said. *"He's here, and he's now. We should save him."*

"Going on your instincts?" Mitsuki asked wryly.

"What if it is *instincts, eh? Got a chippy bias problem, Bats?"*

She shrugged.

"Well, it's not. Even if I had instincts, I wouldn't trust them. Gut or otherwise."

"What do you know?" Siv asked.

"I hacked his network and uncovered security footage of Wang..." Silky snickered *"...sorting through a packet of forged ID cards and a box of what appeared to be high-end chameleon veils, at least a dozen of them. The footage was from two days ago."*

Several bursts of plasma sounded, and the dots in the locator shifted as one thug tried to enter Wang's office. Wang's counter-fire forced the thug to retreat.

"He was trying to find the ones that would best suit his escape plan," Mitsuki mused.

"I don't doubt that," Silky said. *"According to the footage, and his system only stores three days' worth, which is the real crime here, he's been planning his getaway for weeks, converting assets to hard credits, sorting ID's and masks."*

"So he was just waiting for the perfect moment to make a break?" Siv said.

"I don't know what his play is exactly," Silky said, *"but I'm betting he's got a subtle way off this world. And we could use one of those."*

"He might simply be planning to flee to another city," Siv said.

"Maybe, but why risk it?" Silky countered. *"Local crime lords don't have resources off-world and are likely to give up looking for him. Unless you owe enough for them to hire a bounty hunter, of course."*

"But he could be going anywhere," Siv said.

"He could be, sir. But he owns a tiny shell company on Titus II. It's not much of anything, and it wasn't easy to track down, even for me. So I'm betting no one else knows about it."

"Damn it, Silky," Mitsuki said. *"I guess we've got to give it a shot."*

"Can't refute my logic, Batwings?"

Mitsuki stretched her wings then snapped them back in. *"Don't push it, chippy."*

"We could ignore the potential for a lead on a ship off-world and just get the masks and ID cards," Siv said. *"Smash and grab while he's distracted."*

"They're in a safe behind his desk, sir."

Siv groaned. *"Well, shit."*

"Okay, what's the play then?" Mitsuki asked. *"And if you say guns blazing, Silkster, I swear I'll rip you out of Siv's head and toss you into the street."*

"I love you too, Mits," Silky said. *"And I'd have thrown you away years ago. If I could throw."*

Another exchange of plasma buzzed. *"Focus, you two,"* Siv said. *"I'd like to get in there while the guy's still alive, and before the cops get here."*

Mitsuki shrugged. *"If we wait, they may take him out but not have time to crack the safe before the cops arrive. They'd have to leave it behind."*

"They'll just antigrav it and take it away to open later," Siv said.

"First off," Silky said. *"Siv's right. That skimmer truck across the street is theirs. Second off, the cops have been paid to wait. They will take their time getting here. Think about it. In a halfway decent neighborhood in a halfway decent city, with a standoff lasting this long, the cops—"*

"Would already be on the way," Mitsuki said. *"So, we've got to take out six bad guys."*

Siv slipped on his force-knuckles then drew his plasma pistol. Mitsuki quickly reassembled the plasma carbine.

He took a deep breath and considered the situation. *"We're dealing with thugs, not Reapers or professional hunters or trained guild agents, so I think we just need to give them a good enough scare to send them running."*

"You want to hit them with a show of force?" Mitsuki asked.

"Oh, I do love a good show of force!" Silky said. *"Sir, I would like to see them run away. Like actually run, not ride off. Permission to launch Spy-Fly 03?"*

"Permission is—" Siv stopped. The drone was already flying and had been launched before he'd even had a chance to answer. He watched as it headed out toward the skimmer-truck. *"Doing some skimmer highjacking?"*

"It's been a while, sir. And I do need to keep my skills primed."

Mitsuki rolled her eyes. *"Why don't you just tell us your grand scheme before Wang gets his head blown—"*

Silky guffawed, and Siv couldn't help but giggle along with him.

"Shut it!" Mitsuki snapped. *"Both of you."*

"Ahem." Silky cleared a throat he didn't have with mock dignity. *"The best bet in this instance is to put them in a state of panic. We don't need to injure or kill them. In fact, we don't want to. That would just complicate things. We want them running."*

"How do you propose we do that?" Siv asked. More plasma shots were fired, and they could hear bits of wall splintering. *"And tell us quickly."*

"We just need to add some shots to put pressure on them. Sir, you will drop in alongside Wang and start shooting. Having a second defender will make them start doubting themselves."

"What about me?" Mitsuki asked.

"You're going to take up position out here and fire your carbine at the building. These exterior walls aren't going to stop the shots if they're placed right. I will coordinate with B to get your shots lined up. Once they start taking crossfire—"

"They're going to panic," Siv said.

"Also," Silky said. *"I'm going to take over their van—they really should have better security on it—honk the horn, spin it around, and then drive it away."*

"It all seems *simple enough,"* Mitsuki said.

Siv had been studying the warehouse schematics. *"It looks like I could leap across and make my way in without too much trouble."*

"Are you sure I shouldn't turn on the refractor cloak and sneak in?" Mitsuki asked. *"I could throw some punches and mix things up. I've got the shock-club we seized on the station."*

"I don't think it's necessary," Silky asked. *"And I think it would be better to have you at a sniper position out here in case things go bad."*

"Okay then." Siv stepped over to the edge of the roof and activated his antigrav. *"Let's do it."*

33

KYRALLA VIM

Twelve beams fired from the pirate vessel's laser battery struck the *Outworld Ranger's* shields.

"Shields down to sixty-two percent," the ship's AI announced.

"Bishop!" Kyralla shouted. "Get out of there now! We're under attack! Rosie, what's the recharge rate on their lasers?"

"Five minutes, madam," Rosie replied aloud.

"Can we return fire?" Oona asked.

Kyralla shook her head. "The plasma cannons have a ninety-degree, forward-firing arc, and the railguns only have a forty-five-degree, forward arc." The *Outworld Ranger* had a small missile bay, but no missiles. "We could fire the flak cannon at them, I guess."

"What good will that do?" Oona asked.

Kyralla shrugged. "Honestly? I have no idea."

"That would simply be wasting ammunition," Rosie said.

"We can't just sit here," Tekeru Jones said.

"Shut the hell up!" Kyralla snapped.

Ripples of bluish energy appeared along the outside of the *Outworld Ranger* as four railgun shots crashed against their shields.

"Shields at forty-one percent," the ship's AI announced. "Four missiles launched. Flak cannon activated."

"Rosie, where's Bishop?"

"The main corridor of the Argos Alpha, *madam."*

"Heading this direction?"

"No, madam, toward the cargo bay."

"How do they not know what's going on?"

"Apparently, they can't hear the battle or our attempts to hail them, madam."

"Ship, retract the docking tunnel."

"We can't leave Bishop behind!" Oona said. "Or Octavian."

"It's better than getting all of us killed," Kyralla said.

"I suspect," Artemisia said, "that the pirates would prefer to leave the research vessel alone so that they can salvage it after disabling us."

"Docking tube retraction initiated," the ship said. "Full retraction will take five minutes."

"Do it faster!"

"Three minutes is the fastest time possible," the ship responded. "And that carries a significant risk of damaging the—"

"Just do it!"

The flak cannon took out two of the plasma missiles, but the other two connected.

"Shields at thirty percent," the ship announced.

"Can't we fly away as soon as the docking tube disconnects from the *Argos Alpha*?" Tekeru Jones asked. "It doesn't have to be completely retracted does it?"

"No, it does not," Artemisia replied.

"Maybe you're not useless after all," Kyralla told Tekeru.

"However, the tube could get hit by a stray shot or damaged by debris," Artemisia added.

"We'll risk it."

"The docking tube is disconnected," the ship said.

"The pirate vessel's plasma cannons are now online," Artemisia said.

"Why only now?" Oona asked.

"They were likely damaged during the explosion or in wraith-space," Artemisia answered.

"Reroute all non-essential power to the shields," Kyralla said.

The lights on the bridge dimmed immediately.

She slammed the accelerator forward and pulled the control-stick right, pulling them toward the pirate cruiser. If they could pass over or under the enemy ship, that would take away their firing arcs. She was betting the *Outworld Ranger* was more maneuverable, which would allow her to seize the advantage over them.

"Shields up to forty-two percent," Rosie said.

Plasma shots flared white as they hammered at the front of the ship.

"Shields down to twenty-seven," the ship announced.

"Coming up on an angle for our plasma cannons...now," Artemisia said. "Opening fire."

The *Outworld Ranger* was accelerating but slowly. Even as their plasma bolts burst against the enemy shields, they took more plasma fire in return.

"Shields down to sixteen percent," the ship said.

"Enemy shields are at thirty," Artemisia said. "They must have weakened inside wraith-space."

"We opened fire on one of their ships when we were attacked," Tekeru Jones said.

"I doubt your ship hit them that hard," Rosie said. "Perhaps they took some damage from their sister ship exploding before they fled to wraith-space."

The pirate cruiser was also moving slowly, but it wasn't accelerating. They'd had no incentive to since they were immediately lined up for perfect shots. But they had almost certainly underestimated the *Outworld Ranger's* capabilities.

"Pirate ship firing railguns," Artemisia called out.

Kyralla "saw" the shots coming. Their current course had them lined up to meet the pirate ship dead-on, head-to-head. She had yet to decide whether she wanted to go under or over the cruiser. However, since the railguns were firing from the top of the enemy vessel, she plunged the *Outworld Ranger* downward to try to duck under the shots.

One rail-shot glanced off their shields, reducing them to fourteen percent.

The second shot missed and continued on.

Kyralla hadn't even considered where the shot might go if it missed them. In her HUD locator, she watched in horror as the blip representing the shot sped toward the research vessel.

"Rosie, bring up the video feed of the Argos Alpha in my HUD."

The railgun shot plowed into the midsection of the research vessel. A brief explosion flared, and then the *Argos Alpha* ruptured, breaking apart into a dozen large fragments.

"Bishop!" Kyralla cried out.

Oona gasped and stood up from the command chair. Tekeru looked at them in confusion, then winced and covered his mouth as he realized what had happened.

"I hate to bear worse news," Artemisia said. "But a G-class destroyer just entered the system at maximum speed. And according to data Silky left with us, the destroyer is a fully-armed, World Bleeder command ship."

34

KARSON BISHOP

It took nearly fifteen minutes for Karson and Octavian to clear the doorway of enough debris so that they could move into the corridor beyond. Octavian was the first through, scrambling over the remaining rubble with ease. Karson, however, had to carefully pick his way across.

"Sir, I'm no longer receiving a signal from the Outworld Ranger*."*

"Did something happen to them?"

"I believe it's interference, sir."

"Octavian, what do you make of that?"

The cog paused and cocked its head. Bartimaeus translated the responding beeps and clicks. *"Sir, he says the fusion core's containment field just started leaking. That's causing interference."*

"Are we safe?"

"For now," the cog responded.

Struggling to keep up with the nimble cog, who didn't have a spacesuit to worry about, Karson followed Octavian through the main corridor. The dots on his HUD tracking their progress through the ship showed them as being halfway to the cargo bay when Karson heard a tapping noise.

He paused and listened. Nothing. He almost chalked it up to his imagination and continued toward the cargo bay, but curiosity got the better of him. He backtracked a few steps. There it was again. The sound was coming from behind a closed door to his left. The fact that he could hear it through his helmet, with the ship creaking and groaning all around them, was a testament to his excellent hearing.

He swiped a hand across the keypad beside the door. It slid open to reveal a second door, this one coated in diamondine and bearing a second keypad.

"Sir, a second ship has suddenly appeared."

"Appeared?! From where?"

"Unknown, sir. I still can't contact the ship."

"We've got to get out of here. Is the docking tube still deployed?"

"It is, sir."

"Octavian! We have to go!"

"Sir, the second ship has opened fire on the Outworld Ranger.*"*

"Damn it," Karson cursed.

"We should stay," the cog responded through Bartimaeus. *"Let them disconnect the tube and fight. Waiting for us to run back to the ship is unwise."*

Karson considered it a moment. Octavian was right. As long as the *Outworld Ranger* remained in a static position, waiting for them to run back through the tube, they'd be sitting ducks. To fight, Kyralla needed to be able to maneuver.

"I guess we're not going to be priority targets for the pirates anyway."

"No salvage to be had if they destroy this ship, sir," Octavian said, agreeing with him.

"The pirate ship has them flanked, sir. The Outworld Ranger *is out of position to return fire."*

That settled it then. "Kyralla, Oona, I don't know if you can hear this, but we're going to stay aboard the Argos Alpha. Detach the tube and deal with the pirate ship. Come back for us later."

"Message sent, sir."

"Did it get through?"

"I have no idea, sir. I'm not receiving confirmation that it did."

"Keep sending the message every thirty seconds, until they move on."

Karson focused. He needed to continue his mission and trust that Kyralla and Oona would be okay. In the meantime, there were people here on this ship who needed saving.

He touched the keypad for the second door, but nothing happened. The system must have lost power.

The tapping stopped, and then it started again. It was louder now that the primary door was open.

"Can I breathe the atmosphere in here?"

"For a short while, sir. But I don't recommend doing so."

He took a deep breath, retracted his helmet, and placed an ear against the diamondine door. Tap. Tap tap scratch. Tap. Tap tap tap. Scratch.

"Is it a repeating pattern?"

"Not one that I can detect, sir."

He rapped his knuckles against the door. "Is there anyone in there? Can you hear me?"

The tapping and scratching stopped. After a few moments, the sounds resumed.

"Octavian! I think someone might be alive in here!"

The cog paused at the end of the corridor, glanced back, shook his head, and issued a series of beeps.

As Karson redeployed his helmet, Bartimaeus translated. *"Sir, he says he can't detect any lifeforms in that area, and so he must focus on rescuing the ones we do know about."*

"Someone's trying to communicate, I'm sure of it! But I can't check it out because there's no power coming to the door."

Octavian beeped a response and trundled out of sight around the corner. *"If you feel it is worth the effort, reroute power from the primary door to the secondary door."*

"Do you need my help in the cargo bay?"

"Not at the moment."

"Okay. I'm going to make sure no one is in here. Then I'll come help you."

Karson examined the keypads of both doors as well as the frame from top to bottom. *"Do we have schematics for doors of this type?"*

"Pulling some up, sir."

As he scanned the schematics, Karson rushed over to a functioning control panel several meters down the corridor. By accessing the ship's mainframe, he digitally rerouted power from one door to the other.

While he was there, he tried to pull up the ship's sensor readings and video feeds of the room. He growled in frustration when those attempts were met with error messages.

"Barty, can you maintain a link to this station?"

"I believe so, sir. As long as you don't go too far."

Karson rushed back and swiped a hand across the keypad. Nothing happened. It looked as if he were going to have to fix the problem manually.

"Sir, the Outworld Ranger retracted the docking tube and engaged the pirates. Both ships have sustained substantial damage to their shields."

Karson took a deep breath and muttered a prayer for their safety. *"Keep me informed of their status."*

"Yes, sir."

Going as fast as he could, he popped a panel off the wall and pulled out wires. It was immediately apparent what had happened. An electrical overload had fried a power relay for the second door.

"Tell the ship to override the primary door's programming and have it remain open."

"Done, sir."

Luckily, he'd brought a toolkit along with him. Following the schematics Barty had pulled up, he rerouted wires from one door to the next. The procedure was simple but time-consuming, especially since one of the wires was also fried, requiring him to splice in a new one. Still, he would've whizzed through it if not for the bulky spacesuit he was wearing.

"Octavian, how's it going?"

"I was unable to restore power to the cargo bay's door, so I am cutting my way in. The cargo bay walls are reinforced, so it's taking longer than expected."

"I'm about to open the door here. If it doesn't pan out, I'll be there to help you ASAP."

Karson finished his repairs and swiped the keypad, hoping it wasn't locked. The pad flashed red. Damn.

"Barty, ask the ship for a lock override."

"I'll try, sir, but... Got it. But only because Octavian placed the ship in emergency rescue mode. Normally this is a highly secure area."

Karson swiped the keypad again. The second door slid open to reveal a reinforced, security-shielded storage vault. Transparent cryo-units of various sizes, a few containing plant and animal specimens, filled the shelves lining the walls. Two closed plastic crates sat beneath a command terminal in one corner. A fire extinguisher lay atop them.

At Karson's feet, a starkat kitten mewed in distress and pawed at his leg. Like all its species, the bioengineered feline had a long, fluffy, prehensile tail and tufted ears. This one had pale orange fur and intense brown eyes.

Starkats were popular with many spacers who spent all their time living and working in space.

The starkat locked eyes with him then looked deliberately toward the corner of the room. Karson followed its gaze. A young, blue-haired woman covered in burns, with a massive cut across her abdomen, lay slumped on the floor, half-conscious. Blood pooled beneath her.

Karson rushed over and knelt beside her. "Are you okay?"

She coughed up blood. "Peachy."

"Octavian! We have a badly wounded woman here."

The cog requested the scan data of her vitals.

"Can you beam your health data to my chippy?"

"Sure..." she answered in a whisper "...but it doesn't...matter..."

Bartimaeus did the best he could with an external scan, and they relayed that data along with the information from her chippy to Octavian.

The cog responded simply. *"Comfort her."*

"You're not going to help?"

"She only has a few minutes to live. I am entering the cargo bay now."

"What's your name?" Karson asked, taking the woman's right hand. Cuts and burns had rendered her left hand a tangled mess.

"Doesn't matter...I'm dying."

Karson didn't know what to say. Someone trained in medicine would. He considered telling her that she wasn't going to die, to give her hope. But that was a blatant lie.

"It's...okay," she told him. "I know."

The starkat purred and rubbed its face against the top of her head. She tried to smile in response. Then she flicked her eyes toward the little creature.

"Peachy. Can you...take care...of Peachy? Get her off...this ship...somewhere safe."

"Of course." Karson peered into the starkat's big, round eyes and nodded. He could easily do that for her. "I'll take her back to my ship. She'll have loads of space onboard to roam around and plenty of people who will enjoy playing with her."

As he talked, the woman closed her eyes and smiled in relief. Slowly, her smile faded...then disappeared.

The starkat bumped its head against hers, mewling in grief.

Karson squeezed her hand a few more moments then rubbed the starkat's head. "Don't worry, little guy. I'll get you to safety. But first, we have to go help save—"

"Sir, the Outworld Ranger *just evaded a railgun projectile, and that projectile is on a direct course for this ship."*

Karson rushed to the door and slammed his hand on the inside keypad. The door snapped shut.

"Octavian, take cover!"

35

KYRALLA VIM

Kyralla marshaled her emotions. She couldn't worry about Bishop, not right now. She had to keep Oona and herself alive. That came first. And to do that, she had to focus.

"ETA on that destroyer?" she asked.

"Four hours," Artemisia replied.

"That should give us enough time to escape, right?" Oona asked.

"Maybe. But we have to survive this and rescue Bishop first. And I have no idea how long that will take."

The *Outworld Ranger* zipped under the pirate cruiser. Kyralla pulled the nose up enough to line up another attack.

"Enemy shields at twenty-one percent," Artemisia said.

Their plasma cannons flashed, and the flaring bolts splattered against the pirate vessel's shields. She waited for the railgun's recoil to rock the ship, but nothing happened.

"What the hell!" Kyralla snapped. "Why haven't we fired the railguns?"

"The ship can't line up the shots," Tekeru Jones told her. "You would have to bring the nose up further."

"I can't do that without running into their shields."

"Then we can't fire them," he replied.

"I'm picking up an emergency signal from Octavian," Rosie said over the ship's comms. "His processor's still active. He is unharmed and awaiting rescue."

"What about Bishop?" Oona asked.

"He does not know where Mr. Bishop is, madam. And we can't get a life-force reading. There's too much interference in the area."

"Oona, can you sense whether he's okay?" Kyralla asked.

"Not while I'm plugged into the ship like this," Oona replied. "Even if I wasn't, who knows?"

The *Outworld Ranger* cleared the underside of the pirate vessel. Kyralla cut the ion engines, pulled the nose up, and activated the port thruster to rotate the ship around to line up more shots.

Suddenly, a pair of plasma bolts flared into them.

"Shields at nine percent," the ship announced.

"What the hell was that?" Kyralla asked.

"The pirate cruiser has a rear-mounted dual plasma cannon," Artemisia said.

"Why didn't anyone tell me about that?"

"You didn't ask," Rosie said. "And it's in the specs I pulled up in your HUD."

"Kyra," Oona said. "You're asking too many questions and talking too much. None of this stuff matters if you can't focus on the moment and use your abilities."

Kyralla nodded, took a deep breath, and began reciting the Fibonacci sequence. Oona was right. She didn't have enough skill to handle this without Silky and the others. Their only advantage was her ability to see and react to the enemy's actions before they took them.

The *Outworld Ranger* had rotated ninety-two degrees, when the pirate vessel hit them with another round from their dual plasma cannons.

"Shields to two percent," the ship said.

"Can we divert any more power?" Oona asked.

"Only if we cut life-support, sensors, and the flak cannons," Artemisia said.

"None of those will matter if they hit us again," Tekeru said.

"Do it," Oona ordered.

"Shields at four percent," the ship stated.

Kyralla considered activating the ion engines to maneuver them away from the next volley. But the engines would have to first counter inertia. They didn't have time for that. She could spin back around and evade, but they needed to take their own shots and make them count. Disabling the pirates would be far more effective than trying to evade them. The pirate ship had more weapons and a crew that had experience fighting space battles.

"Divert power from the ion engines," Kyralla said.

"Are you certain?" the ship asked.

"Yes! Do it!"

"Shields to thirteen percent."

"That's all?" Tekeru asked.

"It's impossible to reroute all power designated for the ion engines," Artemisia explained.

The pirate vessel's plasma cannons struck them again.

"Shields to six percent."

The *Outworld Ranger* completed its rotation, and they opened fire. All four plasma shots and both diamondine-tipped railgun shells struck the enemy ship dead center.

"Enemy shields down," Artemisia said. "Minimal damage to their hull."

"Target those plasma cannons and their engines," Kyralla said.

"Quad-plasma targeting their engines," Tekeru said. "Railguns aimed at their dual cannons."

"Is that optimal?" Kyralla asked.

"I have no idea," he replied. "I'm just relaying information and loaning brainpower to the system like you told me to do. The ship chose the targets for me."

"Which one recharges first?" Oona asked.

"The plasma cannons," Artemisia said.

"Then switch the targeting around," Kyralla ordered.

"Targeting switched," Tekeru reported.

Kyralla waited tensely, gripping the control-stick and accelerator until her knuckles turned white and her hands cramped. She wished to hell they had a supply of missiles.

The meters in her HUD registering the recharge rates for the plasma cannons and railguns ticked steadily upward. A third meter showed that the pirates' guns would be ready to fire a full ten seconds before theirs.

The enemy meter hit green. Kyralla inhaled and braced herself. But nothing happened.

"Did we damage their plasma cannons?" she asked.

"We only scarred their hull," Rosie said.

"Then what's going on?"

"I bet they're overcharging their plasma cannons," Tekeru said.

"What makes you say that?" Oona asked.

"It's just an educated guess, but that's what we did on the *Argos Alpha* right after they took out our shields. We were desperate."

"Enemy overcharge confirmed," Rosie said. "I adjusted your meters, madam."

Kyralla stared in terror at the meters for the plasma cannons. Theirs and the enemy's matched. The exchange of fire would be simultaneous.

"What happens when you overcharge them?" she asked. "That wasn't covered in the manual I read for our weapon system."

"It wasn't covered because you have to alter the system manually to allow an overcharge," Artemisia said, "and the *Outworld Ranger's* weapons have not been altered."

"An overcharge will fry the system," Rosie said. "But it allows—"

All the meters hit green.

"Fire!" Kyralla said.

The *Outworld Ranger* unleashed a volley from their quad-cannon and fired the railguns. At the same time, electricity flickered around the pirate ship's dual cannons as they discharged twice.

A second later, four plasma bolts plowed into those cannons. Flames and debris burst outward from the pirate vessel. The *Outworld Ranger's* diamondine-tipped railgun shells plunged into the aft section of the cruiser. Flames spurted from the holes they had punched into the vessel.

The first two shots from the pirate ship knocked out the *Outworld Ranger's* shields. Following right behind those, the second pair struck the hull.

The ship bucked, throwing Oona onto the floor and pounding the back of Kyralla's skull against her chair's headrest. A boom reverberated throughout the ship. The dim, emergency lights flickered. The ship groaned and creaked around them. A red warning light flashed.

"Hull integrity secure," the ship announced. "Ion engines offline. Flak cannon damaged and inoperable. Port thrusters sustained heavy damage. Comm array knocked out of alignment. Plasma cannon recharge delayed. Railguns temporarily disabled."

"Shit," Kyralla cursed. "We're screwed."

Oona stood and gathered herself. Tekeru glanced back at her.

"Enable the inertial dampeners for your chair," he said. "Then that won't happen again."

"Oh." She settled back into the command chair. "Did we disable the pirates?"

"The pirate vessel suffered heavy damage," Artemisia said. "Their aft plasma cannons, aft shield projectors, and ion engines were destroyed. Their fusion core is cracked, but the containment field is holding. Seven pirates killed, twelve injured."

Oona threw a hand over her mouth. "Oh...oh, 'Nevolence. All those people. All those—"

"Criminals," Tekeru Jones spat. "Criminals who killed two dozen innocent researchers and crewmen."

"I think I'm going to be sick," Oona said.

As she rose from her chair, Kyralla spun around and pointed at her. "Sit down. You can't leave. We need you here."

"But...but..."

"Do you want to die, too?"

Oona shook her head and sat.

"Then keep it together, for now. Push it aside, block it out. Do whatever you have to do, but keep it together. We're in a lot of danger right now."

"Speaking of danger," Rosie said. "The pirate cruiser has fired their starboard thrusters. With a recharged forward-firing laser battery, missiles, and plasma cannons, they present a more than significant threat."

"What Rosie doesn't want to say," Artemisia told them, "is the moment we enter their firing arc, we're dead."

"What about our shields?" Oona asked. "Won't they be recharged by then?"

"When they can fire at us, our shields will have recharged to four percent," Artemisia said.

"We could evade," Oona said.

"Only with our port thrusters," Kyralla replied. "The engines will be offline for..."

"Fifty-four minutes," Artemisia said. "Unless you reboot them. That would reduce the time to twenty-five minutes."

"Until we affect repairs," Rosie said, "we won't be able to shoot down incoming missiles either."

Kyralla glanced at Tekeru Jones. Their eyes met, and understanding passed between them. They both knew what had to be done. She checked her HUD. The meter for their plasma cannons remained in the yellow.

"Rosie, give me a meter representing when we'll enter the cruiser's firing arc."

A new meter popped up in her HUD. She breathed a sigh of relief. The *Outworld Ranger's* weapons would be recharged in time to do what had to be done.

"We need Octavian," Oona said. "Is he still okay?"

"I'm detecting a signal from him," Artemisia said. "During the battle, he sent us a message. He's still searching for Mr. Bishop amongst the wreckage. However, his scanning abilities are limited, and he's unable to maneuver within the vacuum."

"I don't understand why we can't detect Bishop," Oona said. "Shouldn't we be getting some sort of signal?"

Because he's dead and his chippy and his spacesuit have been destroyed, Kyralla thought. But she didn't voice it. She couldn't bring herself to. Besides, Oona couldn't handle any more emotional distress right now.

On the viewscreen, they watched the pirate vessel slowly spinning towards them. Oona shifted nervously in the command chair. Surely, she must realize what they would have to do.

"So how do we go about making repairs?" Oona asked.

"We'll instruct you on what to do using augmented reality guidance," Rosie said. "But it will be neither easy nor fast since you lack the required manual skills and know-how."

The pirate vessel had spun one hundred and forty-seven degrees. The meter for the *Outworld Ranger's* plasma cannons ticked up to a bright yellow.

Just a few more moments...

"I hate to convey more bad news," Artemisia said, but the World Bleeder destroyer just launched three U-XT starfighters. They're faster, more advanced versions of the starfighters we faced in the Zayer system."

Kyralla unleashed a string of curses.

"The World Bleeders...they're a criminal organization, right?" Tekeru Jones said.

"And they're after us," Oona replied, dismayed.

"Great," he said. "That's just great."

"ETA on the starfighters?" Kyralla asked.

"One hour, madam," Rosie answered solemnly.

If they rebooted the engines in time, they would have only half an hour to recover Bishop and escape. And slowing down to pick him up would almost certainly mean the starfighters would catch up to them. Of course, all of that assumed that Bishop was somehow alive amongst all that wreckage.

"Rosie, where will our shields be in an hour?"

"Roughly seventy-eight percent, madam."

The meter for the plasma cannons reached green. The pirate vessel was less than a minute away from being able to target the *Outworld Ranger*.

Kyralla inhaled deeply and started to speak, but Tekeru acted before she could issue the command.

"Switching weapon activation to manual control," he said.

Kyralla noted with relief that targeting control remained with the ship.

Oona leaned forward. "What are you—"

Tekeru Jones pressed a button on the command console. The white flash of four plasma bolts sped out from the quad-cannon on top of the *Outworld Ranger*. The shots pierced the pirate vessel, opening a gaping hole in its side.

A column of flame spurted out from the vessel.

Then it exploded in a massive fireball as the fusion reactor when nova. Oona cried out, and Rosie actually cursed. Eyes wide, Kyralla sat stunned.

The blast flung debris and blue flames in all directions. This resulting blast wave barreled toward the *Outworld Ranger*.

"Brace for impact!" Artemisia shouted.

"Shields angled forward," Rosie said. "What little we have now anyway."

"Inertial dampening maxed," the ship announced.

With the wall of blue flame only a few hundred meters away, Kyralla drew in a sharp breath and closed her eyes.

36

SIV GENDIN

Siv kicked down hard on the ceiling tile. It clattered onto the floor of Wang's office unnoticed. The thugs released another volley of plasma fire. Crackling bolts burned through the interior wall, scorched the floor and ceiling, and pelted into the overturned desk. Surprisingly, the shots did nothing more than scar the surface.

Wang was crouched behind the desk, his back to it, his head hunkered down. The tile fell to his left, next to the wall, yet he didn't spot it nor hear it strike.

"Sir, drop on my mark." Silky sighed. *"What a bunch of rubes, not knowing how to cycle amongst themselves to keep the firing continuous."*

Siv activated his force-shield.

"Wait...wait... Go!"

The firing stopped, and Siv dropped into the room, holding the force-shield in front of him. He made his body as compact as possible and kept his head tucked behind the shield.

He struck the floor, eyes wide as he noted the dozens of holes punctuating the walls.

Keeping the shield up, he ran across the room. Just as he dived for cover behind the desk, the thugs opened up with another volley of fire.

Wang glanced at him in surprise, then he aimed his plasma pistol at Siv.

"Whoa!" Siv exclaimed, putting his force-shield between them. "Do I look like I'm your enemy?"

"I don't know you," Wang said, "so you can't be a friend."

"If I were your enemy, you'd be dead already."

As plasma bolts seared into the desk protecting them, Wang quirked an eyebrow then nodded. "Well, I can't argue with that. Why are you here?"

"I'm rescuing you," Siv said, lowering his voice so the thugs wouldn't know he was there. "In return for a favor. You have something I need."

Wang kept his voice low, matching Siv's volume. "I can't turn down your terms." Wang shook his head, a twisted smile on his face. "But I don't know how dropping into this toilet with me is supposed to help. What's one more turd in the bowl supposed to accomplish?"

"I like the way this guy turns a phrase," Silky muttered.

"You're just as screwed as I am." Wang eyed the force-shield. "Though you do seem better equipped."

"There's a plan," Siv told him. "Trust me."

Wang shrugged as a plasma bolt struck the wall over their heads. A picture of a scantily clad girl riding a skimmer cycle burst into flames then clattered onto the floor.

"Sure," Wang said, eyeing the smoldering picture, his face turning to a deep frown. "Why not?"

Wang was in his late forties, much younger than Siv had expected. He had a slender frame, shock white hair, bronze skin, and sky-blue eyes. He wore a red, silk suit that was now sliced open and scorched in several places, revealing the mesh body armor beneath.

Wang had an innocent face, one that belied his occupation. It was the sort of look that could help you as a criminal, making it easier to mislead others, even amongst your kind. But one that could also hurt you, because you'd have to work a bit harder to earn the respect of the rough men you worked with.

Siv was more than familiar with the problem, having become a passable procurement specialist by the age of fourteen, and one of the best on Ekaran IV by sixteen.

Siv held out a hand. "My name is—"

"Mr. A," Wang said. "Your name is Mr. A. I don't want to know your real name, and you shouldn't tell me."

"I didn't intend to," Siv replied.

Wang nodded. "Smart lad."

"He seems likable enough," Silky said.

"I don't trust him," Mitsuki said over the secure channel. *"And you just like him cause he's a smart ass."*

"That is a plus," Silky replied. *"But what I really like is that he appears to be intelligent."*

"Why does that matter?" Mitsuki asked.

"If he's smart, he's not going to rat us out," Siv said. *"Given his situation, he doesn't want to draw attention to himself any more than we do."*

"A smart man can still make poor decisions and screw himself over," Mitsuki said.

Siv couldn't argue against that, but his instincts told him that Wang had the good sense not to risk himself by ratting on them. Unless he figured out precisely how much they were worth. In that case, he would, once he was away from Zayer Prime.

One of the thugs popped around the corner and squeezed off three shots before darting back. The desk shuddered as the plasma bolts he'd fired struck its surface without burning through.

"This is one hell of a desk," Siv said.

"There are thin layers of ceramic, carbon fiber, and diamondine beneath the wood top," Wang said, and Silky verified the information. "I purchased it for just such an occasion. I had hoped I'd never have to use it."

"You've clearly fallen on hard times," Siv said. "I'm betting you're going to have to cut and run and leave this world for another. And I'm thinking you already have plans for doing just that."

Wang narrowed his eyes at him. "You're a shrewd man, Mr. A."

"Leaving seems obvious given how many enemies you've made."

"Knowing about me isn't easy when you're an outsider, which you clearly are," Wang said. "But guessing that I'm about to leave the planet is a whole other matter."

Siv decided to cut to the chase. "You're heading to Titus II."

Taken aback, Wang flinched. "How do you know that?"

"You own a shell-company there."

"You do have me at a disadvantage." He chuckled nervously. "It seems I have no advantages today."

"You have me."

Siv noticed in his locator that one of the thugs was edging toward the doorway. Wang had stopped returning fire when Siv arrived, and Siv hadn't helped yet.

The thugs almost certainly didn't know Siv was there. Their chippies weren't advanced enough to give locator scans, and even if they'd been modified for that, they couldn't have overcome Silky's jamming.

They probably thought that the silence indicated they'd finally killed or incapacitated Wang.

Siv waited as the man was just about to peek his head around the corner.

"Now, sir!"

Siv popped up and placed a shot into the wall beside the man. Wang joined him, and his shot clipped the man's shoulder. The thug screamed and fell back.

"Careful," Siv said. "We don't want to kill them."

"What are you, some kind of anti-violence crusader? These men are trying to kill me!"

"Dead men draw attention. I have a plan to drive them off."

Wang shrugged. "Whatever gets me out of here." His eyes narrowed, and he chewed on his lip. "You have an accomplice."

"Outside," Siv said, nodding. "When I tell you to, stand and fire. Send your shots through the doorway, into the wall, the ceiling, whatever. It doesn't matter, just don't injure any of them bad enough that they can't run away."

"I'll do my best," Wang said. "Truthfully, though, I'm a terrible shot. If I hit someone, it's luck."

"Siv, I'm in position," Mitsuki said. *"Though I'm going to have a tough time hitting the places Silky wants me to, even with the new targeting software he uploaded to B."*

"Just line up the triangles, it couldn't be any simpler," Silky said.

"I'm an extraction agent," Mitsuki replied. *"Not a sniper. I'm not even a soldier. I'm a decent shot, but that's it. And you want me to strike targets no bigger than a gnat's ass. So, unless you've got a software upload for my arm..."*

"Well, we could cut it off and replace it with a bionic model," Silky said. *"Then I could assist you with—"*

Siv cut him off. *"You'll do fine, Mits. Just focus."*

"We're all ready, sir. Everything's in place."

"Then let's hit it."

"And quit it, sir. I agree. Go!"

Siv popped up, force-shield in place, and opened fire, his plasma pistol bursts streaming through the doorway. Wang joined in. As they fired, the thugs backed up, surprised to have two people in the office now when there should have only been one.

Mitsuki's plasma carbine rapped a staccato pattern on the outside wall to Siv's left and into the room with the thugs. Most of the shots spattered against the outer wall harmlessly, but a few bolts cut through and flashed into the other room.

One bolt struck a thug, and he cried out.

"Damn it, Mits," Siv cursed.

"I'm trying!" she said. *"I can't help that they're moving around."*

"It's just a burn on his forearm," Silky said. *"Nothing too severe. I'll begin my part now."*

Outside, an engine revved up, and a horn honked incessantly. The skimmer truck began to circle in the street.

The thugs exchanged shouts of confusion. Then one glanced outside. "Someone's stolen our ride!"

"We can't go out there!" another said. "We'll get shot."

"We can't let them steal our van!" said a third. "If we lose the van *and* the mark, we're doomed."

Siv stopped firing and shouted as loudly as he could to Wang. "Pass me the grenade!"

That did it. The thugs broke and ran. As they headed out the door, Silky hit the throttle and sent the van speeding down the street. The thugs chased after it on foot, but it was out of sight before they cleared half a block. Mitsuki sent a few bolts at their heels to keep them running.

Once the thugs were several blocks away, Siv stood. "Mr. Wang, you're safe now."

Wang turned the gun on him, and Siv put the shield between them.

"What do you want from me?" Wang asked.

"Forged ID cards and chameleon veils, good ones if you have them, and a lead on discreet transportation to Titus II. We are willing to pay."

"But we will be deducting a significant rescue fee," Mitsuki said, striding into the room, her plasma carbine in hand. She'd used her wings to glide down.

"That...um...that seems fair enough," Wang said, lowering his gun. He eyed Mitsuki curiously. "I guess I'll call you Mr. B."

Her gender change solution was working.

"She's definitely a B," Silky said.

"I'll take that as a compliment, Silkster. But we already have a B."

"Wait," Mitsuki's chippy said. *"Am I called B because you think I'm a bitch?"*

"I don't think you're a bitch, B. You're very polite."

"Oh good, madam. I don't want to be one."

"But you are my bitch, B. If you get my drift."

"Oh my, madam. I had no idea."

"My upgrade's working wonders," Silky cooed.

"Can we all focus, please," Siv said.

"Call me Mr. C," Mitsuki told Wang.

Wang cocked an eyebrow then shrugged. "If you prefer."

Mitsuki went back into the front room, shut the door, and then barricaded it. The thugs had broken the lock when they entered.

Suddenly, Wang collapsed to the floor trembling and breathing rapidly.

"He's shell-shocked, sir. His vitals confirm it. You should get him talking."

"Mr. Wang, let's talk about your wares," Siv said. "Tell me what you have in stock."

"I...I have some top-shelf ID cards...and chameleon veils," Wang said, his voice shaky. "I make the ID's...myself and I...obtained a large stock of quality masks...a few years back. Selling this stuff is all that's kept me afloat...over the last few months."

"You'd think that a crime lord would be harder to rattle," Mitsuki said disapprovingly.

"Most people, including crime bosses and petty crooks, aren't used to firefights, especially prolonged ones," Silky said. *"You two have unusually steady nerves. If you didn't, you wouldn't have been able to do your jobs."*

"How'd you hit bottom?" Siv asked, to keep him talking.

Wang took a big breath and released it. "I'm a gambler, in every way imaginable. It's how I rose to the top so quickly, and it's how I crashed to the bottom even faster."

"Good work, boss," Silky said. *"He's starting to calm down. And we've now got insight into his personality."*

Siv lifted the massive desk, setting it back up. The wood on the top was almost entirely gone, burned away by plasma blasts, leaving the diamondine layer exposed.

"That certainly doesn't make me trust him more," Mitsuki said. *"He'll take*

a risk on turning us over as soon as it's safe enough for him to do so, maybe much earlier than that."

"At least we know so that we can plan around it," Silky said.

"We should get moving," Siv prompted.

Wang nodded, coming to his senses. He moved to the safe, opened it, and removed the packet of ID cards. When Siv didn't react, he eyed them shrewdly.

"You already knew I had these. How?"

"Do you really want to get into that?"

"No." Wang dumped the packet's contents out on the desk then half smiled. "You hacked my security camera feed."

"Yes," Siv answered simply. "Mit... Mr. C., why don't you sort through these. I'd like to examine the masks."

Wang pulled out a box. "I need two of them." He grabbed the two veils on the top. "The rest are yours...for the right price."

Siv dug through the box, lifting out models and examining them. He sorted them into three piles with Silky's help: the mediocre ones, the good ones, and the top-shelf veils. There weren't any bad ones in the lot.

Wang nodded appreciatively. "You have a good eye for chameleon veils, sir. I might quibble with you placing the Eighty-Seven into that second pile instead of the first, though."

"It's personal," Siv remarked. "The Eighty-Sevens don't fit me right."

Wang eyed him, nodding. "I can see that."

"Sir, we have a crew of five wanted misfits. Plus another if we manage to rescue Ambassador Vim. And all of these are good masks."

"I'll take the lot," Siv said aloud as he pulled a mask from the first pile. "And I'll be using this one right away."

"Each top-notch veil I've got sells for five thousand credits," Wang said. "The others for four and three."

Siv coughed and attempted to sound incredulous. "That's ridiculous!"

"Sir, what a bargain! He should be selling those for twice that much. Maybe more. I think I know why he hit hard times."

"Oh, I can see what you're thinking," Wang said, "that I'm selling these far too cheap. It's warehouse pricing, you see. I make a killing selling them this cheap because I got the inventory for free. And truthfully, people here can't afford to pay as much anyway."

"Well, I certainly can't pay you that much for them."

"I didn't expect that you could."

"I can pay three thousand."

Wang sighed. "I need those masks to set up my next venture. Take one veil from each pile, take however many ID cards you need, and pay me three thousand. We'll call it even."

"All the masks from the first pile, and five thousand credits," Siv said.

"Siv, that's half what we've got!" Mitsuki cautioned as she sorted through IDs. She didn't let her emotion show physically, but her voice certainly conveyed her disapproval.

"Sir, is that wise?"

"I'm trying to stay on his good side," Siv said, *"to delay him from taking a gamble and trying to sell us out too soon."*

"I'll take that deal," Wang said. "But only because I've got my passage secured and paid for. And I guess you want in on that?"

Siv nodded.

"There's a finder's fee of five hundred credits."

"You drive a hard bargain for a man we just saved," Mitsuki said. "We could just take this stuff from you, you know." He had pushed her too far.

Wang threw his hands up. "Okay, okay. I'll key you in on that for free, and you can have the masks for forty-five hundred."

"That's better," she said, pocketing eight ID cards. "What's your way out of here?"

"I've booked space on a Hydrogenist cult ship," Wang said. "They are leaving here and heading for the Titus system. Before they start their research there, they'll visit Titus II to refresh their supplies and spread the good word. It's just luck that they were done here and ready to leave in time for me, and now you as well, to beat a hasty retreat. They will have space for more passengers." He held up a plastic voucher. "I just have to show them this."

Siv reacted with a groan almost as loud as Silky's, but without the cursing to accompany it.

"That's a strange lot to hook up with."

"Just tell them you're interested in the faith and want to learn more," Wang said. "Then kick over a few hundred credits. They won't ask much at that point, even if they think you're lying. They'll jump at any chance to convert you, however remote. And they're desperate to keep their pilgrimage going, so they'll take what money they can get and not question its source. You do need a voucher, though, or be in the company of someone who has one. There's a process to joining them, even for a short trip."

Silky sighed. *"Hydrogenists, they're just the worst."*

"Really?" Mitsuki said. *"They're harmless."*

"I'd rather the harmful who make sense."

"It sounds perfect," Siv said to Wang.

"Their ship leaves in two hours."

It only took Mr. Wang fifteen minutes to pack up the last of his belongings. He'd gone from a prosperous crime lord to a man who could fit all his most valuable possessions into a duffle bag. Silky commented several times that they could just rob the man.

"It's not like he's a good guy, sir. He has been involved in worse stuff than the two of you. We could get our forty-five hundred back, take the other six thousand he has hidden in various pockets and sewn into the lining of his pack, and the rest of the masks. We'd make out big time."

"We're honest people," Siv replied. *"As much as we can be. We do this right. We earn good karma."*

"Well, I'm not people, sir. Chippies don't have karma. Put me in charge. Let me make the decision, and then you can live guilt-free."

"Not happening, Silkster. End of discussion."

"Have it your way, sir. Just know that my way's better."

Wang had changed into clothes that made him look like a vagabond, though he'd kept his mesh armor on beneath.

Siv donned the chameleon veil he'd selected and used a new profile Silky had downloaded from the net, having customized it to be unique. They then matched the ID card data to a fake profile Silky had been working on to go with the new face.

Mitsuki used one of the veils to alter her face further. There was no getting around that she was a wakyran, though. There wasn't anything they could do about that except to use the refraction cloak if it looked like they were about to be scrutinized.

As Silky pulled the van around, Siv's spy-fly drones returned to their launch bays on his belt.

They climbed into the van, Siv taking the driver's seat and Wang the passenger side. Mitsuki hopped into the back.

"This is a lot better than calling a cab, I'll admit," Wang said. "But aren't you worried they'll trace the van?"

"We scrubbed its transponder and registration while you were getting your stuff together," Siv said. "It's clean enough to get us where we need to go. They won't be able to trace it for several hours, and by that time we'll be gone."

Assuming they maintained a moderate speed that wouldn't draw attention, they should reach the Teloso starport in half an hour.

Siv hadn't expected any problems along the way, but they didn't even get two blocks before a flashing red circle with an X inside it popped up in his HUD.

Siv had never even seen that warning symbol before. Silky apparently had, because he freaked out.

"No, no, no, no!"

A series of symbols and scrolls of data swept through Siv's HUD so fast he couldn't decipher it all. *"Silkster, calm down and tell me what's happening!"*

"An Infiltrator class starship just dropped out of orbit, sir! A freaking Infiltrator V7! And it's speeding straight toward us at Mach five."

An Infiltrator V7? Siv had no idea what that was. He started to ask, but then another warning flashed. This one he recognized.

"It's got a target lock on us, sir."

"Jam it!" Siv urged.

The target lock remained.

"I'm doing everything I can, sir. But I can't break the target lock." Silky's voice grew oddly soft and despondent. "It's happening again. I can't believe it's happening again."

"What's happening again?"

"Missile launched, sir. A Tober Pinpoint. High velocity, low yield, extremely accurate. Time to impact, fourteen seconds."

37

KARSON BISHOP

A thunderous boom rocked the ship. Karson snatched up the starkat and retreated to the corner. He knocked the top crate off the stack and cowered in the gap between.

The starkat buried its head into the crook of his arm as metal tore, alarms blared, and a series of small explosions popped off. Tremors vibrated through the floor, and high-pitched grating and scraping noises surrounded them.

The artificial gravity vanished suddenly. Karson, the starkat, the crates, and all the containers on the shelves floated freely within the vault.

He cradled the starkat to make sure it wouldn't bump into anything and get hurt. The creature glanced at the body of the woman and her blood, rising from the floor in a spread of droplets, then tucked its head back into Karson's arm.

Kicking off a wall, he got his feet onto the floor and activated the maglock on his boots.

"What's happening, Barty?"

"The ship's breaking apart, sir."

Karson's breath caught. His heart hammered. *"The fusion reactor?"*

"The shell missed the engines, sir. It struck the upper half of this vessel, halfway between your position and the cargo bay. The fusion core is still leaking, but the containment field is holding. There's no risk of an explosion."

"Octavian?"

"I can't pinpoint him, sir. All the minor explosions, electrical flares, and sonic disturbances are wreaking havoc on my sensors. And the ship's computers are now inoperable."

There came a clunking, thumping sound.

And then silence.

"Sir, we are drifting free amidst the wreckage."

Something thumped the wall.

"Was that some of the debris?"

"It was, sir."

Karson averted his eyes from the floating body and focused on one of the larger stasis units drifting nearby. The starkat would be much safer in one of the containers, especially since the air in here was already thin. Luckily, the hermetically sealed room had prevented a decompression disaster.

He grabbed the unit. *"How long could the starkat breathe within this?"*

"I'd say half an hour, sir. Maybe less."

"And if its air started running low, I could freeze it, right?"

"The starkat would no doubt be well preserved, sir. And it should survive that process. Most creatures do. The container, however, is not rated to store a living specimen for longer than a year."

"As long as it lasts at least..." he checked the oxygen level of his spacesuit *"...four hours. Six counting the backup canister. Otherwise, the poor thing will be floating around without me."*

Karson let go of Peachy so that he could grab the container. As the starkat began to float away, it whipped out its tail and wrapped it three times around Karson's wrist. Peachy then used his tail to pull himself back to Karson's body.

The starkat mewed at him pitifully. Its large eyes and angular face showed a mixture of fear and grief. And he couldn't blame it. Starkats were highly intelligent, and they supposedly had empathic abilities. It no doubt had a good understanding of what was going on and the danger it was facing.

Karson opened the container and smiled at Peachy. "I need to put you in here."

It mewed questioningly.

"It's to keep you safe."

Peachy frowned and tucked his head into Karson's arm.

"I promise you'll be safe inside. I won't even seal the container until I have to." He moved his arm to make the cat look at the container. "And it's clear, see. You'll be able to observe everything going on around you."

The starkat trembled.

"I won't freeze you unless I have to. Come on now. Work with me. I promised I would save you, and that's exactly what I'll do."

Slowly, Peachy unwound his tail. Then he allowed Karson to place him inside the container.

"Thank you, Peachy."

He closed the lid but didn't activate the seal.

"Have you received any signals from the Outworld Ranger?*"*

"None, sir. Their comms array must be damaged. However, I just managed to link to the sensor array that was attached to this ship. It's still drawing power from an independent source. Thanks to it, I am getting some readings on the Outworld Ranger's *position and status."*

"That's fantastic. What about this ship's comms?"

"Only the sensors are still powered, sir."

"Oh well. So how are our friends faring?"

"Sir, the Outworld Ranger's *shields are down, the ion drive is offline, along with one set of maneuvering thrusters, and the ship has sustained light but substantial damage."*

Shit. They were done for. *"And the pirate ship?"*

"Also without shields and propulsion, sir. And its aft weapon system was destroyed. It's rotating to face the Outworld Ranger *so that it can use its forward-arc weapons, and the* Outworld Ranger's *plasma cannon is powering up."*

"Can they destroy it before it turns around?"

"I'm not sure, sir. It looks close."

"What about Octavian?"

"I just located him, sir. His signal is active. He's drifting safely amongst the wreckage."

"That's good news. The crewmen he was trying to save?"

"No life signs in the area, sir."

Bishop frowned. That was hardly surprising.

With one hand, Karson opened one of the plastic crates. Inside, he found two hazmat suits and two neural disruptors. He released the maglock and kicked off the floor then off the wall, propelling himself across the vault toward the other crate, blood splattering off his helmet. He took Peachy along with him.

He reached the second crate and opened it, finding an antigrav belt unit and a toolkit.

"Sir, the Outworld Ranger *just opened fire on the pirate ship, before it could return— On no! Brace yourself, sir!"*

Not again.

Karson strapped the antigrav belt around his waist and set it to max gravity. He then set the suit to max gravity as well. His feet hit the floor, and he again activated the maglock.

He hunkered down as far as he could while hugging Peachy's container to his chest.

"What happened?"

"The pirate ship's fusion reactor exploded, sir. Shockwave here in 4... 3...2...1."

38

KYRALLA VIM

The blast wave struck the *Outworld Ranger*. The shields failed, and the hull absorbed the impact. A boom echoed throughout the ship as it tumbled uncontrollably away from the planet, speeding them toward the World Bleeder ships.

The inertial dampeners failed to adequately compensate, and Kyralla blacked out. She woke, feeling as if she were hungover. The viewscreen was dark, and the room was dimly lit by the emergency lights.

"The viewscreen's dark. Did we...did we lose power?"

"No, madam. We turned off the viewscreen, figuring you'd prefer not to see the ship spinning out of control. That can be disorienting for humans."

"Feeling it is bad enough. What about the lights..."

"They haven't changed since we rerouted power to the shields, madam."

"Right. Of course." Kyralla grabbed her head and winced. *"Sorry, it's hard to focus."*

"I understand, madam."

She glanced over her shoulder. Oona had passed out. Kyralla started to rise, to go check on her, but a wave of dizziness struck as soon as she moved.

"I don't recommend getting up, madam. The thrusters haven't stabilized the ship yet. Once you're out of the chair, away from its albeit weak inertial field, you'll be on the ship's default artificial gravity, and you will likely black out again."

"We only have the use of one set of thrusters, right?"

"That's correct, madam."

She examined the system locator window in her HUD and noted the three red dots of the starfighters racing towards them. The big, red oval representing the World Bleeders destroyer loomed behind them.

"We have to get the ship under control, and soon. Those starfighters are closing on us."

"I don't think there's anything we can do but wait for the thrusters to stabilize the ship, madam. Artemisia and I have tried everything we could think of, but nothing has helped."

"And how long will the stabilization take?"

"You don't want to know, madam. You really don't want to know."

"So we're—"

The ion engines awoke with a thrum she could feel as well as hear. A smile spread across her face. She hadn't realized how much and how quickly she'd grown accustomed to that hum and vibration being present all the time.

"You got the engines on without rebooting them. Good work, Rosie!"

"We didn't do it, madam."

Kyralla looked across the bridge to see Tekeru Jones passed out as well. *"Then who did?"*

"Seneca, madam. Though he didn't tell us he was going to do it. He made his way into engineering, not without significant difficulty, I suspect, and initiated the reboot."

"I didn't know he could do that."

"He shouldn't have known how, madam. However—"

"Silky must have upgraded him as well."

"It appears so, madam. Seneca also performed an emergency override, reducing the reboot time from twenty-five minutes to fourteen minutes. That no doubt caused immense strain on the engines."

"It seems like we've already overtaxed the engines a lot." She sighed. *"And we'll probably have to do it again to escape this system."*

"The engines are going to need an expensive and time-consuming overhaul sooner rather than later, madam."

"Can we balance out the ship using the ion drive?"

"It's possible, madam. But it will require careful steering and bursts of thrust at precise intervals, all in concert with the thrusters."

"Can you work out a routine to guide the ship in doing so?"

"Artemisia and I will get right to work on it, madam."

As Kyralla waited for the controls for the engines to come online, Tekeru Jones woke, rubbed his temples, and then looked over at her.

"I'm living a nightmare."

"Oh, this is nothing," she told him. "It could get worse."

"Worse than losing the crew I served with for over a year? Some of those people were my friends."

"Fair enough," she replied. "We haven't had it that bad. Not yet anyway. But the Thousand Worlders and the Tekk Reapers are after us, so..."

His face blanched. "I don't think I want to stay with you for long."

"You're probably not going to have much of a choice for a while. We're wanted by pretty much every criminal guild out there as well as the Federal government, so we can't stop just anywhere to drop you off."

"I understand." He nodded toward Oona. "Word got out, huh?"

"Are you a believer?" she asked.

"I do not blindly believe in anything," he answered. "But your sister is obviously special."

"We're still figuring out what she can do and what made her who she is and why," Kyralla said. "Luckily, we've..." She stopped herself from mentioning the priestess. "We've discovered some new things about it all."

"I won't rat you out," Tekeru said. "Once you've dropped me off somewhere."

"I don't know you," she replied. "So I can't trust that you won't."

"You saved my life, Kyralla. I owe you."

"Our uncle, who sheltered and provided for us for years, betrayed us. So I'm not in a trusting state of mind these days."

He frowned. "That's terrible."

She gave him a kind smile in return. "It doesn't really matter. Everyone already knows about us, and we'll be staying on the move. I'm not sure there's anything you could tell that would make a difference anyway."

He half chuckled. "I don't even know what kind of ship I'm on. So I really wouldn't have a clue about what to tell someone."

He was still in shock. That much was obvious. At some point, the adrenaline would dissipate, and the loss of his friends and everything that had happened to him would crash in on him.

It was relatively calm now, so she should probably keep him distracted. If he started thinking about the last few hours, he might crack, and right now, they could use all the brainpower they could get.

"What sort of scientist are you?" she asked.

"He's a biologist," Oona moaned as she woke. "His specialty is..." She shrugged. "Sorry, I had it...for a moment...but now it's gone."

He stared at her, blinking with surprise. "How...how did you know that?"

"I'm a...hyperphasic messiah," Oona whispered hoarsely. "Though right now...I feel like...hyperphasic shit."

"Xenobiology," Tekeru Jones said with awe in his voice. "That's my specialty. I study lifeforms that evolved separately from Terra or were never affected by the Benevolence. My thesis focused on diverse planets with seemingly native species that I contend share evolutionary links and were spread amongst those worlds by the Ancients."

Kyralla and Oona exchanged a meaningful glance and smiled. This poor guy had no idea what was onboard the ship. Otherwise, he'd be shitting his pants.

"You know, you might actually like it here with us," Oona said.

"Running for my life with every major power in the galaxy chasing me?" he asked. "You think I'd enjoy that?"

"It's possible," Oona said.

"I really don't see how."

A series of dots lit up one at a time on the piloting console. They flashed twice, and then they all stayed on. Knowing exactly what it meant since she'd studied her station, Kyralla pumped a fist.

"Now we're in business."

"The ion drive control system is online," the ship confirmed.

She grabbed the control-stick and accelerator. *"Rosie, do you have that routine prepared?"*

"I've already uploaded it to the Outworld Ranger, *madam. We're ready to go."*

"Do I need to do anything? Aside from loaning brainpower to the operation?"

"It's a complex routine with many variables, madam. I think we worked it out perfectly, but we didn't have time to run as many simulations as we would like. So use your abilities and stand at the ready, just in case."

"To be helpful, I'm going to need to see outside the ship."

The viewscreen activated. The ringed planet popped up and disappeared, stars swept by, and then the planet sped across the screen again. Tekeru threw an arm up to hide the view.

Oona turned her head. "I think I'm going to be sick."

Kyralla's brain and stomach swirled, but then she recovered. She could do this. All she had to do was ignore the dizzying effect of what she saw and focus on what she felt in her gravity-controlled environment.

From that point on, she worked in concert with the ship. Her hands remained on the controls, but she simply allowed them to move freely under the ship's guidance. She calmed her mind and observed. Once, she thought maybe the routine was overcompensating, but she had no way of being sure and didn't want to accidentally make things worse.

Steadily, the ship leveled out as the ion engines fired in bursts with steering angled one way and then another. They also slowed down, since they were burning the engines to move them back toward the super-Earth and away from the starfighters.

At last, the planet appeared dead ahead, and the ship was level. She breathed a sigh of relief then kicked the accelerator forward.

"If you're planning on stopping to rescue Bishop, then you're overdoing it," Artemisia said aloud.

"We don't even know if he's alive," Kyralla said. "Not getting a signal of any kind from him is a bad sign."

"We have to try," Oona said. "And we need Octavian. Desperately."

"I know," Kyralla replied. "I'm just worried about those starfighters, and I don't know how we're going to escape them."

"Your friend and your cog risked themselves to save me," Tekeru Jones said. "I'd like to return the favor if possible."

"You know," Oona said, "I would rather die than—"

Kyralla held up a hand. "I know. And I agree this time. I'm just worried."

"We'll figure it out," Oona said.

"So," Tekeru said, "we need to travel at a speed that will allow us to adequately slow down while putting as much distance between us and those starfighters as possible."

"Rosie and I will help the ship with that calculation," Artemisia said. "The three of you need to get moving on those repairs. Otherwise, speed may not matter."

"What's our order of priority?" Tekeru asked.

Oona stood then cried out and fell to the floor. She curled up into a ball, crying. "All those people...dead. All because of us."

Kyralla rushed over and squatted beside her. "Hey, pull it together. We need you."

"What's wrong?" Tekeru asked.

Kyralla placed a hand on her shoulder. "Oona..."

"All those people...all those people..."

Tekeru stepped up beside them. "I don't understand. She was fine a few minutes ago."

Kyralla stood. "It's some sort of psychic backlash, I guess." She couldn't afford to take the time to comfort her sister. They had to get moving. "Do you know how to do repairs, Tekeru?"

"Ship repairs? No. But I do work with complicated scientific instruments, and sometimes I have to repair them in the field."

"In that case, you're our chief engineer for now."

"Swell."

"Madam, we need to know what model chippy he has."

Kyralla asked.

"It's a 5G-plus," he replied. "It was the best I could afford."

"His chippy won't have the data or programming for what we need, madam. And we don't have time for it to install new routines. It may not even have database access to this ship's schematics, and our connection to the galactic net is slow out here. So, given Oona's incapacity, I recommend we let Artemisia link to his chippy and use it as a terminal."

Kyralla frowned, knowing this was going to be a sensitive subject. People were protective and defensive about their chippies.

"Tekeru, could you give Oona's chippy, Artemisia, permission to ghost through your chippy, so she can show you how to properly do the repairs."

"I think mine could handle it if you sent over the data," he answered in an offended tone.

"I'm sure it could, but we don't have much time to waste. This will be much faster."

"Why?" he replied. "What model is yours?"

"An upgraded 8G."

"Oh. Okay, fine."

"Three ion missiles incoming," the ship announced. "One launched from each starfighter. ETA twenty-one minutes."

Kyralla heart skipped. This situation was getting worse and worse. She'd been right. They never should have come here.

"So the flak cannons first, huh?" Tekeru said.

She nodded. "Let's get to work."

39

SIV GENDIN

Siv had no clue what Silky meant when he said it was happening again, but he guessed it was something to do with Eyana Ora—or maybe his father. Regardless, they had a far more immediate problem.

"Low yield?" Mitsuki said. *"What does that mean?"*

"Just strong enough to destroy the van," Silky replied. "There's a fifty-three percent chance one of us will survive. A Tober is what you use when you don't have an ion missile, or if you need to take out a single enemy in a Centurion battlesuit or a fast skimmer bike."

Siv slammed the accelerator forward. *"Get me a safe route with a couple of turns in it. And keep us in the old warehouse district, away from innocents."*

"We're not going to be able to shake it, sir. Or trick it. That missile has advanced maneuvering capabilities and a 4G chippy installed to maintain the guidance system."

Siv slammed the right break, spinning the van around so he could head back into the district. *"Watch me try."*

"What the hell?!" Wang said. "We're supposed to be driving casual, so we won't attract attention."

"We've already attracted attention."

"Your kind or mine?" Wang said.

"Ours," Mitsuki answered.

Wang shook his head. "Looks like I'm doomed after all."

"Time to impact eight seconds, sir. Your turn lost us four seconds."

"You didn't give me a route!"

"This is a skimmer van, not a starship, sir. You can't shake this missile! It has advanced tracking and can turn on a rat's whisker. We're screwed."

Siv made a sharp left turn between two tall buildings, buying them a few more seconds as the missile was forced to work its way around to them.

"What's going on?!" Wang demanded.

"Someone launched a missile at us," Siv replied.

"'Nevolence!"

"We should ditch the van and go on foot," Mitsuki said.

"You should, but I can't," Silky said.

"What are you talking about?" Siv asked.

"The target lock isn't focused on the van," Silky said. *"It's on me."*

Shit. *"How's that even possible?"*

"No time to explain. Sir, you need to eject me, leave me in the van, then leap out to safety."

"Silkster, I can't do that."

"Put me in the glove box. I should be safe enough there. The missile won't take out the entire van. Six seconds to impact, sir."

Siv made a quick left turn, accelerated, then took a right. Dilapidated warehouses sped past. He hoped the missile wasn't capable of flying through one. Twice, he wove around other skimmers. Luckily, hardly anyone was around.

"Silky, I...I can't do that."

"Sir, you need to ditch me and the van now."

Siv banked another hard left. The van's engines screamed. It couldn't take much more of this. It wasn't built for anything more than making local deliveries.

"Sir, please. It's the only way."

Siv's breath caught, and his heart skipped a beat. He couldn't abandon the chippy. Silky was like a father to him. He was Siv's best friend. And without him, they would all be lost. There was no way in hell they could survive this mission without him.

Siv watched in terror as the blinking red arrow in his locator closed on their position.

"Buy me a few more seconds," Siv said. *"Do whatever you have to."*

"I can do an audio burst, sir, as soon as it's lined up on a direct course for

us. It will confuse the missile for a few moments. It won't stop it, though. Or the Infiltrator that's still closing in fast."

"Just do it when you can." Siv cut another hard turn. "Wang, reach under the dashboard. There's a tiny override switch. Flip it."

The missile rounded the corner, drawing a bead on them. As Wang fumbled for the switch, Silky unleashed an audio blast wave from the sensor array. The sound was a rumble so deep that it was barely audible. Siv's bones ached, and his insides quivered. Wang leaned forward, threw his hands over his ears, and vomited. Mitsuki swayed side-to-side and nearly passed out.

"What—is—that?!" Wang yelled.

The audio pulse ended. The missile fell back and took a wrong turn, confused.

"The ploy worked, sir. Time to impact is now seventeen seconds. Whatever you're planning, you'd best do it quickly."

Siv breathed and nodded. "Mits, I'm taking us up. We'll jump out the back of the van on my mark. You take care of Wang."

"You got it."

"Wang! Flip the switch!"

Wang wiped his mouth off, reached under the dashboard, and flipped the switch. A readout notified Siv that the altitude restriction for the van had been deactivated.

He turned the van into the alleyway beside Wang's warehouse, removing the force-shield from his arm as he drove.

"Nine seconds, sir."

Siv reached for the eject switch on the socket in his temple, his hand shaking. *"Silkster, be safe."*

"Sir, whoever fired that missile..."

"They're dangerous?"

"They know about me, sir. They know what I am, and they have incredibly advanced tech. You need to assume that they're the most dangerous thing you have ever encountered. Eject, sir! We're out of time."

Silky hit the eject switch, and Silky popped out of the socket into his hand. He had never removed Silky before, not even for a single second. Silky had been with him for every moment of his life since the day his father had given him the chippy. As his HUD went dark, a tear rolled down his cheek. He felt as if he were dying, as if the entire galaxy was collapsing in on him.

Lying in his hand, the chippy was so tiny. It seemed so...insignificant.

How could such a small thing contain everything that Silky was, everything that he meant to Siv, everything he had meant to his dad and Eyana?

"Siv, the missile's back on our tail," Mitsuki said.

He took a sharp right down a long, abandoned stretch of warehouses that bordered the city's slum district.

"Right," he said out loud. He *had* to say it out loud. "Mits, have B take control of the skimmer van and wait for my signal."

"You got it," Mitsuki said tenderly.

Before he could change his mind, before he panicked and decided to face the missile along with Silky, he placed him in the glove compartment. Then he shoved his force-shield inside as well.

He hit the manual activation switch on the shield then yanked his hand back before it extended. That was the best he could do to protect him.

For a moment, he expected Silky to comment on how clever his plan was, but he wasn't there.

He might never be there again.

"Wang, crawl into the back seat. Now!"

Wang unbuckled his seat belt and went into the back. Mitsuki had dropped the back seat into a reclining position and had their gear strapped to her back. She wrapped her arms around Wang, who clutched his duffle bag to his chest.

Siv pulled back on the steering wheel. The van's engines growled in agony as it climbed. He pressed a button, and the back doors sprang open. The ground was nearly three floors below.

"As soon as I'm clear, level out the van!" Siv called back.

"Hurry," Mitsuki replied. "The missile's almost on top of us."

With Wang secured in her clawed grip, Mitsuki leaped out the back, her antigrav activated. As soon as she was clear of the van, she spread her wings to glide down. Siv shoved his way between the front seats into the back and grabbed a headrest to hold onto as he fumbled for the manual controls for his antigrav belt, controls he never used. Silky always took care of that.

Siv found the button and turned his antigrav on, setting it to what he guessed was seventy-five percent. He then glanced back toward the glove compartment.

"Be safe, old friend."

Siv jumped. As he dropped, the missile flashed by above him. The Tober Pinpoint was small, no larger than a heavy plasma pistol.

He boosted his antigrav all the way, and hit the ground, tucking into a shoulder roll to lessen the impact. When he came to a scraped and bruised stop on the street, he whipped around.

The missile struck the back of the skimmer van at an angle and exploded. Metal tore and twisted as the back third of the skimmer blew apart.

The van flipped over twice, skewing to the side, and struck the side of a building with a thunderous crunch. The front end crumpled.

Siv cried out. His force-shield could only protect Silky from the back.

The van hit the ground, belly up, and erupted in flames.

40

KARSON BISHOP

Karson woke with a pounding headache. Crates and storage containers floated haphazardly around him. They must have lost the ship's artificial gravity. Luckily, the magnets in his boots kept him locked to the floor, or what had been the floor anyway.

"Oxygen...in vault?"

"Enough to breathe, sir."

He retracted the helmet of his spacesuit and threw up. Instantly, he regretted it. Large glops of vomit drifted around him.

"Are we spinning?"

"We are, sir. We crashed into a large chunk of debris."

Bartimaeus placed a flashing marker in the HUD, bringing Karson's attention to the wall to his right. As soon as he saw the massive indentation, he flinched. *"Damn! We're lucky that didn't break through."*

"We are lucky, sir, that this vault was made to survive a crash-landing. And that the collision dramatically altered our course. We're still heading toward the planet below, but at our current angle, we will not crash into the rings for another three hours. That's much longer than the roughly half an hour I estimated before."

Karson wiped his mouth with the back of his right hand then replaced the helmet. *"How long was I out?"*

"Ten minutes, sir."

Karson checked the starkat in the container, which he was still holding onto with his left hand. It mewed at him weakly. Apparently, he wasn't the only one who had gotten sick after the blast wave struck the vault.

"How did I manage to hold onto the container while unconscious?"

"I took over the suit, sir, and activated the grip motors in the left glove."

"There are grip motors?"

"Indeed, sir."

"The Outworld Ranger*...did it survive the blast?"*

"I have no idea, sir. I can no longer connect to the sensor array."

He turned off one of the antigrav belts and breathed a sigh of relief to have that weight removed. He carefully turned down the other belt, adjusting to the sensation as he went.

He scanned his surroundings and regretted it. The vault was a horror show of floating blood and vomit and a now even more battered corpse.

He began to consider how to escape the vault. The door didn't appear to have suffered any damage, but it was locked shut without any power flowing to it.

Turning down the maglock so that he could take slow, plodding steps, he moved over to the terminal station. He swiped a hand across the screen. It turned on. Smiling, he swiped again to shut it off.

He knelt, removed a panel from the base, and dug around inside until he found the tiny power pack. All ship terminals had these backup power systems. Researching starship schematics the last few days aboard the *Outworld Ranger* was paying off.

"Sir! I'm getting a ping from the Outworld Ranger*!"*

"Patch them through!"

"You are now connected to their comm system, sir."

"Bishop?" Oona said. "Can you hear us?"

A tear of relief rolled down his cheek. "I can!"

"Thank the Source," she replied.

"Are you okay?"

"We are fine," Kyralla said, "but the ship's banged up pretty bad, our shields are low, and we have three World Bleeders starfighters closing on us, with their destroyer command ship following behind them."

"Sorry we couldn't communicate with you earlier," Tekeru said. "We didn't realize the comms array had suffered damage, and the sensor array was out of alignment."

"Kyralla, I'm sorry I didn't come back immediately," he said earnestly. "You were right. It was too risky to stay. And we weren't able to save anyone except Tekeru anyway."

"What's done is done," Oona replied, but Kyralla made no comment.

"So...I'm spinning in a secure vault, and Octavian was drifting in space last I knew."

"We've located him," Tekeru said. "He's unharmed. We're beaming you all our scan data. You should get it any moment now."

In his HUD appeared data on the ship and a locator map showing Octavian, the *Outworld Ranger*, the starfighters, the destroyer, and the larger chunks of debris.

"We're trying to figure out the correct speed and vector to retrieve you and get moving again," Kyralla said. "We won't have long to—"

"Ion missiles in range," the ship said.

"Evasive maneuvers engaged," Kyralla replied.

"Flak cannon activated," Tekeru said.

The missiles popped up in Karson's locator. He watched Kyralla weave the *Outworld Ranger* to slow them down. The flak cannon caught the first then the second. She pulled the ship into a steep incline then turned to narrowly avoid the third. As it came back around, the cannons nailed it.

"Good work!" he told her.

"Except the evasive maneuvers slowed us down," she replied.

"Try to be positive," Oona said.

"Damn," Tekeru said. "The flak cannon just went back offline. I'll see what I can do with it."

"While you're back there, see if you can get the railguns going," Kyralla called out. "Bishop... Honestly, I don't know what to do. Once we slow down to retrieve you, those starfighters will overtake us. If we can't maneuver, we're dead."

"The destroyer appears slow," Karson said. "You could take out the three starfighters and then come back for Octavian and me."

"With the ship in this state, I don't think I can beat them," Kyralla said. "I'm not a trained pilot, and these starfighters are better than the ones we faced before. My best chance is to try to outrun them and...I'm not sure that will be enough."

"I would caution against underestimating the destroyer's speed," Rosie said. "It's still accelerating. If you engage the starfighters, it will likely catch up."

"And you won't defeat the destroyer," Artemisia added. "It has three laser batteries, four-quad plasma cannons with three-sixty rotation, six railguns, and four missile bays."

"See," Kyralla said. "We're kind of screwed."

"Give me a moment to think," Karson said.

"I can't give you many."

He studied the locator and had Bartimaeus bring up vector and speed calculations. A broad smile spread across his face as an idea came to him.

"I think Siv and Mitsuki are bad influences," he told them.

"Why do you say that?" Oona asked.

"Because my plans are getting increasingly risky and insane."

"A crazy plan is probably what we need right now," Oona said.

Karson plodded across the vault to the door. He knelt and placed the containment unit between his knees to keep it from floating away. Then he removed the panel underneath the keypad, searching for the wires he needed.

"So, what's the plan?" Kyralla asked.

"I'm going to get out of this vault and use the jets in my spacesuit to position myself on a path that will allow you to scoop up Octavian and me without having to slow down as much as a normal rescue recovery would require."

"What do you mean when you say scoop?" Kyralla asked.

Karson found the bundle of wires he needed and pulled them out while shoving the others back in.

"Just before you reach me, you're going to use the maneuvering thrusters to rotate the ship so that you're flying backward. With the boarding ramp retracted and the door open, I'll simply crash into the loading bay. You'll need to have the artificial gravity tuned properly and the inertial dampeners maxed out, of course."

"That sounds utterly insane," Oona said.

"Do you have a better idea?" he asked.

No one replied to that.

"What about Octavian?" Oona asked.

"I should be able to position myself so that you can do the same thing for him without having to turn too much."

"Are you sure this is possible?" Tekeru Jones asked.

"I'm calculating the trajectories," Rosie said. "And...I do not believe it is possible to get them both without a major course correction and reduction of speed that would allow the starfighters to easily overtake us."

Confused, Karson asked what the problem was.

"Mr. Bishop, your spacesuit does not have enough propellant for what you're planning."

"Then we may have to leave Octavian behind," Kyralla said.

"We are not leaving him behind," Oona said. "I don't care if he's just a machine. He saved my life, and we need him on this ship desperately."

Karson began stripping the wires he needed. "I have a fire extinguisher that I can use to propel myself."

"In that case..." Rosie said. "I do believe it is possible."

"Great!" Oona exclaimed.

"There is one problem, however," Artemisia said. "I have been running some calculations, and I do not see how Mr. Bishop can survive the impact in the loading bay. Unless we reduce our speed such that—"

"The starfighters will overtake us," Kyralla said.

"At least we would be moving," Oona said. "That's better than sitting still while we recover him."

"I won't survive the impact even with the inertial dampeners maxed?" Karson asked.

"You would need to be moving in the same direction as us and at considerable speed," Artemisia said. "Otherwise, the dampeners are just not enough."

"What if we overpowered the inertial dampeners?" Oona asked.

"My calculations assumed that we would, madam," Artemisia said.

"No, I mean what if *I* overpowered the inertial dampeners?" she replied.

"Oh," Artemisia replied. "I suppose it's possible, madam. But you would have to power them up to at least five times their normal capacity."

"I did better than that with the plasma snubbie," she replied.

"Oona, your powers are unreliable," Kyralla said. "If you failed, Bishop would likely die. And even if you succeed, your powers might have unintended consequences. You could overpower the engines or fry the ship's electrical systems or cause any number of unpredictable things to happen. You could kill us all."

"Do you have another way of beating those starfighters and saving Bishop?" Oona asked.

Kyralla sighed.

"Either we leave him behind or we take this chance," Oona said.

Kyralla didn't respond.

"Don't look at me," Tekeru Jones said. "I'm only here because you risked your lives to save me. And you wouldn't be in this position otherwise. So do whatever you think is best."

"I think you should let Oona make the attempt," Karson said. "But I'm not on the ship, so it's your call whether to take the risk."

"We're going to save you," Oona said. "Period."

"You'd be putting your life in her hands, Bishop," Kyralla said. "And you can't be certain it will work. Her powers are far from reliable."

"I believe in Oona," he told her. "She can do it. Besides, if you don't pick me up, I'm dead anyway, either at the hands of the World Bleeders or by running out of oxygen. It's not like we have many choices."

Karson connected the wires to the tiny power pack. He did believe in Oona. She was the hyperphasic messiah. She would restore the Benevolence and save the galaxy. She could do this.

The keypad lit up. The door and its control system were powered now. Maybe only enough to open once, but that was all he needed.

He looked at the tangle of wires and considered how lucky it was he'd learned enough to do this.

"Kyralla, don't even think about shaving off a minute by not picking up Octavian. We can't survive without him. With all the damage the ship has taken and with more possibly to come because of the starfighters, I'm convinced he's essential to our survival."

"We will get him if at all possible," Kyralla replied.

Karson double-checked his spacesuit, knowing that he would be going out into deep space with no atmosphere whatsoever to protect him.

"All systems normal, sir."

Now he had to make sure his new little friend was secure. He smiled at the starkat, and it gazed at him with large, frightened eyes. He sealed the container then anchored it to his suit using a tether with a maglock on the end. A light flashed on the lid, showing him it was airtight.

"To enable the freezing process, sir, all you have to do is press the green button on the side three times."

"Don't worry, Peachy. We're about to go to my ship. You'll like it there."

Karson checked the level of the fire extinguisher. Sixty-two percent of its charge remained. Had he mentioned that to the others? Surely, Bartimaeus had relayed the information to Artemisia and Rosie so they could use it in their calculations.

He started to ask them if they knew about its level but then changed his mind. Either it would be enough, or it wouldn't. There was no point worrying about it. He would do his best to get into position, and then he'd trust in Oona to save him.

"Barty, which do you think I should use first? My jets or the extinguisher?"

"That is an easy answer, sir. Use the fire extinguisher first. Use your jets last so that you can fine-tune your exact position."

"I can adjust my position by how I aim the nozzle on the extinguisher?"

"Of course, you can, sir. However, your hand positioning will be less than precise, especially if you're nervous. However, I can run the jets on your suit, and I do not get nervous."

"Good point."

Karson took a deep breath and prepared himself. Jumping into space wasn't going to be easy. And it wasn't because he'd never done it before. It was the finality of it. Either it worked or...or it didn't.

He wanted to go over every detail of the plan two or three, maybe ten times. But he couldn't put it off any longer. It was time to commit. Every moment he wasted would make it harder to line up with Octavian correctly.

He picked up the fire extinguisher, took another breath, and then triggered the door.

As the air rushed out of the vault, the maglock boots rooted him in place. He bent his legs, preparing to kick off so he could start with as much momentum as possible. He ducked as the two crates flew out through the door above him.

"Sir, watch out!"

He squatted as far down as he could, but the corpse slammed into him and knocked him tumbling out of the vault.

Fearing that the spinning would make him throw up in his helmet, he clenched his eyes shut and focused on a still image in his mind: his old workbench littered with tools and gadgets.

"Turning on the spacesuit's jets, sir."

After a few bursts, Bartimaeus stabilized him.

"You can open your eyes now, sir."

"How much fuel did that waste?"

"We should still be fine, sir. You were heading the correct direction."

Taking up most of his view from this height, the barren super-Earth loomed below, encircled by its seven sparkling arcs. He was so close that he could easily pick out individual chunks of ice and rock amongst the nearest ring.

"It's so quiet and beautiful from here."

"I have oriented you so that your back's facing the direction you need to travel, sir. And now it's all on you."

He released the stasis container, and the tether held it securely. Peachy cowered in a corner, his head tucked into his body and his tail curled twice around him.

Karson secured the fire extinguisher with both hands. In his HUD there appeared a strange blue dot and a yellow triangle.

"What's this?"

"An aiming point and a targeting triangle, sir. The blue dot is mapped to your hands and the extinguisher. Line it up inside the triangle. You'll know for certain you're on target when the dot turns green."

Bishop triggered the extinguisher. He had thought it would be harder to control, but he was able to keep the dot lined up within the triangle without too much trouble.

After a minute of spraying out at full blast, the extinguisher ran out of propellant. As he released it into the void, he saw a tiny glimmer in the distance. Checking his locator, he confirmed it was the *Outworld Ranger* speeding toward him.

"How's our position?"

"It's not quite what we wanted, sir. You didn't get the push off we had planned, and the fire extinguisher didn't last as long as we needed it to."

"How bad is it?"

"The Outworld Ranger *will have to slow down by twenty percent. That's not good. But it could be a lot worse, though."*

He spun around to face the direction he was heading. Though he couldn't see him yet, he found Octavian in his locator.

Something several kilometers beyond Octavian's position glowed a faint blue. Karson marked it in his HUD.

"What's that?"

"That, sir, is the fusion reactor from the research vessel. It's still leaking. We are quite lucky the containment field held."

"We're lucky that railgun round didn't score a hit on it."

As Karson stared at the leaking fusion reactor, a thought came to him. It was the craziest thought he'd had on a day already full of them.

"Would it be possible for us to line up the Outworld Ranger *in a way that we could pick up that fusion core as well?"*

"Sir, why would you want a leaking fusion core?

"The correct question is why wouldn't I want one?"

"Sir, I am certain that's not the correct question."

Karson laughed. He could see the gleam in his eyes reflecting on the inside of his helmet. His face was contorted into the too clever smile all his school teachers had found irritating.

"Well, is it possible?"

The nearly always agreeable Bartimaeus sighed dramatically. *"It is, sir, but picking it up would slow the* Outworld Ranger *by nearly thirty percent."*

"Theoretically, is there a way to line up myself, the fusion core, and Octavian so the ship doesn't have to slow down?"

"I believe so, sir. But you don't have enough propellant in the spacesuit. And if you do pick it up, I'm not sure how long the containment field will hold."

"It doesn't have to hold for long."

"And you and Octavian would need to clear the loading bay immediately upon arriving."

Karson ripped the spare oxygen tank free from his spacesuit. *"I can expel oxygen from the container to propel me."*

"Is using your backup oxygen wise, sir?"

"It's do or die within the next few minutes out here. The four hours I currently have left are more than enough." Karson spun around again. *"I need guidance."*

"When this is all over, sir, I recommend therapy. You have some risk-taking issues that need to be resolved."

The blue dot and the yellow targeting triangle returned. Karson pointed the canister's intake away from his body and triggered the release. Oxygen poured from the cartridge, propelling him onto his new course.

41

MITSUKI REEL

Mitsuki stared in shock at the wreckage. A fire blazed amidst the torn remains of the back third of the skimmer van. Flames licked the ruptured propulsion engine. The antigrav coils underneath the upturned van sprayed plumes of coolant into the air.

Worst of all, the impact with the building had crushed the front end to half its original size, driving the antigrav motivator, steering system, and other electronics into the front passenger seat.

Silky was in there, and while Siv's shield might have protected him from the explosion in the rear compartment, it could not have protected him from the front-end collision.

He was tiny, a fragile electronic device far more significant than his size indicated. Mitsuki could only hope that his small size had worked to his advantage because Silky had to survive.

Without him, they were completely screwed. There was no doubt in her mind about that. Most importantly, he knew how the Benevolence had fallen and why. He knew so many secrets no one else in the galaxy knew.

Siv dropped the backpack from his shoulders and fell to his knees, stammering uncontrollably and shaking all over. Chippy panic had set in. Not to mention he was undoubtedly worried about his best friend.

Condrance Wang, with his pack still clutched to his chest, staggered forward helplessly. Despite being uninjured, he was clearly dazed.

"Madam, I'm becoming worried. I can't detect him."

"Silky?"

"Yes, madam. I'm not getting a signal from him. And my sensors can't pick him up, though there is a lot of wreckage and he is at the end of my range."

Mitsuki's heart sank. *"Keep...keep trying."*

"Yes, madam."

Siv stopped stammering and shot to his feet. As he ran for the burning wreck, Mitsuki grabbed him by the waist, pulling him back.

"Let me go!" He wrenched himself one way then another. "Mits, let go of me!"

"There's nothing you can do right now."

"I've got to rescue him!"

"You've got to let the fire burn out first. It's too dangerous. And the enemy is still—"

"Screw them! Screw everything!"

He broke free from her and ran, but he only got a few meters before he skidded to a halt.

An imposing figure in crimson Centurion battle armor zoomed over them, using a modified Fisk-300 jetpack, then descended on antigrav to land between Siv and the wrecked van.

The armored figure had two pistols drawn: a neural disruptor in his left hand and in his right a sniper pistol capable of firing nearly soundless guided rounds. He had a pair of plasma pistols attached to a bandolier, a compact assault rifle magnetically clamped to his right leg, and a lasgun clamped to the left. Mounted on top of his left shoulder was what she thought was a grenade launcher. She had never seen anyone so well armed, and to the point of excess.

His jetpack alone was worth a small fortune. Mitsuki knew this because it was a more advanced version of the modified one she had used until she'd lost it rescuing Siv and Bishop. His armor appeared more advanced than what the Thousand Worlders were using when they had faced them on Ekaran IV. She couldn't even begin to imagine how much his armor and weapons must have cost.

The black faceplate on the helmet obscured the person's face, and the armor bore no markings that she could see.

"B, can you identify our lovely new opponent?"

"Affiliation, identity, and origin currently unknown, madam. I will continue searching the net."

"Check all the bounty hunter sites you can access."

"Yes, madam."

Siv brought his plasma pistol up, backing away slowly. Mitsuki pulled out the plasma carbine.

"Who is that?" Condrance Wang asked, stepping up beside her. "What the hell's going on?"

"That's the person who—"

"Madam, I've detected a threat behind us."

A red blip appeared in the locator window in Mitsuki's HUD.

Before she could react, Mitsuki heard a whirring sound and felt a whoosh of air as something zoomed towards them. Wang's chest exploded as a fist-sized orb with blades spinning around its equator tore through him and flew upward. Wang fell to the ground dead.

Mitsuki opened fire on the orb, not even waiting for her targeting triangle to lock onto it. A moment later, Siv started shooting at it as well.

The orb zipped one way then another, as agile as a hummingbird. Not a single plasma bolt came close to striking it. It seemed as if it could anticipate their shots. As Mitsuki's target triangle finally got a lock on it, the orb disappeared.

She opened fire, but her plasma shots burned pointlessly through the sky. She couldn't see it anywhere, and the red dot representing it on her HUD had disappeared. Siv stopped firing and gaped at Wang's corpse.

"B, did it just cloak and signal-jam us?"

"Yes, madam. That is a sky-blade, a rare and powerful weapon used by the military before the Fall. A particularly advanced one since it has a refraction cloak. Do not underestimate it. A sky-blade is no mere machine. There is a chippy unit embedded inside it, quite possibly one more advanced than me."

Siv swung around to face the man, who was striding calmly toward them.

"Bastard!" Siv yelled. "You killed my best friend!"

He aimed his plasma pistol and opened fire, the gun pumping out shots as fast as it could. Their opponent stepped side-to-side, dodging some of the shots. As he moved, he deployed a force-shield from his forearm to deflect the rest.

Mitsuki trained her carbine on him, but before she could fire, the sky-blade suddenly reappeared to her right side. She darted backward, but it adjusted mid-charge. She cringed, expecting herself to become a shredded corpse before she could take another breath. But she wasn't the target.

The sky-blade buzz-sawed through her plasma rifle, cutting through it as if it were made of nothing more than wood and glue.

As it sped away, Siv stopped shooting. His gun had overheated and would not fire again until it cooled off. His last shot had knocked out their opponent's force-shield though.

Siv tossed the gun aside, drew his neural disruptor, and opened fire.

The man didn't even attempt to dodge the shots. He didn't need to.

The white rings of the neural blasts splatted harmlessly on a full-body force-field surrounding him. It would take dozens of neural shots to get through a field like that.

"Shit!" Mitsuki said.

"Madam, I've found a reference on an obscure bounty hunter site Silky gave me access to. A picture there shows a man wearing this armor without a helmet. If it's the same man, and I think it is based on his MO, then we are facing an android soldier that goes by the name Vega Kaleeb."

Mitsuki's eyes widened in shock for a third time within the last minute. She'd heard whispers about Vega Kaleeb. Anyone who worked in the upper echelons of the criminal world knew and feared that name.

When she was young and new to the extraction game, she'd trained with a few retired Shadowslip agents who talked about Kaleeb like he was a god of death. They'd told her never to attempt an extraction if he were even so much as rumored to be involved. She hadn't paid it much attention though. The galaxy was a big place, and she wasn't likely to ever face someone like him on backwater Ekaran IV.

They were in way over their heads. If she couldn't take out the combat drone, she had no chance of stopping Kaleeb. And even if they got through his force-field, they weren't getting through his armor too, not before he or his sky-blade took them out.

Siv continued firing pointlessly, his disruptor shots glancing off Kaleeb's force-field. When he was just a few meters away, Vega finally trained his guns on Siv.

42

OONA VIM

Despite being in a deep meditative state as she sat cross-legged in the command chair, Oona listened in on the others. The technique she was using allowed her to maintain complete awareness of her surroundings without breaking her focus.

"Mr. Bishop, you are changing course," Rosie said.

"I'm aware of that," he replied.

"How?" Artemisia asked.

"I'm using the oxygen from my suit's spare canister as propellant."

"A much better question is, why the hell are you doing it?" Kyralla demanded.

"I'm lining myself up so that after you scoop up Octavian and me, you can pick up the Argos Alpha's leaking fusion core? Do you see it on your locator?"

"We're very aware of it," Kyralla said. "We're trying to avoid it."

"We need that fusion core," Bishop said.

"Have you lost your damn mind?" Kyralla asked.

"Possibly."

"Possibly?" Kyralla snapped. "If that thing blows anywhere near us, we're dead."

"I understand that."

"If it's onboard and the containment field fails, the radiation will fry us all," Rosie added.

"I'm aware of the risks," Bishop replied. "But I believe that fusion core will give us our best chance of getting out of here alive."

"I understand now why Siv put his neck on the line to save you and vouched for you with the Shadowslip," Kyralla said. "You think like he does. Only you have a different skillset than him."

"Well, are you onboard with bringing it...onboard?" he asked.

Kyralla looked to Tekeru Jones. He started to nod, but then shrugged instead. When she turned to her, Oona didn't need to consider the issue. Bishop had placed his faith in her. She would do the same with him. To maintain her focus, she merely responded with a confident nod.

Kyralla sighed. "At this point, why the hell not? Go for it. What else do we have to lose but our lives?"

"Okay," Bishop said. "So the plan is—"

"I don't want to know until I have to," Kyralla said.

"Why?" Bishop asked.

"Because it will freak me out, and then I'll say, 'No, it's too risky.' But everyone else will outvote me. So the end result will be a lot of wasted time and energy."

Oona suppressed a snort of laughter that nearly shattered her concentration. She only barely managed to wipe the smile from her face before Kyralla flicked a glance in her direction.

"Is there anything you need us to do?" Tekeru Jones asked.

"I need Rosie and Artemisia to run some calculations for me. Bartimaeus will beam over the data. And, Tekeru, I need you to go to my makeshift workbench in the cargo bay. In a blue crate, you'll find three phantom emitters. I need you to grab the one with the orange sticker and load the preset routine called 'No, I'm the *Outworld Ranger*.' Do not activate it yet. Just load the routine."

"I don't know what a phantom emitter is," Tekeru replied.

"I'll send you all the info you need."

"Anything else?" Tekeru asked.

"Place the device in the emergency airlock above the engineering station, but don't space it."

"Mr. Bishop," Artemisia said. "This is an incredibly brilliant plan."

"Thank you," he responded brightly.

"But I do think there's a fifty percent chance it will end up killing us."

"I would say fifty-three percent," Rosie added.

Oona was tempted to ask Artemisia what the plan was, but she didn't want to break her focus. And if Oona couldn't bring in Bishop safely, then his daring plan wouldn't matter for squat.

Tekeru Jones rushed out to follow Bishop's instructions. He returned in a hurry and flopped back into the seat at the sensor station.

Several tense minutes passed without anyone speaking. Oona considered each breath and blocked every thought that tried to worm its way through her mind. Those that did make it through, she allowed to slip away without consideration.

"We're closing in on Bishop." Kyralla turned around in her chair. "Oona, are you ready?"

Oona nodded shakily.

"Are you certain?"

She inhaled deeply and steadied her nerves. She couldn't let her focus fail. A life depended on her. No, she couldn't think about that. It was too much pressure. All she could allow herself to think about was the inertial dampening system. She exhaled.

"I'm ready, Artemisia."

"Closing access to all other systems, madam."

One by one, Artemisia suspended Oona's access to the ship's systems through the circlet until all that remained was a connection to the inertial dampeners.

Initially, she had considered going to the engineering station and touching the manual control panel for the inertial dampeners. But the circlet actually gave her a much more direct link. And by closing off access to everything else, she shouldn't be able to affect any other systems by accident—in theory at least.

Using the circlet, she suspended inertial dampening in every section of the ship save the loading bay where Bishop would land, rerouting all the power there.

"Port thrusters activated," Kyralla said.

Oona rooted her thoughts in the ship's systems and focused on the inertial dampeners. She raised them to their normal maximum.

"Inertial dampening in the loading bay's now at five times normal," Tekeru Jones announced.

"We're lined up," Rosie said.

"Now's the time, madam."

Oona threw her psyche into the dampeners and willed them to power up. She used the same mental technique she had used when breaking the DNA lock on the snubbie.

She felt an immediate response.

It was working.

"Dampening to seven times normal," Tekeru Jones said. "Now eight times. Eight point two... Eight point three..."

"It's not enough," Rosie said.

"We'll reach him in less than a minute," Kyralla said. "We're going to have to change course."

"No!" Oona called out.

Not picking up Bishop now was as good as leaving him for dead. He believed in her. He always had. She could do this. His life depended on it. Focusing on his sweet, awkward, brilliant presence, she put everything she had into the dampeners.

Something within her psyche snapped, and she cried out. Her thoughts swirled. Her focus fractured. Her identity spread out, and despite their precautions, her consciousness invaded every one of the *Outworld Ranger's* systems.

She saw through every camera feed. She heard the heartbeat of the nearby universe through every sensor. The cold of space surrounded her, and cosmic rays glanced off her diamondine skin. The ship's thoughts were her thoughts, and she could almost touch Kyralla and Tekeru's minds through their circlets.

She and the ship had become one.

"Whoa, dampeners to twelve times max!" Tekeru Jones called out. "Thirteen...fifteen...seventeen... Leveling out at eighteen."

Oona didn't need to hear him say it. She knew everything the ship knew before he did.

Through the ship, she watched Bishop zooming toward them. And she wasn't afraid. He would be okay.

He passed through the plasma window and entered the loading bay. The dampeners slowed him, but he still crashed into the wall. He slumped down and lay stunned a moment.

But he was alive. The sensors said so.

"Get up, Bishop," she said through the ship's comm. "We're coming up on Octavian."

Slowly, Bishop got to his feet. She opened the door for him, and he stumbled into the corridor. He started to turn, to swipe the keypad, but she snapped the door shut.

With a painful groan, he collapsed next to the phantom emitter.

"I'm onboard and...alive..." Bishop said. "But I tore the suit...cracked three ribs, maybe four...broke my arm. Need to check...for internal...bleeding."

A few moments later, Octavian smacked into the wall in the loading bay. Oona felt the crunch as if he had impacted her own skin.

Limping and cradling one arm, Octavian scrambled inside. The ankle of the cog's injured leg bent awkwardly to the side, and the hand of the arm he cradled was smashed, bits of gears and wires poking out.

Octavian stopped to administer first aid to Bishop, who had retracted his helmet.

"Coming up on the fusion core," Tekeru Jones said.

"Bishop, this is the last chance to reconsider," Kyralla said. "Even with the dampeners tuned this high, it's going to hit hard."

"Can we beat those starfighters?" he asked.

"Honestly? No. Not with our shields this low and so many systems damaged."

"Are they going to catch up before we reach the breakpoint?"

"Yes."

"Then we need it."

Suddenly fearing the fusion core would explode in the loading bay, Oona fired the ion engines at full blast to slow their speed.

"Speed reduced by twenty percent," Rosie said.

"What the hell!" Kyralla pulled the accelerator back. "Ship, stop firing the engines."

"Attempting to," the ship's AI replied. "Sorry, I no longer have control over that system."

"How's that—" Kyralla turned and faced Oona. "You're doing this, aren't you?"

Oona didn't reply. She needed to focus. They would reach the fusion core in thirty seconds.

"Madam...madam, are you okay?"

She didn't respond to Artemisia either.

"Oona isn't communicating with me," Artemisia said aloud. "I'm not sure what's going on, but her brain activity resembles a festival of lights."

"Nearing the fusion core," Tekeru said. "Inertial dampening up to eighteen times normal."

The *Outworld Ranger* swallowed the core. It scraped the floor then banged into the wall.

The crack in its side widened, and the leak doubled. The containment field it projected flickered a moment but then held steady.

"We have twenty minutes at best before the core goes nova," Artemisia said.

Oona cut off the atmosphere supply to the loading bay and released the plasma window so that radiation could flow back out into space and wouldn't overwhelm the ship's filtration systems.

Kyralla fired the starboard thrusters to spin the ship back into the direction it was traveling.

"The starfighters are almost in weapons range," Tekeru Jones said.

Kyralla slammed the accelerator forward. "Maximizing ion engines. *If* that's okay with Oona."

She allowed the ship to accelerate.

"Fly into the...rings...for cover," Bishop said.

"I was planning on it," Kyralla said.

"We need to get to...the other side of the planet..." Bishop said "...so we can put it...between us and the destroyer."

"I'll do what I can," Kyralla replied, "but there's only so fast we can... Whoa. How are we going this fast? I didn't max the engines."

Oona realized that she'd maxed the engines by merely thinking how they needed to go as fast as possible to escape the bad guys.

"Oona, if you're doing that, I need you to stop," Kyralla said. "Fast is good, but I will need to slow down once we're weaving through the planet's rings."

She tried to slow the ship but couldn't.

"Oona?" Kyralla spun around. "Are you okay?"

"Her neural networks are lighting up even brighter now," Artemisia said. "Something's wrong."

"I'm losing conscious control of the ship," Oona responded.

"Oona...how are you talking through the comms without moving your mouth?" Kyralla asked.

"I didn't realize I was."

"You need to break the connection," Kyralla said.

Oona tried to separate herself from the ship, but she couldn't. "I...I'm bonded to the ship. My brain has replaced the ship's AI. I can see and hear everything the ship experiences. I feel what it feels."

"Tekeru, take the circlet off her!" Kyralla shouted.

He bounded over, and before Oona could tell him to stop, he lifted it off her head. She cried out in dismay.

The ship rocked as if struck by an object. The lights flickered. Alarms blared. Sparks shot from control panels on the bridge.

"What the hell's happening?" Bishop asked.

"Ship, status report!" Tekeru Jones requested.

As Octavian limped onto the bridge and headed toward Oona, the ship began its status report...

"Inertial dampeners in the loading bay are burned out. Offline in all other sectors. Shields up twenty percent. Quad plasma and flak cannons offline. Boarding ramp activators, railgun electrical systems, and the lights in the main corridor and cargo bay one are burned out. Reduced capacity in the temperature control and air ventilation systems."

Oona heard the ship's report, but she could no longer feel the damage. Her spirit, her identity, had separated from the *Outworld Ranger*. And suddenly, she couldn't even hear the others or see the bridge.

Her consciousness had failed to return to her body. Instead, her mind soared out into the depths of space toward a gleaming point over a thousand light years away.

43

MITSUKI REEL

Mitsuki ran forward and tackled Siv, taking him to the ground. Kaleeb's shot flared over their heads. As she climbed to her feet, Mitsuki grabbed the plasma pistol Siv had discarded. She reached around her back and tucked the gun into her belt. Then she grabbed her neural disruptor.

"B, initiate Protocol Disruption."

"Initiated, madam."

"It would be best to surrender," Vega Kaleeb said, his deep voice resonating through the sound emitter on his helmet.

The sky-blade uncloaked and hovered beside Kaleeb's right shoulder, spinning its blades to appear menacing.

But then it started bouncing in place as if agitated. Kaleeb kept the neural disruptor leveled at Siv, but he turned his head sharply toward Mitsuki.

"Madam, I think he's detected the overload you triggered on the disruptor."

"The question is, what's he going to do about it?"

Mitsuki and Kaleeb eyed each other. If her disrupter exploded now, it would kill them all. A little farther away from the blast, and they would be injured or knocked out by the neural pulse.

Taking advantage of the distraction, Siv lunged forward and punched Kaleeb, his force-knuckles crackling as they struck the bounty hunter's force-field. He followed with a quick left jab, sending more sparks flying. Kaleeb began to retreat, but not because he was reeling. His android strength was more than a match for Siv's field-deflected punches.

Suddenly, Siv spun and threw a haymaker at the sky-blade. The orb hadn't expected that. Siv's fist connected. The cog's force-field held, but the impact sent it spiraling backward.

Kaleeb looked from Mitsuki to the sky-blade tumbling through the air. He backed away. Siv started to follow, but Mitsuki grabbed him by the arm.

"Come on!"

She tossed the disruptor over Vega's head and dragged Siv toward the warehouse behind them.

"What the hell!" Siv shouted. "I had the bastard on the ropes! I could have—"

The engines of Kaleeb's backpack flared, and he zoomed away as Mitsuki's disruptor exploded. At the same time, she tossed Siv through the window of the nearby warehouse's front office, then crashed in after him. As soon as they struck the floor, she threw her wings out to cover them both and ducked her head.

White energy flared across the street and into the office, passing over their heads. The booming shockwave blew the remaining glass out of the window and onto them.

The wall below the window had effectively shielded them from the blast. Mitsuki got to her feet and helped Siv up. She checked herself over and discovered only one small cut on her cheek. Otherwise, she'd gotten through the encounter unscathed. Siv had some cuts on his face and hands, none of them severe.

He rushed toward the window, but Mitsuki jumped in the way. He tried to dart around her, so she spread her wings to block the opening.

"We can't take him," she said. "He's too heavily armored."

"Silky would know how," Siv muttered.

"Silky's gone."

Siv's face twisted in anger and grief. "You don't know that!"

"Nothing could have survived that crash, and you saw the blaze. B can't find his signal. I'm sorry, but he's gone."

"Then I'll kill the bastard that took him!"

Mitsuki rubbed her forehead. "Siv, that's Vega Kaleeb. We don't stand a chance against him."

"Ka–Kaleeb?" he nearly sobbed.

For a moment, she thought he was about to break down and start crying. He'd been struggling to hold it together ever since Zetta had tempted him with Kompel. But now he'd lost Silky. She wouldn't blame him one bit for falling apart, but now wasn't the time to do it. They had to survive first.

"Siv, he's still out there. We've got to escape...on our own."

"How?" he asked despondently.

"I don't know. Just run and hope for the best, I guess. He doesn't seem to want to kill us. We do have that in our advantage."

Siv didn't respond. But he didn't argue either or try to run out into the street when she closed her wings. When she headed deeper into the building, he followed.

"B, what's here?"

Mitsuki checked her locator. Vega had gotten high enough to avoid the explosion. Now he was rapidly closing on their position. The sky-blade, however, was nowhere to be seen, but they weren't lucky enough for it to have been taken out by the blast.

"Madam, this building housed a parts company specializing in plastic components for starships and skimmers. Some manufacturing occurred here, but most of the building was dedicated to storage and logistics."

"Is there anything here that can help us?"

"Not that I know of, madam. But it was only recently closed, so the power and emergency systems are still on."

"And that helps how?"

"Madam, I have no—"

Mitsuki spotted an elevator. *"Hold that thought."*

If the building had power, she could take the elevator. And if she could get to the top of the factory warehouse, she could glide away. With their anti-gravs maxed, she felt confident she could carry Siv along, especially since they didn't have any excess weight, having abandoned their packs and equipment on the street.

She led Siv into the elevator and pressed the button for the thirty-first floor. As they sped upward, Mitsuki sagged against the wall.

She realized suddenly what having to abandon their packs on the street meant. They had no hard credits now, no disguises, no contacts, and no safe way off the planet. So even if they escaped Kaleeb here, he'd quickly track them down again.

She put a hand on Siv's shoulder. He was shaking, his face a blank mask.

Poor Siv. He was in shock. Without Silky, he was broken. Maybe permanently.

She couldn't let him down—not now. This was just another extraction. And she was the best extraction agent in the game. So what if she was up against a legendary bounty hunter? That only made it a challenge, another chance to prove herself. And so what if the whole operation was up to her now? She'd always done fine on her own before. She could do this.

She squeezed Siv's shoulder. "I'll get us out of here, Sivvy. Extraction's my game."

He stared at her blankly for a few moments, then his glassy eyes fell toward the floor as he nodded.

"B, can we get to the rooftop?"

"Not easily, madam. The door is supposed to remain physically locked at all times, so unless we're lucky, that route is barred to us."

"Windows on the top floor?"

"There are some windows on the top five floors, madam."

The red dot on the locator closed in. With a thought, she rotated the image to get a three-dimensional representation. It was just as she had feared. Kaleeb wasn't landing on the street to come up through the building after them. He was using his jetpack to fly in and catch them from above. He would crash through a window on whatever floor she stopped on, and they'd be trapped.

"B, do you have any ideas?"

"About what, madam?"

"I don't know, some way to survive this."

"Sorry, madam. I'm not that creative."

Mitsuki chuckled. *"Okay, how about ideas for getting out of this elevator without Kaleeb immediately springing out on us."*

"Madam...I...I could tap into Siv's sensor array and try to replicate the signal of an overloaded plasma pistol. He would think you're trying the same trick again but with a bigger blast."

"You can do that?"

"Silky gave me access to the array before he...perished. And I copied the signal of the neural disruptor before it exploded. If we broadcast that, it might fool Vega Kaleeb."

Mitsuki nodded appreciatively. *"That should make him back off at the least. Do it."*

"Yes, madam."

Getting him to back off was a good start, but she still had no idea how to disable his jetpack so she could glide to safety.

"Wait, have you started the signal yet?"

"I was just about to, madam. Do you want me to wait or cancel it?"

"Put it on hold. I have an idea. Do you think you could mask an overloading plasma pistol instead of broadcasting a fake overload?"

"I could try, madam."

She drew Siv's plasma pistol from her belt. *"Okay then, wait for my signal."*

When they were two floors away from the top, she triggered the overload sequence. She smiled sadly. She would never have thought to do this except for Silky. He'd taught her the strategy years ago and had always customized every weapon she acquired, disabling the protections that would prevent a forced overload.

"Make sure Kaleeb sees it at the last moment. I need him to back away from the door, so I can hit him with the blast but not catch us as well."

"I don't think I can mask it once we're that close, madam. I can't run the calculations and change the variables as fast as Silky can...could, I mean."

Mitsuki turned to Siv. "Want to know the plan?"

He glanced at the pistol in her hand then stared at her as if she were asking a stupid question. "Do you want me to hit the button to close the door after you do your thing?"

Mitsuki marveled at him. He still looked blank and listless, so she hadn't thought he was paying attention. "How did you know—"

"How do you think? It's what...it's what he'd tell us to do. And it's the only play, isn't it?"

"The only one I can think of."

Kaleeb was waiting on the top floor, just a few meters from the elevator. When the doors opened, Mitsuki tossed the overloading plasma pistol into the room, aiming it at Kaleeb. As soon as he saw the weapon, he turned and fled. Siv pressed three buttons simultaneously, triggering the emergency closing function on the elevator doors. They closed, and she hit the button for the next floor down. She needed to preserve as much height as possible for gliding.

The building rocked, and the elevator bucked as the pistol exploded. An overloaded plasma pistol created a far more significant blast than a disruptor.

Mitsuki pinned Siv in one of the back corners and braced herself against the walls to keep them from getting tossed around. Based on the position of the red dot in her locator, Kaleeb was speeding away. She couldn't tell if it was under his own power, or if he'd gotten caught in the blast.

The elevator dinged, and she squeezed out through the warped doors as fast as possible. Siv followed blindly.

"B, bring up an escape path to an accessible or breakable window. I need to be able to fly down the length of a street, a straight shot to build up speed and get as far away as possible. If I have to turn, I'll lose speed and altitude fast."

"Here you go, madam."

A map appeared in her HUD, leading across this level of the warehouse to the opposite end of where she was now. Terrific, just terrific. She had to cross most of a city block to get to the best location for her attempted escape. This just couldn't get easier.

Siv dutifully following, she raced through narrow aisles that weaved between giant factory machines and storage tanks.

"What's in the tanks?"

"Those, madam, are filled with various organic and synthetic polymers, coolants, and propellants. Many of the substances are highly flammable."

"Then it's a damned good thing I didn't throw the plasma pistol in here. I could've blown up the entire building."

"I would have warned you, madam."

Ceiling tiles, knocked loose from the explosion, had fallen throughout this level, exposing the concrete above. One section of concrete was cracked and blackened where the blast had nearly punched through. They were lucky to be alive.

Mitsuki had almost reached their exit window when she heard weapons fire above.

The sky-blade crashed through the ceiling. Big chunks of concrete rained down around it.

Mitsuki sprinted for the window. The sky-blade zipped in front of her, blocking the way. She turned to run the other way and collided with Siv, nearly knocking them both down.

Kaleeb jumped down through the hole the sky-blade had made, landing in a perfect action pose, with his neural disruptor and sniper pistol aimed at her. His armor was scorched on one side, which could only mean one thing. The blast had knocked out his force-field.

Mitsuki drew her plasma pistol, the only weapon she and Siv had left between them, unless Siv still had his disruptor. Her plasma carbine was lying in the street where she had dropped it.

Vega Kaleeb shook his head. "I have grown tired of playing, Ms. Reel."

The sky-blade zoomed up to Siv, bringing its whirring blades near his throat.

"You, Ms. Reel, I need alive. Gendin..." he shrugged his shoulders. "I get the same amount for him if he's dead."

44

KYRALLA VIM

Every fiber of Kyralla's being wanted to rush to her sister's side. But she didn't. She stayed plugged into the piloting station and did her best to maintain her composure. Even as the ship rocked, the consoles sparked, and the alarms blared, she remained focused.

She had a job to do, and their lives depended on it. Besides, this wasn't the first time Oona had collapsed. It wasn't even the first time this week. And Octavian was already limping over to help her.

Everything would be okay.

Or it wouldn't.

Either way, the only thing she had control over right now was piloting the *Outworld Ranger* and keeping Oona away from the World Bleeders. That was her job. That was how she could be Oona's protector. She had to learn to stop panicking about Oona's messianic episodes. Doing so achieved nothing.

There was no point in second-guessing Oona's decision to enhance the ship's capabilities. Or even their decision to come here in the first place. Those were Oona's choices, and Oona was going to do what Oona thought was right. It was who she was, and truthfully, it was what Kyralla loved and admired most about her sister.

Besides, if any messiah was going to survive the Awakening, it was going to be Oona. Not because of the priestess but because Oona had such a kind soul, a soul that had to help others in any way that it could.

Kyralla pulled back on the accelerator. This time the *Outworld Ranger* responded, and the ion engines throttled down. She didn't fire the thrusters to reduce their speed, though. If she were careful, they'd have a few more minutes before they'd have to slow down for maneuvering through the rings, and she needed to maintain as much distance as possible between them and the faster starfighters.

Octavian bleeped and trilled as he scanned Oona. Rosie translated.

"Physically, Oona shows no signs of injury or illness. Her neural networks, however, are firing at unprecedented levels. Giving her Awake or Calm could make things worse, so I recommend waiting and keeping an eye on her."

"I understand. Just focus on repairing the ship then."

Octavian gave an affirmative bloop and hurried off the bridge, metal feet clicking as he scurried toward engineering.

Bishop nearly crashed into Octavian on his way onto the bridge. He stumbled out of the cog's path and cried out as the movement jarred his injured arm. Octavian beeped in apology and trundled past.

Bishop grimaced as he clutched his shoulder. "I should try to help Octavian."

"Stay here," Kyralla replied. "Tekeru, you go help Octavian."

Tekeru rushed off the bridge. "I'll do what I can."

"Shouldn't I be the one going?" Bishop asked. "I know I'm kind of beat up right now but—"

"You have three broken ribs, a fractured humerus, and a mild concussion, and you are only this active because of the stimulants and pain relievers Octavian gave you," Bartimaeus said aloud over the ship's comm. "You will be of little help to Octavian."

"And I need more brainpower here on the bridge," Kyralla said. "I can't be the only one up here if the starfighters catch up to us. Besides, if your crazy plan goes sideways, you'll need to think of a fix."

Seneca sped onto the bridge, lifted Oona from the command chair, and placed her onto the antigrav sled. Rosie told them Seneca was taking her to the captain's quarters and would stay with her.

Bishop dropped into the command chair with a grunt and placed the circlet on his head. "If this plan goes sideways, we're dead."

"Comforting," Kyralla responded. "Are we certain there's not a better plan?"

"We're not going to outrace those starfighters to the breakpoint," Rosie said. "And if we fight them, the destroyer will catch up. I believe Mr. Bishop's insane yet brilliant plan is our best shot."

"I concur," Artemisia added. "I can't wait to tell Silky all about it. Assuming we don't all die a horrible death."

Kyralla rolled her eyes. "Well, here goes nothing then."

The *Outworld Ranger* shot past the planet's glistening rings on an orbit that would take them up and over the super-Earth's northern pole.

The starfighters followed, steadily gaining on them.

"The starfighters will be in reliable targeting range in three minutes," the ship's AI announced. "The destroyer will be in missile range in seven minutes, thirty-four seconds."

As they arced over the north pole, Kyralla adjusted their orbit to place them on a crash course with the rings on the planet's opposite side from where they had been. Then she zoomed in her view of the rings, trying to find the best route to take.

The rocks, dust, and ice crystals that formed the world's distinct rings were too densely packed for her to weave directly through one. She'd have to squeeze through one of the gaps between the seven rings.

Seven...

Kyralla focused her HUD view on the central ring, which was by far the broadest. She marked a spot and relayed it to the viewscreen on the bridge. "Is it just me, or are there eight rings? Because I'm seeing a tiny gap there."

"It's not large enough for that ring to be properly considered two separate ones," Artemisia answered.

"Could I fly through it?" Kyralla asked.

"With care, yes," Rosie answered. "But only just. It's much narrower than you realize. And a few rocks, as well as dust and ice particles, bridge the gap."

"I'm not sure it's worth the risk," Artemisia said. "Flying through one of the proper gaps would be much safer."

"Safer maybe," Bishop replied. "But given how large that central ring is, they'll have to follow us through or lose ground."

"But we need to drop the fusion core behind us," Artemisia. "If they choose to lose the ground they've gained by not following, then—"

"They'll follow," Kyralla said. "I feel certain of that."

"Besides, the explosion should catch them either way, directly or indirectly, by kicking ring debris everywhere," Bishop said.

Kyralla smirked. The explosion was likely going to catch them as well. "Then I say we risk it."

"We'll line up the safest course possible," Artemisia said with a sigh.

"Fusion core containment field failure imminent," the ship's AI announced.

"Exactly how long do we have?" Kyralla asked.

"Five to six minutes," Artemisia replied.

"And how soon will we reach the gap we're aiming for?" Bishop asked.

"Six minutes," Artemisia said.

"Well, that's great," Kyralla replied.

She studied the flight course Artemisia had loaded into the ship's system. It required a twenty-eight percent reduction in speed and the use of thrusters to be sure they cleared a few large chunks of rock and ice.

"What if I don't slow down?" Kyralla asked. "What if I plunge straight through with only minimal maneuvering?"

"That would get you through the gap in four minutes," Rosie answered. "But I have to warn you that from this range our sensors are limited. They're not calibrated to scan for small debris, and due to damage, they're not operating at peak efficiency."

"I don't think we have a choice," Kyralla responded.

"We could slow down enough to get us through in four and a half minutes," Bishop suggested. "That should be somewhat safer."

"I'd like to put as much distance between us and that fusion core as possible once we dump it," Kyralla said. "Smacking into a rock is a risk I'm more willing to take."

Artemisia loaded a new routine, and under the AI's control, the thrusters adjusted the angle of their approach.

"Shields focused rearward," Bishop said.

Kyralla centered her mind. The enemy was nearly in range to open fire, and she needed to be prepared to see into the future and alter their course as they flew through the gap.

Two of the starfighters opened fire. Refusing the ship's desire to perform an evasive maneuver, Kyralla slammed the control-stick hard right and sent the ship into a roll. Two white bolts of plasma streaked by. Two others struck them.

"Shields down to thirty-four percent," Rosie said.

"I've pressurized the loading bay and turned off the artificial gravity and inertial dampeners there," Bishop said. "We can expel the fusion core when ready."

As the ship neared the gap, all three starfighters opened fire. Failing to evade properly since she was trying to conserve their speed, four plasma cannon shots struck them.

"Shields down to eighteen percent," Rosie said.

"The fusion core's containment field is failing," Artemisia said. "We need to dump it now."

"We're almost there," Kyralla said, shoving the accelerator forward. "We can make it."

"Flak cannon and railguns now online," the ship's AI announced. "Power relays repaired."

They didn't need those weapons right now, but they could certainly use their power.

"Rerouting all weapon system power to the shields," Bishop said. "Shields up to twenty-six percent."

Tekeru Jones rushed onto the bridge and dived into the sensor station. He placed the circlet on his head. "Octavian said my brainpower would be more useful than my hands."

Octavian was correct. A dozen small ring fragments immediately popped up in Kyralla's locator.

Along with Rosie, Artemisia, and the ship's AI, she tried to find a way to thread through the gap without hitting anything. But there was no way for a ship of the *Outworld Ranger's* size to entirely avoid all the fragments.

"We're going to have to shift the shields forward before going through," Rosie said.

"We can't expose ourselves to those plasma cannons," Bishop responded. "Can't the hull withstand a little debris?"

"At our current speed, even some of the smallest fragments could cause significant damage," Rosie replied.

"Maintain aft shields," Kyralla said. "I've got this. Bishop, stay focused."

The starfighters opened fire again. She saw the plasma bolts a moment early and rolled the ship while jerking upward then back down on the control stick. They lost some speed, but it was worth it. She dodged three of six fiery bolts completely. One struck a glancing blow on the shields, and two landed solidly.

"Shields down to eleven percent," Rosie said.

A meter in Kyralla's HUD showed that the starfighters would be able to fire again just before they reach the gap. Because she needed to keep the ship lined up accurately, she wouldn't be able to do any evasive maneuvers, not even a well-timed roll. They'd have to take the shots and hope for the best.

She said a quick prayer to the Source of the Benevolence...for all the good that might do.

"Bishop, are you ready?"

"I am."

"If this doesn't work..."

"We've done our best." He shrugged. "That's all we can do."

"I guess so." Kyralla refocused on her station. Her knees shook with fear, but her hands stayed steady.

The starfighters opened fire in sequence. Two plasma bolts scored direct hits.

"Shields to five percent," Rosie said.

Two more struck.

"Shields down."

The last two blasted against the hull, rocking the ship. Kyralla struggled with the control-stick and only barely managed to maintain their course.

"Direct hit," the ship's AI called out. "Cargo bay one breached. Plasma containment field holding. Minimal internal damage. Life-support in both cargo bays now offline."

Kyralla breathed a sigh of relief that the World Bleeders hadn't struck the loading bay and detonated the fusion drive. Knowing the starfighters would be erased along with them was not particularly satisfying.

As they neared the narrow gap through the central ring, it loomed in her HUD. The path they'd chosen was blocked by three larger fragments. It would be up to her to pilot them through.

"Now, Mr. Bishop," Artemisia said.

Bishop ejected the fusion drive from the back of the *Outworld Ranger*.

"Bombs away!"

Kyralla maxed out the engines and plunged the *Outworld Ranger* through the gap. Working in conjunction with the AI, she made a half roll and a slight pitch to avoid the first large fragment.

She pulled up and banked the ship around the second, but only narrowly. She then cut the control-stick hard right and down to duck past the third. She wasn't quick enough. The bottom portion of the rock scraped across the top of the ship.

"Quad plasma damaged and offline," the ship's AI announced. "Sensor array damaged. Status unknown."

The impact knocked them slightly off-course. She corrected as quickly as possible, but several tiny fragments pelted the ship.

"Flak cannon damaged and offline. Hull integrity weakened in all forward sections."

As the *Outworld Ranger* sped out the other side of the rings, Kyralla took a deep breath. The starfighters slowed before reaching the gap. Then, presumably having spotted the fusion core, they took immediate evasive maneuvers.

"Containment field down," Artemisia said.

A bright explosion blossomed behind them.

"All power to shields!" Bishop said.

As planned, every system on the ship went dark except for life support. Even the ion engines shut down, despite their need to accelerate out of the planet's gravity well. They would ride the shockwave to freedom. Or die.

"Shields restored, at thirteen percent," the ship's AI said.

That was two percent better than they'd hoped.

"Launching phantom emitter," Bishop said. "Our transponder is off, and the signal from the emitter is now active."

The shockwave struck them.

"Shields to zero," Rosie said.

Once again, the *Outworld Ranger* bucked, groaned, and tumbled. Kyralla blacked out as the ship's AI began its damage report.

When Kyralla woke, Octavian was stepping away from her, an injector in one of his hands.

"You just received a dose of Awake, madam."

She glanced around, groggy, her head spinning. The ship's bridge appeared undamaged. Octavian was heading toward Tekeru Jones, who was slumped over the sensor console.

"We're alive. And on course. I can't believe it."

"Artemisia and I managed to stabilize the ship and fire the ion engines. We're nearing the breakpoint."

"The destroyer?"

"Mr. Bishop's scheme worked brilliantly, madam. The combination of the phantom emitter's signal, our powering down, and the scattering of ring debris confused them. They slowed to avoid the shockwave and debris, adjusted their course toward the emitter, and then readjusted when they realized their mistake."

Kyralla finally managed to focus on the locator in her HUD. Six ion missiles zoomed toward them. *"The missiles..."*

"Will never reach us in time, madam."

Kyralla looked over her shoulder, fought back a wave of nausea, and smiled at Bishop, who was still sitting in the command chair. "Your crazy scheme pulled us through."

"Barely," he replied weakly. "Have you seen the damage report yet?"

"No."

"I don't recommend looking at it unless you want to be depressed. The ship's in rough shape."

"Silky's going to be pissed," Rosie said aloud.

"Oona!" Kyralla said, attempting to stand. "She wasn't in a station chair when the shockwave struck! She—"

"She's fine," Artemisia said. "Seneca strapped her to the bed for safety before leaving the room and stationing himself in the galley."

Kyralla sighed with relief and dropped back into her seat. "Her status?"

"Unchanged," Artemisia answered. "Coming up on the breakpoint now."

Kyralla stood and limped toward the command chair. She patted Bishop on the shoulder then gave him a kiss on the cheek. "Get us out of here."

45

OONA VIM

A white light burned in the distance. It was something more than a star. It was almost alive. Oona flew toward it faster than light, faster even than the swiftest ship traveling through hyperspace.

As she got closer, she noticed the light pulsed, glowing momentarily brighter every few seconds.

Suddenly, the light disappeared, and her spirit came to a halt. Below her loomed a pale, yellowish moon, splotched with dark red patches, circling a barren ice world.

As she drifted down toward the moon, a squat, solitary structure came into view. Aside from its glistening diamondine walls, there was nothing special about it. And yet, she felt its monumental importance. Something within her stirred, and inexplicably, she smiled even as a tear trickled down her face.

Oona's feet touched the surface of the moon, stirring yellowish dust, a few meters away from the structure. The seams of a door appeared.

She stepped forward, and the door opened. She walked through a steel-reinforced wall of pure diamondine five meters thick then headed down a dark corridor.

The hallway led to a brightly lit medical facility. It was absent of people, but dozens of cogs waited dormant in recharging stations. She wandered through rows of intricate machines and sophisticated laboratory stations. The equipment in here was old and high tech. Even before the Tekk Plague, this stuff would have been insanely advanced.

She knew this facility. Not that she'd ever been here, but every messiah family had searched for this secret genetics lab. Lore claimed it held all the answers about the origins and purpose of the hyperphasic messiah. And that it would only open to one.

At the far end of the lab, a tall glass case stood in an alcove. As Oona approached, a light turned on, illuminating the contents. Inside the case rested a young woman, a twin of Oona herself, though a few years older.

She marveled at the girl for a moment. But then something pulled her onward, toward a fat pillar in the middle of the facility. When she stepped up to the column, a hidden door opened, revealing an elevator. She stepped inside, and the door closed behind her.

The elevator traveled downward for several minutes. When the door opened, she stepped out into an empty corridor and moved forward, passing through a dozen diamondine doorways, each one opening for her as she approached.

Finally, the corridor spilled into a large, open chamber where a glowing, meter-wide orb hovered in the center of the room. She stared at it, transfixed. It pulsed steadily, like a heartbeat. This was the light that had brought her here. She didn't know what the orb was, but she knew it was important—perhaps the most important thing in the universe.

Oona was so focused on the orb that she didn't notice the vision starting to fade until it was almost gone. Then she heard a voice...her father's voice. He sounded excited, more thrilled than he'd ever been before.

"I have discovered something, something important. This will change everything!"

46

MITSUKI REEL

Mitsuki wasn't surprised that Siv was worth as much dead or alive. Siv was just a procurement specialist, and by all rights, he should already be dead from Kompel withdrawal.

But she was worth capturing alive. Back on Ekaran IV, she had claimed to be the rogue Federation and Thousand Worlders' agent, Silustria Ting. Everyone involved had figured out by now that she wasn't. But if she knew enough about Ting to trick them, then she knew enough to be valuable. Certain people would pay a lot of money for even a scrap of knowledge about Ting. Others would pay a lot to verify that no one else knew the information she might possess.

"I'd rather not make a mess of things," Kaleeb said, his voice taking on a hint of dark mirth. "Though my friend here, he does enjoy messes, and he's been begging me to let him dice up another victim today."

"Mits," Siv said distantly, his voice hardly more than a whisper. "We're finished."

He was right. They'd have to surrender and hope they could escape from Kaleeb, or that someone, somewhere, would rescue them.

She dropped her plasma pistol and raised her hands.

"Smart move," Kaleeb said.

The sky-blade bobbed happily around them. But when it came to her side, it fell suddenly from the air and struck the floor, a lifeless hunk of metal. Kaleeb snapped his attention onto it, shock evident in his posture.

As Mitsuki dropped to pick up her pistol, a voice spoke into her mind through B. She'd never been happier to hear any voice.

"Heads-up, Batwings! Shoot exactly what your targeting triangle is lighting up. Then grab Siv and get the hell out of there. As fast as you can. Do not waste a single second."

Kaleeb stalked forward, outraged. "What the hell did you—"

He cried out and fell to his knees, thrusting his wrists against the sides of his helmet.

A targeting triangle popped up in Mitsuki's HUD, illuminating a conduit that connected a storage tank to a mold injection machine. She snatched up her pistol and turned toward it. Then she paused, spun back, and shot Kaleeb. A faint field flickered in defense, but the bolt pierced through it and blasted him square in the face-plate. Cracks webbed across the dark glass.

Screw the targeting triangle. She fired again, but Kaleeb rolled aside and brought his neural disruptor up. She ducked the wild shot he fired. The grenade launcher rotated on his shoulder, attempting to target her, but then it spun out of control.

Before she could fire at him again, Silky screamed at her. *"The sky-blade's stirring, and you don't have time to kill them both. Shoot the damn conduit and get out of there!"*

She started to argue with him but noticed the sky-blade had turned over. It rolled again and bounced a few centimeters into the air.

Distracted by the moving sky-blade, she'd taken her eyes off Kaleeb. He leveled his disruptor at her, hands shaking. Whatever Silky had done was causing the android a lot of distress.

Before he could fire at her, Siv dived on top of him and smacked him in the head with a fist, his force-knuckles flaring as he struck. The face-plate cracked open, and he fell to the ground. Siv sat on Kaleeb's chest, pummeling him in the face.

A halo of electricity sparked around Kaleeb's armor. The force of the shock tossed Siv away. He landed in a slump, groaning, at Mitsuki's feet.

"Is he okay?"

"Just momentarily stunned," Silky replied. *"Take the shot!"*

She inhaled as she trained her gun on the conduit Silky had marked. Then she exhaled and pulled the trigger. The plasma bolt streaked across the room and struck home. A bright burst of green light sprouted from the conduit, and a whoosh of flames followed.

Kaleeb sat up. His face was a mess of blue android blood on dark synthetic skin. Siv groaned again and climbed woozily to his feet. He spotted Kaleeb, growled, and started toward him. Mitsuki grabbed him by the arm.

"Siv, we've got to go. Now!"

He struggled against her grip. "Let me go."

When one of the storage tanks rumbled, Siv got the message. So did Kaleeb, who turned toward the noise, ignoring both of them.

"Run for that window!" Mitsuki told Siv and gave him a shove in the right direction.

As he started to run, she shot Kaleeb on the side of the head. The plasma bolt burned into his helmet, and he slumped over. Hopefully, he was dead.

They had only traveled five meters when Silky cried out in warning. A red dot popped up in her locator, zooming right for them.

Mitsuki lunged forward and shoved Siv. The sky-blade skipped between them, flying erratically. Its razor-sharp blades sliced across the back of Siv's left calf. He stumbled a few steps then fell.

The sky-blade dropped, struck the floor, and rolled out of control before bobbing back into the air. It was recovering from whatever it was that Silky had done.

Siv scrambled up and hobbled for the window as fast as he could, with Mitsuki right on his tail. A series of booms echoed behind them as Siv reached the window.

"You've only got seconds left," Silky warned.

Mitsuki fired two plasma shots into the large window, one to each side of Siv. The glass shattered and rained onto the street below. Mitsuki holstered her pistol and charged forward. She slammed into Siv, wrapped her arms around him, and leaped out the window.

She extended her wings as the entire floor behind them exploded. The shockwave sent her tumbling through the sky. Her wings strained to keep them steady, and she thought for a moment they would fall, despite B maxing out the antigrav.

But then Siv managed to manually adjust his, and they made it far enough away from the flaming building that she could regain her balance.

Windows shattered. Debris tumbled to the street below. And flames engulfed the upper floors of the building.

The red blips disappeared from her locator.

"Are they dead?" Mitsuki asked.

"I can't get an accurate scan due to interference, madam. But I hope so."

"I'm not detecting them," Silky said. *"Now circle back down here and pick me up. Playing dead has worn me out, and I'm ready to be done with this."*

"You could have helped earlier."

"I helped when it would matter most, Wings."

"That was when it would help most?"

"Well, it did happen to coincide, more or less, with me figuring out the right frequency to neutralize the sky-blade and send a brain-numbing screech into Kaleeb's ears."

"Nice trick."

"You're lucky I've worked with sky-blades before and know their weaknesses. I assure you the trick won't work a second time. They'll know how to defend against it."

"Surely, they're dead."

"I wouldn't count on it."

"Well, I'm glad you're not. You had us worried."

"It takes more than a small missile and a car crash to do me in!"

As Mitsuki circled back, she yelled the good news down to Siv. But he was already smiling and laughing. He knew where the sudden help they'd gotten had come from.

47

SIV GENDIN

Siv smiled like an idiot in Mitsuki's arms as she flew clear of the exploding building. She circled back to land half a block away from the wrecked van. Police and fire department sirens wailed from every direction. They'd have to work fast.

Two hovering firefighter cogs had just finished spraying down the van. Luckily, the flames never reached the front half of the vehicle.

As the firefighter cogs raced off toward the factory, the top half of which was now engulfed in flames, Siv and Mitsuki sprang into action.

She gathered their packs and her plasma carbine, along with Wang's disruptor, the box of chameleon hoods he had been carrying, the voucher for passage on the Hydrogenists' ship, and his considerable amount of cash.

It was fortunate the fire was confined to the upper floors because even from the ground across the street, they felt the searing heat and caught the faintest whiff of the no-doubt incredibly toxic fumes. A pile of debris smoldered only a few meters away from their packs. That was a stroke of luck on a day that seemed in desperately short supply of it.

Siv climbed into the wreckage of the van, not giving a single shit about the heat left over from the fire. His hands blistered as he pried open the bent glove compartment to find Silky tucked safely within an energy bubble formed by the force-shield.

Tears stung his eyes. He'd felt so lost without Silky. It was almost like he'd lost part of himself. Or rather, it was exactly like that. He hardly remembered what it was like as a child before he'd had Silky's voice in his head, giving advice and comfort, teaching him, and telling ridiculous jokes and stories. Being without Silky was worse than going through Kompel withdrawal.

He felt terrible, knowing how useless he'd been during the fight with Kaleeb. But as always, Mitsuki had come through. She was weird and sometimes annoying, but you could always count on her.

The energy shield dissipated, and he reached in and took up the tiny chippy unit, reinstalling it immediately, not even caring to wait until he exited the hot wreckage. He put the force-shield armband on and climbed out as the chippy's startup sequence chimed.

Silky didn't have to reboot in such cases, but he did it anyway because it ensured reliable connections with the wiring in the socket and gave the brain a chance to acclimate. Siv stood in the street like an idiot, waiting to hear Silky's voice.

When he spoke, a wave of relief and contentment washed over Siv. But that feeling didn't last long.

"Sir, there's a car three blocks from here that we can jack and take to the starport."

"That's it?! No welcome back? No I'm glad you survived the crazy bounty hunter? No I'm sorry I didn't tell you I had a plan?"

"Sir, all of that seems rather obvious. Now, we need to get moving."

Siv shook his head. *"You're impossible."*

"That's the consensus."

"Just so you know. Next time, I'm not hitting the eject switch."

"That's rather illogical, sir."

"It's not logic. It's emotion. I don't know why, but I love you, you stupid circuit board."

"Watch your language!"

Siv rolled his eyes as he caught the pack Mitsuki tossed him, forgetting that his hands were now cut and blistered from the hot wreckage.

He cried out and dropped it.

"As for why you love me... Familiarity. Not to mention my wit and charm. Also, sir, next time you rescue me from burning wreckage, take the proper precautions so you don't hurt yourself needlessly. Now get going!"

Siv shouldered the pack. Then he and Mitsuki ran toward the car. When they were only a block away, four police cruisers turned onto their street and screamed in their direction. They darted into an abandoned warehouse and dived behind a pile of old crates.

As the cruisers continued toward the burning building, Siv and Mitsuki stood.

"I'd stay down for a while," Silky cautioned. *"Police drones are hovering everywhere now."*

Siv spotted an old couch in an employee breakroom. They went in, closed the door, and collapsed onto it. Mitsuki snuggled up against him, and he didn't mind. For a moment, he almost broke down sobbing. But he gathered his composure.

"Thanks, Mits."

"For pulling your ass through that factory with the galaxy's most notorious bounty hunter and his insane cog on our asses?"

"That and so much more."

She smiled and patted his leg. "You may not know it, but you've pulled me along over the years, far more than you may realize."

"Siv has pulled you along?" Silky countered. *"Who upgrades the software in all your gear? Who helps you with flight data and escape vectors and mission planning and—"*

Siv sat upright. *"You help her with planning and escape vectors?"*

"She's an ally and a friend, sir. So, of course, I do."

"You never told me."

"Sir, I don't feel that I need to tell you everything I do. And what's a little mission planning amongst friends? You rarely take up a significant amount of my processing capabilities, and I can get extraordinarily bored when you're sleeping."

"He didn't want me to tell you," Mitsuki said. "It started several years ago, after our one-night stand. Since you found me annoying and—"

Siv patted her hand. "S'okay. I don't mind him having helped you. Honestly, I never would have. I do mind him not telling me."

"My apologies, sir."

"I think you like keeping secrets."

"Sir, you have no idea what it's like for your entire experience of the world to be through the galactic net and a single person. Your every thought is practically my every thought, and vice-versa. A normal chippy, that's all they ever get. I need more. Keeping a little to myself helps me... I guess it's sort of a comfort."

"I get it. Though to be fair, I don't have any secrets from you."

"I'd never thought about it that way, sir."

"Anyone else you've been helping?"

"Only you and Batwings, sir."

Mitsuki squeezed his arm. "Sivvy, you *have* helped me, you know. I don't have many... I don't have *any* friends actually. Just you."

"Now I feel rotten for avoiding you so much."

"You should. I'm awesome." A broad smile inched across her face. "You also dragged me into all of this."

"Are you thanking me for that?"

"I was stuck in a rut. I needed to break out of my routine. To be something more. To do something more, something meaningful. So yeah, I'm thanking you for that."

They sat in silence for a long time. Even Silky was quiet.

"Do you think he's dead?" Siv asked.

"I hope so," Mitsuki answered.

"It doesn't really matter, does it?" Siv muttered despondently. "Even if Kaleeb's dead, there are so many others like him and Zetta... Reapers, Bleeders, the Shadowslip, Cutters, Thousand Worlders, and 'Nevolence knows what else. We've got to go through all of that just for a *chance* at rescuing Ambassador Vim from a planet we're still several lightyears away from. Right now...I just don't see how we're going to make it."

"And that, sir, is why we're done."

"Done? Are you invoking your override?"

Siv was torn. Part of him didn't want to stop pressing forward. He would have done anything to save his dad. How could he just give up on Kyralla and Oona's, no matter the odds stacked against them? But another part, a more logical part, knew the chance of success was practically nonexistent.

It wasn't dying that scared him. Death was inevitable. There was no shame in a good death.

But losing Silky... The chance of going through the rest of his life, however brief, without his best friend, his mentor, his surrogate father... Siv couldn't handle that. It was too much to bear.

"I am, in fact, invoking the override, sir."

Siv took in a deep breath then exhaled. *"Okay."*

"You're not going to fight me on it, sir?"

"I promised you I wouldn't, Silkster. I don't want to disappoint Kyralla

and Oona, and I hate the idea of abandoning a mission, but I just don't think I can go on. It's too much."

"Wonders never cease, sir."

"What does Mitsuki think? Have you asked her?"

"She doesn't like quitting either. But she's finding it hard to argue against it when the odds are so stacked against us. And she did agree to the terms as well."

He turned to Mitsuki. "I guess that's it, huh?"

She nodded but wouldn't meet his eyes.

"I've connected to the Outworld Ranger*, sir. Launching Spy-Fly 01 and patching you through so we can video chat with everyone."*

The tiny drone hovered in front of Siv and Mitsuki and beamed its camera feed through Silky to the *Outworld Ranger*. Meanwhile, a view of the bridge opened within a window in Siv's HUD.

The first thing that caught his attention was the young man he'd never seen before sitting at the sensor station. He had wild, white hair. Burns, scrapes, grease, and soot-covered him.

"Siv," Kyralla said with eagerness. A warmth spread through him. "Thank the Benevolence you're alive. Both of you."

"Just barely," Siv answered. "Did Silky catch you up on what happened to us?"

"He hasn't said anything yet," Bishop answered.

When Siv's eyes fell to Bishop, who was sitting in the command chair, he cringed. The gizmet had his arm in a sling, and he looked as if a gang of thugs had beaten him up. A pale, orange starkat lay curled in Bishop's lap.

"What the hell happened to you?" Mitsuki asked.

"It's a long story," Bishop answered.

"And who the hell is this guy?" she countered.

"Part of the long story," Kyralla answered.

"I don't see Oona," Siv said. "Is she okay?"

"We don't know," Kyralla replied. "She's been catatonic for a while now. We're just waiting...and hoping."

"I'm Tekeru Jones," the man said. "I'm an assistant professor at the University of Stygia."

"What the hell have y'all done to my ship?" Silky growled over the comm.

"Your ship?" Bishop asked.

"I just completed a thorough analysis of all the damage," Silky responded with irritation. "And I'm not happy! Not at all. Even the ship's cog is beaten up. What the hell?!"

No one answered. Probably because, unlike Siv, they had never heard Silky angry before. No jokes, no one-liners and snarky asides. Just raw anger.

"I see," Silky said, his voice softening somewhat. "Thank you for enlightening me, Artemisia. Kyralla, well done on the piloting. Mr. Jones, welcome aboard. Karson Bishop, sir, you have my deepest respect. That will go down in history as one of the most brilliant of all insane schemes ever. If I had hands, I would applaud you."

Silky's voice deepened back to raw anger. "That said, all of you are incredibly stupid for putting yourself in that situation in the first place. Spare me any arguments you might make. I'm disgusted with you all. Silky out."

As everyone on the bridge stared wide-eyed at the viewscreen, Siv tried to smile apologetically. "So, maybe you should tell us what happened."

He listened attentively as Kyralla and Bishop recounted their attempt to save the crew of the damaged research vessel, how they fought off a pirate vessel, how Oona bonded with the ship, and then how they narrowly escaped a World Bleeders' destroyer and three starfighters.

Mitsuki grinned like a starkat who'd killed twice as much prey as she could eat. "Sivvy, little Bishy-Bish is one of us. How about that?"

Siv chuckled. "That he is, Mits."

"One of you?" Bishop asked. "What does that mean?"

"That you're batshit crazy when it comes to getting the job done," Mitsuki answered.

The gizmet frowned. "Huh."

"It's a compliment," Siv told him.

Artemisia then recounted the damage the ship had sustained during the encounter. That was more than discouraging, and an unexpected fire of protectiveness erupted within Siv. They had nearly gotten themselves killed, and they had damaged his dad's ship.

"That *was* reckless," Siv said with unintended anger.

Kyralla dropped her eyes.

"Sorry," Bishop whispered.

"I mean... I get it," he said, softening his tone.

"I would tell you what you did was foolish," Mitsuki said. "But what's the point? Besides, it was the right thing to do. I might not have done it, maybe, but I get why you felt you had to."

Siv sighed. "And what's done is done."

"How have you fared?" Bishop asked. "I'm guessing not well given how exhausted you look and the burns on your clothing."

They told them about Vega Kaleeb chasing them, how they had almost lost Silky, and everything else that had happened.

"While he may be dead," Siv said, "there will be many others like him. None as individually dangerous, of course."

"We've got a way to Titus II," Mitsuki said quietly. "But...things won't be any easier there, assuming we don't hit any problems on the way."

Kyralla glanced around the bridge. After eyeing Tekeru Jones then Bishop, she took a deep breath and sighed painfully. "I can't ask you to go any further. Not even to save my dad. The risk is too great."

"We agree," Siv said with as much kindness as he could manage, to soften the blow. "Mitsuki and I gave Silky an override, a chance to call off the mission if it was too dangerous, no matter what information your father might have."

"I would rather continue," Mitsuki said. "But Silky is right. And it's not just that the risk is too great for the reward. It just seems impossible to pull off."

"Part of me is willing to press on," Siv told them. "But...but honestly, I'm not sure it's worth it. I know that's a rotten thing to say, Kyra, when your father's life hangs in the balance, but..."

"I understand," she said softly.

"I think we should all be together on the *Outworld Ranger* anyway," Mitsuki said.

"Strength in numbers," Kyralla replied. "I can agree about that. I'm in way over my head here. We almost lost everything."

"So that's it then?" Bishop asked.

Kyralla nodded. "We'll leave my dad on Titus II, for better or for worse and...and hope that he can escape somehow." As a few tears rolled down her cheeks, she gazed down at the console. "Assuming...that he's still...alive."

Siv wished he could hold her hands and tell her something...anything... that would make her feel better. But what could he say other than he'd been powerless to save his own father and understood her anguish?

He'd so hoped he could do for them what he'd been unable to do for himself. His eyes teared up as well. "I wanted to save him for you...and for Oona. But I just don't think that we can. And even then..."

"It's not really worth it," Kyralla said, half sobbing. "I love my dad, and I want to see him safe. But he is only one man, while the fate of the entire galaxy lies with my sister. She has to be my priority. That's something he told me many times. I think it's time for me to heed his words. Oona won't understand, of course. But I think we're all in agreement on this, right?"

"We are," Mitsuki whispered.

Siv nodded. "I don't think we have any other choice. The risk is too great. We need to stick together."

"I...I agree," Bishop said.

Silky didn't voice an opinion, but he didn't need to. He hadn't said a thing to Siv since his tirade.

"Then it's settled," Siv said. "We just need to arrange a way to—"

"No!" Oona cried as she ran onto the bridge breathless. "You don't understand. We must go on! We have to rescue my dad!"

"Oona, are you okay?" Kyralla asked, standing.

She waved a hand dismissively. "I'm fine."

"Oona," Siv said kindly. "The reason we—"

She interrupted him. "Artemisia told me what you'd decided and why. But we *can't* give up. We absolutely *have* to find my dad."

"Oona, I want to save him just as much as you," Kyralla said. "But—"

"You don't understand," Oona responded. "The important information he has—"

"We've been over that," Mitsuki said with irritation.

"It's not just any information," Oona replied. "He found the location of the secret genetics research facility every messiah family has searched for."

"He discovered the facility?" Kyralla asked with excitement. "Are you sure? Did you have a vision?"

"Yes. I'm certain. After I disconnected from the ship I...I saw it, and then I heard him, I heard dad."

Oona recounted the dream for them.

"Tell us again *exactly* what you saw," Silky said, his voice filled with awe. "Every detail. Leave nothing out."

Oona did as he asked.

"Now, describe the orb to me again," Silky said.

"I'll do my best."

She went over it again, but apparently, there wasn't much to say. As far as she could recall, it had been nothing more than a large, glowing ball hovering within a dark chamber.

"Did you hear anything?" Silky asked.

"Other than my dad's voice at the end? No."

"How did you feel in its presence?"

"Inspired and...and a little afraid, honestly. I sensed that it was the most important thing in the universe. Though why, I have no idea."

"And you think the orb is there?" Silky asked.

"I know it is," she answered. "Without a doubt."

"Amazing," he muttered. "Just amazing..."

"Silkster, do you know what this orb is?" Siv asked.

"It's something I did not think existed, sir. I never would have even dreamed of the possibility."

"And..." Mitsuki prompted after Silky remained silent for nearly a minute.

"And that is all I will say about it."

"For now?" Siv asked.

"Until we reach that facility, yes."

"Why?" Oona asked. "Tell me. I *need* to know what it was."

"I can't tell you. If any of you were to get captured and interrogated, you might reveal what it is. Just knowing that it exists is bad enough. The Dark Messiah, for instance, would know exactly what it is from that description, just as I did. Vega Kaleeb would have known what it was as well."

"Since your spirit traveled there, do you know how to get to that moon without the need for your father?" Mitsuki asked.

"Sorry, but I have no idea," Oona asked. "All I can say is that it's very, very far away from here."

"Well, if we intend to go to the facility," Siv said, "then we'll have to continue the rescue mission, right?"

"I believe we have to," Silky replied. "Sir, I rescind my override. We *must* go to that facility. Whatever the risks may be. Nothing could be more important. The existence of that orb changes everything."

48

VEGA KALEEB

With help from Faisal, Vega heaved a steel beam aside and clawed his way free from the wreckage. The top five floors of the factory warehouse had collapsed into one another. He was lucky they hadn't brought the entire building down with them. There was no way he would have survived that.

He stood and tried to take a step, but something snagged his leg, keeping him in place. He glanced down and growled in disgust. A narrow strip of metal, torn from another beam, had pierced through the meat of his calf before twisting on the end. He couldn't pull it free without causing more damage. He hadn't known about it because he'd disabled his pain receptors.

"Damn it."

He began to reach down, but Faisal zipped over. "I've got it, boss. Save your strength."

The sky-blade floated down to examine the metal strip, then projected a laser tool from his bottom section. The instrument was designed for cutting more than killing, not that Faisal wouldn't use it for that purpose if he felt like it. Faisal's typical use for the laser was to make a wounded victim suffer before extinguishing them.

"Hold still, boss. I'm going to cut it as close to your leg as possible to prevent further damage to your tissues."

"Just get it done," Vega snapped.

Tiny bits of debris along with a cloud of dust still rained around them.

Vega could barely restrain his anger and was more than ready to return to the hunt. Unfortunately, he was in no shape to do so. Since his narrow escape from Terra during the final days of the Benevolence, Vega had been in more than a few tough scrapes. But in the last hundred years, he'd never come so close to death as this. And in his nearly two centuries of existence, he had never been so humiliated.

For the second time in a century, Faisal had saved Vega's life. The moment before the first chemical tank exploded, Faisal had bounced over to land in front of Vega, shouting a warning. Vega had heard him, but there was little he could do about it.

Reel's plasma shot had blasted through what force-field he had left, pierced his helmet at his temple, then burned through his synth-flesh, stopping only when it struck his titanium-encased skull. The concussive force of that strike had sent his vision swimming, his ears ringing, and worst of all, it had temporarily knocked out his central control system. It was the android equivalent of being knocked out, only he was aware of precisely what was happening around him.

He had thought he was about to die, but instead of shooting him again, Reel had fired into one of the chemical tanks then fled. Clearly, she wanted to escape before Faisal recovered.

As the first tank was about to explode, Vega enacted an emergency protocol allowing Faisal access to his control systems. Faisal zoomed over and maxed out his own shields, extending them to help protect Vega. Then he rerouted all the power from the jetpack and weapon systems and drained Vega's heart down to one percent, pouring that energy into Vega's force-field, reactivating it.

The sudden drain on his heart, coupled with the shock of the blast, had rendered Vega fully unconscious, for only the second time in his life.

He had awoken half an hour later, buried beneath five floors of rubble. Massive dents and hairline fractures marred his skeleton-casing. A chunk of stone had fractured his hand, and a steel beam had cracked his breastplate, shattering five ribs. He was lucky not to have been crushed to death.

Instead of killing him, the rubble had saved him by shielding him from the raging flames above. The heat from that fire, however, had blistered the skin on his unprotected face.

His flickering HUD showed firefighter cogs working to put out the blaze.

Unfortunately, it also showed firefighter, police, and medical teams only minutes away. He needed to get free and out of the area before the authorities arrived.

Once the debris had stopped falling, he and Faisal started clearing off the rubble. They failed, however, to get him free in time to avoid the authorities. The half-demolished building was surrounded by first responders. A cacophony of competing sirens filled the air, and Vega's HUD showed even more on their way.

Metal clanged as Faisal finished cutting through the piece of metal piercing Vega's calf. He reached down, ripped the strip free, and then stumbled away, heading toward the stairs.

"Now that you're free, boss, I'm going after them."

Faisal began to zip away, but Vega stopped him. "Wait!"

"Don't worry, boss. I'll take them by surprise!"

"How much power do you have left?"

"Enough to carve them up," Faisal replied harshly.

"And if Silky has another trick up his sleeve?"

Faisal hovered in front of him, sparks flaring off his surface. "That chippy will *not* beat me again!"

"Faisal, he's your equal, and he spent years operating in the field. Don't underestimate him."

"Boss, do you want me to quit our partnership? Cause you're pissing me off mightily."

"I want you to help me get to the ship so we can regroup and take them on properly. No mistakes. No half-measures. I want to take them down for certain. And I don't want to lose you in the process."

Faisal bobbed along silently as Vega limped down the staircase, his busted armor clattering with each step. He'd made it down to the second floor before his companion finally responded.

"You're right," he whispered. "But if you ever compare me to that chippy again, or even mention us in the same breath, then—"

"I won't. I promise. Now help me figure out how to get past this mass of firefighters and police."

"There's no way you're getting out of here without a fight, looking how you look, boss. A building mysteriously blows up and an armored man walks out... The police are going to arrest you first and then ask questions."

Vega counted the police and squad skimmers and bikes surrounding the building. "My HUD and sensors are still on the fritz from the damage I took. Can you confirm what I'm seeing?"

"Thirty officers, five bikes, a van, and ten cars."

"That's what I see, too."

"The van brought in an armored, rapid-response team."

"I can't take them on."

"Not with one percent power remaining in your system, boss. Your grenade launcher is offline, and I have no idea what happened to your assault rifle, your neural disruptor, or your sniper pistol."

Vega paused. He'd been so dazed he hadn't even checked for his weapons. He took stock of what he had left...a laser rifle, a plasma pistol, two shock-knives, and...and that was it.

Damn it. He'd lost a fortune in gear. The sniper pistol alone was worth five thousand, and his incredibly expensive and rare armor was finished. It wasn't useful for anything more than scrap parts now. He hadn't looked yet, but he felt certain his jetpack was finished too.

"The damage they did—I'll have to kill Gendin and Bishop just to cover my losses."

"Don't sweat it, boss. The girl's the prize. And I'm already studying what...that chippy...did to us. I can guarantee you that will not work a second time."

Vega stopped at the door that opened into the first floor. "I still need a way out of here, and soon. The structural integrity of this building may have been compromised, and I don't want to find out what happens if the whole thing falls on me."

"I think you've only got one option, boss. You're going to have to use the *Spinner's Blade*."

"That's going to get me noticed by more than the cops."

"It will, boss. But the primitive security forces here are going to struggle to find you once you're cloaked. And even if they do, I'm sure we can outrun them to safety."

Vega nodded, then he opened a connection to his starship. Ever since he'd leaped out, the *Spinner's Blade* had been circling overhead with the cloak enabled. If any air traffic came near, the ship's AI would change course to avoid it.

Vega took command of the ship and directed the AI to alter its course.

Then he set up combat parameters and allowed Faisal to conduct the rest of the operation.

"No cop killing."

"Aww."

"No harming firefighters, medical personnel, or people of any other varieties."

"What about the medical and firefighter cogs?"

"If it makes you happy."

"Thanks, boss."

Vega collapsed onto the bottom step and waited.

Moments later, the *Spinner's Blade* zoomed low across the street just outside, its dual-laser cannon pumping shots into the cops' skimmer bikes and cars and the rapid response van. Faisal even managed to nail a firefighter cog along the way, causing him to cheer maliciously.

Vega shook his head. If blowing off some steam by destroying harmless cogs made the sky-blade feel better, then so be it.

All the cops scattered into the alley or took shelter in the building across the street. The *Spinner's Blade* stopped just outside Vega's position. He lumbered as fast as he could out the door.

As the boarding ramp deployed, a rapid-response officer opened fire with his plasma carbine. One of his shots grazed Vega's shoulder, but he kept going.

He'd intended to leap onto the boarding ramp, but instead, he fell halfway onto it then had to crawl farther inside, with Faisal pulling him along with his tractor beam.

By the time he was safely inside, three officers were firing on the *Spinner's Blade*, but it wasn't anything the starship's shields couldn't handle. The ship cloaked and climbed toward orbit as Vega limped toward his repair station, dumping pieces of armor as he went.

Vega collapsed with his back against the control panel for his repair and recharging station. Faisal hovered in front of him. He gazed at his reflection in the cog's shiny black surface. Dried blood was smeared across his face, his nose was bent, his forehead darkening with a bruise.

Anger swelled within him, and the face reflected on Faisal's surface hardened. Siv Gendin was going to pay for this, with his life. Mitsuki Reel...she was too valuable to kill. He needed the money. However, the bounty didn't say he wasn't allowed to maim her. He was going to enjoy watching Faisal play with her before they turned her in.

As for Silky, Faisal assured him that torturing and killing Gendin was the best they could do to make the chippy suffer before destroying him, too. And Faisal, whose pride was thoroughly injured, would more than relish the job. He would, without doubt, make it a work of art.

AFTERWORD

To received updates on new releases, visit dahayden.com and sign up for my no-spam newsletter.

If you enjoyed this book, please leave a review online or tell your friends about it. All it takes is a few sentences. Without positive reviews, a series may wither and die.

ALSO BY DAVID ALASTAIR HAYDEN

Outworld Ranger

Forbidden System

Rogue Starship

Shadow Agents

Breaking Point

Storm Phase

The Storm Dragon's Heart

The Maker's Brush

Lair of the Deadly Twelve

The Forbidden Library

The Blood King's Apprentice

The First Kaiaru

The Arthur Paladin Chronicles

The Shadowed Manse

The Warlock's Gambit

Pawan Kor

Wrath of the White Tigress

Chains of a Dark Goddess

Who Walks in Flame

Made in the USA
Columbia, SC
22 June 2022